Mary DeMuth is a stunningly talented storyteller and wordsmith. *Life in Defiance*—a compelling read on so many levels—is pure DeMuthian artistry.

Susan Meissner, author of *The Shape of Mercy*

Mary DeMuth is an evocative, beautiful storyteller. She will move you emotionally, she will impact you spiritually.

Tosca Lee, author of *Havah: The Story of Eve*

With uncanny precision, Mary DeMuth has become a master at beautifully exposing ugly truth. *Life in Defiance* is completely compelling.

Allison Bottke, author of *You Make Me Feel Like Dancing* and *Setting Boundaries with Your Adult Children*

Life in Defiance will stir up emotions of anger, and forgiveness. It will disturb you. It will enthrall you. It will draw you out and pull you in. And it will fill you with hope. Beautifully written, it's another proof that Mary DeMuth is one of our finest novelists.

James L. Rubart, author of *Rooms*

Life in Defiance

Other Books by Mary E. DeMuth

Daisy Chain

A Slow Burn

Life in Defiance

BOOK THREE

MARY E. DeMUTH

≡ZONDERVAN®

ZONDERVAN.com/
AUTHORTRACKER
follow your favorite authors

ZONDERVAN

Life in Defiance
Copyright © 2010 by Mary E. DeMuth

This title is also available as a Zondervan ebook.
Visit www.zondervan.com/ebooks.

This title is also available in a Zondervan audio edition.
Visit www.zondervan.fm.

Requests for information should be addressed to:

Zondervan, *Grand Rapids, Michigan 49530*

Library of Congress Cataloging-in-Publication Data

DeMuth, Mary E., 1967-
    Life in Defiance / Mary E. DeMuth.
        p. cm. — (Defiance Texas triology ; bk. 3)
        ISBN 978-0-310-27838-2 (pbk.)
        1. Texas—Fiction. I. Title.
PS3604.E48L54 2010
813'.6—dc22   2010009044

Scripture quotations are taken from the King James Version of the Bible.

Any Internet addresses (websites, blogs, etc.) and telephone numbers printed in this book are offered as a resource. They are not intended in any way to be or imply an endorsement by Zondervan, nor does Zondervan vouch for the content of these sites and numbers for the life of this book.

Published in association with the literary agency of Alive Communications, Inc., 7680 Goddard Street, Suite 200, Colorado Springs, CO 80920. www.alivecommunications .com

Cover design: Laura Maitner-Mason
Cover photography: Chiara Fersini, Trevillion Images; JupiterImages; Veer
Interior design: Christine Orejuela-Winkelman

Printed in the United States of America

---

10 11 12 13 14 15 /DCI/ 23 22 21 20 19 18 17 16 15 14 13 12 11 10 9 8 7 6 5 4 3 2 1

To drowning wives who want to fly.

One

DEFIANCE, TEXAS, DECEMBER 1977

When Hap swift-kicks me in my stomach, the last thing I see is the retreat of one well-polished pastor's shoe. Mama always said you could tell the value of a man by the shine of his shoes. How he treated them reflected how he treated his women, she believed.

"If you can find a man with polished shoes, Louise," she told me, "then you'll find the world."

The world I find today is a dirt-embedded yellow linoleum floor, no longer reverberating from rushing kids preparing for school. I can't even remember what brought on the kick, what inciting words I said to deserve Hap's rage. I try to stand, but the world twirls around me, nearly the same feeling I get when I drink a little too much, though not nearly as sweet, not as beautiful an escape.

I re-taste my breakfast, then swallow it again. I'm terribly good at swallowing things these days—particularly secrets. The children gulp down their share, too. If the church body would dethrone Hap from his pulpited pedestal and truly look him square in the eyes they'd see these secrets, but no one bothers —not even the elders and deacons who actually know more than they let on. So we ingest secrets like gravel, our stomachs distended in the effort, never really feeling fed or alive.

But this is not my only secret. A few months ago, someone killed my son Jed's best friend, Daisy Chance. A waif of a girl, thirteen and gangly, and the love of Jed's life, though he wouldn't say such things. And as sure as I know the streets of Defiance, Texas, I know who killed her. Hap believes I'm slow; he doesn't understand the real Ouisie Pepper. When I'm holding my head in our curtained bedroom, convulsing under the spasm of another headache, I think, and remember the man in the woods.

You want to know, don't you?

You want to know what kind of person would strangle a sweet teenage girl. Isn't it ironic that a woman people pass on the street, nod politely to and gossip about, actually knows Defiance's most horrible secret? But I'm not telling. Not yet. Don't fret yourself, though, I'm pretty sure Daisy will be the only one taken.

I steady myself at the kitchen sink, washing cereal bowls one by one. I scrub in circles, round and round until they squeak beneath my sponge. And I watch the winter from my window. It's not a cruel winter, not terribly chilly as you might expect this season. But this is Texas after all, prone to doing its own thing. As I settle myself into the day's plain mediocrity, the wind musters strength, bending trees, ripping browning leaves from stark branches. There are no clouds shifting in the wind, no birds protesting. It's a silent torrent, threatening to unhinge everything anchored down. Leaves spiral to the ground, but I can't hear them. And even if I could, I couldn't stop their demise.

In the quiet of my afternoon, a knock at my front door ends the day's silence.

I open it to Emory Chance, face afluster, eyes telling a story I cannot understand.

"Can you be married to a dead man?" she asks.

"Let's sit on the porch," I tell her.

She slides slender hands down the legs of her blue jeans. "He was fixin' to marry me. He asked me once." She reveals a simple gold ring, the ring she's shown me several times this week—a symbol of her confusion and a testimony to her grief.

I look at Emory, her blonde hair so much like Daisy's, though the past months have made her old, with tiny lines that crease around her downturned mouth. She smells of smoke, but her eyes don't hold fire anymore. It's a strange thing to me, and should be to you, that Emory has recently become my closest friend on this earth, because standing in our midst is that terrible truth of her affair with my husband.

I wonder if Hap still loves her, still sees the beauty beneath the lines, behind the smoke. Or maybe it was plain, undecorated lust.

"I said no." She sighs then, like she's letting out every hurt she's ever felt into the cool Defiance air. She owes her every breath to a man named Hixon, who rescued her from herself, hauling her from a burning church, though I'm sure she scratched and scraped at the earth as he pulled her from the fire's destruction.

She wanted to die.

And he, saint that he was, wanted to marry her.

"You said no. Now you regret it. I say give it to Jesus. He keeps our grief. Holds it." The words feel like sandpaper on my tongue, the abrasive shaving my taste buds.

Head in her hands, she grapples her skull with thin fingers. "He loved Jesus so much. Me, I'm restless. Loving folks, Jesus in particular, doesn't come easily for me. Religion feels more like a trap."

"Jesus said the truth will set you free." The word *truth* slips out of my mouth like preferred vocabulary, like I'm accustomed to telling the truth with every sentence. But me saying "truth" is its own lie.

"Freedom." She says the word like it's Moon Pies on a high unreachable shelf of the Piggly Wiggly.

"He will bring it, but it's never easy to grasp or understand. God gives His freedom and love like a mystery."

Emory hushes in and out. I know because I see her breath turn to mist. She looks at me. "Do you ever feel you deserve love like that?"

"No," I say. I don't deserve anything but rage. Certainly not affection. They say folks define their relationship to God with how their daddy treated them, but my daddy was benevolent. It's Hap I see in the Trinity now.

She stares at me, examines my face. "Has he been at you again?"

I shake my head, hoping tears won't bother my eyelids. Hap is adept at hurting me so it doesn't show now that the elders and deacons got a sneak peek into his "home issues." He kicks me in the gut like he did this morning, below my ribcage. I see myself crumpled on the kitchen floor, grabbing at breath.

"Ouisie?"

I shake my head. "I'm sorry."

"I'm not the marrying type." Emory holds herself. She shivers too. She pets her gold ring. "I loved him," she whispers — the quietest declaration of love I've heard, yet the loudest. "But I never told him. And now he'll be scattered atop the earth with so many unspoken words hovering above the ground."

With those hopeless words filling the space between us, Hap pulls into the driveway. My heart grows colder than the December afternoon. Emory gives me a frightened look as Hap opens the door to his Chevy, a smile etched into his pastor face. "Well," he says. "Look here."

"I'll see you later." Emory haunts each stair, barely touching the risers.

Hap approaches her, puts up his hand. "What's that?" He points at the gold ring on her left index finger.

"Hixon asked her to marry him." I raise my voice when I say it, then cough, hoping he won't notice.

Hap stiffens. His teeth leave his smile, replaced by a tight-lipped grin. He sighs. "That's one I never pictured, to tell you the truth. Coffee and cream mixed together in Defiance, Texas? It's not the Almighty's plan."

Emory stops, turns and looks Hap square in the face. "I always thought cream tendered the coffee. The coffee's the better for it, wouldn't you say? Or do you like yours black?"

Hap keeps his smile, shoves his hands into his dress pants pockets. "You know folks around here don't like the races mixing."

"Since when have I cared about what Defiance thinks, Hap Pepper?" Words that only a woman not married to Hap could say. I wonder if he's enamored with her sass. Oh dear Lord, I hope not.

"There are norms, Emory. Societal standards that keep a town running smoothly. I'm just saying you and Hixon would've been in for some ugly behavior."

Emory laughs. "I'm touched by your concern."

"What's that supposed to mean?" His biceps twitch beneath his white pressed shirt. I suck in my breath. I want to say something, anything, to diffuse Hap, but the fuse has been lit, and I hear its crackling spark. The sizzling burns my voice clear away.

"I best be going." Emory turns, seemingly unaware of what she's ignited.

Hap grabs her arm.

She jerks it away. "You make your point well." She brisks away before I can beg her to stay.

We are left to stand on the cold porch, anger roaring between us like a campfire baptized with gasoline. Sissy will be home soon. Hap won't have time to take his fury out on me in the next seven minutes, so he looks at me with those secret-holding eyes. I capture a snapshot of his gaze for later examination in my memory, for one of those days the headache plagues me, because for a moment I see the hint of the man I first married, the reason I stay and don't run one thousand miles away.

"I'm hungry." He swallows.

"I'll make us a snack." I open the door, feel the warmth of our house, and thank God for Hap's hunger and Sissy's imminent arrival. That's enough grace for me today. And I guess I don't deserve much more.

In the kitchen, I watch Hap's Adam's apple move up and down his neck, note his broad shoulders, his burgundy patterned tie, the way his pants belt at the waist precisely at hole number three, how his pant legs kiss perfectly shined shoes.

Her shoes enticed the man.

The rough leather straps crudely tacked to the bottom of an old rubber tire that'd been annihilated for the sake of sandals.

He watched her tanned feet from the underbrush, the way her toes struggled to keep the too-large sandals anchored there. Something in that moment, the snap of a twig or the trigger of a grenade, ignited him to reach through the humid air. Forced his strong grip around the girl's ankle.

She screamed.

But the man silenced her with a firm palm around her mouth and nose. Her chest rose and fell to the sound of birds in the sky above him, circling as if they knew. She wrestled and twisted before her eyes blanked and lolled back into her head. When Death limped her, he laid her on the green earth, taking off each sandal like a trophy.

He left her there, staring at the sky, at the birds, at the world. While he walked one thousand paces away holding two rubber-soled sandals.

Two

S tanding at its edge, I don't allow Lake Pisgah to lick my
shoes; the water repulses and allures—so much like Hap, I
shudder.

When Jed near drowned right after Daisy went missing, I
hollered and screeched, but did not—could not—rescue him.
What kind of mama won't risk her life for her son? Muriel, a
friend but at the time a stranger, stripped off her red wig and
plunged bald-head-first into Lake Pisgah's murky depths, pulling herself through the wet, wet water like a snake on the prowl.
Muriel rescued Jed, even with cancer sapping her body. She
pulled him clear out of the murky water and defied his thrash-
ing. She threw a protective arm over his chest and hauled him
back to me—a resurrected son to a scaredy-cat mama.

The gentle lapping of the lake creeps itself closer. I back up.
Clementine sits next to me, waiting. Her muscles twitch under
her fur—her barreled chest touching my calf rhythmically with
her panting. She wants that water. I pat her on the head. "Go,"
I tell her. So she does, splashing the world on a gray December
day that hasn't yet decided if it'll wear a coat or fling it off. The
weatherman called for rain and cold, but the muggy morning
threatens to lift the gray in favor of sun, sweet sun.

What I love about Lake Pisgah is that the land around its
circumference is all mine. Seldom are others here, particularly at

this time of day—or year. The lake's become my place to think, my crazy haven after the bustle of Jed and Sissy racing out the door to school. There's a rickety Adirondack flecked white over gray boards that I've claimed as Ouisie Pepper's. I crunch the mottled distance between the chair and me under steady feet. Defiance has a strange way of putting itself to sleep for the winter—in death, the grass gives up its last green hurrah, turning honey and taupe with a hint of burnt sienna. I wish I could paint grass the way I see it, but when I paint—and I do—my strokes are too broad for such intricacies. I sit in the chair and feel its boards digging into bone. I pull out my sketchbook, place a pencil to the semi-rough paper and drag a line across the page— Lake Pisgah's horizon.

But that's as far as the drawing goes before the liquid Voice comes to me. As a child, I hearkened God's clear and perfect voice, beckoning me to adventures. That Voice enamored my childhood, wooing me into the woods for discovery hikes and fields for romps with butterflies. It poured over me, wooing me toward baptism after I prayed the sinner's prayer years ago, but I didn't heed it enough to risk my life to a gaping, wet specter that would swallow me whole.

Maybe that's why the Voice wrecked my adulthood. To be fair, it did issue a warning in my heart, but then the Voice shifted, taking on Hap's baritone, assuring me God told Hap to marry me. So you see? I said yes. I had to.

He was as serene as Lake Pisgah then, calm as placid waters before a gullywashing storm. I'd been standing by my car, its engine sending steam to the sky, when Hap swooped in like a cowbird, leveled those storm-blue eyes at me, and tinkered under the hood of my car. "I'm Hapland." He wiped a rough hand on workman Levis, then thrust it my way.

"Louise." I blushed then, felt the heat in my cheeks when I saw the admiration in his eyes.

"Louise." He said my given name like it was something to

be savored in the mouth, letting it slowly melt between tongue and teeth.

"My car—is it all right?"

"I'm afraid it'll need to be towed. Why don't you come with me to the station so I can talk to the guys on your behalf." He pointed a lazy finger back to his Chevy. With a white T-shirt, rough jeans, and that car, I thought I'd run into James Dean—a benevolent one. You can bet I jumped inside, noting "Only the Lonely" by Roy Orbison, my favorite song and anthem blaring from AM speakers. I watched his arms flex as he drove me to town. I felt queenly then, riding in a horsepower-drawn carriage, next to the reigning Rebel-King of Defiance.

That reign ended, not a coup d'état like you'd expect. More like dry rot brought on by years of a slow leak; all my life has poured, then trickled, then dripped out at the feet of Hap until I am as dry as an abandoned cistern on the Texas plains. And yet I wonder: is there something inside me that's just too thirsty, and my thirst is what wearied Hap to rage?

My pencil poised above the sketchpad, I watch as Clementine thrashes the water, then wags her dripping tail and smiles my way. She knows not to shake near me so she wiggles her golden fur at Pisgah's edge, that terrifying and inviting place the Voice tells me to go now.

Why do I still obey it? That same Voice led me to Daisy's killer; that's why. You have to trust a Voice that tells you things like that. And if I'm honest, it got Hap right, at first. Maybe my inklings are correct. Maybe it was me that drowned Hap with my neediness. Maybe I wrung him inside out, when God had Hap right.

I walk to the water's edge, feeling the shivers rise inside me. Perhaps the weatherman is right. Perhaps the muggy air will shape-shift before my eyes, darken the sky, and pour merciless rain.

A chill wind sends bristles through me and I hug myself. I watch the clouds above, remembering Sissy. "Mama," she said this morning. "Do you think if an airplane could drop red food coloring into the clouds that it'd rain pink?"

She is an artist's daughter, I thought. "Sure, baby," I told her. And I want to believe such a thing is possible. And for a moment, while the breeze stiffens around me and the lake churns at my feet, I dream of flying to heaven with a watering can full of fire-engine red and sprinkling the angry clouds like a fairy. Imagine their masculine fury when they're forced to spend themselves pink.

A drop of rain wets my nose. Clementine sits next to me, but not so close I feel her this time—she knows I don't relish her wet dog perfume. I pat her head and note her shivering. "We'll go soon."

She nods—such an agreeable dog.

I see the lake dimple under sporadic drops. To my right, I catch sight of lily pads browned by winter, carcasses floating together, linked by tendrils underwater. I want my eyes to rain when I see them because I understand about winter's lot. I've had my springtime. Summer's long gone. The autumn brought Daisy's death. Winter stole Hixon's life. And now the long, terrible coldness has come—in my life and in this town's. I'm sick to death of death. I nearly shout the word to those spent lily pads, but I keep silent in the rain, marveling at the quivering water, trying to capture its dance in my thoughts so I can paint it later. Paint it, yes. Submerge in it—never.

A movement in the lilies startles me. Floating between those carcasses are hiding ducks, camouflaged by umber leaves. Why hadn't I seen them before?

Watch, the Voice tells me.

So I watch.

Clementine barks. And with her voice the ducks soar to the clouds—from near-death repose to spectacular flight.

See? After death comes resurrection, the Voice tells me.

And I thirst to believe such things. Oh I want to.

But something tells me I'll sink first. Perhaps today.

Three

The sacrifice is not lost on me. Hixon rescued a wayward woman and a wedding ring in two trips to a burning, dying church, but my Jed rescued Hixon only to feel the weight of another friend's demise. He wears death like a yoke now, encasing his strong shoulders like Emory's gold ring circles her slender finger. They sit next to each other—an answer to one of my prayers that actually reaches God's ears. Emory's chosen to forgive Jed for his part in Daisy's death, for leaving her alone in the church.

Jed looks taller, Sissy smaller. Jed says nothing, his neck unshaven, his ears red. Fourteen years old is too young to lose so many. And Sissy, whose hand feels fragile in mine siphons in Jed's grief, then wears it on her face. She doesn't frown; it's more like her face weeps without tears.

Emory fidgets with Hixon's ring as she sits in the pew, another coffin like a curse in front of our congregation. Only this coffin is a prop, empty because Hixon's been cremated. I wish, for Emory's sake, that the wooden box could be akin to Jesus' empty tomb, that Hixon's laughter will bellow forth from the back of the church, folks turning their heads to experience their first resurrection. But Sly Owen has dirge in his fingers as he mourns at the organ, a melancholy melody that permeates the pews. I lean forward, place a hand on Emory's shoulder. "I'm sorry," I say.

She shrugs me away, a loner in grief, though she sits between Jed on her left and Big Earl, her boss at Little Myrtle's. I have not lost anyone like she has. But I feel Hixon's absence in Defiance like a kick to my shin. He will be missed. Sissy feels that loss too. She cries beside me while I squeeze her small hand. I hear Big Earl pull in a raspy breath, never been one to hide emotions.

Hap mounts the carpeted stairs, skirting Hixon's coffin. He splays open the big, black Bible, unfolds his notes. He's reigned in this church as its King many years. He scans the kingdom below him, nodding indiscriminately. Then he looks at me for a hiccup of an instant. I see distaste there, nothing more.

He clears his throat. "It's never easy to say goodbye." His eyes are wet.

"Hixon was a friend to many in this town." He grips the lectern. His knuckles whiten. "He fixed folks' houses, fancied himself a handyman. He befriended all sorts of people — even Muriel, the Catholic."

The last words, he practically spits. I feel my neck tense. Sissy pulls me closer, then whispers, "I loved Muriel," she says. "Why does Daddy say her name that way?"

"Shush," I tell her. She obeys.

"We didn't always see eye to eye, me and Hixon, but we both served the same God. That's the beauty of this church, folks. That people so different can come together under the same roof and serve our Almighty Father." He nods Jed's way.

Jed stands. My heart stops up my chest. His stature is Hap's; demeanor too. But when Jed eyes me, he throws love my way. Please God, let him be his own man. With Hap next to him like that, I worry about the inevitability of son becoming father.

Hap steps aside but does not leave the podium — it's his dominion, after all. His head sits directly beneath the cross, as if it rests on his scalp like a holy exclamation point.

Jed does not have tears in his eyes. His eyes are flames, the

same flames that licked at his feet when he dragged Hixon from a fiery belly. "Hixon Jones was a man who loved Jesus." He swallows. I watch his Adam's apple quiver for a moment, then stiffen. He looks at the coffin. "And he was my friend. Besides Daisy, my best friend. But I don't think he knew it. I wish he did."

Emory lets out a gulping cry. Big Earl puts a fleshy arm around her, soothes her with words I cannot hear.

"But he wouldn't like us sitting around here crying like babies, now would he?" His voice is a preacher's, only genuine, scrubbed free of pretense. Perhaps he is the true pastor of the family. Jed's voice gathers itself, stirring into momentum. "He'd want us to throw him a little party. Hixon understood, probably more than anyone I know, that heaven is a real place and Jesus is a real, living person. How many of you here have heard Hixon talk to Jesus out loud?"

Hands rise throughout the congregation.

"How about when he sang to Jesus right in the middle of the day?"

More hands shoot heavenward.

"Hixon would want nothing more than for us to do the same. To talk to Jesus like He was here, standing among us — a fellow citizen of Defiance. Hixon," Jed clears his throat, "loved singing to Jesus. Hixon, this is for you."

His voice, which sounded assured moments ago, is now a whisper of a melody.

" ... this I know," he sings. "For the Bible tells me so."

A smattering of voices join him. I do too. Sissy grips my hand tighter. "Little ones to him belong. They are weak, but he is strong," we sing.

Hap booms, "Yes, Jesus loves me," as if his volume proves his ownership over the congregation. It jars the song, jolting the cadence of quiet singing.

I hear Emory choke out, "Yes, Jesus loves me." Does she truly believe such words?

"Yes, Jesus loves me, the Bible tells me so."

The silence after the song sounds like the nothingness of star-pocked space. Jed leaves the podium. Hap stands there awkward, as if he's unaccustomed to feeling God in his church, doesn't know how to manage the thickness of His presence. Emory stands. Hap's eyebrows raise, but he says nothing. The cross still rests on his forehead.

Emory doesn't mount the carpeted stairs. Instead she steps toward Hixon's coffin. She places a white hand on the brown wood and pulls in a raggedy breath. She caresses the top for an agonizing moment, like a mama stroking a sick child's forehead in the quiet of a midnight fever. Emory shakes her head over something—a memory perhaps?

"Hixon doesn't have a mama to mourn him today, but if I were his mama, I'd understand that kind of grief. I will miss Daisy every day of my life. Recently, I added Muriel, Hixon's adopted mama, to the list of folks who've left this earth far too soon. And now, Hixon."

She sways under her grief, but steadies herself by the coffin. Big Earl inches forward, as if ready to catch her.

"Muriel told me there'd be fire. I wonder if she saw what that fire would do to Hixon, that my fire would take his life, or that his remains would be burned until there was nothing more than a jar of him left."

I feel a scraping in my mouth, a hankering for a drink I cannot quench right now. If only there'd been water to baptize Crooked Creek Church, to extinguish those flames. But no hose could reach that far.

Emory pauses, eyes wet. "I think Muriel knew, somehow. I know many of you made your speculations about me, but Muriel, she saw something different. Hixon too. Maybe that's why he went in after me when Crooked Creek Church was burning. He saw something worth saving."

She wheezes in air. I hear it slide through her throat, con-

stricted. She levels a gaze toward the pew Hixon frequented. "He asked me to marry him," she says.

I hear murmurings around me. Though I know the information, many didn't.

"And I said no." She looks at Big Earl, nods. "I wish I had answered differently." A tear slips down her smooth cheek, touches her lips. She licks the grief and continues. "But with Daisy being gone, and me being a confused woman, how could I? Why would Hixon Jones want me? I didn't deserve him. And in some ways, I think we Defiance folk didn't deserve him either."

I watch Hap as Emory speaks. He seems to agree with Emory's words, but I know better.

"Hixon wasn't perfect. But he didn't pretend to be. He was just a handyman, he'd tell you. He painted my house. He fixed my sidewalk. He put locks on my doors. He made me feel safe. He protected. He loved. And now he's gone. We're all the worse for it, I'm telling you."

More tears wet her cheeks, but she doesn't wipe them away. She touches the coffin again. "I will never hold his hand again. But his hand and his heart changed me forever. I hope you won't see the same Emory Chance when you look at me. And if you see me changed, don't praise me. Thank Hixon Jones. He made me want to be a better woman."

I feel her words in my heart. It has been years since Hap has made me want to be a better woman. I can't look at him now, can't hold his once-kind eyes in my memory. Because he is no longer kind, he's a Doberman, ready to retaliate and maim, never to lick. Even so, maybe it's time I offer my hand again. Perhaps there's one more thing I can do.

Emory raises her left hand, almost in salute. With her other hand, she points to her ring finger, still adorned with Hixon's ring. "Though we didn't get married, I feel like a widow today. And my guess is that some of you have that kind of grief. That's the kind of person I want to be. The kind of person who'd leave a gaping hole if I left. That was Hixon. Now no one's left to fill his place."

She sits between Jed and Big Earl, grieving as a widow, while I grieve as a wife.

Hap speaks of comfort and peace and the hereafter, the wooden cross now an off-centered crown on his head. I watch his lips move, wishing they were Hixon's instead.

Four

Daisy used to say Hixon would marry us," Jed speaks to the space between us in the car. Having Jed with me on the ride home aches my heart.

I clear my voice, hoping it's steady when I release it. "That would've been beautiful."

"None of it will happen now."

I feel his six words in my gut. We share grief in the emptiest, most painful ways. He has lost three friends: Daisy, Muriel, Hixon. I've lost them too, and my marriage—or so it seems. I detour toward downtown Defiance. "Maybe—"

"No maybes, Mama. Death does that. Takes away the future. Wipes it clear out."

I sigh. "But you have your life shining ahead of you. Don't forget that." I almost say at least be thankful for that, but I restrain.

"Muriel said I had good in me, but I'm not so sure she's right."

"She was right. You do have good. But right now ... grief will take its place for a long time."

I see his jaw tense. "Why are we going this way?" Jed's eyes are pink-rimmed. I wish I could change that.

"I need some time to think before we head home."

He says nothing. He doesn't need to.

We're on Elm, Hixon's street. I am floating outside my mind, letting the car drive itself. For some reason, the car stops in front of his mismatched home. I find my car keys in my hand, the car no longer idling, like it died with the memory of Hixon. Or lost its will to run.

"Thanks, Mama," Jed says. He opens the door, steps out into the cold. I stay in the car, letting Jed be with himself and Hixon's home. He stands on the sidewalk, one foot on a rise created by a tree root, the other on a crack. It makes his stance crooked, one shoulder lower. God, how I love that kid. I wonder what job'll suit him when his frame fills out. Will he find another Daisy? Maybe so. But something tells me there's only one Hixon in the world. Never again another Hixon.

Hearing her name in my head reminds me of Jed's losses, the anguish he tries to hide. I see it, but I can't enter it. It's not that I don't want to, it's that I can't seem to figure out how to crawl into his shoes. They're too big for me anyway.

He walks up the sidewalk, then mounts the stairs. His shoulders buckle in a swift moment, heaving up and down. His back shudders while his hands cover his face. I cannot see him cry, as he faces away from me. But tears streak my face now; my shoulders buckle too—and the heaving mimics Jed's. It's as if Jesus has died all over again, but Hixon won't rise again. Jed turns on the porch, heads to Hixon's swing and sits. He rocks to the rhythm of my tears.

Time ends in this moment and a picture forms. It's the most beautiful picture I've conjured since escaping my stepdad—it's Lake Pisgah, sparkling under a wide sun. One million diamonds catch the light and shout it back heavenward in praise. Nothing breaks the surface of the water; it simply ripples there. I turn my head and see a man. He is blurred but he smiles. His arm is around a woman. Faceless, she shivers beneath his embrace. She is not afraid of the water, but I don't know why. Water drowns folks, I want to tell her. He gently pushes her backward into

Lake Pisgah's diamonds. She inhales, then disappears beneath its waters. Liquid dances in response, but she is not to be found. Seeing it all in my mind, I suddenly feel I can't take in air. Just when I grab it, the woman emerges, alive, so very alive. The man next to her dissipates like mist, and I am left to look at her, she at me, as if in a mirror. The resurrected one is me. Baptized and reborn. Another man stands to the side, shoeless, watching as others throw rose petals toward me. He shines like the lake's sun-kissed dimples, everything about him beckons me alive.

I should listen to the Voice, should plunge into the waters of baptism. He's needled me about it most of my life, but I never heeded, letting my fear of watery depths kill my obedience. Perhaps someday you'll see me stir the waters.

The sun angles its way into the windshield, magnifying what little heat it has this time of year. I gulp oxygen, hoping I won't lose my air, hoping Jed will recover somehow. So much to hold on his shoulders. And I've got no shoulders to support him. What kind of mother—

The door opens. I quickly wipe away mascara stains. Jed sits next to me. We look into the sun, blinking, as if we found ourselves here by chance, and we don't know where to go from here. I find the key in my hand and place it in the ignition; the car percolates to life.

"Thanks, Mama." His voice sounds ancient and youthful at the same time.

"I'm so sorry," I tell him.

"I know you are. But Mama?"

"Yes."

"I'm fourteen. I know you think messages on flower petals will help me, but they won't."

I stifle a cry; these messages I've made a habit of sending Jed's way are my link to him, my connection—our private conversation. How can I not write him felt-tipped notes on petals? Years of flowers and notes decayed so Hap'll never see. And now the flow of messages is over. I have no choice but to acquiesce to Jed's request. "I understand," I tell him. But I don't.

I continue down Elm — a street I've traveled many times — only now it looks different. Defiance has altered itself, though I'm not sure how.

We come up slow on Little Myrtle's — Emory's waitressing job. I see Big Earl's car turning in. He parks, then lumbers out of his car, shaking keys, shaking his head. All of Defiance mourns. Is that why God put this town here? So all the grieving of the world would settle in one place? I'd rather mourning would spread its geography. But I'm not God.

At the stop sign, Jed points. "Who is that?"

I'm about to tell him it's impolite to point, but when I see the man standing on the corner, I don't bother to reprimand. He is old, though his face is nearly wrinkle-free. His hair and beard are Santa-white, and he wears Santa's hat. He holds a cardboard sign that says, "Santa is watching. Merry Christmas."

I pull forward through the stop sign. Jed turns, watches the man. In the rearview mirror, Santa locks eyes with me, and winks.

Five

I am not free. I am not alive, really. You probably can see that. But I can make choices, even now. Salvation sits next to my bed. Not the vase full of hidden vodka, plastic flowers drinking its sweet nectar, but a book that beckons me. *The Godly Woman's Guide to Marriage* by Sheba Nelson, bless her heart. Maybe I'll read the introduction. And then I'll change. I'll escape the pain. I'll live.

I have hopes that someday I can be comfortable being me, walking in my shoes, head held high, a bouquet of yellow roses and honeysuckle scenting the path before me. I dream it, you know. See it as clear as Defiance at mid-sun, just as clear as I saw my own rebirth yesterday in front of Hixon's house. In the dank light of my room, I see me walking, smiling, maybe even skipping. But every time I am set free like this, I see Hap's mouth undecorating my dream.

Would it shock you to know I fantasize about Hap dying? It's not like I wish him cancer or heart attacks. It's not an ailment I give him. It's a gunshot wound to the head. But I'm not the one to pull the trigger.

I mourn then, wearing a black veil, while Jed and Sissy cry from relief and grief mixed together. I feel the regret in my gut, sad that I wished the gunshot upon him somehow. Even so, his casket is decorated with flowers — in every color God created — my last defiant act.

It's a dream I entertain for moments at a time, savoring them like a good chicken fried steak, only to chastise myself for the gluttony the next moment. I'm chastising now, choking on my horrid daydream. The kids are off to school. Hap's gone to church. And I'm left alone here with a stash of hidden paint-brushes and paintings beneath me and a book hollering at me from the nightstand.

But first, a drink. I lift the vase to my lips — a mixture of vanilla extract and vodka — hoping its liquid will soothe the hammering headache that woke with me. That always wakes with me. But it does not soothe. It simply gives me cookie breath and makes me remember my Mama's last gasps.

Once my throat warms under the alcohol's influence, I grab *The Godly Woman's Guide to Marriage* by Sheba Nelson. I feel compelled to tame my wild dreams, my death-wishes. My hunch is that my crazed thoughts are best dealt with by godliness. After all, that's what a pastor's wife is known for, right? Godly character and a penchant for playing the piano. I'm terribly rudimentary at the piano, but the character's clunkier still.

I read:

> I believe the biblical truths found in these pages will change your marriage forever. They will free you to be the woman you've always longed to be. We've run amok in this day and age, buying into a false women's liberation. But we wives don't need that kind of bra-burning liberation! No! We need godliness. We need submission. We need a gentle and quiet spirit. These things free you to be happy in your life.
>
> Open these pages to experience the kind of marital healing you've always longed for. I don't promise it will be easy. Revolutionizing a marriage seldom is. But if you're willing to submit and lay down your life, your husband

won't be able to help but love you. Isn't that what we all want? Our husband's passionate love? If that's what you want, keep reading.

I put my finger on the page, closing the book a moment to look at Sheba Nelson's face on the back cover. She wears buttoned up clothes, outdated glasses, and a smirk. How can someone like this know everything there is to know in a marriage? Is there such a thing as a perfect formula, and Sheba has figured it all out? Still, the words ricochet in my head and I open the book again. There's something enticing about all this. If I can do what Sheba says, I can fundamentally change everything. All within my power. After years of feeling like I have no influence, no voice, maybe this subversive text will help me manage my family, my marriage, my home. When there's nothing left in my life but to dream terrible dreams or drink away headaches, it's worth a try. Freedom's worth such sacrifice.

After all, Santa is watching, right?

I turn the page to chapter 1, "The Wifely Barometer: You Set the Atmosphere."

> A wife is the climate-creator in the home—a woman with a very special and beautiful purpose. It's her sunny attitude that creates the optimal environment for the marriage plant to take root, sprout, and grow. Therefore, it's her responsibility to tame the weeds her tongue longs to say, to plow under her stormy emotions, and shower her family with positivity and grace.

Positivity. Grace. A sunny attitude. All the things I am not. If Emory sat across from me at a booth in Little Myrtle's, I doubt she'd say, "Gee, Ouisie, you're sure sunny today!" Not that she isn't prone to praise like that, but I just can't picture it. Sissy, maybe. But me? Not on your life. Not in my life.

I close the book and pull out a pen and paper.

Dear Sheba,

I'm writing this today with many questions, with far too many hopes to put to paper. I'm sure, you being famous and all, are accustomed to hearing the woes of wives who can't seem to get it right. You probably have stacks of letters like mine. Perhaps many of the letters are from holy wives with little problems like meatloaf burning or incompetent laundering. I'm coming to you with another type of problem. Mine's simple. I am not enough. Not positive enough. Not encouraging enough. Not wife enough.

As I spill my worries, I picture Sheba sitting in a wingback chair, a cup of tea in hand, furrowing her brows, wondering at my wayward soul.

I write everything down for Sheba, spell it out in blue ink on white notebook paper. I tell Sheba how hard her words are to obey, that surely I merit some sort of Get-out-of-this-marriage-free card because of Hap's anger and violence. I can't believe I dare to write such words, but they fly out of me, like birds escaping an iron cage.

Thank you for reading my ramblings. That's really all I needed, for someone in this world to know my struggle, to hear me. Now you know.

I address an envelope, lick a stamp, and send my heart into the great unknown, to Rowlett, Texas 75088.

I pull the vase again to trembling lips and take a drink to soften my rough edges. Sometimes vanilla-vodka brings sunshine, though rarely does it welcome grace into my life. More like guilt. Still it helps as its burn races down my throat. It blurs my mind for a blessed moment, only to recoil on me, dousing me with an angry headache, my penance for seducing it.

With the envelope sealed, I cannot write the words I think right now. They are this: Sheba, how can a woman like me be set free?

He'd listened to them, the boy Jed and the girl Daisy, while they bantered from inside the abandoned old church. Talk of marriage and families. Such normal conversation before death. And then the boy Jed ran, haunted, from the old church.

As soon as the footsteps of the boy ran clear away and the night shifted the shadows, he crept up the church's steps. Opened the door. She spun around herself, her face full of life, her voicing trailing, "Jed, you came back."

His deliberate steps creaked along the center aisle.

Unlike the sandaled girl, she didn't holler. Didn't try to run. She faced him, looked him square in the face and said, "And who are you?"

He did not answer such things. Instead he glanced down at her feet, encased in ordinary sneakers. And then he smiled.

Six

The tree framed in our front room window smells like life to me—blessed evergreen, scenting our Christmas. We gather around it as we always have, in varying degrees of sleepiness and anticipation. Only my anticipation isn't of the package-opening variety. Will Hap behave this holiday? Or will he rip us all apart?

I open Sissy's gift first, at her insistence. "You'll love it, Mama," she tells me. A tired plaid bow preens on top of her head—she's her own Christmas present. I wonder if Santa really came last night—if the man on the corner shimmied down our chimney and brought a little parcel of joy just for today.

I lift each flap, bending the tape over. You can always re-use paper if you're careful enough. Besides, Hap watches me, makes sure I am cautious. I slip my finger along the back of Sissy's present, revealing a simple white box.

"Open it, Mama. You're so slow!"

Clementine understands and nuzzles me. I lift the box and cry. Brushes. Beautiful paintbrushes. "Oh Sissy," I say.

"What d'you need those for?" Hap barks from the easy chair. He's slippered and robed. I guess I hoped with such clothing on, he'd be feeble or quiet. No. His voice is dressed up and ready to fight.

I swallow my tears, wiping my face clean of them with the

top of my wrist. Funny how my daughter knows me better than the man who shares my bed. He doesn't know about the hidden paintings. Sheba says there should be no secrets between husband and wife, but this one seems too delicate to share. She says to smile often, to deflect, to entice. So I beg God to give me smiles and subtlety. A sunny attitude.

But I can't help picturing my hidden paintings—flowers, landscapes, portraits—unstretched canvasses under the bed, rolled up and hidden from Hap's eyes. When he's not haunting the house, I paint worlds my feet will never jump into, and I regret my reticence to leap every day of my life. Flowers burst from my brushes, dance in the fickle Texas wind on an undecorated canvas—vibrant colors Hap won't allow in the house. Too racy, he says. Too everything. If it were up to my husband, we'd hang empty canvasses on the walls.

Jed pushes an envelope my way.

I startle, and then smile.

"For you, Mama." His voice is plain, but I hear the anxiety beneath his words, like a wolverine suppressing growls. Always present, ready to release. But Jed has what his father doesn't—a stubborn glimmer of self-control. And a hatred of his father I'm trying desperately to resist in myself, but falling headlong into almost as quickly as I fell in love.

"What's this?" I ask. I note Hap's neck. It's candy-apple red. Another Christmas with tight-lipped sentiments unfolds before me. I steady my worry.

"Miss Emory helped me with it a few days ago—when she moved into Miss Muriel's." Jed's fourteen-year-old voice is deeper than last Christmas, and his eyes are older, wiser and cynical. That's what death does to a young man.

I open the envelope. Inside is a teaspoon of what looks like seeds.

"Hollyhocks," Jed says. "Muriel loved 'em. Every year, she'd save their seeds. Hixon once told me she sowed the whole south side of her property with them. Miss Emory found them and told me I could give some to you."

I tell myself not to cry. My children see my need for beauty. They understand. "They're beautiful. Thank you, Jed."

"I don't want a bunch of flowers decorating my yard," Hap says. "Just look at the jungle Ethrea Ree planted. I'm not having a yard like that, Ouisie." He stands, walks my way.

Instinctively, I cringe, but plant a smile on my face. I am the climate-creator.

He hands me a small package, hastily wrapped. It's our tradition to recognize each other, one at a time. First Sissy, then Jed, then Hap. And perhaps Clementine will come after me because I know Sissy's found her a bone.

"Thanks," I tell Hap. I try to mean it. The package feels light. I rip the paper—it's the Funnies anyway—and wonder if Hap has lost his senses. A square box houses a Magic 8 Ball. I pull it from its case, setting the box on the floor beside me.

"Oh I love those." Sissy sits closer to me, resting her head on my upper arm. I know she wants to try it.

"Why this?" I ask.

Hap settles back into the chair, a smile on his face. "You know how you always ask so many questions when I come home?"

I nod.

"Well, now you won't need to ask. You can pester that ball with all the questions you want, and it'll answer right back."

"Isn't that a little like Voodoo? Or witchcraft?"

Hap laughs. "Shoot, Ouisie. It's supposed to be funny. This way, I can come home and read the paper without you bothering me."

"So it's really a gift for you." So much for grace.

Hap pounds slippered feet toward me. He grabs the shiny black ball from my hand. Sissy shivers beside me. Jed stiffens and flexes. Hap towers over us all, shaking the ball. "It's like

this, Ouisie. You ask it a question, and it answers back. It's a game. Not witchcraft. Let me demonstrate." He looks at the ceiling. I can still smell sleep on him. "Will we have a Merry Christmas?" He turns over the ball. A smile etches into his face. " 'As I see it, yes,' it says. See?" He shakes it again. "Will we find the tattooed man?"

"Hap," I say. "On Christmas?"

He looks at me, "Didn't Emory say she saw a man with a tattoo? That she thinks he's who took Daisy?"

At the mention of Daisy, Jed looks away. Sissy snuggles closer. I close my eyes.

" 'Very doubtful,' " Hap reads.

I open my eyes. Doubtful, indeed. The Magic 8 Ball doesn't know everything, now, or does it?

He hands the ball to Jed. "You try."

"No thanks."

Hap offers it to Sissy.

"Will I ever get rid of my lisp?" Her S is nearly perfect, almost an imperceptible TH, but I fear she hears her imperfections like a bullhorn. She shakes the ball. She reads, "It is decidedly so," but this time the lisp is more pronounced. She hands me my present.

"Try it," Hap tells me, more a command than an invitation. I lack the will to fight him today, especially considering it's Jesus' birthday, and He personified meek and mild. I should follow His example more.

I ask one question, but place another in my mind. Out loud I ask, "Will flowers bloom in my yard this year?" Hap growls— there's really no other way to describe his voice—and lifts his left eyebrow, his angry look. I turn the ball over. I frown at its response: "cannot predict now." My real question is *Will I ever be happy in this marriage?* Seems the 8 Ball's captured my life beautifully. My unpredictable, flowerless life.

"What did it say?" Hap asks.

I tell them it says "without a doubt," which I believe to be true on the flower question, terribly wrong on the happy question.

Hap nods. "We'll see about flowers in the yard. Perhaps I can be persuaded."

Jed and I look his way at once. Is this a joke? A taunt? Or kindness?

"Are you sure there's not more in the box?" Hap winks at me. He's been doing it since I found out about his long-ago fling with Emory Chance—his lighthearted way of repenting, I guess. It unnerves me. I'm not sure if I want to spit or melt or swear or smile. I retrieve the box at my feet. In my haste to pull out the Magic 8 Ball, I missed a small envelope in the bottom. I open it.

My Mama's ring, and it's polished too, as if it'd never been lost in the plumbing this year.

"You told me it dropped down the kitchen sink. Well, when you were out, I unscrewed the plumbing and found it. I took it to Orlean's for cleaning."

Jed stands to see, almost like a soldier saluting. Sissy beckons Clementine to the rawhide chew she bought while I place the ring back on my right ring finger. The emerald glistens green in the morning light. It's surrounded by tiny diamonds, little shimmers of sparkle. And the simple band is more golden than I can remember. "Perfect," I say.

In spite of all the things Hap can do, all the rages, all the flinging of pans, all the midnight hollering, he does something right today. He takes what was lost and makes it found, something I was blind to, but now I see.

Maybe there's something to Sheba's godliness words. Maybe my secret plan is working, and this shiny ring is the exclamation point. With the ring circling my finger, I wrap my arms around my husband who still smells like waking up. I tell him Merry Christmas. I whisper I love you. And when he leaves to

visit Mr. Jenkins in the nursing home today, I'll plant those hollyhock seeds on the bed flanking the house's left side. And hide my brushes.

Something tells me — is it the Voice? — that hiding will keep me safe.

Seven

Dishes bewitch me again, that staid chore I never escape. But this morning while mist rises on the morning and the kids are off to school, I don't mind so much. You have to love how the warm water unchills icy hands.

I look up to see Delmer Ree lumbering his way through the landscape behind my back yard, his large footfalls heavy with each plodding step. He is a strapping man with a boy's careless sensibilities, clad in long sleeves, a pair of too-big pants, and no shoes. I wonder if I should call Ethrea Ree, our rose-loving neighbor and Delmer's mother, and alert her to his wanderings. But my hands are so warm and my will so weak that I watch him meander out of sight toward Lord knows what. Squirrel befriending, probably. Or just plain exploring, perhaps. Surely Ethrea knows.

As I baptize each dish, I realize Lake Pisgah must miss my presence something awful—an orphan from my neglect. You'd think I'd prefer springtime at the lake, when trees burst green and the old dogwoods sing pink and white to the breezes. No. I hope in gaunt limbs scraping across blue winter skies. You can see the birds' nests that way, woven up high—empty little homes soon to be full.

Someone knocks at the door.

I dry my hands, walk down the hallway, and see Emory Chance. I let her in.

"It's cold." She shrugs off an old wool seaman's coat and fuzzy lime-green mittens, unleashing her hair from a woolen cap. It rises from static.

"I'll make tea." I lead her into the kitchen. The teakettle is chipped and its interior is flecked white from too much calcified water. Used to be I'd scrub it spic-clean only to have the spots magically appear again the next day. I've given up on that now. Life's too short, as they say.

"I need to talk." Emory rests her chin on the heels of both hands.

I sit. "What about?"

"Guilt."

I want to say something catty now, about how she wears guilt like a favorite sweatshirt. But I don't. Clementine stares at me with those browner-than-brown eyes. The dog's got my tongue.

Emory sits up, releasing her chin from her hands. She pulls a long strand of hair forward and twirls it around her left index finger. Her nervous twitch. "It's been a long time since Hap and me. But I still feel awful."

The teakettle whistles, freeing me from having to talk in the silence. I pour two cups of Red Rose, bring them to the table. I give her a spoon and place the milk and sugar nearby. I take mine plain. Silence stirs between us. I have no words.

"I never loved Hap," she says. "I only really loved David."

It surprises me that we never really spoke of David much, yet hearing his name kindles me. "I know him," I try to say casually, but I hear the catch in my voice.

"Your first love too, right?"

I take a drink, but it doesn't quench my thirst. "Yes." Maybe my only. He told me he loved me, told me he'd protect me, take care of me. But that's another lifetime. I don't bore Emory with mundane details like these.

"You know about him, don't you? That he's in a wheelchair now."

"Hap was quick to tell me that. He's been jealous of my relationship with David all these years. Seems to think we're still together."

"Jealousy does interesting things to a man," she says.

"Indeed." I want to add that they do interesting things to a wife, but I hold my tongue. I remind myself this is Emory sipping tea before me, a wayward mama who's lost a daughter and a potential husband in the span of a few months. Her landscape is entirely craggy.

She clears her throat. "Back to love. With Hixon, it was this pure love—like a grandfather's, but sweeter. I see myself married to Hixon in a strange sort of way, which means I can't exactly cheat on him, though I swear the loneliness is choking me. Even Angus Day steers clear of me now. Is God some sort of spoiler in the sky, messing with what I want to do?"

"I don't speak well for God. I usually let Hap speak of matters of theology."

"Oh, come on, Ouisie. Just tell me what you think. You're intelligent. You've got opinions."

"I've lost my opinions." I look out the kitchen window hoping to catch a bird in flight or the tremble of a leaf floating to earth, but the world seems just as bare and lifeless outside as inside.

She puts a hand on mine, grabs my eyes a moment. "Were you in love with Hap?"

"Yes." Her clever use of *were* begs for more, but I don't want to add a comma and another phrase to my sentence.

She drinks a sip of tea the color of mud puddles. She throws out the deepest sigh, like her soul is leaving her body. "I'm sorry, Ouisie."

"Sorry?"

"I wish I could say I'm sorry one million times to show you how much I regret Hap. It wasn't love."

I stand. I can't help it; hearing the words so stark in the quiet

kitchen brings tea rushing up my throat. I cough, but I can't hack it back down. I run to the sink and spit out brown, rasping afterwards. I fill a glass with water and drink it straight down, hoping it will calm the angry lake inside.

Emory stands, looks frail. If there were such a thing as wind in our house, it'd blow her clear to the stove. "I best be leaving."

I sit back down, tell her to do the same. "It's okay. Really."

"I'm sorry," she mutters.

"I told you already. I forgive you. I do. Just sometimes it's hard. You know?"

"Yeah." Emory takes another drink. I let my tea cool between us.

I take the adulteress-friend's hand, and look at her. "Love will come someday for you." They are my words of hope and dread mixed together. Hope for her, dread for me—because if love doesn't come, maybe she'll steal Hap again. Then again, would that be so awful? Why am I so afraid to be on my own?

A knock startles us both.

"Don't get up. I'll see who it is. Feel free to pour yourself another cup. The tea bags are on the counter." I leave Emory for the door. I open it to Ethrea Ree, her hair neatly rolled into pink curlers, a gray, ratty bathrobe warming her scrawny frame. "Ethrea," I say.

"He's gone."

"Who's gone?"

"Who else could be gone but my Delmer?" She wrings her hands. Something flecks her gray eyes. Terror? Relief?

"I saw him while I did the dishes earlier, heading through the woods toward downtown."

Her face relaxes. "He wanders."

I invite her in, show her to the kitchen. "Have a seat next to Emory. We're having tea."

They exchange a hasty hello.

"Seems Delmer's gone missing again."

I pour her a cup of tea.

"Your son?" Emory takes a drink. "I'm sorry."

Her sorry is genuine, I'm sure—spoken like only a mama who lost a child could speak.

"Delmer, well, he's special. Leastways that's what the teachers told me when he went to school. Been home with me many years now. But he's never quite been the same since Slim's death. No matter what kind of man you are, you never outgrow the need for a father, now do you?"

Her question has no answer. We sip tea.

"When did you notice him missing?" I touch her cold hand, but she shrugs me away.

"I went to wake him this morning. His bed was made. He rarely does that 'cept on holidays like Christmas or his birthday when I link opening his gifts to the state of his bedding. Sometimes Delmer talks to Jesus, so I checked that out, of course." To Emory she says, "The Jesus statue in our back yard."

"Have you called the police?"

"Thought I'd check here first. My Delmer talks a lot about Jed. How he's his friend."

I try not to look confused, but I'm sure my face gives me away. Jed never sees Delmer, never talks to him. If you ask me, he's scared of the addled man—as he should be. "Well, Delmer's not here. He probably just wandered off. Maybe we best call the police."

"Delmer doesn't wander *much*, just out back sometimes in the field—never beyond. I think that kook out there nabbed him. Same one who took Daisy."

I move toward the phone. "All the better to call the police."

The front door opens then closes, banging on its hinges. "Papa? Papa?" Delmer's voice.

Ethrea Ree runs down the hallway to the living room. We follow. There, dressed in nothing but those loose-fitting pants and a long sleeved shirt the color of green olives stands Delmer,

wild-eyed and shoeless. "Where'd you put him, Mama? Where'd you put Papa?"

She stiffens. "Delmer, we've gone over this." Her words sound siphoned through a too-narrow drinking straw. "He's miles away in a cemetery. I can take you there and we can visit. Bring him some flowers. Some of my roses are still blooming. I promise we'll go again. Just don't go running away. You had me scared to death."

I wonder if I should speak, or let them play this out. I scan his body briefly, landing on his arms, then try to catch his eyes, but he stares at his toes.

"He's not there. You and me, we checked before. There's just a stone with something scratched in it. No man at all. No man at all."

This time I decide to speak. "Delmer, your papa died in the war. He was a hero, but he's in heaven now."

"He can come out of heaven, can't he? Because I see him." Delmer places his thumb between his perfectly white teeth and bites down. Hard.

Emory puts a thin hand on Delmer. "Your papa's keeping company with Hixon and Daisy."

"Hixon's for fixin'. Daisies are for fields and for picking."

"Let Mama take you home, Delmer. You're near froze to death being out there." Ethrea Ree grabs his free hand, opens the front door. "Where are your shoes?"

"Under my bed where they're supposed to be. All lined up."

"But when you go outside," Ethrea says, "you must remember to wear them. Now let's get home."

"Will I get to open presents?"

"No, that's for Christmas and birthdays, remember?"

"It's Papa's birthday today."

"So it is," Ethrea says. "I should've realized." She pushes

Delmer through the doorway, steals a quick look back, and throws an apology our way with her eyes.

I nod in reply.

When the door closes, Emory's face drains. "She brought me casseroles."

"Ethrea Ree?"

"Yes, I thought it was just quirky, but now I'm not so sure."

"What do you mean?"

Emory holds herself, thin arms around a thinner body. She sits in the easy chair by the window—Hap's chair. "I didn't see his arms, and he seems pretty slow. Do you think Delmer can run?"

I sit on the divan. "I suppose."

"He doesn't get out much, does he?"

"No, except for out back where I can see him, he's afraid of going out, which is why today's escape is a little strange. But what are you trying to say?"

Emory sighs. "That Delmer took Daisy."

"I doubt it," I say. But now I'm not sure what to think. But this I do know: No matter if men are slow or clever—you'll never quite understand their ways.

Eight

Santa knocks on the window of the kitchen door. His eyes are red, his smile the same smile I saw when he held that sign up in downtown Defiance. I do not open the door. I look at the ticking clock—an hour to go before the kids get home. Still, what can it hurt?

I open the door.

He stands at the threshold, not entering, not backing away. "God told me something."

I think of the Voice, wondering if He whispered my rebellious refusal to be baptized to Kris Kringle. "Oh really," I say.

"He said to give you this." He stretches his hand through the doorway. I place my hand under his while he drops something light as air into my palm. My heart beats; the clock ticks.

I look at my hand. In it sits a tiny paper box. "What is it?"

But Santa says nothing.

I touch it. It's one inch by one inch, made of thin cardboard, perfectly glued. A doll-sized green bow adorns the top.

His hair is white, his eyes the color of a winter sky. He clears his throat, and when he does, his beard shakes. "God told me to make boxes, and that I was to give the first one to you." His voice is graveled as if it trailed down many roads.

So Santa does bring presents. "It's beautiful." I try not to use that word, but it slips out of my mouth like a robin's flight, taking on wings of its own. The word *beautiful* lingers in the room's atmosphere.

"A sign from the Almighty," he says.

I look at the box between us, a little square island of buffer hovering in my palm. "What's inside?"

"Love," he says. "God's love."

"It's such a small box."

"Ironic, isn't it?" He backs away. "I best be going, ma'am. No need to overstay my welcome. Besides, I did what I was supposed to do."

"Thank you," I say, then I realize I don't know Santa's name.

He extends a dirty hand my way. "It's Elijah." He bows slightly. "But let's keep this meeting between the two of us, shall we? Our little secret?" He shuts the door and walks away through the back gate into the woods.

I am alone holding a green-bowed box, coddling a burning desire to talk to this Elijah again. And not tell a soul. Our little secret.

The man haunted the Defiance woods. He memorized its trees. He ran rough hands over tree trunks wherever he went, feeling their girth, their life. They'd sheltered him, hiding the girl who hollered too much, who begged to be silenced. And they never told a soul.

From holes in the ground to branches reaching to the humid sky, stealthily he waited for the moment to silence her sentences. The trees deemed the day, providing an opening, a place. He dug the hole with a shovel stolen from a careless gardener, then carried it back to its home, never the worse for wear.

He pulled her there, dragging, lurching, silencing her cries with his thick hand. She let out one last yelp to the heavens when he choked her breath the final time. Just as he had with the sandaled girl.

But he felt no relief as he held her shoe in his hands. And took to watching her mother through a canopy of branches.

Nine

The cool of the day beckons me to the Lake Pisgah's edge, daring me to remove my shoes, take a toe-dip. But I don't. Water is like that quicksand you see in B-movies—it sucks you into the ground in a drop of a second. And I have my own prison, my own lock and key.

And again I am visited by this Elijah, his hair white and wooly, the way I imagine a prophet. He walks toward me as I straddle Lake Pisgah's shore. He wears a ratty woolen coat around wide shoulders.

He utters no greeting, doesn't raise his hand in hello. "Your husband is the preacher." He says it with eyes like dark clouds.

"He is." Saying it so stark like that reminds me of the start of Hap's preaching career, how he'd been a carpenter—a good one—before he ventured off into the hinterlands of ministry when he turned thirty-three. We've been in this wilderness too many years.

"From what I hear, he's an interesting man." Elijah walks toward the lake's eastern shore. He doesn't beckon, but I follow. How can I not? His hair is January white. Old Man Winter.

We walk the circumference of the lake in silence. The only sound is the crunching Bermuda grass beneath my sneakers and his black shoes. It feels right, circling the lake this way—alone, and yet not. I feel safe next to this man who could be my father. I know I shouldn't trust a stranger, especially not in light of

recent events, but I can't help but walk alongside him. He exudes something intoxicating, a delicious wonder I can't seem to capture or understand.

"He's got some demons," Elijah says once we've circled the lake. How would he know such a thing? We are standing where we started, a whisper of air between us, swirling in the cool January atmosphere toward leafless trees kissing the sky. I wonder if he means actual demons or the kind you get when you've had a hard childhood and the memories haunt you as an adult. But he interrupts my thoughts. "He'll have to battle them. Tame them, if he's going to come out on the other end of this thing."

"What thing?"

Elijah shakes his head, rubs his bearded chin with a gloved hand. "That, I don't know right now. I try to say the words the Lord says to me, and that's what came out."

"I need to go," I tell him. The sun's near its zenith, and I've got to clean the house.

"Godliness," he tells me, "is great gain." He nods as he says it, as if that should settle everything. I remember my book and think maybe this whole walk is a sign from God, another confirmation from the Voice that I should continue forward with my hesitant plan to woo Hap. "That's good to know," I say.

"I haven't told you my story yet. Can you spare a little more time? Dishes can always wait, and I feel compelled to spill it here, while the sun casts its shadows straight down, nailing us to the earth." He gestures with his hands, then points to my Adirondack chair. "It's not a long story. I'll stand; you can rest in your chair."

I make my way to the Adirondack, pulling my coat further around me, if that's possible, and pray I'm not making some sort of cardinal mistake by listening to this stranger who seems to have accurately pigeonholed my husband's soul. Sitting down, I think of Emory and suddenly I want her here. Not to protect me, but to experience Elijah alongside me so we can share something that doesn't consist of affairs or death. Shouldn't friends — if you can call us that — share joys too? And stories?

But Elijah said not to tell, and I'm strangely inclined to obey. He paces in front of me, his hands shoved deep into coat pockets, exhaling like coffee steam. "My real name's a killer," he says. "And it all makes sense, if you ask me. I was destined, you might say."

"What is it?"

"Well, you've got to remember my folks weren't religious. They didn't cavort with Christians, didn't swing in their circles. And when I came along, his wasn't exactly a familiar name."

I want him to tell me everything at once, but I sense his desire to spin a story, to elongate information in a perfectly agonizing manner, so I keep silent.

He bows. "I am Billy Grammer."

I laugh.

He stands before me, his hands raised like fists, as if this story needs exact motions. He throws a few punches into the wind. "Well, it didn't mean much to me as a kid. I made my way through elementary school relatively untouched by the Reverend Graham. Then in high school, a pretty little girl invited me to a concert, so she said. I thought she was awfully forward, doing such a thing, but her beauty hoodwinked me and I followed like a lamb to the slaughter. Only I didn't get slaughtered. I got preached at. By the real Billy."

"How old were you?" I ask.

"I was seventeen — a cocky kid with an attitude. Every time Billy said Jesus, I'd say his name too, only my rendition was swearing. I think the Lord must've had himself a mighty fine laugh from heaven watching one Billy Jesus-talk another Billy. It's as if we were dueling the name."

"So what happened?" I've heard so many conversion stories that I know what is coming next.

"I left the stadium, deserting the pretty girl."

"And then you met Jesus."

He smiles, and I notice his teeth—some chipped, others browned. "No. I ran away. I don't know why I did such a thing. I didn't hate my parents—they were good, earthy parents. But I felt like God was chasing me and I didn't want to be caught, so I ran clear to Vegas. I had no money, no skills. I worked odd jobs and lived in the sewer pipes beneath the city."

"You lived in the sewer?"

"For a good long time. It's not what you might think. It's quite spacious down there. Plus, I couldn't hear the voice of God. I surrounded myself with other folks who were running away from him. Their voices bounced off the pipes; they chattered mighty loud. God couldn't get a word in edgewise."

He paces now, back and forth; he whispers like he's arguing with himself. I glance behind me, noting my car and the distance between it and me. I finger my keys in my pocket.

"It was in the sewers my hair turned white. Not sure why, but folks called me Santa once it did. So I grew myself a beard and let the name stick."

"It just turned white?"

"Yeah, over the period of a year. I figured each hair willed itself to be brown only to turn white against its will, like God was converting each strand. But I'm a stubborn one, you see. After I'd whitened, it took a good amount of years for my will to bow to God's. Forty-three years after I first heard about Jesus, I surrendered it all—white hair, body, soul."

I calculate seventeen plus forty-three and get sixty, my guess for his age. "So you haven't been a Christian long?"

"Twenty-six days," he says.

I look behind me again, pray for protection.

"On the day I read in the Tyler paper that Hixon Jones died, Jesus appeared to me. Told me to go to Defiance and fill in. Told me to make boxes. And He told me you'd be here today."

I stand, chastising myself for circling the lake with this madman.

"You want to leave."

"I have dishes to do."

He raises his hands in surrender—his eyes squinting like a painter concentrating on a difficult stroke. "I won't keep you. Far be it from me to imprison you by rambling on and on about my story. You've got prisons aplenty."

Ten

I know it's supposed to be Jesus who does all that freeing from prisons aplenty. I know he's the One who has to perform heart surgery on Hap, but Sheba seems to think I can help him somehow, by conjuring up a compliant, teachable heart. But I am a woman of secrets, secret wishes, secret desires—by now you know that. Can that sort of woman revolutionize the unrevolutionary? Will my family ever shine? Ever reflect the joy I long for as Lake Pisgah reflects the sunlight today? It's been a week since I encountered Elijah—and kept him secret from everyone but you. The other times I walked the lake, he didn't appear like a mist on the water. So for company, I take Sheba's book with me, along with some gloves and a hat, hoping to read in the January chill, to glean just a bit more about reigniting the family I've always wanted.

When I arrive, the woods ringing the lake stand skeleton-bare and their shed leaves scratch a noise under my boots. I look for my familiar chair, but it's been moved four feet to the north. Nothing looks right. I am unsettled, praying that my discomfort blows away. Or that my heart will settle itself.

Elijah is not here to ruffle my worry—or fuel it either—but I feel his strange presence nonetheless. Like he's watching me behind grayed trunks and tenacious vines, lurking in and out, in front and behind. The thought of him sends shivers through me.

And yet, there's enticement—the very thing I'm supposed to use to woo Hap back to the straight and narrow. I am intrigued by the wrong man. It's not like I think Elijah handsome, or compelling, even. No, it's something deeper than that. He reminds me of someone.

I open the book with gloved hands, but I cannot turn the pages, so I take them off. The chill kisses my hands. I jump over chapter two, the chapter titled "Submission—God's Gift to Women." My eyes refuse to crawl over the words. I'll come back to it on a better day, when I finally make the decision to always say yes to the Almighty and submit to Hap. But I cannot obey completely today.

Instead I skim the chapter entitled, "The Secret of the Shunammite Woman." Sheba quotes from the book of Second Kings:

> "And it fell on a day, that Elisha passed to Shunem, where was a great woman; and she constrained him to eat bread. And so it was, that as oft as he passed by, he turned in thither to eat bread. And she said unto her husband, Behold now, I perceive that this is an holy man of God, which passeth by us continually."

I see Elijah in this passage, so close to his name that I wonder if I didn't hear him wrong. I know the Voice sends surprises my way, little delights, perhaps angels unawares. But how does meeting Elijah relate to my family? Should I invite him into our home, hoping his eccentric faith would rub off on Hap? Is this the secret to a better marriage?

I continue reading while a hint of fire carries on the wind, snapping me back to the day Hixon died and Jed played the hero. Jed's hair smelled like charcoal, his face hot and dusted black. He escaped the lick of fire, but Hixon didn't.

I continue reading and stop at this sentence: "The barren Shunammite's reward for her hospitality is her son's life resur-

rected—a renewed family from the ashes. Could welcoming a stranger like Elijah be rewarded lavishly like that?

"Ouisie, this is the best chicken fried steak I've ever had." Hap smiled as he said it, wiping gravy off the corner of his mouth, that place I wanted to kiss one hundred times. We sat in my home. My mama and stepdad were out for the evening, so I was playing house, trying desperately to impress this man who stole my heart. I was ravenous for his words, his praise.

"Thank you," I said. "Did you try the potatoes?"

"They're perfect. Not a lump. Not only are you beautiful ... " He pulled me onto his lap, " ... but you're full of hospitality. I like that. I like it a lot. Because I want that in my family—a home folks want to come to—strangers, needy people, folks needing family." His eyes wet, he turned away from me for a hesitant moment, pulling in long breaths. "Family's all a person ever has." I looked at my home, remembering Mama's haunted stare and how my stepdad ruled the place with wrath. How it never used to be that way when Daddy shepherded our lives. Yes, Hap was right. Family, when it worked right, made all the difference. Hap turned me to face him and gently kissed me, his right hand cradling the back of my neck, his left hand warm on my back. I gave him everything, as much as a kiss could offer, my own invitation to family. When he moved away, he looked farther into my eyes.

I returned the favor.

"I love you, Ouisie."

I told myself not to cry. Tears emerged; my head spun. I saw every color God created all at once, a Jackson Pollock daydream I couldn't erase if I wanted to. I saturated myself in Hap's love, relished his words. I knew he wanted me to speak, but I was mute in the moment, utterly bamboozled by his declaration. He wrapped his carpenter arms around me. "I'll need good food when I'm building things, you know."

I found my voice. "And I'll need a home to cook in. Away from here." I gestured to the kitchen, my mama's. My stepdad's boots decorated the corner, muddying it. I caught elation then. Hap became my escape from my stepdad David's tirades, from his harsh words, his violence. I didn't have to have that kind of family. I didn't have to settle for violence and intimidation. For a hesitant moment, I worried about my mama, her safety, but that moment fled as Hap kissed me fiercely.

"I love you," I finally said. I loved him for his kindness, for appreciating my cooking, for freeing me from this home. For accepting my paltry hospitality. All I thought about in the circle of his arms was how safe I felt in his embrace and how beautiful, truly beautiful, my family might look.

I shiver, remembering how Hap smelled like soap and hard work, how I couldn't keep from smiling after his declaration of love. It'd come on the heels of my hospitality—at the time, the most surprising gift of my life—until he asked me to be his wife.

So I thrill at the Shunammite's joy, and I rejoice that she has her own Jed to love, just like me. But I continue to read. I grapple with Emory's grief as the son dies. I picture the Shunammite woman as she finds Elisha, tells him off, then begs him to return. The prophet enters her home, lays flat out on the boy and somehow blows new life into him. "And the child sneezed seven times, and the child opened his eyes. And he called Gehazi, and said, Call this Shunammite. So he called her. And when she was come in unto him, he said, Take up thy son. Then she went in, and fell at his feet, and bowed herself to the ground, and took up her son, and went out."

Sheba explains that the Shunammite relied only on God and his prophet to restore what was dead. She continues:

Some of you reading this might be discouraged. You might believe your marriage is as dead as the Shunammite's son. Don't give into that fear. You have a God who sees you, who undergirds you with strength. And a God who loves to breathe life into that which is decaying or dead. Would

you spend some time today praying that God would resurrect your marriage? That He would breathe vitality into it? Your job is to boldly ask, to chase after God as the Shunammite woman chased after Elisha. Grab His cloak if you must.

I cradle this belief to my chest, as I breathe in the cool scent of Lake Pisgah. If my family's to be saved, perhaps Elijah will play a part. What part, I don't know exactly. But perhaps it involves the most important propheting he'll ever do—laying himself out on the shattered pieces of the Pepper family, breathing life.

Eleven

T hey say you should never grocery shop when you're hungry, or you'll want to buy everything in sight. I'm hungry, but the money in my purse prevents me from grabbing chips and ice cream and cookies from the shelves of Piggly Wiggly. I do touch a package of Oreos screaming my name then place them back on the shelf while my stomach grumbles back at me. I can almost taste the Crisco-white frosting.

"I like 'em too," a voice behind me says. Elijah.

I let out a breath, then look into Elijah's dancing eyes. "You shopping?"

"Nah," he breezes. "Just looking."

He walks beside me as I push the cart down the breakfast aisle. I plant my feet smack dab in the middle of the cereal section debating between Cheerios and its store-brand counterpart, as if the decision were between heaven and hell. I have eighteen dollars and forty-eight cents in my purse. Nothing more. Not even two stray pennies to make it an even $18.50.

"It really doesn't matter," I hear him say. I turn to face Elijah. It's been seven days since I decided I would invite him to dinner, seven days of Hap's instability. Happy one moment, growling and pacing the next. No matter how much I follow Sheba's tutelage, his mood still swings. I'd hoped Elijah would find me much faster. But he hasn't.

"I suppose you're right." I drop Tasty-O's into my cart—they're a few cents cheaper anyway—and push my way through the colorful aisle, Elijah walking beside me. Ask boldly, I hear Sheba say. And even though I worry about this man, how he can be so close to God in such a short glimmer of time, I remember the way he seemed to know me, my situation. I say: "Do you mind if I ask you a question?"

"Not at all. I can't say I'll answer it, but you're free to ask." He chews gum, smacking it between some of his words. Loving that gum to death, it seems.

I feign interest in canned tomatoes, worried about the prices, calculating just how much more I can buy before Hap's grocery allowance runs out. Holding a can of stewed store-brand tomatoes, I say, "Do you believe in miracles?"

"Only certain ones."

I put the tomatoes back on the shelf. "What do you mean?"

"Some folks say a thing's a miracle when it's really just happenstance. It has to have God's fingerprints all over it for me to deem it so. Why? What kind of miracle are you after?"

I sigh. Do I say it out loud for the tomato cans to hear?

"You're afraid to say it, aren't you?"

"Yes."

"You want a happy family. Problem is husbands aren't easily tamed."

He says the words I long to say but can't. Does this mean he's really in touch with God? Only God can type a person's thoughts then send that memo to another soul, right? Only God, I hope. I notice Elijah's shoes then, terribly worn, missing a lace in one. Where are his black shoes he wore when he walked the lake with me? It occurs to me that I have no idea where Elijah lives, or if he has a place of his own. "Where do you live?"

"Now why would you ask such a silly question?"

"Call me curious."

"The Good Lord provides a place to lay my head, which is more than He had when He walked this earth. I can't complain."

"You're not going to tell me, are you?"

"Some things are better kept a mystery."

"Well, mystery man, here's something concrete for you: Why don't you come for supper? I make a great chicken fried steak, with lumpless mashed potatoes."

He smiles, looks hungry. "Sounds like heaven, but I can't impose. My food is to do the will of the Father, and he's asked me to trust him for my food."

I try to examine his expression, but he turns his head and pulls off a box of brown sugar.

"Perhaps," I say, "God's avenue of provision is me—I mean our family."

"I can't change him just by eating at your table, Ouisie. I'm not that kind of man."

Then what kind of man are you? "Suit yourself. But the invitation's always there."

"I appreciate it. Being hungry's its own cross, I can assure you."

His words trigger a mad adding in my head, tabulating the prices of the items in my cart, always rounding the prices up. I remind myself of the $18.48 in my purse. I must not go over that, though I can't bear to put things back again. Flo at the counter knows and understands the heartache and never adds more grief to my embarrassment, but I'd rather not force her to re-ring my order. I remove a tub of sour cream and turn toward the milk case.

Elijah smiles. He places a warm hand on my other wrist, then turns my palm heavenward. In it he places a dollar—enough for the sour cream and a little extra. "It may not be a miracle, but it's small proof that God concerns himself with you. He clothes the fields. He'll take care of you."

I nearly cry. "But you—you need it."

"I need very little. You have a family to feed." He wraps large arms around his large belly. "Besides, I have reserve."

"Thank you," I say. "I'll repay you."

"Here's how you repay." He takes the shopping cart from me and maneuvers it toward a smiling, denture-wearing Flo whose silver-blonde hair is higher since it's Monday and she's been to the beauty shop for it to be teased. Then he stops behind the ice cream freezer and shuffles through his pockets. Flo waves at me, and I return the favor, but Elijah is hidden. I wonder if she knows him.

"Here's your answer." He hands me string.

"String?" What do I need a string for?

"Not just any string. It's for something."

"Is this to tie around my finger so I won't forget something?"

Elijah laughs. "No, but sometimes that's a good idea, particularly if God's burdened you with praying for someone or something, don't you think? If you have a string around your finger, you're apt to pray."

"True."

Elijah moves close to me. I smell his gum. "It's a bracelet," he says.

"Not much of one, if you ask me."

"You make of it what you will, but it's part of the miracle, Ouisie. I won't tell you more because God's silent on that. It's up to you to figure it out."

"Okay." I pocket the string for safekeeping.

"I need to run. You take care, okay?" He winks. "And keep our little secret, you hear?" Before I answer back, he retreats to the back of the store, which strikes me as odd. But Flo hollers my way, tells me to get to getting because she's almost done with her shift and she'd rather it speed by with clicking register keys than staring at her nails.

"What was holding you up?" says Flo. "You dilly-dallied so long by the ice cream I thought you'd turn into Neapolitan right then and there."

"I guess I'm slow is all." I'm not ready to mention Elijah,

though she may have spied him there. I hope she won't tell Hap such things.

"Time is slow." She clicks her nails on the chipped countertop. "Like how it snails along during Pastor Pepper's sermons."

She says his name hushed-like, as if he's the Pope and she's a mouse near his feet. I don't say anything, preferring to count my money once again, careful to add Elijah's dollar, praying it will all add up in the end.

Flo's fingers fly over the cash register. She keys in bologna, and I worry. I forgot to figure it in the total, having hidden it under the Tasty-Os.

"Don't take offense at my comment," Flo says to me, picking up the conversation I never started. "I didn't mean no harm. It's just that I'm not good at following your husband. He's loud and passionate and all, but half the time I don't understand what he's talking about. I'm a simple woman." She keys in the Tasty-Os while I finger my grocery money again.

"I'm not offended," I say. I wonder if Hap knows what he's talking about half the time. He strings scriptures together in the same rapid-fire progression as Flo's unbroken nails to the number pad, I'm not sure he even knows how they all add up. Or how they relate to regular folks' struggles — like the struggle I have right now, measuring out my bills.

She continues clicking. "You know what we need at Defiance Community Church?"

"What's that?"

"A place just for us."

"Us?"

"Women. You know, one of them women's Bible studies."

I try to picture such a thing, but Hap usually pooh-poohs women taking any sort of leadership. "I guess — "

She takes my last item, and taps those maddening keys. "You do me a favor and ask him, will you? Maybe you could lead it!"

I try not to laugh, but I do anyway. "I'll ask him, but I'm the last person on earth who could teach one."

"Which is why you should," she smiles. She smacks the same gum as Elijah; I can smell it. Then she winks. Her mascara cakes her lashes together momentarily before they part. "That'll be $19.48," Flo says.

I hand her everything and say a polite thank you as I wheel the cart toward the parking lot.

If only Elijah were here, I'd thank him for his extra dollar. But instead, out of eyeshot of Flo, I rip open the Tasty-Os, plunge my hand into its belly, and take a handful of oat goodness, wishing all along they'd turn into Oreos. One can always dream.

The man followed Ouisie, close enough to hear her voice. He traced the line of her body. He lived as a fugitive, crawling on his belly like the snake that inched across a muscled forearm. Huddled in camouflaged tree houses, buried like a mole underground.

She walked from grocery to car, igniting the roar of an idling engine. He walked behind houses, in alleyways, dodging the eyes of Defiance's gossips, all to follow her tire prints.

And when he arrived at her home, he camouflaged his whereabouts. But not so much that he couldn't watch her unpack her groceries, one by one.

Twelve

Emory called me this morning on the heels of Hap's departure for work, exploding into tears, finally regaining composure to ask me to join her in scattering Hixon's ashes. So I'm idling in front of her new home—Muriel's place she left for Hixon and Emory—wondering if my shoulders are strong enough to bear her burden or my ribs to hold her embrace. Around my wrist is a simple piece of string, unadorned. Though it doesn't encircle my finger, it helps me to pray for Hap, to keep a weak shred of hope alive. Though aching ribs suck most of the hope away and my wrenched neck feels like fire.

His eggs weren't cooked right, he told me. The yoke was too hard, not gooey like he likes it. What a burden I am to him, he said.

I see it all play in front of me on the screen of the blue sky stretching beyond the cracked windshield Hap refuses to have repaired.

I turned to leave, too quickly, kinking my neck as Hap fastened an air-stealing grip around the arch of my ribcage and compressed, slowly, painfully, until I cried out. His arms held a different sort of hardness, an ironclad anger, and I had to struggle against them or give into hopelessness. I wondered if Sheba's husband ever grabbed her.

"You make it hard for me to control my temper." His sentence seethed out of him. If he could spit the words, he would've.

"I'm sorry. I thought—"

He sneered as he vice-gripped my ribs further.

I heaved in, hoping that the air would bulwark my bones from breaking altogether. I wanted to massage my neck from its sideways wrenching, but I told myself to be strong, to appear fine. He doesn't like it when I act hurt. Doesn't like it one smidge.

"I love that you actually fancy yourself a thinking woman, Ouisie. Here's the thing, wife. You don't *think*. That's why God gave you me. I help you understand what is necessary for this life, for *our* life." He let go of me.

I felt release, but didn't experience freedom from his terror grip. How could I? I looked toe-ward, noting chipping pink polish peeking out of overworn slippers. "You're right," I told him. "I don't think."

His leaving settled the matter.

I turn off the car, rub my neck. I don't dare touch my ribs, though. I open the cranky door to the sun's brilliance. I shade my eyes. I'm sure Hixon sent the sun our way just for today's holy scattering, so we could see to do it right. The chill of last week has been cut in half by a warm front. I'm thankful for sixty-five degrees. Thankful I don't have to inhale chilled air into my burdened lungs.

Emory greets me at the door before I can knock. Bloodshot eyes, flushed cheeks. Her hair is pulled back severely, magnifying her pink-hued blush. "Come in," she says.

The house is tidy. Near the fireplace sits Emory's tired couch, next to some furniture I don't recognize. She reads my mind. "It was Muriel's," she tells me. She plops herself on a couch, crosses her legs like a child ready for storytime, and gives me a hard look. "Are you okay?"

I may not be a thinking woman, but I am quick enough to know when it's not the proper time to air dirty laundry. "The question is," I say, "are *you* all right?"

"You know what I want right now?" She smiles when she says it.

I sit on her old paisley coach, noting the ashes in the fireplace and smiling at the lingering wood smell. "A piece of cherry pie? Because that's what I want." I try not to grimace as I shift in my seat. It's as if my ribs are daggering me.

"No, just one smoke of weed."

I cover my ears. "I don't want to hear that, Emory. Please don't talk about it."

She releases her hair from its ponytail prison and shakes it free. "It's the truth, plain and simple. It takes the edge off. And believe me, I've got plenty of edges. Especially today." She untethers her gaze from me and settles it above my head. I turn to see Hixon's urn on the mantle.

"It's time, isn't it?" I stand and look full on at Hixon's remains in the urn. I don't know if it's right to hold the recepticle, but Emory motions me to, so I do. He feels heavier than I expected.

"I wanted to wait until spring, when I could see the hollyhocks burst forth. I know that's where he'd want to be—with them. But I won't wait that long. He's there on the mantle, watching me, and I can't seem to get his voice out of my head. He's like a dog that's stir-crazy, who needs to run wild outside to get his stink blown off."

I hand the urn to Emory. "Your grief's in there too." I suddenly wish God would make a clean-cut exchange—Hap's raging life for Hixon's peace-loving ways. Why can't Hap's ashes weight the jar? Why can't his anger burn away in the flames? An insistent voice inside me whispers, *"Because he needs you to burn."* I know Sheba tells me I am to be a sacrificial wife—but a burnt offering? Is this what God requires? The best I can do these days is to douse Hap with water, hoping he's not a grease fire.

"Where are you, Ouisie?" The question comes from Emory's

lips, but I can't quite trace her words backwards and realize what she asks.

I shake my head instead.

"Let's go," she says. Her words are heavy, then heavier. I feel the weight of them.

We walk outside, both squinting under Hixon's sun. Ours is a processional of determination, I think. Emory's feet plod steadily over brown grass. Dried, spent flowers bend their brown heads toward the dirt, as if they hoped to kiss it in thanks before their chilly death. I wonder if I could do the same, lie flat-stomached on the earth, and view the decay up close. I wonder if I could paint such sadness as a flower under death's sentence.

"He was a good man," she says. I choke at *was*; such a final, terrible word.

We pass a woodshed, no paint left. It leans to the right, and the door is long gone. A tiny yard surrounds another shack, chicken wire the only remnant of what must've been a henhouse. She points to a tree stump. "That's where Muriel butchered her chickens," she says.

We stand above the stump. I marvel at the cuts, how they crisscross the darkened wood like the scars on Hixon's wrists. Jagged, angry, swift cuts. Blood has stained it a sickly mahogany that shimmers under the weighty noonday sun. There, beneath the stump, is something I must hold. I bend low and pick it up— a bleached white vertebra from a doomed chicken's neck. It's simple in its construction, a perfect piece of God's handiwork. For a few months, this piece of neck helped a chicken peck the dust for food, and now I hold it between thumb and forefinger.

In the distance, Emory calls back, "What are you doing?"

I place the vertebrae in my pocket and follow Emory into the open field. It seems fitting she walks ahead of me in her own empty world—a "widow" alone in her grief. So I follow her, but I feel the weight of sadness in my own chest too.

"Here," she says. "Right here."

We are standing in a field, several stones' throw from the house. I can nearly see the curvature of the earth here, the earth's scoliosis, while the sun illuminates dried grass and a field of decaying hollyhocks. I remember Jed's gift, how I spirited those hollyhock seeds into an empty garden bed, praying for their resurrection in spring while I grabbed handfuls of dirt, nearly pressing them to my nose. Someday I'll have a flower deathbed too, but it will be evidence of a life once lived — all because of God's sovereignty, Hixon's sunlight, and water, water everywhere.

Emory sits cross-legged on the earth like a hippie child. I follow, but I cringe as I sit, my ribs feeling the compaction as I ease to the ground. Though it's warm, the earth stubbornly clings to last week's cool.

"I don't know how to do this," she says.

"I've never scattered ashes either." Oh, I've scattered my own — the ashes of dreams, hopes, scattered long ago, released to eternity on wild winds. But not a real person's substance. Not real ashes like this. Under the sun, she lies on her back, arms spread wide like she's embracing the day. She holds the world inside her chest until it nearly bursts from her. "I daydream a lot," she says.

"About what?"

"The what-ifs."

"You wonder what it would've been like to be married, I imagine."

"Yeah."

I envy her in that. To have the romantic notion of possibilities never shattered by the reality of men — how they act once the ring is firmly placed, how swiftly the promises get broken, how anger replaces tenderness. She can spend the rest of her life daydreaming. "What exactly happened with Angus?"

She laughs. "When I started wearing Hixon's ring, he told me I was a crazy-woman. Said he had himself some big plans —

to expand his empire, he said. What that really means is that he moved to Mineola to sell more marijuana."

"He was handsome."

"Yeah, he was. But he wasn't Hixon."

"No one was." Three true words, uttered from my pressed-in chest.

"Here's what I've been thinking." She props herself on one elbow, not worrying a bit about the dirt or her clothes. "You know that phrase, 'joined at the hip'?"

I nod.

"I can't help but think Hixon and I would've been joined a different way. He and his simple ways and me with my love for stories and adventure and escape. I'd like to think if he were alive today, we'd be joined by the imagination."

"That's beautiful," I say.

She reclines back onto the earth. I join her there, watching the clouds morph into diaphanous shapes, propelled by a slight breeze. I feel small here, but alive. Smelling the earth wakes me up proper.

Emory stands, pushing herself up from the dust. "Should I just dump his remains here?" She points to the spot she once flattened. "Where I warmed a spot?"

I think of the hollyhocks as she asks me, remembering their need for fertilizer and care. "Maybe I can help a little." I dust off my gardening know-how and stand again, telling myself not to wince. "Hixon will make these flowers brilliant, but you must scatter him wide and long so the whole field can benefit."

She nods. She hands the jar to me and stands. "Is it okay to touch them?"

"I don't know. But I suppose it's allowed."

Emory shakes a bit of Hixon into her palm. He is gray and gritty. In a flurry, Emory scatters the dust like a farmer scatters seeds. A weight seems to release from her shoulders as she does it.

You may wonder why I can say such a thing; it's only because I still carry my burden like a trusty pack mule. When a woman's free of a burden, a burdened woman can see it. And gets jealous.

We spend several moments scattering Hixon under a sunny sky, giving hollyhocks permission to flower in glory this summer. When it's all done, Emory is left with an urn, leaking eyes, and no words. We walk back to the house in silence while the sun pushes our shadows long and elegant in front of us. I see no indication of Emory's grief as we walk back until she stops at the henhouse, plants her feet like Jed pitching a baseball, and hurls the clay urn at the dilapidated building. It crashes against the wood, shards littering the ground where hens once pecked. She says nothing, cries nothing, and retrieves nothing. When we find ourselves back in the house, each sitting on the same couches we sat on an hour before, it's as if none of the scattering, the unburdening ever happened. She crosses her legs the same. But she doesn't look above my head this time, doesn't nod Hixon's way. We make no small talk. The room absorbs us as if it were a henhouse's walls seeping in the smell of nesting chickens.

I leave Emory sitting just like that. She is quiet in her grief, but I see the pain she holds near. She grieves a beautiful man's death. Me? I grieve my life.

Sitting in my sun-heated car, I pull out the stark white chicken neck. I untie Elijah's bracelet string by pulling one end with my teeth and then thread the cavity through. Where the chicken's nerves once pulsed, my bracelet string backbones the chalky piece. It reminds me of the fragility of life, how quickly the axe falls, how simply death tacks "The End" on our stories, how one minute you're rescuing your love from fire, fertilizing flowers the next. Life, indeed, is too short. Retying the knot, again using my teeth as leverage, I pray for Hap. But mostly I pray I will live. Really live.

I feel mostly, though, that I am nearing death.

He traced a finger over the gray-green snake on his arm. He hated getting the thing—but felt he must. A deserved punishment for taking the sandaled girl's life. He didn't yowl while each needle pricked his skin, while the snake took maniacal shape, coming alive, boa-constrictor-like, wrapping its leathery slick body around the man for eternity.

And like a snake, he spent his days searching for prey. Watching. Calculating. The light emanated from the Pepper's kitchen window announcing her presence, haloing her head as she washed dishes, then stopped. Sometimes she stared through the panes right at him, but she didn't see.

And when she turned off the light at this time of day, he knew right where she'd be.

Thirteen

The beds made, the floors vacuumed, the morning dishes scrubbed meant one thing for me: time for reflection, to sit quietly in the beauty of the day. Of all the things Hap steals from me, he can't touch my relishing of nature. He can't see me during the day when I pace before my seemingly empty flower-bed, praying for hollyhock resurrection.

I fold the kitchen towel, catching a last look out the window. The trees seem to preen under my scrutiny, brown-limbed, yet proud. Barrenness is its own kind of stark beauty. Because without all that foliage, the sky feels all the more blue, more true, beyond the clack of limbs. I open the back door and breathe in the remains of the morning, wishing I could smell such beauty every moment. If I could capture the smell of winter, I'd win a perfumer's heart, I'm sure.

I shut the door to the day and turn off the kitchen's incandescent light. I scold myself for the dead flies that lie in the opaque reservoir beneath the light. Another day I'll dump the little black carcasses in the garbage, rid the light of death. Or maybe I'll watch those bodies, unmoving, and capture the display in an abstract painting. But today I don't have the will to do either. My momentary whiff of the outdoors beckons me to the front of the house, to the porch swing.

When I open the front door, Elijah stands at the base of the porch, his head bowed as if he were praying. He nods, says nothing. He walks up the stairs and sits on the swing as if he'd been invited. He assumes a strange hospitality on my part. I wonder: Will Hap come home and discover him here? Will it fuel more rage-infused sermons about my adulterous heart? Part of me fears, really fears, this will happen, confirming his ridiculous assumptions that I'm also madly in love with David, my first love. But even so, I do worry. Am I a perfect heathen for entertaining a drifter-grandfather on my porch? The chicken vertebra brushes against my skin and I wonder if Elijah sees it. Or perceives it.

Elijah rocks. He watches me, but his eyes are kind. They don't hold the anger Hap cages inside. At least that's what I hope. I suppose you hope this too.

"Can I help you?"

"No, I just thought I'd come and swing a bit." He winks my way, then pats the seat next to him.

You might ask why I sit. What is it inside me that automatically obeys a man's voice? Have I lost my own will completely?

These are good questions. Unanswerable ones.

"Do you worry?" he asks.

My head aches again. I think about the vase next to my bed. I need a drink. I have to have a drink. I worry about not having a drink. "Yes," I tell him. "All the time."

"You worry about your children."

"Not enough," I say. And that's the truth. When Sissy went missing, just for a little bit, it was on my watch. I slept while she...

"None of us can do it all right. Mothering. Marriage."

I laugh. "I don't suppose you do either very well."

He joins my laughter. "I'm not much of a mother, but I do remember something my mother taught me. And it involves what we're doing right here." He pats the swing.

"Talking?"

"No. Swinging." He pushes himself a little higher, not that he could swing very high on this rickety contraption. "She used to say, 'Worrying's like swinging on a porch swing. It occupies your time, but it doesn't take you anywhere.'"

We swing in the silent day, the trees with their crooked arms pleading toward the sky. The creak of the swing beneath our weight is the only noise in the world. Not even Clementine stirs behind the front door. "She's right," I say to the silence, but I say all sorts of things, believing they're right, only to act as if they're not. It's one thing to believe worry is a porch swing going nowhere, another to bridle my worry so it doesn't take flight.

"Mothers aren't always right," he says. His voice nearly holds tears. He notices my bracelet. "You've added something."

"Yes, from Emory's place. It's a chicken bone."

"Mind if I look?"

I shake my head no. He doesn't touch my hand or my wrist. Instead he places rough fingers around the chicken bone. "Ezekiel, he wanted life on bones, didn't he? And God gave them flesh and blood."

For knowing God so few days, he sure does know a lot.

He lifts his head toward the bead board where a cobwebbed lamp teeters from the porch ceiling. "Lord, do it now. Bring forth life where there's death. Hear Ouisie's prayers. Hear mine too." He lets go of the bracelet in a whisper of a second. "I have another bead to add." He fishes around in his corduroy jacket and hands me another tiny box. Tiny red, yellow, and orange dots are pointillism wallpaper on each face. A narrow grosgrain ribbon in white ties it up. And on either side, a small hole punched through the cardboard makes it the perfect charm. I remember the other box, hiding in my makeup drawer behind my lined up collection of church lipstick. "Let me help you," he says.

From his pocket he pulls out a spool of thread, a needle embedded there. He pulls it out, pricks his finger, licks the blood. I have since tied on a clasp to the bracelet from a broken bauble, so he unclasps it, still careful not to touch me. He licks one end of the thread, poking it through the needle. One eye pirated, he pokes the needle and string through the box, creating a loop. Through that loop, he threads the bracelet string. Next to the chicken neck, the pierced box looks stunning, like Picasso next to an Egyptian sarcophagus. He returns the bracelet to my wrist and smiles. "Now you have two."

"Thanks." I touch the small box, wondering how I will explain it to Hap, worrying about how I will hide this obvious gift, grappling with the familiar fear that Elijah is not who he says he is. That he's an imposter, bent on my destruction, not my welfare.

"It's to remember to pray for beauty," he says.

We rock a few moments more before I say goodbye. He leaves in a flurry, like he's called to important business. I open and close the front door, then watch the porch swing through the living room window in the safety of my home. It swings still, as if it remembers our cadence. A gentle rock back and forth, going nowhere. Nowhere but the beautiful porch.

Fourteen

It was a lifetime ago, when Daisy's missing was fresh as spring green grass after winter brown. A week after she'd disappeared, Hap spent the morning hollering about my headaches, the unorganized living room, anything he could pull from his mind to berate me. I absorbed every word like I was a thirsty desert and he was my sole source of moisture. But part of me escaped into another place, a safe home somewhere else between the four walls of my imagination, when Mama and Daddy loved each other and me, and I never heard hollering. Just singing and tender words.

Hap paced the living room. My offense? Sissy forgot her sleeping bag for a sleepover, and I'd asked him to deliver it on his way to work. And why on God's green earth would I let her sleep over at a friend's when Daisy'd gone missing?

"Life continues," I told him. "Even after death."

But I felt his accusations like a slap to my face. I was an unfit mother, a wayward housekeeper, a blind-leading-the-blind parent. I had too many headaches. I succumbed far more than I fought through them. And, although he rarely brought it up, I knew I had a hungry craving for alcohol—my secret, liquid lover. I'm not sure, in the recollection, if the hatred I heard in my head was purely mine—my own voice telling me how terrible I was—or if Hap's joined the chorus too. Hard to tell with a memory.

"Always looking on the bright side, aren't we?" He smiled, then fisted his right hand. "While the world's going to hell, you play your own oblivious fiddle."

I looked at my feet, counted my toes three times. Thirty toes in thirty seconds while his words bounced off the walls and gained ferocious strength.

"Look at this dust!"

I looked beyond the dusted windowsill and watched the springtime trees sway in a lazy breeze. Watched as cottonwood blossoms floated like snow in midair, hovering, and then dancing lightly to earth. These are the kinds of musings you do when a man shouts at you.

"The kids are ashamed of you."

I nodded to Jed and Sissy's school photos, smiling back at me from $1.98 Piggly Wiggly picture frames I repainted and spruced up.

"I don't know what I used to see in you."

The mirror above the mantle captured me in those words. Exhausted eyes blinked back at me, a pale face. An expression of death, not life.

While my husband who'd vowed to cherish me said those words, I watched his angry mouth, pink tongue, white teeth for signs of humanity. Instead I saw a deep, yawing mouth of a dog bent on ripping me to shreds. His eyes held murder. He hit me then, in frenzied fury. It hadn't been the first time; it certainly wasn't the last. But it was the time I remember as fresh as if it were happening in the great Right Now.

His open hand hammered the side of my face in a hellish rage. In an instant, a new headache roared. I cried out, said, "No, please," but he didn't obey. His words ceased, replaced by a low growl. I closed my eyes, praying God would take me away. Please God, I said. Please. To heaven. To anywhere. But it wasn't God's pleasure to deliver me. So I accepted the gift of Hap's hand across my face while lightning flashed behind closed eyes and a stab of pain knifed my jaw. While I'd tell you in casual conversation that I was a tough woman, that I could stand physical violence, I always recounted that in retrospect, after the blow-by-blow fury. In the moment of it, I embodied the smallest coward, only to rise up afterward and nurse my wounds. Strange, but I forgot his fists soon after, like how I forgot the pain of childbirth. Only in this instance, I didn't have a baby to salve my pain—just the memory of Hap's jumbled words haunting my tired head, the violence of his sentence that would poison me thereafter. And kill me in little deaths day by day.

I tasted copper blood, felt it warm my teeth. I ran my tongue over each tooth, praying I could count them all, hoping there'd be no gap, no jagged edge, no looseness. Because how could I explain that to the kids? Jed would know the truth, which would make his hand become a fist too. Sissy would believe my excuse, but her confidence would melt into her, accentuating her lisp. I sat in my rocking chair, and for a moment let its steady momentum lull me into another world, another time, another marriage while I felt a painful throbbing heartbeat through my chin.

He loved me once, right? He did. Didn't his hand once hold mine, cradling it? His voice cooed—didn't my ears register that? He'd caught my gaze and smiled. I strained to remember these traits, these bits and pieces of Hapland James Pepper the years had crucified. For the life of me, though, I couldn't conjure up a tangible full-color memory of Hap actually being kind to me, couldn't fish one tender moment out of the pool of memory. Other times I could, but not now. While my head throbbed, I could let my mind rest on platitudes, but those were untethered traits with no root in reality—drifting on a lazy Texas river, slowly meandering out of my sight. Maybe recalling his hand-holding was blind hope. Maybe Hap had never been any of those things.

As calm as Defiance after a hell-clapping thunderstorm, Hap sat on the couch while I clutched my jaw and rocked.

"I hate you." He spoke the words without emotion. The sentence echoed in the air of our stale living room. Not emotion-packed words. Not sad words. Just true words. Cold, hard truth.

I nodded in response. "I know," I said.

And when I dared to look into his soul as he splayed his fingers in front of him, examining his hand for injury, I knew. I *knew*. The man I married, who whisked me away from a life under the tyranny of an angry stepdad, was merely his substitute. I would relive the life I escaped, unless death took me first.

Fifteen

Who am I? I ask this of the bathroom mirror, but only the bags under my eyes answer back. I pull my hair into a ponytail, exposing my cheekbones. They seem hollow today, bony.

I didn't make breakfast for the kids, didn't shower, didn't bother to holler a goodbye when the front door opened and Jed and Sissy ventured out.

I slip out of my nightgown and into my day clothes in a hurried moment, deciding a shower could wait. I sit on the bed, eyeing the vase. I take a drink for breakfast, hoping it will dull the voice inside that tells me I'm unfit to be a mother. But one drink can't hush. Maybe two. Or seven. The room lolls and moves with the last drink, and I sigh.

There was a time when I felt content to be the four walls of my house—the woman who held her family together, protected them, nurtured them with peanut butter and jelly sandwiches and bandages on scraped shins. I lived Sheba Nelson's words long before I read them, savoring domestication, reveling in motherhood. But the walls shifted, moved in toward me, crushing my will. I don't know if Hap pushed them, or I did, but I felt the crush nonetheless.

A knock shakes the front door. I startle at it, wondering who could be here unannounced in the morning. Emory likes sleeping in. Perhaps it's Elijah making good on my invitation to dinner. Only it's not exactly the dinner hour. And I'm not exactly sober.

I pull on socks and shoes and walk on unsteady feet to the front door. I peek around the door through the side window and see a woman standing there, looking back over her shoulder toward a car I don't recognize. She holds a black Bible in her hand. I wonder if she's going to witness to me, or sell me a new religion.

I open the door. "May I help you?" I expect her to ask for directions, as she looks nervous and out of place here.

"I'm Bathsheba Nelson." She extends her Bible-free hand my way. "You sent me a letter."

I try not to register surprise on my face, but I'm afraid she's noticed it.

"I've come to minister to you," she says.

I back up. She steps through the threshold anyway. "Bathsheba," I say into the shrinking space between us. "But I thought your name was She—"

"My given name's Bathsheba, but that's not exactly the kind of name you want to see on a marriage book, now do you?" Her plaid suit, not understated, screams at me. Candy apple red, forest green and shimmering gold crisscross her torso. She stands at the intersection of my life before Sheba's presence and my life after, which I'm convinced, will never be the same. She wears cat glasses, the kind that tilt toward the sky on an impossibly narrow nose. She smiles, not asking to be invited in, but insisting nonetheless.

So I invite her in, but I taste alcohol on my tongue. Am I unsteady? I place one foot in front of the other, deliberately, telling myself not to wobble as she follows me to the kitchen.

She takes tea, just as I expected. Two teaspoons of sugar, no milk.

"I don't like the way the English embellish their tea," she says. She speaks to me as if we've known each other for years, as

if I would know the reason for her distaste of English tea habits. Like I'm her dearest friend.

"How did you find me?" I ask. My words feel slurred on an overthick tongue.

"How does anyone find anybody these days?" She won't hold my gaze, her eyes flitting over my cabinets, no doubt looking for dust or grime. Or maybe she has x-ray vision, seeing how pale my vanilla extract looks from all that added water. My chocolate chip cookies never do taste right anymore.

"You tell me." For a brief moment, I float my eyes around the room as she does, just to understand the appeal. It only makes me dizzier. My stomach feels like it's taken a turn on the tilt-a-whirl.

"You put your address on the envelope. Simple as that. I figured you were reaching out for my help, and as I prayed about it, God seemed to confirm your dire circumstances. I guess you could call me a marriage doctor."

I sit across from her, no teacup to steady my hand. "So you're happily married."

"Was," she said. Her eyes catch mine for one moment. A feeling passes between us like milk gone sour.

"He died." I say the words like nails pounding a coffin.

"No, not exactly."

Not exactly? I lean further in, curious. But re-tasting my saliva settles me back in my chair. "Where is he then?"

"I don't know."

A scenario flashes my mind. Before, it's always been me thinking about escaping Hap. Now I picture him pulling out of the driveway in his precious Chevy, churning gravel in anger, and backing out of my life for good. He could leave. This settles my heart for a moment until I realize there's been a terribly long pause in our conversation. I clear my head of the dream and ask, "You don't know?"

She shakes her head, drinks tea with a slight slurp, and smiles. "He will be back."

"Did he say he'd be back?" Suddenly my dream of Hap disappearing becomes cloudy. If he left, I'd constantly worry about his return.

"He didn't say a thing, dear. Didn't even leave a note. Just didn't come home from work one day. His place of employment said he never returned there either." She sips tea again. "He's on his prodigal journey, I'm guessing. And I'm learning to be patient like the Father in the prodigal story, the one who waits on the hill for his son to come back. Sometimes I wait on tiptoes. Sometimes I weary from the waiting. But there's something beautiful about waiting on someone whose return is a mystery."

Do you think there can be beauty in such a thing? In waiting? I don't say it out loud, because to be honest, I can't believe that today. I've waited for Hap to change. A lifetime, it seems. I look out the window, away from Sheba and see someone in the clearing. I pace to the window, but the hint of a person has vanished. My heart pushes against my ribcage. I will it to slow down, but it won't.

"Anything wrong?" my new friend Sheba asks.

I sit again. "Nothing. Just thought I saw something outside." I look at the ticking clock on the wall. Sheba's not been here long, but it feels like forever. My head throbs, begging for more drink. I'm so thirsty, but tea won't satisfy.

"It seems to me your blood's curdled. I understand unnerved. When my Benjamin left, I swore I saw him lurking near the back flowerbeds. And sometimes things in the house didn't seem right. A plant under the window moved to a side table in the living room. Or my haphazard laundry suddenly neatly folded in a pile near my bed."

I wonder if Candid Camera will burst through the door. I'm sure my face registers shock. Is this some sort of spooky joke? Maybe I should introduce plaid-wearing, ghost-husbanded Sheba to dollar-doling Elijah. Seems they'd make a good couple.

Instead, I throw something her way. "So, you're a marriage doctor without a marriage."

"Yes. That's right."

"How does that work?"

"Don't you believe in God's grace?"

"Of course." I have to believe in that. The alcohol makes me. She shifts in her Christmas suit, her eyes flitting again. "That's how I can help marriages when mine remains a mystery. It's all about grace."

She elongates *grace* like a cat's slow yawn. I notice the clock again—it seems to be ticking in my head. Hap's due home for lunch today, and I was supposed to be cleaning the house and paying the bills—his to-do list for me. "I'm sorry you drove all the way down here, but I really have to get back to housework."

"Housework's next to holiness. It's God's beautiful way of keeping women's nails clean." Her words grow in intensity as she preaches domestication.

"I know you must have a long drive ahead of you."

"Two hours, but who's counting?"

I keep my tongue in my alcohol-tinged mouth.

She stands. "I see I've overstayed my welcome. But I felt I needed to meet you face to face before I started counseling you."

"Counseling me?" I stand and start toward the hallway. Thankfully, she takes the hint and makes her way to the front door. The walls feel like they're pressing in on me, hemming me in, dizzying my stomach.

She takes my hands in hers, squeezes them. "Sometimes folks call me Abby. As in Dear Abby. That's what I'm to be to you. You send me letters, asking me questions, and I'll write back. Now that I've met you and felt the fear in this house, I'll know better how to advise you. And when Benjamin returns, he'll send letters to—now what's your husband's name again?"

"Hap. Short for Hapland," I tell her. I will intercept the mail if Benjamin ever comes back and starts penning letters Hap's way.

"Hapland. Such a strong, joyful name."

I laugh. "Well, there he is." I point to a picture of him framed at the end of the hallway. Olan Mills gave the sitting to him free. He smiles in his three-piece-suit, a Bible tucked in his right hand. An American flag ruffles behind him.

"He's a godly man. I can see it." She holds my hands again, hers clam-cold, mine, sweaty. "You don't see with the right eyes, dear."

"I see things the way I see them." Not terribly profound words, but true.

"The more you become the Ouisie that man needs, the more joyful he'll be. I promise you. It boils down to plain undecorated obedience. He will become happy again, but you first need to become the wife who chooses to makes him happy—who serves him as priority one."

She lets go of my hands. They fall to my side, trembling. Suddenly I feel the guilt of my drinking, the tasks of the day, and my inadequacies full force on me. I am weighted with it all, so much heaviness now that grace has left. All while a smiling one-dimensional Hap holds his Bible.

"Trust me," she says. She smiles, but her upturned lips don't seem real. They are a clown's painted smile—a grin I don't bother to return. "You're lucky to have a man who stays. A man who is strong, who leads a congregation. I don't think you realize the gift you have." We walk through the living room.

"I'm sure I don't. Thanks for the reminder."

"I'll be in touch." She jingles her keys, rattling my headache. She opens the front door and turns back to me with an upturned hand. "By the way," she says, "would it trouble you to lend me gas money for my trip home?"

I sit inside my four walls—the walls I intended to hold up, but let crash around me. Twenty-seven dollars and thirty-eight cents stares back at me on the table, the money I have to feed the family this week, having given five dollars to the Sheba Nelson Transportation Fund. Why did I do that?

All I know is that someone seems to be watching me out behind the woods, Sheba's bent on fixing me, and Hap's not going to be thrilled with the state of the house when he gets home. It's all too much, really. Too much for a woman to bear. I stand, forsake Hap's money on the dinette, and push through the door to the waiting backyard.

"Who in the world am I?" I whisper it to the winter wind, my arms shivering, my heart nearly dead in my chest.

From the woods I hear something, a voice—but it's just the alcohol tricking me.

"You are mine" he said, but it didn't reach her. She stood in the backyard with a half-frightened, half-curious look on her face. Then she sat on the stoop in front of the kitchen door, placed her head in her hands and pressed her forehead like she had a headache. Perched halfway up a tree, behind several other trunks, he spied on her, fully hidden. Shoulders slumped, feet angled outward, she stayed like that for several minutes. He adjusted his position, his foot cramped between two jutting branches. He made no noise, but she looked up anyway.

"Who am I?" she whispered again.

And he said his answer again, this time whispering behind the trunk.

You are mine.

Sixteen

Hap stands at the table, counting his money. He fists the dollars and throws them; they float like dried leaves, hushing to the linoleum. So he takes a chair and crashes it to the floor, nearly breaking the leg. I watch it all, shivering inside, yet knowing I deserve it. I always do. I right the chair.

"Where's the rest of the money?"

"I'll explain."

"I'm sure you will, but I'm not convinced it's the truth. Besides being a deceiver, you can't seem to get it through your thick head that a man has to toil day and night to make money, and you fritter it away like it means nothing to you. Like *I* mean nothing to you."

"You mean everything to me," I tell him. The words sound awkward on bewildered lips, like truth leaked out despite wanting to keep it inside. Hap is the summation of my small world. Pleasing and appeasing is what I think of every minute of every waking day. What he likes. What he needs. What makes him happy. What gives him joy. What I need to do to improve my chances of winning his favor. He is everything, as the song says, and everything is him.

Hap laughs, then wags his head. "Really, now. If that were true, I could count on you spending our money wisely, not hiding it away. Don't you believe for one moment that I'm not keen on your plans, Ouisic."

"Plans?"

"You know what I'm talking about."

I picture Watergate wiretaps in my house, and Hap at church hearing my every word. "No I don't."

"Either you're spiriting money away to feed your devil habit of drinking, or you're saving it for your rendezvous with David."

It's my turn to wag my head. It's always these two things. Part of me wants to admit to his face that I sneak a bit of money here and there to buy alcohol. But I'm not to the place where I'm ready to say words like that out in the open. I have very little of my own—paintings under the bed, garden dirt under my nails, and, yes, a drink now and again. They are mine. Just mine. But David? When will Hap give it up? I straighten myself, readying for his wrath. "In case you need to know, I gave the money to someone."

"David?"

"Please. I don't even know him anymore. Maybe you should ask Emory. She's seen him recently. He lives in Burl."

"Don't change the subject. You know you were in love with him. How am I supposed to know you don't love him now? I read how women are crazy for handicapped men."

I nearly holler. Why does he say things like this? "You'll have to take my word for it."

He rolls his eyes. He clears his throat. "Who'd you give the money to?"

I shake my head. "A woman who visited me today."

"Someone from the church? Who?" His eyes would growl if they had a voice.

"No, a friend from Rowlett."

"Where in the world is Rowlett?"

"Up north."

"Let me get this straight. You befriend a mystery woman from a town we've never been to?" He narrows his eyes. "She is really a *he*, isn't he?"

"No, her name is Sheba Nelson. She's a Christian writer."

Hap cackles. "You do spin good stories, Ouisie. Maybe you should become a Christian writer too, penning those God-dishonoring, dimestore novels that lead the masses astray."

"Maybe I should." I've gone this far. I can't help these words.

Hap's pupils grow fierce. "Defiance doesn't become you," he says.

"I know." My inside shivers emerge. I hate that Hap sees my weakness. He grabs my hair, but I encircle it beneath his grip so he can't rip all of it from its roots. This fuels more fire behind those eyes.

"I work hard," he says, panting. He removes his hand from my hair. Blond strands poke between his fingers like limp spaghetti. "Only to have you give money to strange men."

"Men are not named Sheba," I say. "Besides, you'll be happy to know she has agreed to counsel me to become a better wife. A godly wife. An attentive wife."

"Well, if that doesn't beat all."

I leave the kitchen, locate the book, and return, handing it to Hap. "See? *The Godly Woman's Guide to Marriage.*"

He grabs it from me, turns it over in his hands. His white shirt cuffs contrast the dark brown of his suit. I can smell his musky cologne.

"Well." He traces his thick finger over Sheba's name. "She was here?"

"I wrote to her. Asked her advice. You may not think so, but I listen to you. I hear every single word. I know I need help, so I sought it. I had no idea this Sheba woman would drive two hours and visit unannounced. I felt bad, so I gave her some gas money."

His eyes soften, a rare occurrence usually spurred only by Clementine fetching and bringing back, or Sissy's spindly arms around his waist. Maybe Sheba will save us all. He says nothing else, just stands there, flipping through the book. No I'm proud of you, Ouisie. Or I'm touched you're trying so hard. I have grown accustomed to eliminating my expectations for Hap's tender words, but there are times those expectations surface. I want him to love me enough to encourage me. But silence is his answer. At least for now. I've logged enough miles in this marriage to know he'll find a way to holler at me about Sheba again. Or about something else. He does not seem satisfied unless he has anger and someone to direct it at.

"You want to be a better wife?"

I nod. It is true. I do want that. You know that, right?

He moves toward me in the afternoon light of the kitchen. I try not to hesitate, but I can't help stepping away. Still he places a strong arm around my shoulders, pulling me to himself. "You know I don't mean half the words I say. And you don't need to be afraid. You know why?"

I shiver under his touch. "Why?"

"Because I'm not mad about the money anymore. I consider it your kingdom investment—money spent to better the kingdom of God under our roof. I'm proud of you."

I let out a measured breath, telling myself to believe his words.

He kisses me on the head, then turns to leave. He stops himself in the doorjamb between the kitchen and the hallway. He points to the money scattered on the floor. "Don't forget to clean that up."

I get on my hands and knees and do just that, sneaking a dollar or two into my bra for safekeeping.

The man held the sharp-bladed knife between dirty hands, then ripped it across the Chevy's long metal flesh. The noise screamed to the trees beneath his gashing, but he didn't pay any mind. He pulled, flecking paint to the gravel, and as he did it, he smiled.

Voices, one melodic, one deeper, interrupted when he neared the headlight. He retreated, just out of eyeshot around the corner of the house. He caught a glimpse of the neighbor's house behind him. He backed further away, hiding behind an evergreen shrub that flanked the corner of the house.

"Don't worry," the boy Jed told his sister. "When kids make fun like they do, they're just jealous."

"I doubt it," his sister said. "No one's jealous of a lisp."

"You haven't lisped in months."

By now they should've been even with the car's back bumper.

"Look! Hap's car!"

"Daddy's going to holler!"

He heard the scuffing of feet, the groans of oh-no.

"I don't want to tell him," Jed said.

"You have to. You know I can't do it."

"Let's go."

So the man rustled himself out of the bush, fighting the thing to be set free. He loped around the back of the house into the woods. And when he climbed a lookout tree, the wind fierced through him, threatening to fell him and the tree alike.

He turned the knife over in his hand, then licked its blade clean of flecking paint.

Seventeen

I feel guilty for the dollars in my bra. I feel them as if they're made of metal, not paper, impressing themselves into my skin permanently. But my temporary remorse doesn't change me. It's my one small way of giving myself a present, of cherishing me just a little. So I keep them there, replacement parts for the love Hap withholds.

The kids are a little late. Before I can walk the hallway to peek out the front room window, I hear the open and close of the screen door, then the front door. Sissy and Jed don't rampage into the kitchen, hoping for snacks like they usually do; they meander on tentative feet. Won't look me in the eye. Seeing Jed's face, how his brow furrows and his mouth takes on that panicky look freezes me to the floor. "What's the matter?"

I look at Sissy who is as pale as an over-bleached dishtowel, her face telling the same story of doom.

"Someone scratched Hap's car." Jed runs a hand over his mouth, shakes his head.

"Just now?" I swallow, wondering when Hap will return from our bedroom, weighing how to share this news. His temporary happiness at my Sheba-following will die with this news. His car. His father's car.

"A little scratch?" My voice squeaks. I tell myself to relax, but the rhythm in my chest accelerates.

"No, Mama," Sissy says. "A great big scratch all the way down its side. Clear to the metal."

I sit at the kitchen table, tell the kids to go to their rooms and do homework.

"It's critical you do it right, Ouisie." Hap took my hand, wrapping it in his while I clutched a terry cloth rag. The car's coat was dusted white with polish, swirled by his elbow grease thirty minutes ago. He pushed my hand in circles while the white rubbed away, leaving pristine paint underneath.

"You know you've got it right when you can see your pretty face in the shine."

I looked at my distorted face.

"Beautiful," he said.

But when I peered up to catch his gaze and accept his praise, I found him staring at his own reflection in the Chevy's paint.

Hap returns from de-suiting, now comfortable in cotton pants and a white t-shirt.

"Would you like something to drink?" I move toward the fridge.

He smiles. "Well, I see you're working hard at this being a godly wife thing. Yes, as a matter of fact, I'd like some orange juice."

I force a smile. No juice is made, so I'll have to make it from frozen concentrate, one of my least favorite things. But I need to keep him here with me with the car out there, waiting for his gasping inspection. I can't bear this right now. So I remove the can from the freezer, open the metal lid, and try to squeeze until my hands freeze to the frosty sides. I run warm water over the can, secretly cursing the state of my iced hands. Eventually the pulp frees itself after I knife it, beg it silently, and shake it into the pitcher.

Hap taps his fingers on the table. "The kids home?"

"Yes, they're doing their homework." I stab the orange cylinder with a knife over and over again, then pull it out, opting for kneading it with clean hands. Sufficiently sticky, I run my hands under water, praying for warmth, begging God for words. Not yet, the Voice seems to say.

"Emory says Big Earl squeezes all his orange juice by hand."

"He's got big enough hands." Hap still taps.

I stir water into the pitcher, plus one cup more to stretch it, and pour a tall glass. Hap drinks, exhales a long orange-juiced sigh, sets the cup down, then demands another go-round with his eyes. I oblige, and set two store-brand cookies on a plate next to him. His last supper before the news crumbles him. I feel the turmoil in every part of my body—a sour stomach, anxious shoulders, a tight throat, weakened knees. Still, I smile. Feign normalcy. Then clear my throat. "Hap?"

"Yes."

"The kids saw something on their way into the house."

"Are they okay? What's wrong?" He empties another glass. I fill it.

"Yes, they're fine. It's your car."

"What?" I hear the yell coming. The kids must too because they appear on cue at the rise of his voice.

Sissy slips through the threshold, putting her hand into his. "I'm sorry, Daddy."

"Did you touch my car, Sissy? I don't know how many times I've told you not to touch it."

More volume. My neck muscles tighten.

"No, Daddy. I'm just sorry is all. We saw it when we walked in from school."

Jed's jaw is taut, his mouth unspeaking. But I catch a hint of amusement on his lips.

"Jed, what did you see?"

"Go see for yourself," Jed tells him.

Sissy leads Hap out the front door, a sheep leading a shepherd to the slaughter. Hap nearly swears when he sees the scar: a keyed gouge running from headlight to taillight. He catapults

himself toward it; there's just no other way to describe the lunge. He kneels, panted knees on gravel, caressing the marred paint, and lets out a cry. I have never seen him kneel like that, not in anguish. Sure, he does it for show at church, demonstrating to the congregation what it looks like to repent, but never as a natural, propelled-from-within act. Sissy whimpers. Jed stands halfway between Hap and me, an intermediary. With stiff steps, he closes the distance and places his hand on Hap. Hap does not shrug it away, probably too occupied with the scratch to notice. He rakes his hair with trembling hands. "What in God's green earth have I ever done to deserve this?"

And all at once, I understand. Hap looks at me, his hair disheveled from his anguished finger combing. His eyes press through me, weakened, needy. I see his grief, his need for the daddy that left life when it got too hard, the man whose shoes Hap spent his life trying to fill, only to realize he chased the footsteps of a ghost. This car was his father's—a piece of machinery that meant more to Hap than the sum of its carburetor, windshield wipers, pistons and tail fins. This car *is* Hap's father—a junker Hap resurrected into a showcase, all for the sketchy memory of a dad who never really loved him.

"Why would anyone do such a thing?" He shakes his head. "I need to take it to the body shop. Right now."

Interesting how five dollars lost meant the world to him, but no expense will be spared in fixing his precious car. Still, I place my hand on Sissy's head, feeling guilt. The gash saves me from explaining lost dollars, and for that I'm nursing relief. "Shouldn't you call Officer Spellman first?"

"Right. Yes. Come on Jed." They tromp to the house, shoes on near-clean floors. While Sissy runs her fingers along the car's scratch, I swing on the porch, listening to the rise and fall of Hap's voice, the animation and angst filtering through the house.

If only I were a car.

Eighteen

Sissy runs inside to finish homework. I swing to the rhythm of my marriage, back and forth, rising with hopes and falling in reality—but going nowhere. Ethrea Ree opens her front door. She determines her feet down each step and stands by Hap's car, not seeing the gouge. "What's all the hollering about?" She is all angles and pokes, but I smile despite her horseradish tone.

"Hap's car was vandalized." I point to the scratch.

Ethrea Ree examines the gouge, then looks up at me swinging in the cool winter afternoon. "And who do you suppose did it?"

Elijah's face pops into my mind all of a sudden, but I shove it back down. He wouldn't do such a thing, would he? "Got me. We were inside when the kids came home and told us. Any chance you were pruning roses?"

"No. Delmer's got himself a cold. He's terribly fussy when he can't breathe through his nose, so I was tending him. I did hear something, though."

"What?"

"I'm not sure. A rustling."

"What kind of rustling?"

"Like a tree bending back on itself in a windstorm, when the leaves slap each other because they can't help it."

"But you didn't see anyone."

"No, just heard rustling. You know, I moved to Defiance be-cause I heard this was a safe town, only to have that Daisy girl kidnapped and things like this happen. And with folks dying like flies, I'm wondering if we have ourselves a bad omen. A deathly pall hangs over this town, if you ask me."

I walk down the porch steps and examine the scratch up close for the first time. I hear Hap's voice still on the phone. He'll be out here again soon, but I can't help but caress the gash — a part of me wishing I'd have the guts to do such a thing. "Sometimes I think that too — that Defiance has a curse."

"No matter. We make our lives, don't we? We lie in the graves we dig for ourselves." Her words sound like she has it on good authority, that she's telling the truth, not just about Defi-ance, but about every person in every town on the planet.

"You are right." I trace the scar down the length of the car as Ethrea walks toward home. I watch as she mounts the porch, wiry leg to misshapen step. She waves at me from up there, then points to the rose bushes flanking her. "I do know one of your secrets, Ouisie Pepper." She pulls a bony finger to her gray lips and shushes. "And I won't tell a soul, not even Delmer. You prune 'em any time you want, you hear me? A woman with a man like Hap needs the Garden of Eden to make up for the grief."

She closes the door before I can say thank you.

Hap opens the front door; he catches me with my hand on the car's wound. I pull it off as if it's fire. I step away. Wait for the blast of words.

He walks around me like I am a statue in a British garden, mossed over and blending into the landscape. He touches the door, caressing the metal line that mars its once-mirrored paint-job. He opens and slams the door. In a heartbeat, he is churn-ing gravel — destination anywhere but here. Once the engine rumbles away and I know I am safe, I find my way to Ethrea Ree's dormant rose bushes. Beneath a thorny bough, I see a hint of color way down deep. A single tea rose flushes violet before me. I have no shears, so I bite the rose's stem until it breaks. I pull the rose to myself, clinging to one horticultural fact: you can root roses and make them your own. Ethrea Ree will know. She'll help me.

Flower bush one in my Garden of Eden.

A wind whirls through me. Is it the same one that brought the rush of leaves Ethrea heard? I protect the flower's head from decapitating and usher it into the house, away from the cursed Defiance weather. As the chill breaks through me, I remember shivering another time when flurries brought a well-shoed man into Mama's life.

Nineteen

It snowed the day David, my mother's second husband, pad-
ded into our lives. I saw him from our living room window
as I drew the ice-charmed landscape in a worn sketchpad. He
paced back and forth in front of our house in shined shoes, a
black robber's hat, and a brown scarf. I called Mama's name,
beckoned her closer, because something in the way the man
walked made me uneasy. She'd been sewing Christmas gifts in
the back room. I was not to turn the knob to ruin her concentration, so I hollered instead.

Amid my hollering, I hoped she wasn't sewing something
for me. At twelve, I would rather buy my own clothes from the
local TROUNCY STORE. It'd been called COUNTRY STORE
for years and years until someone else bought it and felt Defiance needed a decent clothing store. But the new owners were
as thrifty as the Depression, so they wouldn't buy new store
letters. They simply rearranged Country to Trouncy, birthing a
quasi-stylish store on Defiance's main drag. I'd spotted a pale
blue blouse, saving my pennies and dimes, but I was still short
by several dollars.

Mama emerged slowly, closing the door behind her with a
quiet click. "What do you want, Louise?"

"That man. Who is he?" I pointed to the hatted and scarfed
man.

"I have no earthly idea."

At the exact moment she said *idea*, he stared at us both. Snow swirled around him, polka dotting his hat.

"But look at his shoes," Mama said.

I should've been out in the snow, enjoying the East Texas rarity, but being prone to hatching shivers in the cold, I'd stayed inside nursing hot chocolate, taking refuge under a fuzzy blanket. Thick wool socks couldn't keep my toes from embracing the day's icy ways. But watching the snow, bundled in the safety of home, had roused the sleeping artist inside me — a furious desire to capture how I saw the world. I determined that day to draw the snow, how it clung to black branches, blanketed the fence posts, whitened the world. I tried to capture the shadows of snow, how the light muted itself beneath the trees, which is what I was doing until the man tamped down the white beauty under thick-soled shoes. I refused to draw him into my sketch.

"He looks cold," Mama said. Her voice lilted in the quiet, a hush of tone.

"No he doesn't."

Before I could restrain her, she flung the door wide, letting in the cool air.

I shivered.

"Hey!" she hollered. "Are you all right?"

"You're Shelby, aren't you?"

Mama stepped onto the porch. She shielded her eyes from the snow with her left hand. I wanted to shut the door behind her, but thought the better of it. I didn't trust that man in his too-nice shoes. "Why do you want to know?" She blew out into the day in beautiful, tangible tendrils of air.

"We were childhood friends, you and me. I'm David Kennedy. Remember?" He crossed the yard, not bothering to find our sidewalk. His footprints made neat impressions in the virgin snow. Grass peeked out from each indentation. I wanted to shout at him. How could I draw the yard now? At this point in

my painting adventure, I tended toward idealism, not the harsh footprints of reality.

"David?" Snow fell on Mama's hair but she didn't shake away nature's dandruff.

David bowed slightly, then smiled. He winked too. He removed his hat, revealing red hair. His face appeared entirely happy, with snow on his face—little petals of ice forming, then warming into wet streams down clean-shaven cheeks.

I stood next to Mama in the silence between their words. I don't think she saw the imperceptible shift, the ever-so-slight hardening of his smile, the narrowing of his eyes when he first looked at me straight on. But I saw it. "And who is this?" he asked.

"My daughter Louise," she told him.

"Louise. How pretty."

I withdrew behind Mama like a shy child at an overloud grown-up party. His *pretty* stayed in my head that evening, the way the word slid out of his mouth like a snake's lie. I hated him right then and there. Hated his stupid polished shoes.

But Mama was smitten, apparently. I harrumphed around the house, slamming my own shoes to the floor, rousing her from The Beverly Hillbillies. "Mama, can't you see?" I stood between her and Jed Clampett. "That man is a creep. He'll bring nothing but trouble."

She tried to look around me, but I turned off the television. "Louise, your father's been gone a long time now. At least for me it seems long. And I'm lonely. Who will take care of me when I get old?"

"I will. How could you ask such a thing?" I sat next to her on our goldenrod couch.

"You'll have your own life soon enough, with love and marriage and children. It's what I had once. But not what I have now. I miss it."

"Aren't I enough?"

She wrapped an arm around me, settled me into her. "You're everything a mama would want. But you'll never be my husband."

"What would Daddy think?"

"We talked about it once. Did I ever tell you that?"

I noticed the graying of the night, the wind moving through dark branches outside. It shivered me. "No," I finally said.

"He told me if he ever died, he wanted me to find another man. A good man. A man to take care of you and me."

"This David—he's not that man."

"First impressions aren't everything, Louise."

I nodded. "I just have a bad feeling about him is all. Like he'll bring hard times."

"I'm not afraid of hard times, just lonely ones. Hard times are God's gift to us, to keep us hoping in him alone."

I wanted to believe her then. That God would trump any pain that blew through our lives. But the sick feeling in my stomach wouldn't allow for such hope.

The truth of the matter was this: Mama fell heart first into love under that rare canopy of snow. And forgot to fasten on her head.

The man touched all the shoes, every day except Sundays. Some he stored under the earth; others he kept up high, cradled in a wooden box in his home. And a few he strung above his head like talismans in the tree house he constructed from Defiance's trash. He spirited the shoes day by painstaking day, taking from the children of Defiance.

The shoes told him stories through their scent. He smelled each mateless shoe, whispering to the sky, wondering aloud about whose feet they once embraced.

But it was the sandal he always returned to, clutching it to himself before he went to bed. He asked it out loud to please relinquish the nightmares, to hush the roar of voices in his sleeping head.

This shoe, his totem, protected him. Sometimes.

Twenty

It will take a week for Hap to get his car back. Officer Spellman, a deacon in our church, and a policeman to boot, told us they've got no leads on the perpetrator of such sacrilege. He wore such empathy in his expression that I had no doubt of his strange affection for my husband, almost like he worships Hap. So I'm left without transportation, alone in the house, feeling those walls push in, thirsting me again.

Valentine's Day nears—a fact I realize only by Sissy's red-heart-cutting this afternoon. She labors over paper like a mama cat with new kittens, fussing, licking Publisher's Clearing House "stamps," working hard to spell everyone's name right. I love her for it, wishing I had her capacity for giving to folks. Because the reality of the matter is most kids tease Sissy. And her home-made Valentines are one of her ways of wooing them back. I'm not sure if the pain in my stomach is worry for her potential heartbreak, or something else. I push away the something else.

"I gotta get 'em just right, Mama." Her tongue sticks out on the left side, just a tip of pink proving her concentration.

"I know, baby." She hands me a bead—a tiny pink heart seemingly alone in the paper jungle on the table.

"You can have it. I found it on my way home from school. Isn't it pretty?"

"It's beautiful." I allow my bracelet to slip below my shirt cuff. It dangles on my wrist.

"What's that?" Sissy touches the string bracelet, turns it around, inspecting it.

"It's a funny little bracelet. I'm going to put your bead on it."

"Like a charm bracelet? I've always wanted one."

"Yeah, kind of like that."

She fingers the chicken bone. "What is this?"

"I found it when Emory and I scattered Hixon's ashes. It helps me remember him, how kind he was." I don't tell her that it also reminds me of my marriage, bones without flesh.

She touches the next charm, Elijah's second box. "What's this?"

"It's a box from ... an old friend." I take off my bracelet carefully, letting her touch the box.

"It's beautiful. So small."

"Like you." I kiss her head, smell our rose-scented shampoo. She smiles.

I take the little bead, tie a short piece of thread through it, making a loop, then tie it around the bracelet: charm number three.

Sissy re-clasps the bracelet on my wrist. "Why don't you show it?"

"It's my little secret," I tell her. If she only knew how many secrets I cherished to myself. But that's a thought for another day. "Something that makes me happy."

"Like the vase next to your bed?"

I pull in a haggard breath. Does she know that secret? Dear God, I hope not. I don't say anything in response to her question, weighing my words, measuring them out in little quantities in my head, wondering how much to dish out.

"You love flowers," she says, as sweet as spring.

I sigh. "Yes, I do. I guess that's another one of my secrets." Thank you, God, I silence to the heavens. Flower confessions. Nothing more.

"Why don't you write messages to Jed anymore?"

I run my left hand through my hair. "Jed's too old for my petal messages," I tell her. "But you're not, are you?"

"No, ma'am. You can write them all to me now."

I smile. "That's my hope."

"Hope is good." Sissy's voice makes the simple words a beckoning melody. It's almost enough to make me believe hope might just puncture my world again.

I nod and point to her bead. "And this heart bead, dear Sissy, is to remind me about love. Your sweet, beautiful love that comes from a pure heart." I hide the bracelet beneath my cuff. Perhaps someday I will love again. And be loved in return. I know my children love me. Emory too. And Ethrea Ree, in her own way. But the love of a man? Of my man? There's not enough hope in the world to muster such a thing.

Sissy resumes cutting. I watch as paper lace, fashioned from doilies, falls to the kitchen floor, but I don't rescue its scattering.

Sissy picks it up instead. "Valentines need lace, don't you think?"

I nod.

"I'm going to make one for you. And Daddy." She smiles my way, throwing her love around like she's not afraid it'll be devoured. But she's understood devoured, all too well. I remember her haunted face when that tattoo-wearing snake-man nearly stole her from me. I thought he and I had a silent pact between us months ago, that Sissy wouldn't be marked. Jed, neither. Perhaps that's why that man gave her back so quickly, and maybe that's why she recovered, never bending into cynicism or falling headlong into fear of people. She cuts hearts, methodically, to the rhythm of childhood around my kitchen table while I chop lettuce for tacos.

Me? I'd rather be sensible. Smart. Detached. Not prone to declarations of love on lace and red paper. I've given my heart to Hap for so long that it ceases to beat romance.

While Sissy works on blessing classmates with paper gifts, I notice the purple rose at my window, cradled in an empty 7-Up bottle, while I wash the knife and cutting board. The rose's stem is not as smooth as it once was. Little grafts of buds emerge in rooting compound given by Ethrea Ree, longing for the soil of my yard someday. And for a moment, I'm perfectly content using a bottle for such a thing. I stash what I need in the bottles around the house, but this one promotes life. When the hollyhocks surprise us all this summer and next, perhaps a purple rose will sprout strong in its new soil as well. Maybe it will grow to the sky, reaching, reaching for what brings it life. And maybe, just maybe, Hap will smile at the beauty.

"I have a question." Sissy interrupts my daydream.

I am still at the sink, finishing the dishes, readying them for dinner.

"You have to turn around."

So I do.

She grins as she unfolds a large red piece of paper with bits and pieces of lace and stickers and "Happy Valentine's Day" scrawled on a misshapen heart. "Will you be my Valentine?" Sissy giggles.

I smile, but quickly force a frown. It's been a long time since I've heard such valentine words. I hold the construction paper, remembering, while Sissy cuts and glues and writes, her tongue still pinking out.

The rose-scented wedding behind us, we'd scraped together a few dollars here and there from Hap's carpentry business, hoping to buy a home in this town. We'd looked and scrutinized dozens of houses, but none seemed to meet with his specifications—perhaps you know what this is like. "They have to have good bones, Ouisie," he told me. So I waited while we saw so many "bones" I'd grown tired of the anatomy of Defiance houses. I could nearly detect the floor plan just driving by—long front room, galley kitchen, three bedrooms, a dining room with a door to the back yard, a few bathrooms scattered in between down a long dark hallway. With most of the town burning to the ground in the 50s, there hadn't been a lot of variety—mainly ranch style homes, some fixers, and a few remaining antebellum homes in need of paint and wiring and plumbing and drywall that Hap was unwilling to tackle.

"I have a surprise," Hap told me one winter afternoon while I cleaned the apartment. He caught me mid-vacuum, sweeping me off my feet, carrying me beyond the threshold of our apartment, and dropping me gently into the Chevy. "Just you see." He had a glint in his eye I've since nearly forgotten—a flirtatious mischief. He drove through downtown, the windows rolled down. I remember the winter air, warmed to sixty by the sun, how it didn't absorb us like summer air did, how it ignited joy. Hap placed his carpenter hand on my leg, tapping it, smiling. I wrapped my hand around his rough palm, feeling his strength and heat. The radio played a song he liked, so he turned it up. We sang together.

Something about a highway and love. We laughed as we confused the words. Hap inserted my name into the song, warbling like a pretend crooner, one hand in mine, the other on the steering wheel, lifting now and again to accent his performance. He turned the corner from Forest to Dyer, then slowed into the driveway of a nondescript house with a thick crimson ribbon tied around the front door like a present. Beneath the ribbon—a pink heart preened.

"Well?"

"Well, what?" I asked.

"What do you think?"

"It's a house." And that it was. Peeling paint. A broken window. An overgrown lawn. It looked abandoned, condemned.

"It's *our* home."

"Ours?" Tears let loose. I touched my hand to my face, not sure what else would fly out of my mouth. An oh-no? A you've-got-to-be-kidding-me? Yes, I would've liked to be a part of this

monumental decision. Absolutely. But Hap had gone out of his way to secure our future, to get us out from under apartment living. To give us a home.

"Will you be my Valentine, Ouisie Pepper?" He jangled the keys in front of my wet face. "Are you okay? Do you hate it?" I sensed his vulnerability, the way his eyes shifted, how I could nearly detect him recoiling and lashing out if I didn't have the right response. I couldn't stand to disappoint him then.

I choked out "home." Hap pulled me to himself in that in between moment, the fulcrum of joy and wrath. I didn't know that starting off fresh in a need-to-be-remodeled house would prove a chink in Hap's romantic armor, among other things. I felt Hap's arms around my heaving body, the comfort of his strength, the settled beat of my heart when I knew I was safe and taken care of. I would have a home. Finally. But home would prove to be nothing I hoped it would be. And that Valentine's Day would nearly be his last surprise.

Twenty-One

Emory picks me up today, freeing me from the house—the kitchen in particular. She tells me to bring my paints and canvas, so I do. It's a warm day, low seventies, and the sun opens the day with long shadows. I wish I could paint in the dusk instead, where the light is near golden, making particles dance, but I choose to revel in this moment, my paintbrush poised above paper while I try to capture decay.

Emory rebuilds the henhouse nearby, pounding a hammer, swearing on occasion, and sawing boards. She's making Muriel's house into her home. I wonder if Hixon smiles down upon her, whispering encouragement.

I pull brown paint vertically, trying again to capture the sway of the grass. But movement eludes me. I add gold, a taste of shimmering sun on the field, but still it does not move. I want to crumple the paper, send it hurling toward the sun, but I steady my hand. One day the pasture will live beneath my paintbrush.

I am smitten with Hopper, the artist who paints houses and stores and big skies over wheat fields, but I cannot capture his vitality. Pretty is as pretty does, folks say, so maybe it's my stale life that deadens my paintbrush. If I were alive, I can't help but think my paintings would be too.

"That's beautiful," Emory tells me. She's wearing a wide-banded straw hat, a pair of worn out jeans, and a moth-eaten cotton sweater—*Little House on the Prairie* meets Joan Baez.

"Nothing I do is beautiful," I whisper.

Emory looks me right in the eyes, and says, "You are not allowed to talk that way on Muriel's place. You know she'd scold you for such a thing."

I smile, imagining Muriel wagging her finger at me, telling me things about the Almighty's grace and favor. I can nearly hear her voice, the lilt in her laughter. "I know," I tell Emory. "It must be awful quiet around here."

She sits in the dirt beside me while I try again to resurrect the grass on the canvas. "It is." She rubs her knees, but the iron-rich dirt clings. "But you want to know what helps?"

"What?"

"I'm reading Hixon's Bible. It brings me comfort." She pulls a handful of dried grass, bunching it to form two stalks into a cross. "It's like he's here with me, teaching me what I never really understood, as if he's answering my unspoken questions through his own notes."

"That's great." I truly believe it's great, though I sometimes wonder about my own faith. Sure, I want others to believe, and I thrill when such a thing happens, but I feel so disconnected from God that my joy at other's nearness seems sacrilegious to me. I dab my brush into black.

"Like today, you know what I read?"

I shake my head, then mix black with green.

"I memorized it. From Exodus 12:14. It says, 'And this day shall be unto you for a memorial.' Isn't that beautiful? It got me thinking. Maybe God wants me to capture not only this day, sear it into my memory, but to remember Hixon's days too. Like the last day I saw him."

"When he pulled you out of the fire."

"Yeah. I remember strong arms, his voice, the feeling of fear leaving me the farther I emerged from the smoke. I felt the light, but couldn't open my eyes. My throat was so dry I couldn't form a thank you. And then, just like that, the arms slipped away."

"To go fetch the ring." I clean my brush on an old rag, then dab it into a buttery yellow.

She touches the golden band. "Yes. If he hadn't—"

"What's done is done. You can't remake the day, giving Hixon different marching orders. Life's not like that."

She takes off the ring, holds it toward the sky, and looks through it as if it's a portal to heaven. "I wish it were."

"Me too."

She continues looking. "Ever think there might be an entire world just outside our reach where everything's peachy and beautiful?"

"I suppose that's what the hereafter is like."

She puts the ring back on. Then looks at me, her eyes anxious. "There's something I've been meaning to tell you."

"What?"

"Sometimes I hear things, Ouisie."

I set my brush on the paper plate I'm using to mix colors. "What kind of things?"

"Rummaging, mostly. Sometimes right outside my window. Only there's nothing there to rummage. At night I hear trees."

Her words echo Ethrea's a few days ago. "Rustling?"

"Yes, that's it. Only my trees are there." She points to the stand of fruit trees, and further beyond a forest of pines. They are nearly an acre away. "And the orchard doesn't have leaves this time of year."

"You sure you're not just lonely, making up noises in your head?"

"I've considered it, but I don't think so. Sometimes I hear the noises even when the radio's blaring."

I join Emory in the red dust. We sit facing each other like girls about to perform "See See Oh Playmate." I swallow, blink away the sun in my eyes. "You know what happened to Hap's car, right?"

She nods.

"When it was happening, Ethrea Ree said she heard something—a rustling, she said."

I can't see Emory's eyes; the hat shades them, but her head nods slowly. For a long time neither of us speak, letting our thoughts twirl and intersect in the quiet buzz of the day.

"You think this has something to do with the tattooed man?" She pulls a dry piece of grass up from its roots, breaks it in half, and chews on it.

I shake my head. The tattooed man? No. But then what do I know? "I don't know, but it gives me the willies. Marring Hap's car seems to be inviting trouble. He isn't exactly someone to be trifled with. Hap has guns, you know, so whoever did this is fearless. Or has a death wish."

"I know Hap has guns."

I want to ask her to say more, but I stop myself. Knowing details about their affair is something I cannot delve into right now. But since he apparently only came to her house, how would she know about the guns?

Emory blushes. "I'm sorry."

"Don't be. At least you understand how precarious life is with the rustling, the car's scratch, Hap's temper."

"I'm not that afraid, really. What can someone do to me that hasn't already been done?" Emory caresses her ring. She turns it in circles, her finger smaller than its circumference. "The rustling is something that makes my skin crawl, but it's nothing compared to what you deal with every day."

Instinctively, I try to turn my ring around my finger, but it's stuck to my flesh—an indelible part of me I can't move or remove.

"He's going to kill you someday. You know that."

I laugh, really laugh, as the sun warms my hands, my face, my mood. "You can't be serious."

"I'm as serious as the grave," she says.

"He loses his temper, sure. But a killer? Come on Emory. You don't really believe that."

"I may not be much of a Christian. I know I'm confused. But I do have eyes and maybe just a little more insight than you. That man is no good, and someday his temper will blind him."

I look away, noticing the orchard again, how stark limbs move slightly under the bluest wide-open sky. How they look like death, only to resurrect in the spring with blossoms, then fruit as the summer ripens. So much like my marriage—sometimes brittle, other times blossoming. Only I can't remember picking the fruit for the life of me. I throw out, "Well, he would never hurt the kids."

Emory just looks at me. "It's no secret, Ouisie. He hurts you all. Even Sissy."

I swallow her words. I've been careful—concealing, hiding, keeping private. At least I thought so. "It's that obvious?"

She shrugs. "Maybe it's just me who knows. I'm not sure. Big Earl seems to poke around a bit, too, wondering about y'all. But I know enough to watch for the signs, and I've seen 'em."

"Hap's under a lot of pressure."

"So was Hixon, but you didn't see him hauling off and hitting folks, did you?"

"No."

"You really ought to think about getting safe."

"I'm working on things. I'm handling it."

"Oh really." She spins her ring. "Just how are you handling that man's unruly temper?"

"I'm seeking counsel from a godly woman."

"What does that even mean?" She pulls another blade of dried grass and pretends to smoke it.

"Sheba Nelson—she wrote this book, *The Godly Woman's Guide to Marriage*. I've been reading it, trying to obey it. And sometimes it really works."

"Who's named Sheba these days? And how does she know a hoot about your marriage?"

"She visited me."

Emory raises her eyebrows. "The author?"

"Yes. I wrote her a letter, and the next week, she showed up at my doorstep."

"That's weird."

I laugh. It *is* weird. One of the things I love about Emory is that she's not one to skirt around what she really thinks. I used to be that way when Daddy made jewelry from home.

"Ouisie, I don't know much about marriage. Heck, I've never been married. But I don't think there's anything you can do to change a person."

"I can't believe that. If I believe that, then all is lost."

"How about being honest with yourself and me?"

I look at my hands, stained with paint. I'll have to scrub them with Ajax to remove my treachery. "I'm not good enough. I can't keep the house clean. I don't manage our money well. He works hard, and comes home to a mess. And—"

"And what? You're normal? You try, don't you?"

I let out a sigh that emerges louder than I expect. "Yes, of course I try. But evidently not enough. Sheba says—"

"Forget about Sheba."

"I can't. I need godly counsel. My marriage is the way it is because I can't seem to learn to submit to Hap. I'm stubborn."

"You don't make any sense. Have you ever thought about Hap submitting to you? Serving you?"

"That would be selfish. And it's not the way God made things. You're new to all this, so I don't expect you to understand."

"I may not understand the Bible, but I know Jesus through Hixon. And I know Hixon would not treat me the way Hap treats you. Funny thing was that I mistreated Hixon something fierce, but did he return the favor? No. He retaliated with kindness. I hope he's smiling down on me right now, because at least this thick-headed girl learned one thing from him. I learned that Jesus is gentle and patient and kind. I haven't seen Hap be any of those things."

I let the words spin around my head, but I don't absorb them into my soul. I can't. Emory is naïve and doesn't understand the intricacies of marriage. She's stuck in that great happy adventure of courtship that never materialized into matrimony. She'll spend the rest of her life comparing ordinary men with extraordinary Hixon. And anyone can be extraordinary for a time. It's when you live with someone that you discover otherwise. You can't hear a man snore when you're dating.

"I really don't want to talk about this anymore," I tell her.

"That's okay. But please think about what I said." She reaches over, puts her hand on mine. "I've known bad men before. They never go from bad to good; it's always bad to worse. If you ever think you're in danger, you call me. You promise?"

I nod my promise, but I doubt I'll need to call. If I can just be like Sheba, improve myself for Hap, there'll be no more need for his tirades.

"And for what it's worth—I mean I'm no art critic—I think your paintings are beautiful." She removes her old-fashioned hat. The sun responds by bronzing her hair. In that moment, I see what my lifeless grass is missing—a hint of shimmering golden bronze. I pick up my brush as she haunts the pasture and I add Emory's sun-blessed hair color to the field on my paper. A hint here, a sliver there. The grass still doesn't dance off the page like I'd like it to, but at least it moves. Ever so slightly, it moves.

Twenty-Two

I store my paintings and supplies at Emory's place under the watchful eye of Muriel's farm. They are safe there, I know. After all, Muriel was the inspiration behind the beautification of the rendering plant wall behind Emory's house. Muriel's mural changed the graffiti into art, thanks to Hixon, Jed, and even a few of Sissy's amateur strokes. Part of me wonders if Muriel understands why I didn't help paint her legacy, why I didn't lend my artistic touch to something I deem as beautiful. You may say I'm selfish with my creativity. I prefer to say I'm private, not akin to scores of people gawking at my painting.

Somehow I think, though, that Muriel forgives my private ways, that she would've never ridiculed my nearly-swaying grass or questioned my need for paintbrushes. She is in heaven, I know, but I sense her right here, encouraging me, looking down on me with understanding, blessedly cancer-free. When I painted under Muriel's sky today, I felt like maybe life could be happy again, as if God were painting redemption with my brushes. If I spent more time dabbing colors on canvas, maybe Hap would see the change, the joy. I tell myself again that whatever makes me happy might just translate into the husband and home I've always longed for. And maybe the children would laugh in a joyful house.

As the landscape whirs past, Emory's words rip my peaceful

picture in half. Hap will kill me someday. He will kill me—leaving my children motherless. Emory's words are unreal—twisted fairy-tale words. Motherless Hansel and Gretel strike out on their own away from their father. A corner of my mind believes such things, the corner where I store all the dark thoughts about my future. That little voice lives there, not the Voice, but hissing words that say if Hap raised a gun my way, I'd deserve it. But my kids? They wouldn't.

I shake my head, take note of Emory at the wheel. Her face has softened in grief, the harsh lines blurring into something that looks strangely like contentment—a look I doubt I'll wear in this life. She is Impressionism. I am the harsh lines of Modern Art.

"Just so you know," she says. "I wasn't trying to scare you. Just warn you."

I don't want to say any more words about Hap's anger, the guns he has, so I divert. "About how I painted?" Defiance proper rolls out in front of us, the sun casting shadows easterly over dormant cow pastures.

She laughs. "You know what I'm talking about. There's only so much a person can take before it's too late. I worry it's headed that way. And no matter what you do, you won't be able to change its trajectory."

I nod. I know. But all I say is, "Trajectory. Nice word."

She says thank you. She seems to understand enough about the delicate nature of friendship not to press. We watch the horizon together, and I wonder if she's memorized every tree, every rise in the road, every house and trailer along this stretch, as I have. Defiance has changed little in the past several years. A few folks have moved in; others have died. But its skeleton remains reliably familiar. Even the birds tend toward sameness, singing the same songs they sang when railroad men founded the town. It's this monotony that soothes me and drives me batty all at once. It reminds me, though, that Hap has not obliged with such

monotony. He began that way, but then shifted like a Defiance summer wind, and enflamed the sameness with his temper while I tried to douse it with little bottles of liquid sunshine, while my children suffered from both.

When we pull into the driveway, Sissy streaks by the corner of my vision. She opens and slams the front door. Her gait is not a carefree girl's set free from school. It is pure anguish. I holler a quick goodbye to Emory and run into the house after my daughter.

I find her in her room, huddled under her covers, rocking back and forth, weeping. I pull back her bedspread, but she wrenches it back over herself. Wailing erupts from underneath. Sometimes I wish I could hide like that, but then I remember the bottles around the house. They are my blanket. They become tears I lap up.

"Sissy, what's wrong?" I pet the bed, hoping to coax her from her linen prison. But she cries steadily—hiccups of grief. A minute passes. Two.

"They hate me," she whimpers from beneath.

"Who hates you?" I am still stroking the blankets, feeling her sorrow heave through them. I wish all at once I could remove every painful thing from Sissy's life. But I am not big enough to do such a thing.

"My entire class." She throws off the blankets, revealing electric hair, waving in the cold air of her room. Her eyes are pink-rimmed, her nose the color of spring roses just blushing.

"What happened?" I pat the bed next to me. She cuddles underneath my arm. She feels right, cradled beneath like that, like I was made to be her mama, and she was made to be hugged. If only I could hug away all the pain.

"My valentines," is all she said, and then burst afresh into sobs.

"Didn't you have enough?" It's the question I ask myself at the end of the day. And I am never enough. Never have enough. Never give enough.

"I made plenty." Her voice is small, quieter than when Hap corners her for answers. She sniffs. "They said only babies *make* Valentine's. Everyone else had Scooby Doo Valentines. Or Bugs Bunny. I was the only one with homemade—with paper lace."

I touch her hair, a wave of understanding lapping up on the beach of my mind. Slow, relentless, devastating. To give the very best of yourself, only to be ridiculed and found lackluster, not enough. "I'm so sorry, baby."

"Jeremy Keith called me artsy fartsy."

I smile. In trying to erase it, I smile more. "Jeremy Keith is jealous," I tell her. "He probably wishes he could make things like you do."

Sissy lets a smile tease her mouth. "Once he said a tree I drew looked real."

"See? Besides, boys who tease are typically hiding the fact that they have a little crush on you."

"Is that why Daddy teases you, Mama? Because of his crush?"

Her words startle me. There was a time when Hap had a crush on me, though now I think he's more bent on crushing. "Daddy has a hard time at work, and sometimes I don't make his life easier when he comes home. That's probably why he teases."

"You're the best mama," she says—always trying to soothe my sorrow.

"You're my cheerleader, Sissy, you know that?"

She nods, wipes her tears. "You know what Jed told me once?"

"What's that?"

"He said the Bible says to rejoice always. Even when things are hard."

"When did Jed say that?"

"After he got home from Hixon's funeral. We played checkers in his room, and I started crying, carrying on about Hixon. He stopped the game, opened his Bible, and shared that verse."

Jed shares verses? "He's a good brother, isn't he?"

"The best kind of brother. He takes care of me at school, watches over me when he walks me home."

I remember Emory's killing comment, mull it over briefly, and rest a little in Jed's ability to parent Sissy. Maybe they'd be just fine without me.

"Mama?"

"Yes, Sissy?" I look into her trusting, sweet eyes.

"That verse about rejoicing didn't make sense yesterday, not really. But I think I understand now." Clementine joins us in the room, her big golden head resting on Sissy's lap.

"How so?" I join her in petting Clementine, the dog who can't stop loving and protecting this family.

"I'm happy for one thing about today." She shows me a crooked smile.

"What's that?"

"I did make a card for every kid in my class. Every one. And I made some for the kids in other classes who probably wouldn't get Valentines. I know for a fact that Bobby Eller was happy to get one. And Sheryl Root, too. They said their thanks in their own ways, like Delmer would."

"That's sweet." I think how her lisp has tortured her in one respect, but also made her deeply empathetic for kids who are different. She's the most beautiful girl in the world.

"At least, maybe, everyone knew they were loved—even if most thought I made baby Valentines. I think Hixon would've said I did my best."

I choke at Hixon's name, pull in my tears. Death is terribly final. "You *did* do your very best. And by saying what you're saying now, I think Hixon is smiling down upon you. I know I'm proud." And inspired, I almost say.

"Thanks, Mama."

I breathe in, reveling in her little girl smell. She's held the weight of this family, always trying to make sure everyone's loved—even Hap. In truth, she's made us all Valentines every day of her life. I just hope I've recognized her for such valiance. We sit on the bed for I don't know how long, rocking to the rhythm of mother and daughter. Sissy's Valentine story meanders through my head, teaching me again that the world is sometimes a place I want to pull the covers over, but that doesn't mean I give up trying—or being thankful for the small things.

Today I am thankful for this: Sissy's small hand in mine and her blessed, blessed life.

Twenty-Three

Sheba's advice in *The Godly Woman's Guide to Marriage* reverberates through me the next Sunday morning:

> There must be no secrets in the circle of marriage. Secrets at first seem like little delicacies to be savored until they become like cyanide-laced sawdust in the mouth — unappetizing and lethal. The Bible says that Adam and Eve were naked and unashamed, which is God's ideal for marriage. Naked means no secrets, nothing hidden, everything revealed.

My fingers still bear a remnant of speckle from last week's art indulgence. No matter how much Ajax I scrub into them, the stain remains. And as I read Sheba's words just an hour before church, the pointillism near my palms seems to awaken, darken, and scream my sin at me. I have hidden both my art and a secret garden that'll emerge in spring. And my need for the demon liquor, although he knows that. But most of all, I've hidden Daisy's killer — from you, from everyone. Does Sheba really think it wise to share all of this with Hap? I have no doubt what Hap will do if he knows who strangled Daisy. I shake the thought from my head.

"What are you reading now?" Hap tightens his tie while looking into the mirror above our old dresser. His white pressed shirt is starch incarnate. He retains the build he had when he swept me off my penny loafers so many years ago. Lean, strong chest, small waist, hands with muscles I can see. And all his hair, yet grayed above his ears.

I shut the book, almost slap it closed. Sometimes I worry Hap reads the mail of my mind. Will he know if I lie right now? "Sheba's book about being a godly wife." That's not a lie. Not a secret.

Hap smiles. He brushes hands down the front of his shirt, smoothing perfection. He sits on the bed next to me, takes my hand. My heart discos in my chest. Such a rare show of affection. "I'm proud of you." He removes his hand and pats me on the head, ruffling my newly curled hair, but I don't scold.

"Thanks," I tell him. "I'm trying."

"I'll need my coffee sooner rather than later."

I take his hint and enter the kitchen, the place of my liquid trial. I scoop coffee, add water to the percolator, and pray it comes out perfectly. I think coffee tastes like cigarette butts, to be honest, so I am no judge of flavor. I can only hope my formula of three leveled off tablespoons of Folgers to three cups water does the trick. Even though I am careful to do it exactly the same every day, Hap finds fault most mornings. He calls it amazing every tenth day—his personal tithe to me, I suppose.

Sissy and Jed enter as if the smell of coffee lures them. Sissy wears a short-sleeved yellow dress in winter, one that's above her knees now and a little ragged. I've begged Hap for clothes money, but he says we all need to learn the joy of frugality. "The Apostle Paul learned to be content in all things, with lack and with plenty. Surely you can follow his example," he told me the last time I asked. I'm ashamed of Sissy's dress, Jed's pants that brush above lean ankles. And my own clothes are stuck in the women's magazines of seven years ago. I sigh, feed the kids Tasty-Os and frozen concentrate orange juice—now reconstituted with Defiance water, then pour a cup of coffee for Hap.

"Ouisie, someday you'll learn to make coffee right."

Day nine, I should've known. I smile. I tender my words today considering Sheba's advice to spill all my beans. Maybe if I act more pleasant, I can keep my secrets and lessen Hap's temper. "Yes, I need to learn. You're right. Perhaps tomorrow will be better."

We ride to church in silence cramped in my car. I've learned quiet is Hap's preferred way to start his Sundays, so he can preach the sermon in his head while we watch the same birds fly and the same cows graze. When we pull up to the church, ours is the first car there. Hap parks in his space, next to the front entrance. Unlike our home, Hap has allowed for Defiance Community Church to have gardens surrounding its foundation. Hixon used to tend it, and now Emory stubbornly took up his job, though I begged Hap to let me. He simply put up his hand like a stop sign, signaling his decision.

I find it odd that Emory won't come to church, but sometime each week she makes her way here, pulling weeds and prettifying the dirt, even in winter. It's seems to be her way of keeping Hixon alive for the congregation, without words. No one ever sees her dragging her hands through the dirt, but she does her work anyway. I love her for it. Envy her too.

We mount the wooden steps to the white door entrance. Hap felt it wasn't grand enough as a plain white door, so he surrounded it with ripped in half Doric columns, topping them with a decorative header that he carved himself and painted the same Roman white. It's stunning, really, but it looks like jewelry on a donkey. Roman columns and bricks don't match no matter how much Hap says they do. I'm no architect, so I keep my mouth closed.

Just as the landscape of Defiance rolled on and on in tedium, the center aisle of the church with its dark brown pews echoes the same repetition. The people, once they've arrived and are seated, will play their roles in the same seats. We will sing, offer some money to the red-velvet-bottomed plate, listen to Hap as he waves hands to the heavens, say a few polite amens, mull around the foyer, and drive the same roads home to a supper of pot roast and potatoes. No one will dare put two and two together about our upstanding family. Sure, a few elders and deacons know of Hap's penchant for anger, but they fear him more than they like me, so all will be left unsaid. Which is why it's up to me to change this all around. To stop violence with kindness. Or die trying.

Emory giving words to Hap's ways has hijacked me, if you want to know. It's one thing to be stuck in your head with worries and fears aplenty. It's quite another thing when a friend points them all out, throwing words out into the world, making them truer than even your thoughts. When Hap touches me, I jump.

"I'm making an announcement today. One you'll be pleased with." He winks at me, then paces to the pulpit. He shuffles his notes.

Jed pats the pew. "What do you suppose he's going to say?"

"I really don't know." And that's the truth. But my stomach tells me it won't be good.

"Maybe he's quitting," Jed says.

For a moment, I hope that Jed's words are pure prophecy, that Hap will let go of his royal hold on this church, his insatiable need to be revered, and return to his carpenter ways. Back to the life where he didn't hit me as much, when his patience was longer than a Texas summer day, when he smiled as he read the comics. While Jed and Sissy form their own theories, I nurture mine, dreaming of a day where I no longer make my husband hate me. When I feel free to share my secrets. When I'm finally worthy enough. Good enough. Perfect enough. Or just plain *enough*.

The sun angles through the windows of the church, spreading light in several colors through the sanctuary as folks take

their seats and mind their business. I wonder: do they have secrets? What about Flo from Piggly Wiggly? Or pristine Emily Mohler, an elder's wife with the perfect life? I nod to Officer Spellman, say hello to Heloise Dickson, who feigns friendship but gossips about me behind my back. We stand, sing songs, sit, give offerings, then wait as Hap ruffles papers and clears his throat. I swallow. Jed pats me, as if he knows what's coming.

For a long time, nothing comes. Just exegesis, Greek transliteration, and many words about the Body of Christ being made new. Brand new.

"It's like my Chevy," Hap says. "Some of you may have heard that a terrible thing happened to my car this week. In my own driveway, someone gouged a line from the back of the car to the front." He looks at Officer Spellman, who nods in agreement.

"The car had been new once, but it lost its luster. I spent several years in my teens cleaning it up, replacing engine parts, sanding, bonding, and painting. As you all know, that car's a beauty. And in one terrible moment, it's scarred." He scans the congregation. "Isn't that a lot like us? The Bible says if we're in Christ, we're new creatures. We're like that Chevy. Used to be old and broken, but now we're new and running. Here's the problem, though. The devil doesn't like our shiny paint jobs, now does he?"

The word *no* echoes through the sanctuary. I don't add my no.

"The Bible says he roams to and fro throughout the earth, seeking to devour folks. He wants to gouge out your life, friends. To mark you. To scar you."

I steady myself. So far, so good. It's about the car, nothing more.

"Take marriage."

Oh no.

"Marriages may become broken, but then God comes and scrubs 'em clean, doesn't He?"

Amens.

"Sometimes, though, the devil makes his sneaky way into a marriage and starts troubling our spouse. Scars 'em in a way, so they no longer look like they used to, or act the way they did when they were first in love. It's really no different than my Chevy."

So I'm a car now—a vandalized Chevy. I fold my hands, look at them, feel the eyes of one hundred folks on me—like they're spotlighting me with headlights. Emily Mohler, who perennially sits behind me, puts her hand on my shoulder. I want to shrug her perfectly groomed hand away, but instead, I pat it, whisper a thanks.

"But there's hope, folks. Because spouses can go to body shops. They can be fixed. They can be retooled, remodeled, spray-painted clean. Next week, you'll see me smiling behind the wheel of my car, happy."

He smiles my way.

"And that's why I'm so proud of Ouisie. She's had her share of scrapes and bumps, I can assure you. I don't know a mother or wife around who doesn't deal with bad decisions or loads of guilt. But she's not letting that scar her anymore. She's growing. She's changing. And she's becoming new."

I am not sure if I should smile or cry.

He looks away from me. "And don't tell her I told you this," he laughs. "But I have a surprise for her."

He is saying these words in a mock whisper. Emily pats my back again. I hear chuckles around the congregation. Oh how they love to see their pastor bless his wife!

"She's studying a book called *The Godly Woman's Guide to Marriage.* I've read through it, and I'm here to tell you it's full of biblical lessons written by a brilliant author."

He's read Sheba's book?

"I am here to promise you, wives, that if you want to be all that God wants you to be in marriage—no scratches, in pristine condition—then you need to read this book. No, cross that out.

You need to *live* this book. My Ouisie is doing just that. I can't tell you how proud I am. So here's her surprise—and yours too. She's going to lead a study of this book every Tuesday here at the church at ten in the morning. Come one; come all. Be transformed!" He pounds the pulpit with a closed fist while I'm sure my face drains of all its color. Me? Teach Sheba's book? Is he kidding me? I thought he didn't want women teaching Bible studies!

But he is not kidding. He never is. And as we sing the closing song, I steady myself for the onslaught of wives who will sign themselves up to be renewed by none other than me—a failure of a wife who keeps secrets, who fears teaching nearly as much as I fear saying no to my husband. Dear Lord, help me.

I am no Sheba, but as a bevy of women shake my hand and hug my neck, I pray I become her, or at least can regurgitate her words.

The man could picture flowers springing from Ouisie Pepper's empty footsteps, flowers that would follow her around the lake. But she was seldom one to turn around and see their glory, smell their fragrance. She lived her life in the great now; that was his observation. And she was not one to expect surprises, like blossoms emerging from her shoeprints.

He watched her feet, how they caressed the earth. He watched each place where those shoes touched the ground. It had been several days since she circled Lake Pisgah. He sat quietly perched in a familiar tree, absorbing her route, memorizing each hesitation. The sun played upon her hair, how she pushed it away when it shielded her eyes, how long her fingers were.

Daisy's fingers were long too. And her nails, sharp. But her face? He couldn't remember. Nor was he sure he wanted to. One thing he did know: Ouisie wouldn't resist like Daisy did. No scratches, he was sure. Which is why he allowed himself this fascination, watching this solitary woman from a high, high place under a fickle sun.

Twenty-Four

My coffee was stellar today, according to Hap. Another day-ten praise. His words meander through me as I drive to Lake Pisgah, thankful Hap's car is fixed and ready. I open and shut the car door, take in all of Lake Pisgah to myself. Hap's Sunday words continue with me as I walk around the lake; they are praise words, kind words that feel alien in my head. I've shaken hands with angry, fighting words, but meeting gentleness scares me. Perhaps this is the beginning of our new life — a house full of joy, maybe even laughter. Or, as Emory warns, maybe it's the beginning of the end.

Elijah startles me from behind with a low-toned hello.

I scold him for sneaking, but he doesn't say a word. He simply points to heaven. I shake my head, keep walking. Today is Tuesday, you see. The day of leading my first women's Bible study — something I've never done, until his bright idea became the main selling point of his sermon.

"I hear you're becoming a Bible teacher." Elijah keeps pace with me.

I am too tired to ask him why he seems to find me, why he seems to know my life, my schedule, my thoughts. Sometimes I think I'm an unwilling actress in a movie everyone else is making. Hap. Elijah. Sheba. I'm here on this earth to play a role, but I have no say in how that role plays out. And if I deviate —

"That's okay, you don't need to answer." He is all Santa Claus jolly right now—his cheeks rosy against white skin and white hair. Only he doesn't ho-ho-ho.

I face him. "Yes, you heard right. But I'm no teacher, and to tell you the truth—"

"Sorry to interrupt, but I really don't like that phrase, *to tell you the truth*. Because when people say it, I seriously doubt they are going to tell the truth. Most folks lie with every sentence, which makes me crazy."

"Lots of things make you crazy." I keep my pace brisk, and he has no problem keeping up.

"I'm sorry. You were going to expound some truth about yourself."

"I'm not who I appear to be," I say. But the moment the words come out, I regret them.

He laughs. And when he laughs he sounds younger, like Hap when we first fell in love. I smile.

"No one is," he says. "I used to be shocked by people's sins, you know? I'd hear about a pastor who had an affair, and I'd be gape-mouthed. And that's just when I was running from God in the sewers in Vegas. When I reacquainted myself with God, I continued being surprised. But now," he pauses. "Now I am not shocked. I expect it. Because we're all broken. Every one of us. We're all hiding deep dark secrets we feel will ruin us if they ever see the light of day, never realizing that sharing those out loud will give us wings."

"Don't you think folks ought to be who they pretend they are? Why can't we live up to what we want to be?" My feet are cold; I nearly feel the cool ground through my soles.

He points skyward again. "Without Jesus it's impossible."

"That's the problem," I tell him. "The folks I know love Jesus, or say they do. So if they have him, why all the problems? The hiding?"

"What we fear, we become." He says these words without laughter, not even a hint of happy lilt to his voice.

I watch the horizon, the way the mist dissipates under the awakening sun, and hold his words close to me. What do I fear? I let our steps cadence my thoughts, footfall by footfall, afraid to say a word. Because if I tell him what I really fear, he'll know more about me than any other person in Defiance's borders.

Elijah points to the sky. "I feared God fussing with me. And, ultimately, there was no place I could run that He wouldn't bother. So my fear came true, in a beautiful way. I don't know where I'd be without him meddling."

"My fear is ... Well, I'm not sure it's proper."

He places a hand on my shoulder—the way a father would when he gives a child advice. I place my hand on top of his, pat it, then remove it immediately. "Fears are like snakes," he says. "They may wriggle and coil and slink away elusive, but they're still snakes if you get right down to it."

Snakes. The word slithers through my mind; my stomach broils. Still, I sense the Voice telling me to trust this once, to spill my story. So I tell my stomach to cool. "Here's what I'd like to say: I fear Jesus. So in fearing him, I'll turn into him, his loving ways, his perfection, his sacrifice. But it's not true. I've worn the uniform of pastor's wife so long that I've mistaken it for following Jesus. Because playing a role is much easier than surrendering, don't you think?"

He is silent. Which means I don't have to spill my real fear, at least for now.

"I'm still shocked," I tell him.

"That's your fear?"

"No, I'm still shocked by others' sin."

"You shouldn't be."

"I am tired of the word *should*."

"I can imagine."

"Listen, the truth is—" I catch myself in mid-lie and laugh. My laugh frightens a bird in a bush ahead of us. It struggles briefly in the branches then soars upward into the blue and white sky, free.

We finish walking around the lake, the bird a quiet lesson. It is comfortable in this place—birds above, earth below, secrets secure. In one hour I face the women. But now I think I can. All because of a man who listens, really listens.

Twenty-Five

O f all the surprises I feared walking into Defiance Community Church, the one I didn't prepare for was Ethrea Ree ever setting foot in our church. That fact alone shimmies through me, lodging worry firmly between my heart and ribcage. Why her? Why here?

But here she is, seated primly in a circle of chairs, no one on either side of her. Which makes sense. The last time some of these women met, it'd been at our Elder/Deacon picnic when Ethrea Ree burned rugs in the fireplace and shouted at Hap across the fence. She interrupted Hap's tirade against Emory, how she somehow deserved her daughter going missing — a sermon every woman here amen-ed. I sit next to Ethrea. "It's so nice to have you here," I tell her. I want to ask how she found out about my study, but I already know the answer: Defiance is a small town. Word makes its way to every soul within minutes.

"Thank you." She smiles at the other women, but several women deadpan back. So much for a happy, fellowshipping bunch of women.

"Just in case we don't know each other's names, let's — "

"Let's not," Emily Mohler says. She's an elder's wife. She wears a permanent pink-lipped smile, though her eyes shoot fire. "We all know each other." She levels a look Ethrea's way, but Ethrea seems oblivious.

"Even so, I'd like to have us say a few things by way of introduction." Heloise Dickson smiles, but she shakes her head. I clear my throat in the quiet. "Let's say our names and our favorite ice cream."

"It's a bit cold outside to be thinking about ice cream," Emily Mohler says.

"Just the same, humor me. Ethrea?"

"M'name's Ethrea Ree, but I suppose y'all know that. My favorite ice cream is licorice."

"There's such a thing as licorice ice cream?" Heloise laughs as she says it, a rare show of humor. She wears her typical denim jumper with terrible shoes.

"I make it myself with one of those ice cream makers. I grow my own anise—the plant that makes the licorice taste. Only problem is, the ice cream never turns black like I want it. Seems like licorice ice cream should be black."

I nod to Flo Sanders, who must've taken off today from Piggly Wiggly to be here. She's perennially perky. "I'm Flo Sanders. And I like vanilla. And can I just say, this meeting is an answer to my prayers. Why, just a bit ago, I told Ouisie we needed ourselves a Bible study. Just for women. And I thought she should lead it! She didn't seem to think so, but I still did, so I prayed. And look, we're here! I say prayer works, wouldn't you?"

No one seems to agree, or at least say so out loud.

"What a coincidence," Emily says. "I'm Emily and I like vanilla too."

"I'm Heloise, and mine's vanilla too. My cats prefer it as well, only melted." Heloise has at least a dozen of them, all starting with the letter F: Frisky, Fiasco and the like. Poor woman can't have kids.

I search my mind for ice cream flavors, but come up blank. The last thing I want to say is vanilla. In the silence, the door to our fellowship hall opens, revealing Emory Chance. The women gasp all at once, like she's that woman caught in adultery.

Our Bible study just got more interesting.

"Sorry I'm late," Emory says breezily. She sits between Ethrea Ree and Flo. We are now a complete circle of women.

Emily clears her throat, shows her perfect white teeth. "I hate to be picky, Ouisie, but isn't this a study about godly wives? Last I checked, neither Miss Ree nor Miss Chance have husbands."

Emory saves my shock by lifting her left hand in the air. She points to the ring. "I may not have gotten married, but according to this ring I'm married to Hixon. And I believe he attended this church, right?"

Silence answers.

"That's true," I say. "And he was a good man."

"I was married as y'all know," Ethrea Ree says. "And I'm here to figure out what I did wrong. He died when things were unresolved."

Her vulnerability shocks us all into picking our hangnails — a perfect time to pass out the books. "Here are our books. This week we'll end our time by praying for one another. By next week I want you to read chapter one and come with your questions."

The shared prayer requests are like vanilla ice cream — impersonal requests about remote relative's bouts with bunions or shingles or broken wrists. Until Emory pipes up. "I have a prayer request."

"Oh, do tell." Emily exaggerates her interest and leans forward.

"I know Hixon would like me to attend church, but I can't stand going. Folks stare. The pastor preaches sermons about women like me. Whispers follow me into the sanctuary like humming mosquitoes. It's uncomfortable. But if this is what I'm supposed to do, pray I'd become brave. Because you women scare me."

Heloise the cat lady raises her hand.

"Raising your hand's not necessary," I say.

"Well, I just want to say welcome to Miss Emory. I, for one, like her candor, and appreciate what she has to say. It's not easy being different in a church, especially not this church."

"If we're taking requests," Ethrea interjects, "then please hear mine. It's for my boy, Delmer. He's just not been himself lately. He's in the dumps. Keeps muttering to himself. I think he misses his father."

I close our brief meeting in prayer, trying to remember which great aunt battled vertigo, and which cousin had bunion surgery. It ties my mind in a knot, but I finish by praying, "Lord, help Delmer come back to himself. Heal him of his sadness. And give Emory the bravery she needs to come to church. Help us all to welcome her. In Jesus' name I pray, Amen."

Heloise and Emory talk briefly about Fatty's need for a peaceful home away from all the other cats. Emory offers Fatty her place, but Heloise says she's not quite ready to part with her. They follow behind the other women who leave in a flock, squawking to each other—the sound of women's friendship.

I walk out of the church, not bothering to stop by Hap's office. He'll want a full report, but I'm not exactly sure what I will say. Ethrea Ree is standing beneath the Roman-flanked white door, her hand shading her eyes from the sun. The others have dissipated like the morning mist. We are alone.

"It may just be the perfect spring coming. Seems like the sun is telling us so."

I place my hand on her shoulder like Elijah did to me, but she does not return my gesture.

"I hope so." I remove my hand. "I'm afraid, though."

"Why's that?" Ethrea looks right at me, the sun behind her.

"I planted hollyhock seeds without Hap knowing it. And come spring, he'll know. I know enough to know they're biennials and they probably won't bloom until next year, but the green'll emerge once it reaches seventy for a few days in a row.

When that time comes, the rooted rose bush will be ready to go in the ground."

She smiles so I can see her teeth—the first wide smile I've seen since we've met years ago as neighbors. "Hap can't stop nature, you know. You may think he can, but he can't. A seed planted can't help but grow." She makes her way down the stairs and waves a small goodbye. I watch her step into her car, put it in reverse, and drive away.

She is not as I thought her to be. She's like a mottled ruby red grapefruit that looks like decay on the outside, only to peel it away to find bright pink. Used to be I'd eat grapefruit with yellow flesh, the kind that tasted nearly like lemons, requiring a tablespoon of sugar. The first time I had a ruby red, I scolded myself for the pile of sugar because it didn't need one crystal. Ethrea's a ruby red, hidden by leathery skin.

Squinting in the sunlight, I pray that Hap would surprise me the same way. Maybe he's not been peeled away yet. Maybe I'm supposed to do the peeling.

Twenty-Six

But Hap proves himself sour when he comes home early from church. He slams his fist on the kitchen table, upsetting his glass of orange juice. It topples to the ground, the glass shattering. "Look what you made me do! Clean up this mess!"

I scurry beneath the table, a shard of glass biting my knee clear through my pantyhose—new ones too. I pull out the glass. I tell myself not to cry.

"Emily Mohler told her husband all about your supposed 'Bible study' today. I got an earful. What do you mean by inviting Ethrea Ree and Emory Chance? Are you out of your mind?"

I cradle glass shards in my blouse, stand, then deposit them with a crash into the trashcan. "I didn't invite them. They just came. I have no idea how they even knew about it."

His hand slams across my face. I fall onto the garbage can. It topples over, spilling the glass pieces.

"You can't do anything right. Anything! Just when I thought you finally got it, Ouisie, you screw up something as simple as a Bible study. How hard can it be?"

He says more words, in increasing volume, but they sound like the roar of a fire. I inch away from Hap toward the corner—not exactly the best escape route, but it's the only place I can get away. Glass cuts into my left foot. I pull in my arms to protect my head from his impending blows, but he catches my left arm in the effort, lurches me to my feet, and stares at me. "I don't know why I married someone stupid."

His words rip into me, steal my own.

"The world needs to see just how pathetic you are. They don't know what I suffer at your hands, how hard it is to live with a woman like you. You know what the Bible says, right?" He shakes me.

I know my line. "Better to live on a corner of a roof than live with a contentious woman."

"Close enough. Only I don't think it's fair for a husband to have to rearrange his life to suit his wife's sin."

I look outside, watching the clouds hurry through the sky.

"It's time you learn your lesson." He gestures to the clouds I'm watching. "Outside you go."

I say nothing. At least outside I can be free from him. I try to turn in his grasp, but he holds me in one place, his hand etching itself into my skin like a tattoo I never bargained for. I crane my neck behind me, noting the time. The kids will be home any minute. I pray, asking God to please calm Hap down, but even as the words leave my soul and take flight heavenward toward those moving clouds, he pulls at my blouse, then rips it. I shiver, struggle, scratch. He is not going to do this. Not again.

"Dirty laundry should be made public." His voice must carry to Ethrea Ree's ears. Does she hear it? I think about Emory's ominous words, and I close my eyes, let my mind wander back to blue skies and cotton clouds.

But even that snatch of peace suffers Hap's violence. He tears my blouse from me, shakes the tattered fabric like a victory flag. I am exposed in the kitchen light, my bra the only thing between Hap and my dignity. He lunges for my skirt, rips it from me in a wretched tear. Nylons are my armor. Underwear too. Bra. But he is insistent. I kick him, but my kicks mean nothing, stop nothing.

His eyes aren't pleading, nor wounded. They are as cold as frost on a winter windshield—the color of hatred.

I know enough to remain silent, but my mind races with words I'd like to say if I were brave. Words like, *What kind of man bullies his wife into respect? What will the children think of me, half-clothed? You're not very creative, Hap—it's the same old abuse in different packages.* But none of these words fly from me. They can't. Because Hap has doubled me over his fist, my stomach imploding with the blow.

He grabs my knee-high nylons, pulls them off, then my underwear while I curl into a protective ball, crying, nursing my stomach, telling myself not to vomit on the kitchen floor. My knee bleeds from the glass shard. My face swells, I can feel it. And soon, I am nude, bereft of clothes except for my white polyester bra. "The children," I manage.

Hap looks around, his eyes steeped in fury. He counts to ten.

I know this routine. I see a hint of softening around his eyes. He will come to himself, fall over apologizing. Soon I'll be in bed; he'll bring me aspirin and tell the kids Mama has another one of her headache spells. For a few days he will cherish me, will walk around with sheep eyes, docile and complacent. My retching stomach, bloody knee, and swelling face are the fare I pay to gain a few days of peace. I try to stand.

He lifts me. I bend to pick up my clothing scattered at my feet.

He grabs my chin in his hands. "Oh no you don't." Panic the size of Texas overtakes me, suffocates me.

In a swift movement, he reaches into the knife drawer. I try to back away, but he holds me with his other hand. He places the knife between my breasts underneath my bra. The blade is cold on my flesh, but his eyes are colder still. He pulls the knife toward him, ripping the front enclosure, letting the knife clatter to the floor. The bra flies off me like a rubber band released. I

am unclothed now. I cannot cover myself because he holds both arms. "Out you go."

"No, Hap. Please. The children."

He opens the kitchen door, then shoves me down the stairs. I am under the Defiance sky, my legs tangled in the fall. From the corner of my vision, I see someone in the woods—a brief hint of movement followed by nothingness. I shiver, sit up, and wrap my arms around myself, trying to protect myself, but there is nothing left of Ouisie Pepper to protect. Not in the cold. Not with the lock clicked shut on the back door.

I hear another door slam. Is it our front door? It's hard to say. I don't hear the rumble of Hap's newly-shiny Chevy, so it can't be Hap leaving.

Lord, I tell the Almighty, I need your covering. Please.

To my left I hear the crack of branches underfoot. I cringe my eyes shut, not knowing what to do, whether to look up, or be like Sissy when she was a toddler and hope that when my eyes are shut, I'm invisible. I inhale and exhale, letting the cold air ground me to the earth. I am alive. Despite what Emory warned. I am alive.

In a moment, I sense someone's nearness, but I don't open my eyes. I hope it's not Hap, working on his cycle of repentance again. I pray it's not Jed or Sissy. Dear God, don't let Elijah find me here naked. I feel something pulled around my torso, something soft, something warm, and the sound of someone saying shhhhh.

Once covered, I open my eyes.

Ethrea Ree is pulling a quilt clear around me. Of all ironies, she is the answer to my prayers.

The man didn't expect to see her white skin under the Texas sky. But there she was, her body radiating heat under a cold, cold sky. He slipped away into the woods quiet-like, slithering stealth. He watched her shiver. Watched her startle. Watched the old lady cover Ouisie with a ratty blanket.

A cry almost left his lips. Seeing Ouisie like that brought Daisy's missing face to Technicolor—a rainbow of a face, full of light and life and laughter. He groaned inside, felt the guilt like a worm eating its way through his undeserving gut. He killed two girls. Two human beings. Both shoed. Both crying. Both begging. He silenced all those pleas with a thick, strong hand.

He was a murderer. A liar. A strangler. That's who he was.

He watched as she walked barefooted under the watchful arm of the stoop-shouldered neighbor. He pushed back his sleeve, watching the snake recoil itself around a hairy, muscled arm. And waited.

Twenty-Seven

The other David married Mama; that was the fact of it. Got down on one knee and placed a diamond ring around her slender finger. She choked out a yes as I swallowed my tears. David felt I couldn't do right, but he kept it to himself prenuptials. But after, he spewed all his opinions, and I took them in like sulfuric acid on the face. If I wore makeup I was a hussy. If I plain-Janed myself, I was white trash. He spent the time when Mama was out of earshot whispering damnation to me. "I wish you'd just up and leave," he told me nearly every day. His teeth were now stained with chewing tobacco, his scent like sour milk. I never hated a soul prior to David sweeping Mama off her feet. But I hated him soon enough.

And even though I did my best to deserve his kindness, he returned the favor with bitter words and hidden bruises. So much like Hap I wonder if they exchanged notes prior to my own simple wedding. Under the canopy of Ethrea Ree's blanket, I remembered David, remembered how the only time he treated me kindly was when I sunbathed. How he made comments about my body, sly ones so Mama wouldn't notice. My shape under the sun was the only thing that tamed him — for a time.

Ethrea Ree tells me it's time to stand up, time to go to her house for a little while so Hap can settle himself.

"But the children?"

"Delmer, he listens. I promise you, he does. If he hears hollering, he'll come and tell me. He's one thing: consistent."

I stand, but I am wobbly on my legs. "He hears us?"

"We both do. Now come on, or you'll take the cold to your lungs and catch something worse than a broken heart."

She leads me to her home, up crooked wooden steps that creak with each footfall. The paint on her house is weathered gray and peeling like a sunburn. It occurs to me that in all our time next door to each other, I've never been inside her home. When she opens the door, a wave of heat hits me.

"Delmer likes it warm," she says as she shuts the door behind us. "It's his job to stoke the fire."

I am standing, blanketed, barefooted, in their foyer. To my right is their front room, decorated in antiques from what looks like frontier days. Old, old oak. An upright piano with swivel seat. A settee with burgundy brocade. A few wingback chairs. An ancient Oriental rug faded by years. And at the room's right end a fireplace ablaze.

"It was Delmer who told me you were in trouble. But I warned him to stay in his room when I brought you over here. Sit here." She points to one wingback chair, in worn leather.

I sit.

"I don't think we're the same size, but I have some clothes that might work. You wait a moment. Warm yourself."

I shake now, fully warmed, but completely befuddled. I sat in only my skin under a winter sky and now I'm covered in a quilt in my neighbor's house. Yet I don't feel safe.

I think over the day—the walk around Lake Pisgah with Elijah, the Bible study brimming with tension, Hap's ripping at my clothes, the way the earth felt on my unclothed body, the touch of a quilt on quivering flesh, the crackle of the fire warming me. I wonder what Sheba would think. What would she say? Am I free to walk away, spiriting the kids to some other Texas town, praying for safety? But the Bible's pretty clear, isn't it? Divorce

isn't an option, not for me at least. A pastor can't have his wife running away, now can he?

Ethrea returns with a small pile of clothing. "It ain't much, but it'll cover you. The bathroom's just down the hall."

Safe inside, I see my reflection in the mirror. This is one of those tirades Hap will have to deal with for several days, since my face is the evidence of his anger. I touch my cheek where he fisted it. A tear leaks out my eye, confirming the pain. I place the clothes on the oak toilet seat. The toilet is one of those re-production ones, with a tank near the ceiling and a long brass chain swinging from it. I pull it. The water rushes down the pipe, flushing nothing. I pull on Ethrea's underwear, bra, feeling queasy. Wouldn't you? A pair of sky blue polyester pants hides my bleeding knee. A home-knitted sweater the color of coral completes the strange ensemble. Her socks are black, and she's provided a pair of men's slippers that fit just right. I splash water on my face, fold the quilt neatly and place it on the closed toilet, and open the door.

Delmer is there, his eyes to the floor. His feet shuffle in front of him, as if I can't find my way and he's leading me back to the fireplace room. He points to the leather chair. I sit again.

"Thank you, Delmer, for sending your mom to me."

"It's not right, what that man does." His words are thick, slurred.

"Sometimes folks get angry," I tell him. "Do you get angry?"

Ethrea Ree returns with hot tea in china cups. She hands me one. "Chamomile," she says. "I grew it myself."

I sip it into me, letting the warmth spread down my throat into my aching stomach.

Delmer sits on the settee. He looks odd, his large frame draped over a Victorian couch like a moose lounging in a tea-room. "I don't get angry. Not like that. I don't like angry."

Ethrea Ree looks nervous. "Delmer, don't you think it's time to finish chopping the wood out back?"

"It's my job," he says. "I'm good at my job. Papa says I'm a good chopper."

Ethrea turns to me, whispers, "He still has a hard time with Slim being gone."

I nod.

Delmer walks to an ancient piano strewn with framed photographs. Some are dusty and upright, others fall prostrate. He lifts one. It's of a man in a uniform. "My papa." He points a thick finger in his papa's belly. "He killed people over there."

"It's hard to explain war to Delmer," Ethrea adds.

Delmer examines Slim Ree, who looks more stocky than slim, then sets him facedown on the piano. He waves a hand my way. He is wearing long sleeves again—a thick wool sweater, long pants that hang off him, and old tennis shoes. "I'm a good boy, Mama says. Especially when I do my chores. No matter what, I'm a good boy."

I nod. "I'm sure you are, Delmer."

"I don't hate women like that man over there does. He hates 'em." He points toward our house. "Girls too."

"Never you mind," Ethrea Ree says. "It's none of our business." She scoots Delmer away. She turns to me. "Delmer gets a little confused sometimes."

"He seems sweet."

"He was sweeter before Slim dropped him on his head as a toddler. Never been the same since. Head trauma'll do that to a person."

"I thought—"

"He was a normal baby before the dropping." Her eyes take on a wistful look. I can almost see Ethrea as a young woman, full of life, no harsh angles.

"I'm sorry," I say. And I really am.

"Nothing to be sorry for. Some folks get dealt their hand and they like it. Others fight the hand, asking for new cards, only to get the same ones. I'm that person. But no matter. What's done

is done. Besides, I have a companion now. He's not a husband, but in most ways he's better. He does his chores, keeps his room clean, and listens to me."

"I could use a Delmer," I sigh.

"I'm not sure why, but in a way you have one."

"What do you mean?"

"Delmer watches out for you, for Jed and Sissy too."

"I never knew."

"He's quiet. And he worries. Ever since Slim died, he's become a worrywart."

"Losing a father's a hard thing," I say.

"Especially for him. He worshipped Slim."

"My children — "

"It's okay. I know. They're afraid." Ethrea walks over to a large sideboard and pulls out a drawer. Dust unsettles with the pulling. "I have something I want you to have." She unfolds a piece of white lined paper, then smiles. "I had me a girl once."

She splays the paper out for me to see. Two tarnished silver charms rest there side by side — a girl in pigtails and a boy with a fishing rod. "My mama gave me one with each birth. The little girl, Emma Jean, died in the first month. I kept her charm, knowing that someday I'd let it go. I can't say why I knew that, other than I just did. Kind of like how I know that red wigglers make great composting worms. It's just inside me like God plopped the knowing there. And the boy came with Delmer's birth. I know he'll be with me until I die, so I don't rightly need him in silver. Not anymore." She picks each charm up with earth-kissed fingers. I can see the dirt under her nails. She places both in my hand, then folds my fingers over them. "You need to hold your children close," she says. "There's no telling when the dealer will deal a terrible card. Just no telling."

"I can't take these. They're yours." I open my hand, move it her way. I see that the charms have already tarnished my hand, a subtle greening.

She closes my hand back over them. "It's a gift, pure and simple. To remind you."

I shake my head. My mama-hood is something I blame myself for over and over again. I don't take my kids into account. I forget their needs. I treat them like adults when they're really like kids. These charms feel like an indictment of my inadequacy. "I'm not a good mama."

"Are those your words? Or his?" She still stands above me.

"What does it matter?"

"Listen to me." Ethrea Ree stands, then hovers over me until I give her my eyes. Hands on hips, she is the authority now, and I shudder a bit beneath her eyes. "He's bent on making you into nothing, you hear me? Don't ask me why I know; I just do. And if you know what's best for you and the kids—"

"He gets angry, is all. He doesn't hurt the—"

"Yes he does. Don't lie about it. Not to me. I hear it all, Ouisie. I know. And if you don't take some steps toward getting safe, the next time I hear hollering, I'm calling the police."

My voice strangles inside me. If the police come, and if it isn't Officer Spellman who is bent on concealing Hap's imperfections—oh I shudder at the consequences. Defiance news spreads like the old Defiance fire—raging and complete. Hap would be finished. I would be too.

She takes her hands off her hips, then bends near my left ear, "This ain't grade school bullying. He will not be satisfied until you're dead. Or you flee. Throwing you out buck naked into the yard is the beginning of the end." She moves away, sits on the couch. Her eyes are distant again, thinking of Lord knows what. But her words sink deep into me, mingle with Emory's words, and bubble a cauldron of fear.

Sheba, what would you say to this?

Even as I think my words to the author in Rowlett, I feel the bracelet around my wrist. The chicken's vertebrae, Elijah's box, Sissy's heart. I'm surprised Hap didn't rip it from me in his

rage. And now I have two more charms: Sissy and Jed tarnished. This bracelet will become my prayer, whether I pray out loud or not—for my chicken-hearted self, for my need for God's love, for the pure love of a child, for an awareness of my need to protect. Funny how none of them really relate to Hap like I thought they would. This was to be his bracelet, the bracelet that saves my marriage. Perhaps so. Maybe not.

Twenty-Eight

Dear Sheba,

I'm sorry I haven't written since my last letter and your impromptu visit. Did you make it home all right? I wanted you to know that I'm leading a Bible study based on your book. I hope the women get a lot out of it.

Before I jump into teaching chapter two about submission, I have a question. You mention submission at any cost—that the man is the head of the wife and she should respect him and submit to his authority. I understand that. But I'm confused. What if the husband hurts the wife? Yells at her? Throws her around? Bruises her? Is she still obligated to allow him to hurt her? Can she run away? Or must she subdue herself under his every whim? And if she has secrets that if she shares will put her in danger, should she share them? You said no secrets, but I'm having a hard time obeying that one.

Hap threw me outside—without any clothes. The neighbor lady saw it and covered me with a blanket, thank God. And he's sorry, apparently. He's returned to his old self, that sweet man I married. So for now, I'm happy for his pleasant attitude. Folks have warned me he'll get more violent, that I should have a plan of escape. But wouldn't that be disobeying God? Not trusting him?

Thank you for taking the time to read this letter. I
know it must be a burden to be an author, answering
folks' questions and all. No need to come and visit, Sheba.
A letter will suffice. But would you please address it
differently? Please send to:

Ouisie Pepper
c/o Emory Chance
RR 358 Box 24H
Defiance, TX 75801

Sincerely, Ouisie Pepper

I pour cold water into a glass over several tablespoons of
vanilla, and lift it to my mouth, but Jed interrupts me before I
can take a drink.

"Mama, we need to talk." Jed eyes me like he knows my
thoughts.

"Sure, honey," I tell him.

"Not here." He waves at the kitchen. "Can we take a walk?"

I tell him okay. I put the glass on the counter, wishing I could
take it with me, hoping I'd have the gumption to dump its con-
tents down the sink. But I can do neither, so I let it sit, mocking me, beckoning me. With Jed and Sissy now polished on my
bracelet, dangling there, I am trying to be a better mama, a
mama who listens, who sacrifices, who doesn't turn to sleep or
the bottle of vanilla.

We leave out the back door. He opens the picket gate for
me, then shuts it behind us. "I want to walk to Crooked Creek
Church," he says.

"Are you sure?"

"I'm sure. No one'll be around, and I'd like this to be private."

The way he says *private* worries me. But I say a breezy, "So
what's on your mind?"

"Can't we just walk?"

We pass behind Ethrea Ree's house. In the yard's brambles,

an untamed gaggle of vines surrounds a statue of Jesus. She's made him bleed, painted mahogany on his brow where real thorns pierce.

We walk the field. I pull my sweater around myself. The belt around it falls, and Jed picks it up, offers it back. I tie it around my waist with cold fingers. With one deliberate step placed after another, I wish Sissy were with us. Because maybe we could walk and walk and walk and never come back. Maybe bleeding Jesus would stand as a watchman, blinding the way between Hap's steps and ours.

There's always maybe.

But her hand isn't slipped into mine. And Jed's face is full of torment. So my crazy whim will have to wait for another day.

The church's charred ruins come up on us all of a sudden. Jed stops. "I want to know what happened to Daisy," he says.

"I do too. But I'm not sure we'll ever know."

"Really, Mama? Because I think you know."

I hear his words. I really do. But I cannot believe they are coming from a fourteen-year-old's mouth. The tone of accusation cuts through me. I smell ash in the air. Still.

"Jed, the police are doing their best."

"Just shoot straight with me, will you, Mama?"

"I am."

"You know more than you're letting on."

"Emory says the man has a tattoo." This, I know.

"So she says."

"I try not to trouble myself with things outside my control. There are folks who can manage just fine finding Daisy's killer. My own world's enough to worry about."

"How did you get that shiner, Mama? And why were you wearing those weird clothes after you 'visited' Ethrea Ree last week?"

"There are things mamas don't talk about with their sons, Jed."

Jed stops, faces me. "It's my job to protect you. From him."

I want to reach through the space between us, to soothe his guilt, his unction to protect, but I sense it's not appropriate. So I walk. He follows. And the silence between us says so many words.

We stand in front of what were the steps to the church, the last place he saw Daisy alive. I feel Jed's grief as if it were my own. It spreads through me, an ember of grief under a cold sun. My feet are cold, but there is no place to warm them. My hands too. But my heart beats at a steady, thankful pace. I have deflected Jed's curiosity; he does not know what I know. He can't.

Jed spits into the ashes, liquefying into a gray nickel-sized lake at his feet. "I hate the way he treats you, the way he hurts—"

"He's got a lot of worry on his plate is all."

Jed turns, faces me. His cheeks are flushed. "You always take up for him." He shakes his head, his eyes aflame. "And I'm sorry to say this, but I'm sick of it."

"I don't always take up for him." My words sound small in the air, like a wind's come by and stolen them, scattering them higher than the trees, out of earshot.

"Mama, you know I love you, right?"

"Of course."

"The problem isn't that *we* love each other. It's that Hap doesn't *love* us right."

"He has his days, I'll grant you that."

"His days? How about his years, Mama? Why can't you just admit it? He hates us all, and he's bent on taking us down." Jed turns, leaves me at the back of the sooty church. After settling myself, I walk after him, noting his gait, how very similar it is to Hap's.

"Jed, wait."

He stops. "What?"

"It's not that simple."

"How simple can it be? You leave him, taking us with you.

Let him holler at himself, see how he likes that. To me it's as simple as arithmetic. You leave, then he can't throw you out into the cold without your clothes."

I didn't know Jed knew about this. But now in the light of day, it's clear to me. He came home while I sat near Delmer's fire. My clothes must've been heaped in the kitchen. "This doesn't concern you, Jed. It's between your daddy and me."

"It concerns me too. You know why? Because someday Hap's going to go too far, and I won't be there to—"

"What do you mean?"

Jed hurries ahead of me, steps pounding the field. I see the indentation of his soles. He speaks in front of him, as if the field is his audience, but he doesn't turn my way, doesn't catch my eyes. "I mean, I can't stay in this house any longer. Maybe you like getting beaten up black and blue. Maybe it's all you've ever known. But I know better, Mama. And I'm ready to burst out, leave everything behind. I'll get me a job, find me a place to live."

"What about Sissy?" I hear the catch in my voice, try to settle it down. I can't live without Jed near.

Now he faces me. "That's something you need to ask yourself. What about her? Have you noticed her lately, Mama? Have you looked at her hair?"

I must look confused, because he sighs when he sees my face. "You need to pay attention. She's got gray hair. It's hard to see since she's blonde and all, but it's there. I don't know much about doctoring or anything, but I know grade-schoolers don't get gray hair. Unless they're scared out of their gourd. Sissy's worried herself old, Mama. And you haven't noticed."

I play with my hands, noticing my dry skin, how the skin is slackened over the years. That, I can see. But I haven't taken notice of Sissy, not closely anyway.

"All I'm asking is to make her safe. Make a home for her where she doesn't worry about getting hit, or you dying."

"She worries about me dying?"

Jed shakes his head. "We both do."

"But I'm not sick."

Jed leaves me again, walks toward Ethrea Ree's, his pace percolating, determined. I follow, but my steps are slow, full of grief. I will never measure up. Never be the mama I need to be. I'm a miserable failure, just as Hap says. Nothing I touch turns out right. I don't deserve—

"I'm leaving at the end of the school year," Jed shouts my way before he's out of sight. He says nothing more. He doesn't have to. His words are an ultimatum—leave Hap or I leave. I cannot imagine either one. And all I can think of as my cold feet grudge along the dampened earth is how thirsty I am. How very thirsty.

Twenty-Nine

I wasn't thirsty the day Hap proposed to me. When I saw him that morning, I felt like I'd taken a drink from a cool spring, overflowing. He stood outside my house, a savior from my stepdad. I would've run into anyone's arms to be rid of David. Hap held wildflowers in a bunch, extended my way, motioned for me to jump in the Chevy, said he had a surprise for me.

The bouquet of flowers between us, Hap drove to Lake Pisgah. The hills filled out nicely that spring, dotted here and there with bluebonnets and Indian paintbrush. Redbud trees screamed purple blossoms against what once were stark brown trunks. Brown-green leaves unfurled from beneath the nearly spent blooms, proving that winter had passed, that rebirth awaited. The Chevy's windows were down—like its interior wanted to huff in the scent of spring. The music pulsed loud. I laughed for no particular reason while the wind whipped my hair into strings. Funny how I didn't care a hoot. Hap was my ticket to freedom, my way out on this verdant day.

We walked the lake's perimeter, saying nothing. The air smelled of violets and earth. Dogwoods rained down four-petaled blossoms when the wind picked up. It blew lazily, like it needed to let out its breath once in awhile. Hap picked up a blossom, raised it to the sky. "They say the dogwood's a holy tree."

"How so?"

"Legend has it that the tree used to be mighty like an oak—a strong tree with wide branches. Folks believe they nailed Christ to a dogwood."

A bird chirped an amen nearby; another answered back.

Hap continued. "After the dogwood bore Christ's weight, the tree became cursed, never again to be large enough to be forged into a cross."

I smiled. I let my eyes linger on a bent dogwood nearby against the backdrop of an oak that towered over it like a mountain to a hill.

"Its blossoms form a cross, see?" He placed the flower in my hand as he faced me. He traced the cross over the flower, but I could feel his touch through the petals. It sent joy through me. I held his eyes.

"See the nail prints?" He pointed to the outer edge of each petal. "And a crown of thorns to remind us." There, in the middle of the blossom, lay a crown just as he said.

He closed my fingers around the blossom, crushing its scent to my palm, then took my other hand in his. "I'll love you like that, Ouisie. If only you'll let me."

Tears wetted my eyelids. For a moment, I heard the Voice, way down deep. A tiny catch in my heart fluttered inside telling me to think this through. I did love Hap, it was true. But I wondered in that moment as he held my hand and my future in his, if I loved escaping David more. I didn't say a word, letting the Voice battle my will. In the silence, Hap tossed more words.

"He told me, you know." He opened my hand, removed the dogwood blossom, and let it flutter to the ground. "God. He said, Hap Pepper, that woman's to be your wife. And you'll be dishonoring me if you don't ask her to marry you this very day. I'm obeying his voice, Ouisie. Your lack of an answer means you're fighting his will. And believe me, you can't fight him for long without serious consequences."

The birds silenced at his voice. The smell of earth and violets shifted on the wind. In their stead, I inhaled the rendering plant. And I knew. I knew in that moment I had a choice. To follow after what Hap Pepper thought was God's divine mandate, or go my own sweet way, back to stepdad David, who was bent on marrying me in his own way. The choice was clear. I breathed in the stench of death, then exhaled. I took one step toward Hap Pepper, crushing the dogwood blossom between us. I reached my hands to his face, pulled his lips to mine, and whispered, "Thy will be done."

Thirty

I find my vanilla cocktail right where I left it. Jed is nowhere in sight. I am too thirsty to look for him, so I kiss the lip of the glass, begging for drink. It slides down my throat slowly, whetting my appetite for escape. That's what Ouisie Pepper does. She drinks. She escapes. She pays no mind to her daughter. Her son, either. She only minds Hap, Hap, Hap. His moods. His needs. His hopes. His tirades. His expectations. His anger. You know the drill.

I wonder how I will make it without Jed. Or will I suddenly become un-Ouisie-like and spirit the kids away to a new Hapless life? As the vanilla slakes my will, I try to forget about such things. Instead, there is dinner to be made, dishes to do, laundry to fold. These are my life, if you want to quantify it. Holding secrets used to be, but I'm seeing more and more that I'm no mystery woman. My inclinations are wild imaginations. No, I will housemake my way through life, deadening my worry with drink. That's the only way I know how to live.

Sissy breaks through my blurring thoughts as she skips into the kitchen. I grab her to myself, smothering her with hugs and kisses and motherly words. She backs away. "Mama, are you okay?"

"I'm fine. Just fine." I cradle her head beneath me. She reaches my ribcage now. And that's when I see them. Gray hairs wiring through her blond, ancient intruders on her innocence. They shout at me, holler my inadequacy, my neglect. Her teenaged brother saw them first. I rock back and forth—holding her head, my baby. If I stay this way forever, will I atone for what I've allowed her to face? I'm not sure miles of rocking could release my guilt. And I have to stop because she fidgets beneath me, shaking my bracelet.

"I'm thirsty," she tells me.

And I understand.

But I wish I didn't.

Thirty-One

When the kids are at school, I rummage. Though Sheba says I shouldn't keep secrets, I try desperately to preserve them, hiding notebooks and paints and mementos Hap might find offensive or superfluous. In rages, he pilfers, grabs, then throws out anything and everything that smacks of me loving it. What I find today is not something I love, but something I remember. It's not a fond memory, nor is it sad. It just is. But holding the metal eyelet in my hand shakes my resolve to keep this particular secret.

It was days before they found Daisy's body that I heard the Voice telling me to take a walk in the same woods where searchers scraped the ground for Daisy clues. There *he* stood, muttering something, pacing back and forth. He startled when I came upon him, nearly jumped to the pines. And yet I sensed his muscles through his shirt, and the strength that emanated from his jump.

"Interesting day for a walk," I said.

"The sun is out." He said it as if it was all the convincing I needed. His voice sounded like an echo, deep and reverberating off the trees, like he could voice-over movie trailers.

"Mind telling me what you're doing?" I inched closer. With each foot forward, he took his own step backward. I could smell him—a mixture of sweat and cheap cologne.

"I didn't mean it to happen," he said.

I scanned the woods for others, knowing his admission needed secrecy. "Daisy?"

"She's beautiful," he said. "Like a shiny copper penny."

"Where is Daisy? You can tell me. You know that, right?"

He looked at the sky, then shook his head. "She's not right here."

"Then where is she?"

"I have this," he said. He stopped his backing up, opened his hand.

I tiptoed closer, my heart beating as if I were running a race. In his palm was a tiny ring of metal, like a mini-washer. "What is it?"

"It's from her shoe. Where the shoelaces go through." His eyes are both vacant and sad, his face unshaven.

"Why do you have this?" My words catch. I don't know why I wasn't afraid. Were there angels encamping around me? Or was I in that place of sheer terror, unable to feel its talons until too late? The air stiffened between us, charged with electricity. I coughed.

"I can't have this. It's evil." He said it with the kind of fear I should've had.

In one swift movement I still can't recount, he delivered the tiny circlet of metal into my hand and ran swift from the woods. But I couldn't hear his footsteps for the train roaring in my head.

I knew what I needed to do. Knew whom I needed to alert. But instead, I closed my fingers around the tiny circle and walked the Crooked Creek gully toward home, hoping my footsteps would instruct me where I should go. They did. They walked me through the woods, to the clearing behind our house, through the picket gate, up the back steps, through the kitchen, down the hall, into our bedroom.

From the dresser, I spied Hap and me. I crossed the room to pick up the frame. In wedding white, a veil puffed over my head

ignited by the wind, I wear a genuine smile—all the way up to my eyes, which bear no secrets. He held my shoulders in one strong arm, protecting me, loving me. He didn't look at me in the picture; he bent toward my ear, whispering in his Sears suit.

You're curious, aren't you?

I'll tell you this much: he said he wanted to make my life with him better than my life without him, that he'd do what it took to make sure I smiled every day of our marriage. And he did that, for a time. I might tell you such a thing, but there's no telling who killed Daisy. The man didn't mean it. It was a terrible accident, nothing more—and the act did not define him. If I spill it, I'd be giving up on everything, cementing untruths in folks' minds. The man in the woods would always be a murderer. Sure, men do bad things in a flurry of a moment, but those fleeting things do not define them forever, right? I have to believe that's not true, have to believe Hap can change, that these instances of abuse don't measure the whole man.

Which is why I frustrate you in not telling.

I placed the wedding photo back on the dresser. My free hand opened the bottom left drawer, unfolded a hankie laced with pink roses, and placed Daisy's shoe eye inside. I tucked it in, then spirited it back to the drawer. For safekeeping.

For him.

For Hap.

For me.

Sometimes Daisy's eyelet calls to me. Hollers my name. Tells me to tell. And when it does, I take another drink, trying to deaden its pleadings. But today, I hold it, roll it around in my fingers, peek through it. I remember the man who dropped it in my hand in a wink of time, and I pray he won't ever do such a thing again, forcing myself to believe that truth. My prayers have been enough. And my inclination tries to assure me that I'm right. The man with the piece of Daisy's shoe made a terrible mistake—the kind that can't be repeated. Won't be. Though

Sissy's quick escape from his capture a few months back pushes itself to my consciousness, I argue with myself, knowing it won't happen again. Believing it won't. That man can't do such a thing.

It's my strange assurance that a man can change, that he can do one despicable act but regret it and reform. If this man stays put and kids stay safe, maybe there's hope Hap will turn course. I was the fulcrum between the man taking a life and choosing never to do it again. And now, I'll be the center of Hap's teetering ways, tipping him back to good.

I unclasp my bracelet, slip the metal ring onto the string, and re-attach it. It's positioned between Jed and Sissy—my eyelet-hope for protection. I drop to my knees by the bed, weary of the secrets, but resolute in keeping them. I have no words for the Almighty. I clench the bedspread, but it's so threadbare, I reconsider. Instead, I grab at my hair by the roots and pull, really hard. I've forgotten my sanity, it seems. Or lost it. I fist my hair, suppressing the wail that I've held in my chest for so long. A lifetime, it seems.

Yes, I cried when Jed rocked on Hixon's porch the day of the memorial service. But the torrent released was only a trickle of what would happen if I really let my secrets out. More than baptism, the whole world would be engulfed in a torrent. Its banks will flood, and send me drowning on a river I never knew was there.

From way up high, he had command over the window, the roofline, the fenced in yard. But no woman appeared through the small kitchen window, hands to dishes, eyes to the trees. He craned his neck to see, squinted his eyes. Still, she did not appear. He agitated at the thought, peeling bark from the upper branches, letting flecks of tree float to the ground. He tested the strength of his hands on the small but strong branches, snapping one in half like a toothpick.

Thirty-Two

"It's my study, and I promised I'd lead them," I tell Hap. He sits at the kitchen table, grimacing at my eggs.

"I don't care about your empty-headed promise. You forget I started the whole thing in the first place. And as such, I will be with you when you do the study today, and that settles it." Another fist to the table, his exclamation point. Hap terrifies me with his words today, but not in the way you might expect. I don't fear him right now, even as he grimaces at my coffee and pounds the kitchen table. I don't worry about his fist in my gut. I fear instead I'll die of embarrassment.

"But it's a ladies' study. And last I checked, Hap Pepper, you are no lady." I pour him more coffee, a nervous tension settling into my stomach.

"I'll drive you there, then bring you back home at lunchtime. I don't like you traipsing around Defiance with Daisy's killer still on the loose."

"But I need to spend some time alone, filling up. I do that at the lake. You know that."

Hap stands. I stare at his collarbone. I almost wish he'd just hit me and get it over with. Anything but this. I back up, grab a dishtowel, and dry already-dry dishes hoping that he'll throw up his hands and think his idea lacks sense. Or merit.

But he is as resolute as President Carter's desk. "What does

it look like for Ouisie Pepper, the pastor's wife, to be by herself at Lake Pisgah?"

"It looks like a woman taking a walk."

He grabs the towel from me, lets it hit the ground. He holds both my hands firmly in his. I cannot move away in his grip. He tells me to look at him. So I do, but I wish I didn't have to look into his soul because what I see there isn't anger. It's a strange emptiness. He pulls me down the hallway, through the front door, down the porch steps. "Stay here," he says, his voice echoing off the front porch rafters.

He returns from the back shed with a short length of green hose that's been severed on both ends — no fittings. He starts my car, backing it into the driveway so it's practically touching the Chevy. He runs between the cars, almost as if he's trying to sustain his rage by hurry. He opens my gas tank, his too. Then he places his mouth on the hose and plunges the other end into my tank. In an instant, he removes his mouth, then drops the other end of the hose into his tank. I hear the quiet rush of fuel emptying my freedom. My lake. Myself. What do I say to this?

When the last gurgle exclaims an empty gas tank, Hap stiffens, looks at me. "Don't just stand there open-jawed. Get your book, your Bible, and put some decent clothes on. We'll be leaving in five minutes." He delivers his words like my mama measured sugar, deliberately. Only he doesn't scrape the excess off the top like Mama did. He heaps words until they overflow me.

I haven't done my hair proper, haven't gathered my thoughts, haven't filled up with God's wisdom. Five minutes is never long enough. But it has to be.

Elijah asked me what my real fear was, or at least he implied the question. I've been mulling it around in my head since our last Lake Pisgah meeting. You'd think it would be Hap. But as I sit next to this man while Defiance rolls by in brown monotony, I know all at once what my fear is. I'm afraid my life will be nothing of consequence. That I'll never really be me. That I'll fade away from this earth as nothing. That my life will be typi-fied by the word *unremarkable.*

I think about my death as I put my head to the pillow at night, while Hap grunts and snores his own melody. Other than the seeds I sowed, the rose I secreted into the soil, the paintings I've hidden, what will show the world I ever counted? Sheba says my children are my heritage, that they are the testimony I fling to the world in glorious display of my motherhood, but with Sissy's gray hair and Jed's intention of leaving, I've failed. I cannot point to my marriage. I can't even say Hap would miss me if I left Defiance for streets of gold. I'm terrified of myself. My vanilla, unremarkable self.

Hap clears his throat, a sure sign of a lecture. "I read through chapter two, Ouisie."

I know full well what that chapter's about, but I haven't re-ceived word back from Sheba about my question of submission to an angry man. I say nothing.

"It's interesting. A little paradoxical too, don't you think?"

"How so?" My words are as empty as the road we're travel-ing on.

"You teaching a Bible study about something you have no intention of doing. I find that the pinnacle of irony."

"Paradoxical irony," I correct.

He pounds the steering wheel, then apologizes to the Chevy. "Criminy, Ouisie. You wonder why sometimes I blow my top?"

"Sure."

"It's you. You do it. You force my hand. It's your stubborn will, your inability to keep a clean house, your neglect of the children. I've been a saint through all this, trying to push down my anger. But you don't seem to care. Which begs the question: do you even love me?"

"Do I love you? How could you even ask such a thing?" I feel tears, but force them to stay lidded. "Look what I do for you. I clean. I cook. I take care of the kids. I budget. I shop. I have

sex when you want it, on your terms. How can you ask such a thing?" And with each act, I feel like more of *me* siphons out; the precious part of me spills onto thirsty, ungrateful ground.

"Duty, that's all it is." His voice is hardly a whisper above the hum of the motor. He pulls up to the church, cuts the engine, and looks at me. "We used to be in love, you and me. But you've changed. It's like the real you has left, and this empty imposter took over."

For a moment, I see again the Hap that's been wounded, the Hap who has more needs than any woman can fill. I feel pity, then place my hand on his hand. "I'm sorry," I hear myself say. *I am sorry for your anger.*

He slips his hand out from underneath mine. "That's my girl. You're getting it. Slowly, but at least you see it," he says. "That's why God put you in my life. To console me. To submit. You'll be the perfect object lesson today." He smiles a pastor smile. I stay in the car as he gets out, trying to steady my nerves for the inevitable. He must've called the deacons and elders to let them know he'd taken over the reins of the ladies' Bible study because I see everyone's car in the lot. Hap crosses in front of the Chevy, then opens my door. Emily Mohler watches us from the perch beneath the church's white door. "Such a gentleman," she gushes. "I wish my husband would open the door for me."

"Let me get that," Hap says. He runs to the church's entrance, leaving me to carry my gaggle of books.

"Thank you, Pastor." Emily shoots me a look, but I can't discern it. Envy? Hatred? Kindness veiled? Hard to tell with Emily.

In my peripheral vision, I catch Emory's car. I moan to myself. Thankfully, Hap is inside when Emory sidles up to me. "I'm looking forward to this," she tells me.

"You're kidding, right? I didn't figure you for the Bible study type."

"I'm not. But the more I think about Hixon and his words to me, the more I want to learn. I'm no saint, mind you. But I want to learn. The Bible is becoming exciting to me."

"Well, you're in for your share of excitement, believe me."

"What's that supposed—"

But before she finishes her question, Hap appears in the doorway. He gives an amused look Emory's way. "Glad to see the mystery gardener's here. I'd show you where the shovels are, but I suppose you've figured that out."

Emory mounts the stairs. "I'm here to get my fill of the Bible. Your wife's an excellent teacher."

Hap looks my way, his mouth a thin line. "Is that so?" They are nearly even with each other. "Well then. You're in for a treat. This week I'm helping her."

We sit in the same circle, except there's one extra chair Hap pulls in from his study. Its plush contrasts the metal ones we occupy. Ethrea Ree smirks when she walks in. "Well, you're on your throne, Reverend. That's interesting."

He acts as if Ethrea hasn't said a word. His glance grazes over her, landing on me. "Ouisie here said she needed some help with our study. And since this is all about being a godly wife, I figured I could offer a husband's perspective." He pauses. "A much needed perspective, I might add."

"I speak for all of us," Emily says as she looks Emory's way, "when I say we certainly welcome your words."

"I can hardly wait." Emory shifts in her chair, then opens her Bible. "As a matter of fact, I was just reading some words from Jesus about Pharisees and whitewashed tombs I found particularly interesting."

Hap leans forward. "I'm sure that would be a good study for another day. We all must be careful we're not becoming legalistic like Pharisees. But today's study is about women submitting to their husbands."

Ironic how it's the chapter I have the most difficulty with. Is this God's strange sense of humor? But if I can't teach it, then Hap can do it in my stead, take up for me. If only I could leave, extricating Emory and Ethrea Ree for our own little community

of three. But no good pastor's wife would do such a thing, would she?

Emory shakes her head. "Submission?"

"For the wayward," Hap says, "submission is a dirty word. But for the faithful and believing, it's the most beautiful word in the world."

Heloise Dickson frowns again, adjusting the strap on her denim jumper. "Sounds painful, like an ox submitting to a yoke."

"That's the amazing part," Hap says, his eyes animated. "Remember when Jesus teaches that his yoke is light? That's how it is with submission. When you do it, you are free, more able to live for God because you have yourself out of the way."

I wonder how much of Hap is out of the way.

Flo Sanders curls her hair around her ring finger. "I have a question." She abandons her curl, placing her finger in her mouth and tearing away a painted nail, then spitting it on the floor before she speaks again. The silence in the room echoes off the stark church walls. "If submission's so great, why is it up to women to do it? Does that mean we're more privileged? Because we get to submit? Do men have to submit?"

"The Bible's clear." Hap turns to his favorite passage—it's earmarked by a bookmark he received from a traveling evangelist. "In Ephesians 5 it says this: 'Wives, submit yourselves unto your own husbands, as unto the Lord. For the husband is the head of the wife, even as Christ is the head of the church: and he is the savior of the body. Therefore as the church is subject unto Christ, so let the wives be to their own husbands in every thing.' It's pretty clear what the apostle Paul is saying here, don't you think?"

"Wait a minute." Emory is turning pages, searching for something. "What book is that?"

Hap rolls his eyes, his seeming apology to the more refined women in the group. "Ephesians. It's in the New Testament after the Gospels, Acts, Romans, Corinthians, then Galatians. Ephesians follows." He looks at Emily Mohler. "'Course you learned all that in Sunday school, I'd reckon."

She laughs. "Yeah, as in General Electric Power Company."

Emory pays no mind, thumbing through the pages. I point to chapter five for her. "What verses?" she asks.

"Verses twenty-two to twenty-four," I whisper.

She presses a dirt-stained fingernail to the text, then moves it northward. I watch her mouth the words, then see her straighten her back. "I'm confused," she says.

Hap waves a finger. "If you don't mind, Miss Emory, I think it's time to work through the study."

"I'm no Bible scholar, Reverend," she says. "But you've missed a few verses. Let me read them for you. "Giving thanks always for all things unto God and the Father in the name of our Lord Jesus Christ; submitting yourselves one to another in the fear of God." She looks at Emily, who returns her look with another frown. "So here it says we need to submit to one another."

Her words linger between us all. I open my Bible, scurry to Ephesians, and re-read the words. I'd never seen that part of the passage. I've seen the Bible as Hap's tool to prove my worthlessness and incapability, but suddenly the words leap at me, ignite hope. What would it look like for Hap to submit himself?

Emory continues. "After that wifely submission stuff, it talks about husbands." She reads, "Husbands, love your wives, even as Christ also loved the church, and gave himself for it; that he might sanctify and cleanse it with the washing of water by the word, that he might present it to himself a glorious church, not having spot, or wrinkle, or any such thing; but that it should be holy and without blemish. So ought men to love their wives as their own bodies. He that loveth his wife loveth himself. For no man ever yet hated his own flesh; but nourisheth and cherisheth it, even as the Lord the church." She stops.

Flo Sanders raises her hand. Hap doesn't acknowledge it. I

can see his neck splotch pink. Still, Flo persists. "What does that mean that a husband is willing to give himself up for his wife?"

"That's how God planned marriage," Hap finally says. "To have the husband provide for his wife and children, to sacrifice at work. And later, you'll notice the passage says a wife should reverence her husband. That's because of God's divine order. She should praise the office he takes as provider of the home. She should not spend her days in idleness and gossiping." He lands a glance my way.

We spend the next half hour bantering around about wives, how they should act, what submission looks like, while Hap tells his cautionary tales and looks right at me. I want to run into the sanctuary and crawl under a pew. Emory seems to have lost her fight in the matter, as she's stopped talking. In fact, no one speaks, not Ethrea, Emory, Flo, or me. Just Emily chatting friendly words with Hap while Heloise says a word or two and doodles kitties in the book margins. Maybe the four silent ones should form our own study. I dream up names for the study like HHC, the Hap Haters Club; this, of course, proves my own debauchery.

Hap says he's going to close us in prayer. Before he can say *Lord*, Ethrea Ree pipes up. "I just have one thing to ask, Reverend Pepper."

Hap pastes on a smile. "Of course. What is it, Mrs. Ree?"

"Seems to me this submission thing is a hard pill to swallow for anyone. It's not easy for me to submit my will to anyone. I can be strong-headed."

Emily Mohler nods, but not like she's making a similar admission.

Ethrea nods back. "But what about the idea that God loves us all?"

"What do you mean?" Hap leans back on his comfortable chair.

"Well, as I see it, the church teaches that God loves everyone, right? Well, if He loves everyone, then why does He favor half the population?"

Hap leans forward, tents his fingers in front of him. "Haven't you been listening? It goes back to Adam and Eve, and Eve taking that fruit. It's part of the fall. Sometimes Biblical truth is just something you swallow and believe."

"I understand what you're saying," Ethrea Ree says. "I know about faith. But what if someone in your life, a man in particular, asks you—well forces, really—to break the law. Is it right to submit then? Because that doesn't make sense."

"Here's how I see it." Hap stands, then motions for us to join him. He holds hands with Emily and Heloise, but I notice his grip tighter on Emily's hand. I watch how her manicured fingers coil around his. "Some things are mysteries, to be sure. Right now we need to finish our study in prayer." He bows his head. The women follow. But Emory and I keep our heads up and our eyes open. It feels like rebellion to me, so I say a quick prayer for forgiveness. "Lord," Hap prays. "Help these women to be obedient to your divine plan for marriage. Help the single women to know their place in your order. Teach these women to work hard at home, to respect and revere the men in their lives as a testimony to their reverence for you. Give them energy to ready themselves for service. Fill them up with your love to give away. In your holy name, Amen."

He lets go of hands, though Emily's lingers. "I'm sorry to say I won't be leading this study next week. Now that Ouisie's seen the right way to handle things, I'll let her resume her study. But thanks for letting me be part of your circle. I'm humbled."

The women disband, all except Emily who loiters. It's now laughable to me that I worried about Hap having eyes for Emory again. His eyes have clearly wandered elsewhere. Emily touches him, "I have some additional questions, Reverend. Do you mind if we talk privately?" She shoots a look my way, then smiles. Her hand is on Hap's elbow. I cannot tell if he is pulling her toward his office, or she's pushing. Either way, I'm bothered.

Before I can thank Ethrea for coming, she's gone — her car no longer in the parking lot. Emory walks with me to Hap's car.

"Looks like the most right Reverend has his hands full."

"Indeed. I'll have to wait for him before I can get home."

"Nonsense. I'll take you."

"Hap won't like that."

Emory jogs up the church steps. "I'll tell him. It'll save him time, anyway."

Before I can caution her, she's escaped into the church's mouth.

In Emory's car, silence sits between us like a sleeping child. It takes me a long time to say, "What was Hap doing in his office?"

"Just talking to that Emily lady. She was crying."

"That's odd." I fiddle with my cold hands, then relegate them to the space under my knees. They remain cold.

"Yes, it was."

Hilltops give way to small valleys as Defiance proper comes into view.

"All you can do is pray."

I still find it strange that Emory throws words like this toward me; I am the one who shoveled them her way just weeks ago. "I know all about prayer, thank you."

"With a husband like that, I'm sure you do."

"What's that supposed to mean?"

"You know what it means. He's cheated on you once before. He'll do it again. And he beats you up, Ouisie. I'm telling you, he's going to hurt you."

"You're beginning to sound like a broken record."

"Sometimes folks need friends who repeat the same words so the friend will understand the danger."

I turn toward the window and the winter scene rolling beside me on Forest Lane. Texas is unclothed come winter — even the green on the evergreen trees seems dull. I turn toward Emory.

"And sometimes friends know when to leave well enough alone. This—" I stop as tears come. I extend my hand toward all of Defiance in a sweeping motion. "This is my life. I have to live it. There's no one else to be Jed and Sissy's mama. No one else to feed and tend Hap. Sometimes that's just the way things are." I wipe a tear.

"I didn't mean to make you cry."

"Well, it happened, now didn't it?" We pull into my driveway. I open my car door, say a quick thanks, and run up the stairs. I keep my back turned while I fiddle with the front door, waiting for Emory to leave so I can crash into the house and find a hidden bottle, let the liquid release me from all these jumbled thoughts. I hear her back up, her tires catching on Dyer Lane. The car kicks into drive and speeds away. I realize all at once that Hap has the key to the house, and I'm left in the cold to rehash my fight with Emory Chance.

Thirty-Three

I am cold; that is true. But in some ways it feels like apt punishment for hurling words Emory's way. I venture over to Ethrea's, but I don't see her car. I knock anyway, wondering if Delmer is about. If he is, he's not coming to the door. Ethrea probably warned him about folks knocking on the door when she isn't there.

I pull my sweater around myself and decide to take a walk. I walk past my empty-gassed car, through the side yard, admiring the fresh garden bed. It's naked dirt now—there's no mistaking that—but come spring hollyhocks will poke through the soil, eventually flowering my life. I bend to the ground, run my hand along the iron-rich earth. Oh dear God, make these little seeds grow. I'm like those faith teachers, laying hands on the thing in need of resurrection. I wipe my hands on my pants, then move to the house's corner where I've planted Ethrea's purple rose shoot. It's a greening stick saluting the gray sky today, but someday, Lord willing, it will reach magnificence.

In this light, I think of painting. My fingers itch to capture this muddled day, to dabble in shades of gray and brown and black. I remember that vision of me in the sparkling waters— my baptism. And I pray I'll be able to capture such a miracle with paint, brushes, and canvas someday. Or maybe just embody that kind of joy when I finally heed the Voice and sweep under the waters. You think these kinds of things when you're alone and wandering outside.

Pushing through the back gate, I smell the forest, breathe pine into myself. Suddenly I'm not forlorn, needing shelter. I'm taking a walk, beckoned by smells and sights my soul needs.

But as I step into the woods, I shudder.

Someone is near. I hear his panting, but cannot see him. My heart quickens as I step further into Crooked Creek's gully. The earth is smooth, awaiting spring rains, but in a very real sense, the spoon-shaped earth welcomes my feet. This narrow slice of earth keeps me safe, though there is someone near me in ghost-like shadows. I tell myself this. I must believe such things.

Halfway through the woods toward Emory's old place, I stop. The forest is quiet, the birds napping, it seems. I hike up the gulley, leaving my sanctuary. I cannot abide the silence so I whistle my fears into the bracken. But as I tweet, I hear footsteps behind me and in front of me. When I stop whistling, the footsteps cease. I swallow.

My right foot takes its next step, but it doesn't land on earth's flesh—it hits something sounding hollow. My left foot confirms this. I bend to the ground and wipe away dirt. Beneath the woodsy debris is a worn slab of plywood, gray as the day. I whistle more, hoping to keep fears and footprints at bay while I reveal the rectangle. I claw around its perimeter and lift. The wood opens like a yawing mouth, hinges at the other framed end creaking as I push it toward the sky. I have to move to the side to lay the hole beneath it bare. The door moves to the opposite side with a thud. I whistle.

Earthen steps descend into black, reminding me of my grandmother's canning cellar that doubled as a tornado shelter. But there is no house here, and I doubt there ever was one. I forget to whistle. The footsteps return.

I step into the darkness, then move deeper into the hole. The steps nearby are muffled now. I turn in the hole, my head

popping out like a gopher found, and I see boots, then legs, then a torso streaking through the woods away from me. I run up the stairs, return the door to its place, and holler. "It's not like I don't know who you are." The pine trees absorb the words.

A single dove's melancholy answers back, but nothing else. Not even footsteps. I trace the line of trajectory where the man sprinted, but can't see the shiver of bushes, or stirred up dust. A ghost sped by, leaving no trace.

Except that I find footprints. Deep-into-the-earth footprints. Man-sized boots made these impressions. I don't know why I follow them. My mama used to say I'd inherited a feline gene for curiosity because I couldn't seem to leave well enough alone. Like God wired me to need to know every mystery. Maybe that's why I've stayed with Hap all these years.

I follow footprints through the woods. Problem is, they lead to Love Street, almost to Emory's old house. The dirt impressions last several paces, then dissipate on the gravel. No one is in sight. Today must not be the day to uncover the mystery, though I know more of it than anyone in Defiance. And the truth is, the creepy woods shivered me — not just because I was cold, but because the feeling of him watching me frightened my soul.

I pass Emory's old house on the right. A light is on in the front room. I wonder if Elijah lives there, but I don't mount the stairs and find out. Instead, I make my way down the same old roads of Defiance, heading toward church, wondering if I'll find dirt on Hap.

She was the wind, and he was the emptiness that received her breath. He followed her closely this time, the fear of discovery thwarted by the thrill of being near his salvation. This madonna, this mother of children, would tell him the words he needed to hear. Those forgiveness words. He'd heard them once ...

"I forgive you," Daisy Marie Chance choked out while he tried to snuff her life. The words came in stuttered spurts, but they were sincere words. Dying words. He let go of her when she delivered the "you." In fact, he let her fall to the earth.

"Why did you say that?"

"I don't know," she whispered, touching her neck. "I feel sorry for you."

Shock re-emerged as anger in that moment. No one should feel sorry for him. He was a man, strong and able. His mama said to keep his elbows off the table, and he did. An obedient man who followed orders. But Daisy's words ignited the fuse of anger and he could not douse it. In that firestorm of hate, he could only cough on the smoke of rage. So he pressed both strong, able hands into Daisy Marie Chance's neck, stopping the flow of air that would say such words. He didn't know then he'd need her forgiveness, and by the time he longed for it, she had no more oxygen to fuel the words again. Crumpled, lifeless, her silence spoke more than the voices in his head.

He heard Ouisie's holler saying she knew who he was. For a fleeting moment, he believed her and nearly dropped into her line of vision to form their alliance. But her voice had an edge to it, a dissatisfaction that made him worry about her intentions. No. Best wait until the moment was right, when her voice held longing, not irritation. He'd been waiting a long, long time. He could wait a few more days.

She was strong to open the earth's mouth like that, but she shouldn't have ventured into its secrets where shoes without children hurled cacophonous accusations he needed, but hated

to hear. He turned, made more noise, then sprinted away, believing she hadn't seen him, but savoring the deliciousness that perhaps she had.

And when he saw her in the clearing, her feet touching the very gravel he'd traveled, he knew her time was near. Just as he knew Daisy's had been when she offered forgiveness.

Thirty-Four

I hear laughter—Emily's laughter—emanating like poison gas from Hap's chambers. His shoes might be dirt-free, but his heart would not. I fling open the door and say a cheerful hello.

Emily is standing next to Hap, her hand on his forearm.

"Your husband is hilarious!" Her words sound strained, and her smile reflects the tension.

I return it, then nod Hap's way. "I don't have the house keys, so I walked back. Can I drive your car home? I'll pick you up later, if you'd like."

Hap's face is flushed. He stands, moving away from Emily's hand. "Emily, if you don't mind, I need to discuss something with my wife."

He says *wife* like a declaration. I'm not sure what, exactly, he's declaring.

She scoots around the desk, gathers her Bible, Sheba's book and her sweater, and says a hasty goodbye. Before I can shut the door, she pops back into his office, a pasted smile decorating her face. "Thanks for the godly counsel," she says. She leaves like the wind, the door sucking itself shut.

"Well," I say.

"Sit down."

I obey. Or more appropriately, *submit*.

"Here's the thing, Ouisie. She's having some difficulties and I'm helping her. There's nothing more to it than that."

"Really."

He wrings his hands, looks above my eyes. "You know I feel bad about Emory Chance. And I gave you my word it won't happen again."

I see shame on his face, but not regret.

"The Bible says I have grounds, Hap. You sleeping around like that makes you the adulterous one." I watch him contort under my words. And for a moment, I feel like a queen, able to disseminate perfect judgments. To enact my own laws, cure my own life. But his gaze hardens in an instant, and it's me who fiddles with my hands now. The roar of a cornered lion is coming. I can feel it in the air between us.

"You will not say a word about my past indiscretion, you hear me?"

"I hear you." But I shake as I say it. Funny how his prey-seeking look can change the temperature of our relationship in a second.

He stands, both hands on his desk. I count his fingers, noticing the hair above his knuckles. I don't give him my eyes. "Here you are rehashing an old sin, one that's been buried, forgiven, and flung from the east to the west. I'm at your mercy, held prisoner by your stupid whims. I don't relish living this way. I have more eternal things to do with my time, like lead a weary congregation toward the Lord. Do you have any idea what kind of responsibility that is?"

"You mean, like the kind of responsibility that makes a man love his wife and be faithful to her? That kind of responsibility?" My voice frightens me. My words will not return void. They'll invite blows. I back away.

"How can you look yourself in the mirror, Ouisie Pepper, and call yourself a Christian?" He seethes hatred. I can see it. Hear it too.

I shake my head. It's a good question. There are times when I wonder the same thing when my empty face stares back at me.

Is Jesus in there somewhere? Growing me into him? Or have I relegated him to the Emergency Responder, the one I shoot frantic prayers to? "I don't know," I say. My words don't seethe; they weep.

"A woman who throws accusations against an elder in the church without proper witnesses is in danger of reaping a whirlwind."

"It's no accusation. You admitted it." My words are the smallest whispers.

He moves around his desk, almost prowling. He places his hands around my neck. He doesn't squeeze, and I don't move. It's his same position when we're in bed at night, when he "needs" me. He enjoys seeing me squirm, likes the feeling of my jugular under his thumb, apparently. He applies the slightest pressure to my neck. I send a prayer to Jesus—me with my renegade heart who calls in emergencies. I ask him to intervene somehow. I know where this is headed.

"You're worthless," he growls. "Right now I can't think of one reason why I even married you." His grip squeezes.

I labor under his touch. My heart throws up a shield from his words. I escape back to Mama, her smiling face, a swing near our backyard. I am carefree there, legs extended to the clouds, laughing my joy. It's my citadel for now. Even so, I struggle for air.

I shoot another prayer to the ceiling, but it bounces back to me. I know Hap runs this church on his strength—no secretary, no youth pastor, no children's coordinator. He *is* this church. Which means there will be no one out and about to rescue me.

My vision blurs.

My lungs beg for oxygen.

His hands don't relent.

And in this moment, I cradle a delicious thought. Maybe this is it. Maybe it's finally over. He can take my life from me. He's taken everything else. Why not my heartbeat? I fight to

remember Sissy and Jed. In the struggle, I finger Elijah's brace-let under my sleeve, touching the boy and girl charms, hoping they'll forgive me for giving up so easily. But as light halos my vision, and I sense the warmth of a love I've only tasted, I give myself to it, rest in it, feel its warmth. I hear the Voice, beckoning, whispering the kind of words I've longed to understand my entire life. Such beautiful, beautiful words.

Thirty-Five

The light flees in one gasping moment. I choke. I open my eyes, but see only shadows. I shake my head to make sense of it—one second hearing angel-music earthly folks don't hear, the next a wavering of a woman's voice.

"Pastor?"

Hap leaves, the scent of his cologne lingering. I hear footsteps on the church's floorboard, then the slam of the white door, the revving of the Chevy.

I shake my head, then turn toward Heloise Dickson, Bible study member, cat lover, finally focusing on her face. I cough the blurriness away. My voice can't yet form words, but I feel her hand in mine, and I listen to her breathing.

"It's a good thing I had Sunday school work to attend to," she soothes.

"You can't tell. Not a soul." I settle myself, but I can't limit the panic in my voice.

"I heard about Reverend Pepper's anger, Ouisie, from Harold, but I didn't realize it was like this."

"Please, it's just a misunderstanding. Really."

"I see your eyes."

I look down, notice Heloise's sensible shoes, the way her pants reveal yellow socks above narrow ankles that can't support them.

"I understand."

"You do?"

She sits in one of Hap's counseling chairs. I sit in the other.

"When I rescue cats from bad homes, they look just like you."

I don't say anything. Instead I examine my nail beds, noticing how I've peeled away my hangnails until my fingers turned raw. When did I do this? I can't remember.

She places a warm hand on my shoulder. "I'll be praying for you," she says.

"Please don't tell. Really, everything's fine. It's just a misunderstanding."

"Oh, I wouldn't dream of telling. Don't you worry your pretty head. He's the pastor, Ouisie. You can't touch the Lord's anointed without getting hellfire shoveled back on you. I'll keep your secret. And I'll pray."

I don't know what I feel. Relief? Anger? Will no one stand up to Hap? My head roars; my eyes sting. I wonder how I'll get home.

"I need to go." Heloise gathers herself, pats me again on the shoulder. "You'll get through this. They say God won't put us through more than we can bear."

I've been to hell and back, but his anger doesn't die; it enrages. But I stay quiet, trying to force myself to remember the appropriate platitude to interject. I find it. "This too shall pass." The words feel like lies on my tongue. Probably because they are. Sometimes things don't pass. They stay.

Oh, how they stay.

"That's a good wife." She pats me again, painting on a smile. Then she breezes away, as if we just shared coffee and gossip.

In Hap's empty office, tears come to my eyes. The reality of my life hits me all at once—how hard I've tried to mother—and failed. How much I've worked to be a godly wife—and failed. How others have seen or heard of Hap's temper—and failed to protect me, the children. How my own little secrets point to mediocrity, or even betrayal. All I can think about right now is my own mama, how each year married to David sucked the vitality from her—he a thirsty toddler manning a straw, and she the emptying cup of juice. I swore I would never let a man do that to me. And now the swearing seems ridiculous because I wear my mama's face.

I walk outside, run my hand along the Doric columns, feeling how smooth, how loved they are. Hap fashioned them, painted them, admired them. But he doesn't oblige the same for me.

The parking lot sits vacant. I sit on the stoop below the columns, running my hands over the cement steps, dirtying my hands and shuddering. I look down at the gardens Emory tends in secret, sigh, and make my way to the flowerbeds. I hunch over dormant azaleas, and pull off a small shiny leaf, turning it in my hand. Used to be I'd gather ten or so and write Jed a progressive note on the petals. But I'm pure out of inspiration, and Jed's made it clear he wants no more messages.

A car turns into Defiance Community Church's lot. I hear it first, then look up. It's Emory, thank God.

She parks the car in Hap's special pastor's place, turns it off.

"What are you doing here?"

"Came looking for you. I didn't like how things ended."

I wonder if Hap's strangling has left a mark.

"Where's Hap?"

"Home, I think."

"And how are you getting home?"

"I'll walk." I stand, dust off my hands, and drop the azalea leaf to the ground.

"Nonsense, I'll take you." She motions to the car, and I follow.

Safe inside, I say, "I'm sorry."

"For what?" She starts the car, backs up.

"For my words to you earlier today."

"I just wanted to help. You helped me, you know."

"I did?"

"Well, you forgave me, for one."

"It wasn't easy." And it's not so easy to forgive Hap, especially after today.

"I know." She turns to me. "You don't look so good."

I smooth my hair, longing to pull the visor down and make sure I'm presentable, but I don't. "I'm tired, is all."

At the end of the parking lot, she says, "How about this? Why don't I take you back to my place. To settle you."

"But Hap will be expecting me home, and there's dinner to make."

"Would it kill him to make dinner?" She turns on the right blinker, heading away from Defiance. "Well? Would it?"

"Yes." I laugh when I say it, because the whole thing is quite ridiculous. Of course it won't kill him, right? But not coming home just might end up killing me.

She turns right. "I'll call him on your behalf, say you're not feeling well."

I don't argue. I am a fugitive, speeding away on a road in the opposite direction of home, alone in my thoughts, but wearied by their ferocity. What kind of woman deliberately leaves home? What would Sheba say? I pull out my bracelet, fingering the Jed and Sissy charms, feeling fear in my gut. "The children," I say to the dashboard.

"We can pray." Emory turns into her driveway. "I have a special place." She stops the car. "Gotta get the mail."

She leaves in a flurry, jogs to the mailbox, and returns thumbing through several white envelopes. When she's in the car, she hands one to me. "Looks like the author lady wrote you a letter."

Sheba's handwriting is third-grade-teacher perfect. While we bounce on Emory's potholed driveway, I open the envelope. Colored bits of paper spring out, littering Emory's car.

"What happened?" Emory turns off the car.

"I don't know. Looks like she put some confetti in here."

While the fire starts to crackle and Emory bangs pots in the kitchen, I read Sheba's letter:

Dear Ouisie,

I'll start off by answering your question. Yes, I made it home just fine, thanks to God's provision of gas money. And in case you're curious, no, my husband hasn't returned, but I maintain my faith that he will. God never forsakes His godly ones. I'm clinging to that truth, and standing on the promises.

You asked about submission. Let me assure you that the word's gotten bad press. It's a privilege to submit to your husband, to arrange your life to suit his. God sees all that. He rewards wives who choose to do the right thing by their husbands, even when their husbands occasionally lose their temper. The Bible doesn't say you can leave a man just because he hits you. And just think of the reward! God says we're blessed when we turn the other cheek. He tells us to go a second mile when someone's asked us to go one. He rewards what is done in secret.

Your submission to Hap is your secret obedience, only seen by him and rewarded by him. By even sharing what you did about your husband, you've risked losing your recognition by the King. Kind of like when folks spout on about how they gave such and such money to missionaries. If you say it out loud, you have no reward.

It's time to buck up. Choose to be a woman after God's heart. Walk the long journey, just as I have walked it without a husband. You must not lose faith that God is up to something. But it's never up to you to make your husband change, or even mention that you'd like him to. Remember, our husbands will be won without a word from our wayward tongues.

Do not leave. Even entertaining the idea of escape is offensive to God. He joined you in holy matrimony until death. If you sever that, God will un-bless you. I'd hate to see that happen because I like you.

Fondly,

Sheba

I reread the letter, fold it back up, and put it in my purse. When Emory returns from the kitchen, I say nothing, afraid my thoughts will make no sense. With so much advice, who am I to believe? Emory's not been a Christian for very long. Sheba's is probably the correct advice. Problem is, I like Emory's better.

"Well?"

"Well, it's a letter." I shake my head. "I need to go home."

"Let me look at it, will you?"

"I don't know." I remember Sheba's words about secrets, how the secretive God rewards every time I take a fist from Hap. If I let it out, everything will be for naught. After hearing sections of the heavenly choir this afternoon, I'm not sure I want to jeopardize my reward. Breathtakingly beautiful, that place was. Would it be less so if I botch my wifely duty?

"It obviously upset you."

"You can tell?" I pull my feet underneath me. Emory gives me a flannel blanket. I pull it over myself, but I still shiver.

"Yes."

"I can't show you. All I can say is that if I don't get home soon, things will not go well for me. At least hear me when I say that. You haven't called Hap yet anyway, so he won't even know I came here."

"I'll take you home if you promise me one thing." She walks over to the fireplace, adds a hefty log to the fire.

"What's that?"

"You will promise me to think about getting safe."

I wonder if getting safe is some sort of abomination. But

more than that, I wonder how I'd possibly walk back to my home on Dyer Street at this time of day, in this cold weather. "I promise," I say. Promises are meant to be broken, right?

Hap breaks them all the time.

Thirty-Six

The house smells burnt. And it sounds like chaos and pain. My welcome home committee consists of a barking Clementine, a crying Sissy, a stomping Jed and a hollering Hap. He won't meet my eyes when I find him in the kitchen. He is fishing burnt toast from the toaster, trying not to swear—substituting with *gosh* and *shoot*.

I'd noticed at Emory's that Hap's fingers have made an impression on my neck. There is no disguising the imprint. Soon the blush-colored finger marks will mellow to brown and purple, beckoning turtlenecks to conceal them. Just another secret I can cover up for the Almighty to see, to reward.

Hap throws the charcoal toast across the room. It hits the butter-yellow wall just below the clock, leaving a dark smudge. I am not afraid. I pick up a sponge and wipe the spot clean. "Why don't you leave the kitchen and let me handle dinner." It's more of a command than a question.

In one quick motion, he grabs me to himself, holding me chest to chest. He searches my eyes. If you watched us like a movie, you'd see the old Hap, the Hap who rescued me years ago—all blue-eyed sincerity. "I'm sorry," he says. "My temper." The last two words are a whisper. As if the kids didn't already know about his anger. But I take his words to myself and offer forgiveness because I know if I do, I will buy peace for a few days.

"I know. I forgive you."

He touches my neck, tracing the line of his fingers. "I did this."

"Yes, you did."

"Why do you stay with me?"

This is a question he sometimes asks, particularly when he's feeling shame. I've tried many different responses, tried them on like garments at the department store. Only one fits right. "Because I know you don't mean any of this, and I know you're sorry." Just like the tattooed man.

He smiles. "There's my girl."

But as he leaves the kitchen, all I can think of is *who is his girl? And where has Hap taken her?*

Thirty-Seven

B eing homebound has its advantages. I cannot shop until Hap takes me, which makes him come along and bear the burden of groceries with me. I have more time to think. I don't have to visit Emory at her house and listen to her "encouragement" about making a ridiculous plan that we both know won't work. It's really quite nice. In the weeks since Hap siphoned my car of its energy (Jimmy Carter would be proud), I've reorganized the house, made curtains for the living room, taught my Bible study without Hap's interference, and cooked up a storm. The house is cleaner, more welcoming, and Jed and Sissy seem to thrive on the routine I've created. Sheba's words are reachable again. Maybe this whole thing with Hap's temper really has been my fault—my stubborn rebellion, you might say.

Today I revel in joy because I'm outside, digging into burnt sienna earth with willing hands. Although Sheba's admonition to keep secrets at bay tickles my ears, I can't seem to help myself. I must touch the dirt, must give it life, or at least pray God will make plants grow. Under a peek-a-boo sun, the February cold has given way to March warmth. My shadow works before me, proving the sun exists. I wonder if heaven changes shadows to reality. In my dreams I hear the angel choir, reminding me that heaven is a real place and God means it when he says he loves his children. I wish life weren't so loud, shouting away God's voice. It's only when I sleep that I feel his embrace.

Perhaps that's a fitting metaphor for the baptism I'm so afraid of. Sleep in the caress of waters, wake to the sunlight.

Sometimes, like today, I can nearly hear the whisper of God. He is the Creator, the One who made the earth where my knees kneel. The One who gave the birds reason to sing. The One who fashioned Jed and Sissy in my womb. I smile in the recollection.

I pull out a packet of sweet pea seeds from my pocket—yet another secret. I spied a circular rack of seeds at the grocery store last week and hid the sweet pea seeds between two boxes of cereal when Hap performed price comparisons on coffee crystals. I made sure Flo was the checker when we came through, quickly placing the seeds up front while Hap thumbed through a *Reader's Digest*. I told her with my eyes to quickly enter the seeds. She understood. Flo handed me the seeds in a mini-moment. I spirited them away in my purse. And now I hold them.

Armed with a rusty trowel I found in the woods, I pull a long line of dirt beneath the kitchen window. One by one I press a hardened pea into the ground, praying they'll see spring's light, that each will send a green tendril to the sky, daring to push through the tomb of earth. I pray with each seed planted.

Lord, help me to love Hap again. I can't seem to find my affection. Or the will. And yet, I have the will to plant this seed.

I press another seed into the red earth, further down than the last seed. Be with Jed. Keep him home. Don't let him leave.

I pull a stick-a-burr from the soil; it cuts into my thumb. I wipe it on my pants, then suck the rest. Protect Sissy from bullies. And lisps. And her father.

I crunch a wayward leaf into the soil. It breaks completely in my hand, creating life-giving mulch to my next seed. Give Emory peace while she grieves, I pray.

I continue down haphazard rows, feeling the elation of dirt beneath fingernails. I stop at the rose bush that's simply a shoot. Thank you for Ethrea Ree. She's more gift than menace. Just goes to show you can't judge a person by her demeanor.

I find another weed, this time an intrusion of Bermuda grass. I pull and pull, uprooting a weed two feet long. I shake its dirt onto the bed, then toss it behind me. Help me to understand Elijah. Should I stay his friend or walk away?

I don't say my garden prayers out loud, but as the gate creaks behind me, I wonder if I have, if I've voiced them without realizing it. I look up just as I smooth gritty covers over my sleeping seeds. Elijah. He is less Santa Claus, more vagrant. And he twitches as he walks. And once again, he finds me alone. Do you see him here? He is not a ghost, is he?

"Hello," I say.

"Hello yourself." Imaginary friends don't have actual voices, right?

"Where have you been?" I am glad to see him, if I allow myself to be honest.

"Around. You know, a prophet's without honor in his hometown. I understand that now."

He motions for us to sit at the back picnic table. So I sit next to him. "You been back to Burl lately?"

"Last month. But folks there can't see me like a prophet. I'm more of a nuisance. So I'm back. And I'm sorry I've been gone. How's that bracelet of yours coming along?"

I do not want to show him, and I'm not sure why. It's tucked under the elastic of my jacket. "It's in the house. I take it off when I garden."

He turns and stares at me a good five seconds. I look away.

"Well, you keep praying for whatever it is you've found to put on that bracelet. You need to make it a habit, like brushing your teeth."

I notice his teeth—they haven't been brushed in a very long time. "So, where are you staying now?" His clothes are the same as the last time I saw him. He smells worse.

"The Good Lord provided me a place rent free. I'm so blessed. I've got a nice, big table I've set up, making my little boxes. He rifles through his pockets, grimacing for a few seconds, then smiling. "Here." He places a smashed box on the picnic table.

"It's broken."

"That's my intention." The sun grabs the blue sky in that moment, pushing away the cloud that's hidden it. It shines directly on the broken cardboard. "It's for you." He picks it up in dirty hands. He opens my hand, then places it there, closing my fingers around the box. His hand lingers. I pull away.

"Thanks," I say. I may be mortified, but at least I've maintained what Mama called "Southern Charm." I remember her words in this moment, about hard times being God's gift to us, to keep us hoping in him, and I wonder if being broken also keeps us hoping in God. Or does it lead to despair?

"It's only when we're broken beyond repair that God can finally get a word in edgewise. That's how it was with me. And that's how it will be with you."

"I'm not sure I want to hear such words." Haven't I been broken enough already? Isn't my life a smashed box as it is? And with me doing my best to shove the walls of my collapsing box back out, and finding some success, I don't like the way this conversation is headed.

"Folks never want to hear about broken stuff. They want stuff to be fixed in their lives. But that's not how God works, now is it? He breaks, then He repairs. Only he doesn't rebuild what was, he makes something new. Like this." Elijah pulls out another box from the same dirty pocket. It's golden, perfectly shaped, never smashed. "You set these two boxes next to one another as a reminder. Because God will restore the years the locusts have gnawed at you. He'll bring a new crop of life. I see it. I see it as clear as I see the sun hopping in and out of the clouds today."

Tears force their way out, though I didn't give them permission. I sniff in, wipe my face, and wonder if Elijah's golden box is simply the promise of heaven after Hap squeezes too hard on

my neck. This big, beautiful earth, the way it smells, the dirt it deposited under my nails—I will miss it. Oh dear God, how I will miss it.

Elijah places his right hand on my left knee.

I scoot away as fast as I can and run into the house. When I turn to look out the window at Elijah, to gauge his response, he is gone. And nothing is left but a turned over picnic table bench—tangible evidence that I'm not losing my mind, that he sat there with me for a moment.

You saw him, right?

Thirty-Eight

Two times men's hands touched my leg unwanted. One persisted, the other apologized. And both shared the name David.

My stepdad David started touching me a week after the wedding, but it was his words that tore through me. "You dress like a slut," was his favorite thing to say. But then he'd pull me near him with arms much stronger than mine and tell me how pretty I was, always with his hairy hand squeezing above my knee. The fifth time—I had counted—I gathered enough gumption to say, "Take your hand off my leg."

He squeezed harder like he was trying to juice me.

"I said, take it off. Now." I tried to make my voice sound brave. I was anything but.

David laughed. "That's how it is with you types of girls. Teasers. Parading around the house in the get-ups you wear, just welcoming my leer. Then playing hard to get. I see how this goes." He moved closer, put an arm around me.

I smelled his perspiration, felt his strength. I knew all I had left were words. "Mama wouldn't take kindly to you touching me this way. She'll be home soon." I looked up at the clock, willing it to move faster. Mama would be home, but it would be longer than I hoped. I prayed David didn't take note of her schedule.

He let go of my knee and removed his arm in a flash. He stood above me, a look of hatred sneering his face. "You will say nothing of this," he told me. "Or I'll kill her."

I took his words to heart, letting them finger their way through me, taunting me, waking me up at night. Mama was all I had in this world, my own saint. I would not jeopardize her. So I became busy or evasive when David and I were alone. As the year wore on, he'd taken more and more of me, though I fought and kicked him away.

He appeared the protective father when my boyfriend David came to pick me up for dates. He lectured David, telling him about the proper way to treat a girl, all the while pointing out his unique gun collection. He said I was worth my weight in gold, that I was to be cherished, adored, protected. These words float back to me even now as I try to imagine God saying them to me instead. God cherishes me? Adores me? Protects me? Really?

On one date, David drove us to Tyler to catch *Swiss Family Robinson*. It was a long car ride, so we spent our time chatting about everything—our favorite TV shows, dreams for the future, even a few secrets. I found myself falling in love with David on that car ride, if such a thing can happen. He asked me about my father—not David, but my real father who died when I was seven.

"I came home to a quiet house, which was strange because I always heard my father whistle. He was a jeweler, but he worked out of our home, mostly doing watch repair. He had a wide wooden workbench he'd brought into a spare room at the front of the house—his workstation, he called it. I set my books on the floor, hollering for Daddy."

I watched David's jaw tense as he drove. "Are you sure you want to hear this?"

He nodded. Before I continued, I studied his face again, marveling as a tear left the corner of his eye and traveled down his cheek. Maybe he loved me too. "I ran into Daddy's office only to find him slumped over the big wooden work bench, his head and neck in an uncomfortable angle. Knowing Daddy to take a few afternoon naps, I shook him, telling him I was home." I looked out the window, the landscape becoming the horrible scene before me. I could smell death, taste it even. And I felt it when I touched Daddy's hand.

"He was dead, wasn't he?" In a hesitant moment, David looked my way.

"Yes. His hand—it was colder than winter, but the day was muggy hot. I shook Daddy, begged him to rouse, hollered at him. Screamed. But nothing woke him. Not even God could do such a thing. I called the police before I called Mama at work. Both arrived at the same time. I still remember the calmness of the officer, how it contrasted to the hysterics of Mama. And me in the middle trying to make sense of it all."

"I'm sorry." David removed his right hand from the steering wheel and squeezed my knee. He was just about to let go when I backhanded his forearm. The car swerved in response. He pulled it safely to the side of the road and looked at me. "What did I do?"

"Don't you dare touch my leg again."

And he didn't because he loved me.

But the other David didn't, on either account.

The treetop hideaway was sometimes silent. Not often, what with the rain pelting the metal roof or the birds singing soliloquies. But right now, quiet. So the man hummed, quelling the voices in his head.

As the sun cast its light straight down onto Lake Pisgah, making brilliant the muddy waters, the ripples stilled under the heat, forming into a movie screen, glassy pure.

He crouched in the grass as an actor in the scene flickering on the lake, but he wasn't in his skin. He watched like God. The man—him a lifetime ago—followed anyway, stealthy, quieter than the rustling of the grass. She gasped when he grabbed her ankle, but the man knew how to silence her. One hand over the mouth, the other arm stilling battling limbs. The man dragging her to a secluded place, thick with jungled trees. The man listened for sounds, but heard only birds and his own breath.

The enemy shivered, which surprised him. She didn't scream, this girl. And that's when he noticed how different she was. Slower. Addled. Her slowness made him scream inside. He knew addled. Loved it. Hoped to, at least. But he had come this far. The woods pressed in on him. The heat of the day seemed to confirm his need for thrifty speed. She was his enemy.

But she had the look. The eyes. And now, the fear.

Later, he would recount the moment the sandaled girl breathed her last as the final time he shed a tear. The last time he wept under a hung-over sky. It was the day the old him passed away, when the new him came roaring to life. Goodbye, he said to the lifeless girl as he removed her sandals and put them in his satchel; goodbye, he said to himself.

Thirty-Nine

E mory's car rumbles out front. I look out the window, wondering what it is she's doing here. She didn't attend my latest Bible study about heavenly beauty—oh how I missed her presence—and she hasn't returned my calls either. She sits behind the wheel, her head down. The exhaust smokes blue out the back of the car, no doubt polluting Ethrea Ree's roses. I see her fingers thin as French fries, curled slightly around the black wheel.

Having organized the house to oblivion and gnawed on the bones of boredom, I welcome her intrusion. I pull on a sweater and venture outside. I knock on Emory's window. She shakes her head no.

I knock again.

She throws her arms in the air, her eyes wild.

I try the handle. Locked.

I move to the other side of the car, try the door, and find it unlocked, so I slip in beside her. "What's wrong?"

She makes no noise. Instead, she bangs her head in a rhythmic beat on the steering wheel.

"Care to talk about it?" I smell that familiar Emory smell— marijuana seeping into the cushions and dashboard of the car. "Have you been smoking?"

Emory lets out a yaw, hollering her groan of anguish from here clear to Tyler. Clementine responds from the house.

"I have. I did. God hates me."

I place my hand on her shoulder, and she lets it rest there. "He doesn't hate you."

"Yes, He does. Hixon too. I'm sure of it."

"Are you high right now?" I worry whether she's driven here under drug duress.

"No, not at all. It was last night."

"I know where we can go so you can spill this whole thing and get clean."

"Clean? Is that even possible?" She bangs her head on the steering wheel again. Just once this time.

"Yes. Drive to Lake Pisgah. We'll talk there."

The doors slam in the unshaken universe that is my dear Lake Pisgah. Metal against metal is dissonant against birds chirping their songs to welcome springtime around the bend. It's a pleasant day with the sun warming our heads as we walk toward the shoreline. I hear our feet crunch against brittle grass, Emory's steady humming, and a hint of wind through still-bereft trees. In light of the beauty beckoning me, I push down my fear that Hap will return home early as he's been prone to do lately "just to check," and find me a fugitive from my exile.

"I am no angel," Emory says.

"Neither am I."

"All my losses crushed me last night. Daisy, Muriel, Hixon." Her voice catches.

I put my arm around her. A wild goose circles ahead of us, its wings broad against the leafless trees and tangled bracken. "It's really too much for one person to handle. You should've called."

"Yeah, like Mr. Kindness would let you talk to me. He's not exactly keeping you on a long chain these days."

I sigh in the wind. I know I'm living on borrowed air. "You're right."

"Listen, I know you have your own fish to fry, so I've tried not to burden you. After all, I've made a mess of your life. How dare I think I have a right to share my problems with you."

"You need to let the affair go, Emory. I'm learning to. And I've told you I've forgiven you."

"*I* haven't forgiven me." She walks ahead of me, grabs a rock, and hurls it into the stillness of Lake Pisgah. Ripples circle outward from small to large until they nearly kiss her toes at the shore.

"Perhaps someday you'll believe me." I pick up a flint-shaped stone and throw it sideways. It skips above the surface of the now-disturbed lake. Four, five times. It sinks to the great unknown, worrying me afresh about the dream I had about my baptism. I would sink like the rock and never come up.

"I will never be what Hixon saw in me. He treated me like I was a queen or something—when really I'm a homeless wreck."

"He saw something in you. Something beautiful."

She acts as if she doesn't hear me, which frustrates me. It's not like I have a lot to give out. I feel like a squeezed out pastry bag, emptied of frosting. She's received my last sweet teaspoon and not even tasted it.

"It happened last night—when I took a hit." She walks ahead of me, then stops. She removes her shoes, then her white socks. I watch as she shoves the socks into her shoes and carries them with her toward the lakeshore. She steps in, winces at the cold, then steps further, wetting the base of her jeans. She doesn't roll them up, just keeps walking deeper. She stops and looks at me. "I was fine, all alone in my home—Muriel's home, actually—until I picked up an art book I checked out from the library. It was for you actually, knowing how Hap's kept you from everything, I figured you'd enjoy a good art book. Well, at the end of the day, I coaxed the fire until it roared and smelled like heaven. I held a warm cup of hot chocolate in my hand. I put it down to thumb through the book. That's when I knew I couldn't face the evening alone."

"It is quiet out there. I can only imagine." For a moment I consider ridding myself of shoes and coming in after her, but I choose to keep my soles on.

"No, it's not the quiet, it was the book—something I read inside." She throws the shoes my way. I catch them before they hit the mud. She spreads her arms wide, clears her throat, and orates, " 'I saw the angel in the marble and carved until I set him free.' Michelangelo said it. Right after I read it, I sucked down a joint like a pixie stick."

"Why?" I back up the bank and sit down, Emory's shoes my only company. I watch the woman gesture to the sky, to the water, to me. If she didn't have such a pained look on her face, I'd consider myself her audience for her one-woman comedy show.

"I realized when I read Michelangelo's words that God is the one who carves us, Ouisie. He chips away at all that rock until we're better. More whole. Except when I read that quote, I knew for sure God didn't see an angel when he looked at my unformed substance. He saw trouble. And a devil."

Devil stays between us. It's as if the Defiance air has taken hold of that word and hurled it like a whirlwind around the lake, blowing through and around us. "We are all devils if you peel away the happy-clappy facades we muster. We're all broken."

She walks my way. Her toes, white with pink nails, squish through Lake Pisgah's red-brown mud. She sits next to me, then laughs. "That's an easy thing to say, equating us all as Raggedy Anns that God wants to clean. Some are messier than others— way more messy. You don't do drugs. You aren't a neglectful mother."

I smile at the irony, but I'm not happy. A dove moans in the trees behind us, calling me. If I strain enough, I believe it says, "It's time, time, time." You'd think I'd be someone to heed a dove's mandate, but I can't. Won't. The breeze blesses my face, and I close my eyes, waiting for another sign from the Almighty—perhaps the Voice telling me to come clean.

"Sometimes I think I'm the only one in the world who struggles with being good. Maybe I am."

I hear Emory's words, but they come from the heavens, nearly with the timbre of God's breath. He is asking me to set this girl free through my own awful confession. My heart grabs my lungs, squeezes them clear of air in a rhythmic wringing. How can I say such a thing? Reveal who I really am? If Sheba were here, what would she say? And you—what would you do?

Tell her.

I feel tears weep down my cheek. "Emory?"

"Yeah." She caresses the dry grass with her right hand as if it were her sleeping baby.

"I'm just like you. No different."

She looks at me. Her eyes are the color of the pale winter-nearly-spring sky, and they hold tears. "You?"

I nod, then let out the air I've been holding for Lord knows how many years. "You know I drink. Too much. To cope. I'm addicted, I think. And when I'm in a state from drinking, I sleep, letting the kids do whatever they want. We are the same, Emory."

She pats the earth, then walls off her face with dirtied hands, and lets out another cry. I put my arm around her, wanting hers around me, but she is too crushed to think of me right now. "You may not see the angel. And I may not see an angel in myself. But I have to believe God is bigger than both of us."

She shakes her head. "Not as big as my need for dope, apparently. Why didn't he stop me? He could've."

"He hasn't stopped me from drinking. Last I checked, I keep making that decision on my own. And somehow I've convinced myself that I can't *not* make that choice."

"Hixon is looking at me. I know it. He's shaking his head, frowning down from heaven."

"He adored you. Loved you. And I bet he would rather you go forward today than to wallow in your worthlessness." As I say the words, I wonder if they are for me too.

"You think so?"

"Yes. They say that's the wonderful part about following Jesus, though I'm really no expert. He takes you where you are, dusts you off, sets you back on your feet, and shines his love down on you. The only thing you need to do is recognize that you made a mistake, ask forgiveness, and pray he will help you resist temptation in the future." I sound like Sheba.

"I am sorry for everything. Terribly sorry."

"I know."

"Are you sorry?"

I shake my head. "I hope so. I mean to be."

She stands, then lifts me to my feet. "It's just that it seems too good to be true. I screw up and then God forgives. He makes me that angel in the marble. Why? What's the catch?"

"No catch. He does it because he's a good father."

"I didn't really know my daddy," Emory says. "I'm not sure what a father's supposed to do."

"Mine loved me. His eyes lit up when he saw me. I'm sorry you haven't had that."

"Maybe I can borrow your memories for the time being. Maybe that's enough for right now."

I can loan the beauty of my father to Emory. And in the process, perhaps I'll be stirred up to remember more, to understand what a daddy's supposed to do. All of Hap's yelling and marauding through the house has nearly made me forget such extravagant love.

We stop in front of a boulder, taller than a crepe myrtle. Emory touches it, her fingers caressing the rough, ash-colored surface. "You think I'll ever be set free? Be carved into God's angel?" Her questions are beggar's words, thrown out in hope of a scrap of love in return.

I touch the rock and say a silent prayer. I clear my throat for a declaration. "Dear God, I hope so. For both our sakes." Let it be, dear Jesus. Oh, let it be.

Forty

The angel in stone flutters around my mind as Emory presses her foot to the accelerator. I inspire her own paranoia when I look at my watch and fluster that I had to get home before Hap. So we speed.

As the trees blur by and the sameness of the town's landscape dulls my eyes, I wonder if Hap is his own angel. All those angels in the Bible were burly man-like creatures with names like Michael and Gabriel. Do you think Hap is an untamed one? And that God is using my own obedience to chisel away at Hap's rough edges? Could I set Hap free? I want to believe this. I need to believe this. But as we turn into my driveway, every belief I want to harbor flies out Emory's wind-leaking window. Hap is here—to check on me. And he'll be no angel, I can assure you.

Emory shoots me a look of sympathy. "I can take you back to my place if you want."

"No," I tell her. "It's best I face my fugitive ways head on."

"I'm not even sure if God hears me." She traces one finger along the curve of the steering wheel. "But I'll be praying for you." She reaches her hand my way and squeezes. I return the squeeze, but find little comfort.

I wave goodbye as she pulls out of the driveway, praying for the protection of Michael and Gabriel, but mid-prayer, the front door opens behind me. Without a word, Hap places a warm hand on my back. I shudder. It's the beginning of the end.

"So, you were out with your little friend, I see." His hand moves to my shoulder.

"She was upset. I took a walk with her around the lake." I do not turn around.

His hand tightens on my clavicle; my bone feels its chisel. "I thought we agreed that you would be a godly wife, a woman who kept to her home, who managed the affairs of her family. I thought," he squeezed harder, "we had an agreement."

Jed and Sissy will be home in less than an hour—enough time for Hap to compress every bone in my body. My stomach lurches—a hiccup of a jerk that sends stinging fluid up my throat. I cough.

Hap releases his grip. I let out the air I've been holding. "You're right. We had an agreement. Emory came here. She was upset. Wouldn't Jesus help an upset friend?" The moment the question flies from my lips I know violence lurks.

Hap turns me to face him. His eyes are half-anger, half-pity, but so full of coldness I shiver beneath them. "Jesus wants wives to obey their husbands." He grabs me and shakes. My head is not its own in these moments. It doesn't obey my will to stop shaking. Like a spent stuffed animal, my head flops back and forth on my neck. I try to speak, but Hap has shaken out all my words. When the world dizzies, he stops. But Defiance and my home still spin on an unstable axis. I cannot form a thought.

"It is better to live on the corner of a roof than live with you, Ouisie."

I say nothing. Maybe he'll get sick of me and leave. Maybe. Or maybe I'll help God make him into that angel. I pull in a breath. Decide to say something. "You're right. I'm hard to live with. I admit it. I hope you can forgive me, that you can see I'm trying so hard to make you happy."

"Happy?" His face softens.

"Yes, you and I—happy. Remember? How we used to laugh, relax, enjoy each other's words?"

"I don't remember," he says, his voice cooling.

"You have to remember. You have to. Please, Hap. We can be happy. You don't have to be angry."

At the word angry, his face becomes it. "Once dinner is over, I'll have to restrict you to our bedroom. I'll install a lock while you cook."

His words float beyond me like a child's let-go balloon toward telephone wires. Eventually they'll hit the wires and explode, but right now they drift through me, not making sense. Locked in my own bedroom? What am I—six years old?

"I will lock you in at night and unlock you in the morning."

"Where will you be?"

"Out and about, or maybe on the couch. The lock will keep you inside, to help you think about things—alone. Do I make myself clear?"

I nod. And I thank God there's a bottle hiding under my bed.

Forty-One

The words blur before me while Sissy knocks on the door around bedtime. "Mama, please. Come out."

I set the book down and wobble toward her voice. "I can't. Your father locked me in. Where is he?"

"I don't know, Mama. He left. I'm scared."

"Is Jed there?"

"He's in the shed out back rummaging around looking for a key or something to break the lock."

Thank God. "Sissy, go ahead and color for awhile, okay? Or work a puzzle. Keep Clementine near. Jed will figure this out."

"Your voice sounds funny."

I clear my throat, hoping to steady the quaver in my voice. When the liquid warms me, it's hard to control the slurring. "I feel a little sick," I tell her.

"I'm sorry. Do you want me to shove some aspirin under the door?"

Knowing a headache will come, I tell her yes. She scurries away, returning quickly. Two white pills roll under the door. I down them with the last of my drink.

"What about the windows, Mama?" Her voice is full of worry, I can hear it.

"Baby, you know they're painted shut in this room."

"Can't you un-stick them?"

"I've tried. The only thing I can do is wait for your brother. You sit tight. It'll be just fine. I'm right here."

Beneath me a small hand slips underneath the doorway. I touch the fingers, marvel at how innocent they seem. How could such an angel sprout from Hap and me? I bend to the ground and kiss each finger. "Don't worry, okay? Everything will work out."

The fingers slip away as quickly as they came. I hear Sissy leave the hallway, listen to the click of Clementine's nails on the hardwoods. She will be fine. I have to believe that.

I return to Sheba's book. The chapter I'm reading is toward the end. I read slowly now. You might call me superstitious, but if I finish it, I worry I'll face further heartache and disappointment. Because when a person reaches the end of a book that's supposed to help and everything remains the same as before, despair crowds in. I've let Despair live in me before. He's not good company.

While Sissy colors and Jed plots my release, I read the chapter entitled "The Formula for a Perfect Marriage."

As one who floundered in the early years of marriage, I want to spare all of you the pain I experienced. I didn't know then that there was a simple formula to make my marriage great. It's a secret formula that so few know, and I'm going to share it with you. It's simple because performing the formula doesn't take intellect, charm, or beauty. It's wholly related to your ability to simply obey and trust. Remember the words of the hymn? "Trust and obey, for there's no better way — to be happy in Jesus is to trust and obey." I would contend that trusting and obeying makes us happy in marriage as well. So here's the formula. Come close while I whisper it to you. Are you near? Good.

First I need you to read a passage of Scripture to set

the foundation for the formula: "Ye have heard that it hath been said, An eye for an eye, and a tooth for a tooth: But I say unto you, That ye resist not evil: but whosoever shall smite thee on thy right cheek, turn to him the other also. And if any man will sue thee at the law, and take away thy coat, let him have thy cloke also. And whosoever shall compel thee to go a mile, go with him twain. Give to him that asketh thee, and from him that would borrow of thee turn not thou away. Ye have heard that it hath been said, Thou shalt love thy neighbour, and hate thine enemy. But I say unto you, Love your enemies, bless them that curse you, do good to them that hate you, and pray for them which despitefully use you, and persecute you; That ye may be the children of your Father which is in heaven: for he maketh his sun to rise on the evil and on the good, and sendeth rain on the just and on the unjust. For if ye love them which love you, what reward have ye? Do not even the publicans the same? And if ye salute your brethren only, what do ye more than others? do not even the publicans so? Be ye therefore perfect, even as your Father which is in heaven is perfect."

I place the book on my lap like an old woman's covering. I let the words play through my mind. Turn the cheek. Walk another mile. All things Sheba's written before. Is this what Jesus calls me to do? To live a life of subservient fear, waiting for ethereal rewards? Heavens, how will I do it? I open the book again, reading where my finger left off.

After reading this passage, think about those times of harmony in your marriage. When were things good? And what were you doing to make them such? Before you turn the page to discover the secret formula, I'd like you to write your own in the blank below. What makes a happy marriage in your estimation?

In the blank is this: _____ + _____
= a happy marriage

I take out a pen, but then think better of it. I want my answer to match hers. If I'm wrong, at least I can correct myself by erasing. I take a pencil and write in:

Hap's guilt over hitting me + *my perfection* = a happy marriage.

The house is calm when I'm doing everything the way he wants it (mostly). But it's really calm when Hap feels guilt over harming me. In fact, tomorrow, once he sets me free, there will be that un-mistaking sorrow in his eyes. That regret. It'll buy several days of peace. Yes, this is what makes a happy marriage—which means I do what Jesus said and give him my other cheek to hit. I turn the page.

The secret to a happy marriage is:

joyful obedience + servanthood = a BLISSFUL marriage

Why joyful obedience? No one likes to be obeyed from duty. It's your gift to your husband to smile when you fold his socks neatly. He will see more beauty in you when you laugh your way through dishes, diapers, and drudgery. But it's more than that. Not merely obeying with a happy countenance, but seeking ways to serve him when he least expects it. Throwing his towel in the dryer while he showers, and then presenting it toasty warm when he gets out is a prime example of this. Or choosing to have marital relations with him any time he asks for it, and even when he doesn't. Or perfecting several recipes his mother cooked for him. Or polishing his shoes. You will set your husband free to love you when you lavish him with service like this.

I close the book, choosing not to rewrite my formula—it's more realistic. Do you think I will set Hap free by taking my

service to another level? How can I do that when I'm imprisoned in my bedroom?

My head whirs, begging for more drink, but the bottle is empty. I slip onto the floor, my knees aching when they meet it. I am lost. Alone. Cut off. I fold my hands, whisper my voice. "Lord, I can't do this. I'm incapable of Sheba's formula. You'll have to help me. I can't see the angel in the stone. Hap looks more like a monster to me. And the more I try to set the angel free, the more his talons emerge. I'm at a loss now. Show me the way. And if you do, I promise I'll get baptized, promise I'll overcome my fear of the lake for your sake. Protect my children outside the door. And help me to know how to be. I'm losing me. I'm losing me."

I say amen, wondering if the Lord hears, or if he's too busy dealing with poverty and war to pay attention to our microcosm of the same. When I stand, the door unlocks. An angel stands at the door, tears running down his chiseled face.

Forty-Two

I'm sorry," Hap says.

"Where were you?"

"Having it out with the Lord. He told me to come back here and make things right."

So is God on my side, then? Could it be that my prayer changed Hap? That it made God move a magic kindness lever inside my husband? After a few seconds tick by, I tell Hap thank you. He pulls me to himself, but I don't smell him. I smell perfume. And it's not mine. I jerk away, arguing in my head whether I should start climbing this mountain or let it be. Seeing his eyes wet makes me turn the other way. Sometimes it's better to stay in the flatlands of safety than to trudge on the hills of confrontation. At least that's how I see it right now, held by too-strong arms. A violent rapping at the front door interrupts us. Hap moves away, alarm in his eyes. He walks down the hallway. I follow. Through the living room window a patrol car's lights strobe silently.

Hap faces me. "Did you call the police?"

"How could I? There's no phone in the room."

"Did you tell anyone to?"

"No!" I wonder where Jed is. Sissy too. But Hap must wonder the same things. He crashes through the house while the knocking continues. I tell myself to calm down, to relax, to be the epitome of decorum. I'm thankful I wear a turtleneck to conceal my bruising.

"It's Officer Spellman," I tell Hap.

"Open it, then," he hollers.

Officer Spellman moves into the house in a hurry, closing the door behind him. "Where's Hap?"

Before I can answer, Hap is standing behind me — my shadow.

"What can I do for you, Officer?" I hear fear behind his words, and I've seldom heard him refer to Hank Spellman as Officer. As the head of the elders and deacons, Hap ruled them all, kept his shoulders above them.

"A break." Officer Spellman motions for us to sit. We do.

"I'm not sure I understand." I hear Hap's fear. It occurs to me in the split second of silence that Hap actually does have fears — fears of exposure. I file this away.

"We found a lair."

Hap exhales. "You mean this is something in conjunction with Daisy's killer?"

"Of course. What else would it be?"

"Nothing," Hap says. "I just wanted to be clear."

I stand. "Would you like some coffee?" I smile as I say it, wondering if my hair is unkempt, my eyes red.

"That won't be necessary."

"What did you find?" Hap sits back on the couch, his arms stretched along the back of the couch.

"A trap door in the woods leading down to an earthen hideout."

I sit. My stomach's in full revulsion mode, topsy-turvying inside. "When?"

"Not long ago. We're taking in the door for fingerprints and making casts of footprints inside."

"You think it's the killer's hideout?" Hap bends forward, his elbows resting on his suit pants.

"We're pretty sure. We found children's shoes down there."

"Oh dear God," I say.

Jed enters the living room with Sissy on his tail. He gestures to Officer Spellman. "You found shoes? Where?" His voice no longer cracks—it is fully Hap's now—low and strong.

"In the woods to the west of the burnt down church."

"Did you find him?" Jed paces.

"No, but we're closer. It's a strong lead."

"How can we help?" Hap asks.

"You can all be on the alert for anything strange. I have a feeling the perpetrator knows we're on to him."

"Why?" I ask.

"Because when we flashed our light down the dirt stairs, the entire way was crisscrossed with what looked like spider webs. But as we got closer, we noticed the webbing wasn't natural. It was like someone had threaded a thin substance back and forth. If it was broken, he'd know. The top portion had been broken through, but the bottom remained intact."

I wonder if the webbing is on my pants, still balled in the bottom of the laundry bin. I never imagined Daisy's killer would go to such strange lengths. "But you found shoes."

"After a bit of debate, we decided it best to break through the little lines. At the bottom we found an eight by eight room with smooth walls and a few sacks of onions. And a few other things."

Jed kept pacing. "What other things?"

"That's sealed right now. I'm not even supposed to tell you this much. But knowing how much Reverend Pepper has taken an interest in the investigation for your sake, Jed, I thought it right to at least let you know." Officer Spellman rose, shook Hap's hand, then Jed's. He leveled a look at Sissy who stood in the corner with her arms wrapped around herself. "Please hear me. Daisy's killer is highly unstable. If you see anything out of the ordinary, or even if you feel afraid, you call me."

"Will do." Hap walked with Officer Spellman to his car. I watch them talk back and forth, as if Hap were a fellow officer. They laugh—something I don't understand given the news of the day.

"I want to see that lair," Jed says.

"No, Jed." Sissy grabs Jed's hand, pulls it to her cheek. "Don't go. You don't understand."

"Of all the folks roaming Defiance, Sissy, I think I know the most. Besides, Daisy was my friend. I left her alone for some maniac to find her and kill—"

"Jed, please," I say.

"Sorry Mama. I just feel like my world is stopped until we find out the truth. I can't stand just sitting around the house."

"I need you here. Sissy does too."

Jed sits on the couch with a thud. Dust swirls into the air. "Everyone needs me, but I'm not much help."

"You are. I need you."

Jed shrugs. "You didn't need me tonight."

"What are you talking about? I was locked in my room, waiting for your rescue. If Hap hadn't opened the door, I fully expect you would have. You're my hero, Jed."

"I'm not much of one."

Hap returns from his chat with Officer Spellman. He pats Sissy on the head. "I have a good feeling about this. We're getting close. In no time we'll have Daisy's killer behind bars."

"Excuse me," I say. I head to the bathroom. I kneel before the toilet while the water runs in the sink. I pull back my hair and empty my stomach. My footprints will be there where Daisy's killer stood. And then the questioning will follow. Like why didn't I tell anyone? And who do I suspect? And why have I kept it all to myself? Isn't there something about obstructing justice? I stay on the floor, letting the cold linoleum ground me, steady me. But it only makes me shake.

All the prayers that come to mind, I throw away. Every ounce of confusion baffles me, torments my thoughts. What kind of woman am I? What kind of mother? I pinch my stomach skin, twisting the flesh between my fingers until I nearly cry out. Yes, I am alive. In this panicky moment, I feel pain.

She found his lair; he saw that. Then the cops found the dugout with its collection of shoes—even the sandals. He knew they wouldn't find him. The shoes were clean. And he'd raked over his footprints. But they would find her and start asking questions.

Later, her son Jed circled the lair, disappeared into its belly for more seconds than he could hold his breath. The man climbed down the tree, quiet-like, to stand above the hole and scare the daylights out of Jed, but stood back instead behind an ancient oak. Jed said Daisy's name into the canopy above, a halted cry, then ran in the direction of the burned down church.

He now saw her through the kitchen window. As his mind caressed the shape of her cheek, he knew his time separated from her was coming to a close. Soon she would be in his arms, wrapped around his heart. She would hear his words, pardon him, and then he'd disappear like a mist.

It would have to be soon.

Forty-Three

Jed is all angles and seriousness, thin, yet growing northward. We're sitting at the kitchen table, enjoying a Saturday.

Should I ask? Yes, I should. Because I need to know. "Have you looked—"

"Mama, I don't want to talk about Daisy. Or what Officer Spellman found. Or what I found."

"You found something?" I pull a cracked teacup to my lips, grimacing down the tepid liquid.

He stands. Hovers over me. And then leaves the kitchen, the sound of his sneakers squeaking down the hall. I sigh Jed's sudden absence, but the sun coerces me outside as if it knows I need the wide world beyond my home.

Two weeks I've passed alone at home—full of my own empty thoughts, my mountainous worries. The spring heralds itself by welcoming nubile sprouts in my secret garden. Little stems of hollyhock emerge from the earth. I touch my strange prayer bracelet, hoping and praying that both children will somehow understand. Throwing my marriage up to the heavens in hopes of something better. Begging God to save me, to give me life beyond the dried chicken bone I finger. Asking God to show me that he sees me here, doing the best I can. I am an empty little box, full of nothing but fear and sadness and guilt. *Give me love, Jesus. Real love. And help me to sacrifice my fear of water to be baptized. To finally give you my life.*

I slake my worry by dirtying my nails, by wooing seedlings, by beckoning Ethrea Ree's rooted rose bush to stretch to the sun. It's my place of refuge, this yard. My little cathedral. Clementine sits beside me, alert. I stroke her head, tell her, "Good girl."

She growls in response.

I look behind me to the woods. I catch a glimpse of someone high in the trees.

Seeing him there in that hesitant moment, the ridiculous house of cards I've mortared collapses as it should. If I pull away the sleeve of the man I'm convinced took Daisy, will I find a tattoo, or canvas-white flesh? I need to know. Have to.

The man disappears in a flicker, but I hear the rustling of underbrush through the woods. Without dusting off, I burst through our back gate, sprinting in the direction of his trajectory, hollering at Clementine to stay. My chest hurts in the effort, but I don't care. I shout, "You better just leave. They're looking for you." But my words are answered back by the lone caw of a distant crow. I am in the midst of the woods now, not far from Jed and Daisy's sky chapel—the place they built their friendship. I bend forward, placing my hands on my knees, hoping to breathe in enough air to rejuvenate me. I pant instead.

The ground rustles again to my right, so I take off, this time at a walk. You would think I would be full of terror-thoughts, but I am not afraid. Just resolute. It's time to pull off the sleeves of this mystery, to find out once and for all if my theory's correct.

A branch cracks underfoot. Another distant caw answers. I catch another glimpse, see a muscled arm. I want to make chase, but my age has caught up with my verve, and my bravery is like water poured onto the ground. Suddenly I feel alone, lost, confused. Did the arm have a tattoo scrawled? I couldn't tell. I turn around and around in the woods, saying nothing. Dread seeps into me. I cannot see the sun here. I wish Clementine, for once, had disobeyed me and followed suit. But I am completely alone.

With Hap, my fear has dried up. Maybe because I know him. I can predict his responses. Sure, he's gone overboard at times, but at least when I see anger fill his eyes, I know to duck. But out here in the silent, cool woods, under the shade of a too-thick canopy of newly leafing trees, I have no such anticipation. And the silence only prolongs my worry. I should walk home, but which way is that? I turn again, seeing the same trees, the same stickered underbrush, the same decay of last winter's leaves at my feet. I tell myself to think of the garden, to remember what I've read about the beauty of the forest floor—how the decay of leaves feeds the soil, makes it rich with tilth. I concoct a little scheme—determining to return with a large garbage bag to fill so I can "hide" my hollyhocks a little longer and provide some nutrients too. Yes, that will do.

Someone grabs me from behind, a strong hand over my mouth and nose.

"You think you know," a muffled voice says.

I squirm beneath his arm, trying to maneuver my way around to see his face, but lack of air won't allow for much effort, and his hand has me pinned to himself. I only can see trees—and even if I screamed, they'd not offer their branches in rescue.

"Tell your son to stop poking around."

So Jed did look.

A wind swirls around us, picking up leaves from the earth and sending them helter-skelter around us. And still I need oxygen. I try to elbow the man, but he laughs—an indistinct sound, more like hyena than human. The world of flying leaves and bending trees tilts around me. I see the darkness at the edges of my peripheral vision close in on me. The light in the middle lessens the more I struggle, morphing into the tiniest pinprick. My legs jelly beneath me, but I am still upright because he holds me suspended above the earth, my shoes dragging through the leaves I meant to steal.

The angels sing their songs again. Warmth surrounds me.

I am in a garden ablaze with hollyhocks of every color, colors I've never seen. They aren't biennials here, bound by the laws of earth. They just bloom. I am running free in that garden, smelling roses and peonies and stephanotis. I tell that garden world I can't stay long, that I need to get back to my kids. I finger my bracelet, an anchor to my other world. But the world I'm in seems more real than the metal figures on my bracelet. More alive than the chicken neck. More complete than the eyelet. More dimensional than the little box. I lay down in the field, feeling the sun, but not seeing one in the sky. I try to hold the bracelet, but I can't find it now, can't feel much of anything but sheer joy. I can live in this land. I can be happy here.

Finally.

A cold rush of wind and a sudden burst of light slaps me back to Defiance. I am laying on my back, staring at the swaying branches while Clementine licks my face awake. I reach for my bracelet, but it's gone.

Forty-Four

I am slow to my feet. A headache threatening to unleash its anger throbs through my head. Clementine barks at me, grabs my pants and pulls at me. I shake my head of the memories—the beautiful garden, the smell of the man's strong hand, the way his voice marbled through me. With Clementine on alert, I have little time to evaluate such things. She pulls me, and I follow. I stumble through the brambles, allowing the thorns to cut through my pants. I don't cry out in pain; I simply plod, my feet a slow drum rhythm hitting the earth.

The smell of rain comes first—that dewy, nearly wet shiver in the air. And then it plops wet through the canopy of trees. It's probably mist-like as it hits the top, only to regroup in the branches and dollop itself on Clementine's fur and my aching head. The ground beneath us muddies slowly, making our journey slick. Still, Clementine beckons. Sometimes she whimpers like she detects evil behind every bush, every climbing vine. And I obey her murmurs of encouragement.

I stop for a moment, to recapture my senses, and realize Clementine and I are standing dead-center in Jed and Daisy's sky chapel. The trees have broken open here, so the drops have become mist again, wetting my face, dampening my hair instead of pelting. I know where I am. If we take off east, we'll run into the ruins of Crooked Creek Church where Hixon died. And

directly south is my home. I sigh, "Dear God, get us home." Clementine cocks her head as if she's listening. She barks, then trots southward, obeying my prayer.

No one is home when I open the back door, with Sissy at a friend's, Jed who-knows-where, and Hap preparing his sermon at church. I tell Clementine to stay in the kitchen, otherwise she'll muddy the entire house. She sulks, but listens. I walk to my bathroom, take off my shoes and socks, not bothering to remove my wet clothes. I turn on hot water and step in, waiting for the warmth to seep through my clothes. Earth and leaves dirty the bottom of the tub, eddying at my feet. For a moment, I wonder if this shower could become my baptism. I am wet, right? And filth is being washed away. I'll be clothed in "clean" clothes as I exit. But as I decide this, the Voice says "No."

With the water warming me to the core, I am surprised when tears come. They are warm too, bursting from a place inside me I seldom allow a channel. I am on my knees, bent under their weight, weeping my grief. My mama used to say grief was for those left behind when a person died, but I'm not grieving simple death. I'm weeping over my life, how empty it is, how little it matters, what sacrifices I've made that meant nothing. I'm crying my fear, realizing the man in the woods would've taken me. I'm shedding one thousand tears for my marriage, how much I've failed to be the right wife. The world collapses on top of me in this shower, my own baptism of sadness. I sit in the tub while the water stings my face, hoping someday I'll feel alive again.

But the water cools, and I shiver under its touch. The time for warm tears passes. I turn off the water. It drips from me in a hesitant chorus. I step out of the shower, pulling a towel around me, but it cannot contain my shivers. Instead I'm left with undoing my stupid decision to shower fully clothed. Agonizing pull by agonizing pull, I free myself from pants, shirt, bra, underwear. The threadbare towel is no comfort. Nothing is. So I let it drop to the ground. I open the door to my bedroom, dripping wet.

And there, standing in front of me is Hap in his three-piece suit.

Forty-Five

"Well, what do we have here?" He wears amusement on his face, but it doesn't seem to fit.

"I took a shower."

"At the end of the day? Why?"

"I took Clementine for a walk and it started raining."

"So I saw. Clementine's quite muddy, wouldn't you say?"

"She wanted to go into the woods." It was the truth, after all.

He throws a fist my way, but I duck. I back away into the bathroom, reach for the towel near my feet, and cover up.

"What kind of brain do you have, Ouisie? One like Delmer's?"

I almost agree, but he interrupts.

"You were there when Officer Spellman issued his warning. Or was I just dreaming it?"

"You're right. I was there." I hope he won't notice the wet clothes at my feet, but then again, when does he take stock of laundry?

"I am charged by God to be your protector."

I think Clementine's doing a much better job, I want to say.

"And as your protector, I've forbidden you to leave the home without me."

"You've forbidden me."

"Don't be snappy with me. It's for your own good. For your sake. And when I come home from sermon prep and hear the shower running and running, letting our water bill explode, I get angry."

"I'm sorry," I say.

"You don't sound like it. Sheesh, Ouisie, do I need to send someone here to babysit you? To make sure you don't run off into the woods. You could've been hurt!" He moves closer to me.

I back up, but the sink counter stops me. I am pinned.

He puts a hand on my cheek, caresses it like he would his car. "You know it's only because I love you. I worry about you. I want you to be safe and sound."

I nod.

He places his right hand around my neck, pulls my lips to his, and kisses me fiercely. I taste his toothpaste. He kisses me so long I can barely breathe. In the season of his kiss, I am back in the woods, a firm hand over my mouth and nose. In both cases I cannot breathe. And I can't decide which is worse — the strong-handed man or the hungry lips of my husband.

He lets go of me, pushes me from him. His face registers the same disgust when he finds me cowering under a headache. He slaps me, open-handed. "You've been with another man," he says.

Forty-Six

Hap's calling to be a preacher and his first accusation of infidelity started the same season he fixed our new-to-us home, though it's taken me some time to trace it back there. I used to blame it all on Bible school, but in retrospect it all becomes clear.

He built our creamy yellow cabinets from pine out back, skill-sawing on a makeshift work bench. I brought him lemonade in the hot, hot summer sun. My belly bulged with hopes of Jed safely tucked inside. Hap knew he'd be a boy, already named him.

He patted my belly, a twinkle in his eye. "How's my Jed doing today?"

"Well, he's fine, but I'm hot, and my back is killing me."

He took a thirsty drink of lemonade, then handed the glass back to me. I slid it against my face, relishing the coolness, while my sweat and the glass's perspiration mingled and warmed.

"You make a fine glass of lemonade," he said.

I turned to leave, but he stopped me with his hand—a "don't go" request. "I can't help but think there's more to this life, honey."

"Than what?"

He motions for the shade, a command I quickly obey. I sit in a rickety lawn chair. He leans against the tree trunk. We face the woods, away from our home-in-the-works.

"Than sawing wood, mending things, and making furniture."

"But you're gifted. And so many people here appreciate you."

"But a man's got to go beyond hammering and fixing—there's got to be more. Adventure. Purpose. If I do this the rest of my life, I may end up dwarfing into the mundane."

"Those are pretty high words, Hap Pepper."

He smiled, then brushed the sweat from his face. "I read them today in a book. It's helped me change gears, so to speak. To think on things. To reevaluate my life."

"You're not old. You have your entire life ahead of you. Why are you thinking of this now?"

He ran one rough hand against the trunk. With the other he gestured. "Because I don't want to end up like my father."

"Your father was a confused man. He took his life. I doubt you'll ever do that."

"I have his genetics, Ouisie."

I waited a moment, collected my thoughts. "But not his constitution."

"Maybe so. But I do know this, he wasn't happy when he took his life, and I'm not happy right now."

I touched my belly. Jed kicked back, as if he were kicking against Hap's surprising words. If I could've been so bold...

"I mean, I like you, and I'm happy about being a father, but my job. It's—"

"You like me? What ever happened to love?"

He shook his head, ran his hand over his mouth, then stared at me like I was a bearded lady in a freak show. "Of course I love you. Wrong word—sorry."

Jed kicked again. I shushed him by stroking my belly. "What's wrong with your job? You just built up a good clientele. We're getting steady income now. And it supports our dream of living in a home of our own. I guess I don't get it." I was so thirsty, I was tempted to lick the glass Hap had returned, but I told myself to wait out my thirst.

Hap squatted so he was eye-level with me. "Building things is not meaningful."

"Since when?" I always thought he loved working with his hands, creating something useful and beautiful out of two by fours and joists. How could I not have known his unhappiness?

"Since forever. I know this is going to sound like it's coming from nowhere, but I don't think I'm supposed to fix things the rest of my life. I'm supposed to fix people."

"You want to be a doctor?"

He sat on the grass, massaged my water-retaining ankles. "No. A preacher."

I stood, freeing my needy ankles from his grip. "A preacher? What for?"

"You're a God-fearing woman, Ouisie. What do you mean, *What for?*"

"I know why folks preach, Hap. But why would you change careers right now — when your baby's kicking around inside me? We've got bills to pay. It's hardly the time for a cockamamie dream." My voice squawked — there's just no other way to describe it.

"Since when did you use the word cockamamie?"

"David's favorite word," I said before thinking. I covered my mouth with my left hand, wishing I hadn't let those three words fly.

Hap grabbed my shoulders.

"Wrong word." I repeat his words back to him, hoping for the same grace I granted him. "I should've put 'step dad' before his name. I mean David my step dad. Not the other David."

He vice-gripped my shoulders in carpenter hands. "Wrong words? Are you sure you didn't let something slip out you shouldn't have?"

"You know for yourself how awful my step dad was."

"That's not who we're talking about and you know it."

"Hap, that was years ago, way before we — "

"That's what I worry about. You know how I feel about him. How you felt about him."

"Felt is the appropriate word." Jed kicks me again. Like he wants out. I want out too.

"You been hanging around with him?"

"No," I told him. "You're hurting me."

He released his grip, then looked at my belly. "It's my baby, isn't it?"

"Of course."

He turned away, walked toward the back fence, gave it a kick. It bent beneath his boot, but didn't break. He paced toward me, something in his eyes I couldn't read. So I decided to calm him, reassure him. "I love you. I chose you—not David. Remember that."

He stepped back from me. "The Good Lord's given me charge over you and the children he blesses us with. It's our family I'm to cherish. So I ask you kindly not to ever mention David again."

"But—"

"Promise?"

Jed settled inside me then, seemingly thankful the tension passed. "I promise," I told him, but a snake of fear slithered its way into our marriage that day, eventually morphing from garter to rat snake to water moccasin. Hap's jealousy and paranoia began when one name carelessly slipped from my lips. Stupid, stupid me.

"I hope you know I'll take care of you."

I nodded.

"I'll go to Bible school after we've saved enough. And then I'll be a preacher. I'll fix folks' problems, mend their issues, heal their relationships, and prevent them from destroying themselves. It's God's will, Ouisie."

I walked away with God's will rumbling through me—more like a death sentence than a shred of hope. And I felt guilty for such thoughts. A preacher's wife was many women's dream! But somehow I knew even then that a preacher's life would change my husband. He'd become as hard as the pulpit he pounded.

God, I was right even then.

He wandered Defiance replaying his first and last meeting with Sissy Pepper, how chance had happened him upon her in her daddy's big Chevy. It wasn't hard to lift the small thing, wasn't difficult to pull her closer to his lair in the middle of the woods. But she fought him every step of the way, her will to live as strong as Daisy Marie Chance's and her eyes as wide and crystal clear as her mother's.

But when the waif child lisped, "Please, sir," it startled him. She took off in the hesitant moment between her lisp and his paralysis. He followed her, but stopped when he saw her refuge—a thorn-pricked rosebush he dared not enter. For a moment, he nearly did. But he held himself back knowing what particular thorns were capable of.

He watched as she ghosted her way to Jed, hoping he hadn't been seen.

Forty-Seven

"Why does he accuse you like that?" Emory places a cold compress against my cheek Sunday morning while my children and husband play church.

"I deserve it, I guess." I look out the front window, noting Emory's car there. We don't have long before they all come home.

"Don't say that."

"Why not? It's true."

She sits across from me on our blue-flowered chair. It was my mama's once. Next to the chair on a side table sits Mama's Bible. Emory picks it up. "I keep reading Bibles," she tells me. "Everywhere I go. In the doctor's office. At Little Myrtle's, since Big Earl has ten or so stashed around the restaurant to 'fill his soul' as he works. If I'm not careful, I'll turn into Hixon, only I'll never be as tan."

I laugh despite my aching face. The sun angles its light onto Emory's smile. Her hardness seems smoothed over somehow in that light. "You seem happy," I tell her.

"Well, I'm irked you're not getting to a safe place, if you want to know what's what. But I am happy for other reasons."

"I told you before. Hap's pretty much mostly talk."

"Pretty much mostly. And that's why your cheek is bruised? Cut to it, Ouisie. I'm not as stupid as I look."

"You don't look stupid."

"Quit changing the subject."

"Do you want some tea?"

Emory laughs. "No, I don't want tea. What I do want is for you to listen to me and obey."

"You sound like God. Or Hap."

"I'd make a poor deity, an even worse Hap. Don't put either on me." She pulls her hair back and slips it into a knot at the back of her head. "Just promise me you'll consider a plan."

I cross my heart. "I promise." I lift one hand and two fingers, Jed's scouting pledge.

"All right, now I'm going to change the subject." She flips to the beginning of Mama's Bible, runs her fingers along one page, then another, pokes a particular place, then opens it midway. "I read this and it's freaking me out—in a good way. It's from P-Salms 30."

"P-Salms?" I smile. "It's pronounced Salms."

"Don't rub my ignorance in. This is pretty new to me, you know. I mean I went to Sunday school and all, but I can't remember much of anything. So I'm coming to this Bible stuff with virgin eyes."

"I'm sorry. Go ahead. Psalms 30."

"It's from verse ten until the very end. 'Hear, O LORD, and have mercy upon me: LORD, be thou my helper. Thou hast turned for me my mourning into dancing: thou hast put off my sackcloth, and girded me with gladness; to the end that my glory may sing praise to thee, and not be silent. O LORD my God, I will give thanks unto thee for ever.' Isn't that beautiful?"

"It is."

"I mean I don't necessarily relish the thees and thous and all, and what is a sackcloth?"

"It's something you wear, I think, when you're mourning."

Emory points to her ripped up jeans. "Like these? Am I wearing my own sackcloth?"

"I guess you could say that."

"Here's the thing." She sets the Bible back down and stands. "I've been dancing lately, just like this P-Salm says. Like this."

She gets to her feet, then twirls and jumps and kicks her legs in the air, dancing more like Big Bird than a ballerina. But at least she's exuberant. I worry that Hap will somehow let out church early and pull in any minute, take one look at Crazy Emory's dance, and tighten his restrictions on me even more. But Emory doesn't pay any mind to my unspoken worry. She shifts and jaunts and sweats and laughs, finally plopping on the floor, her hands resting on her knees. "Like that," she says.

"I don't think you'll be on American Bandstand any time soon."

"I don't suppose I will." Her cheeks flush rose.

"But I'm glad you're dancing."

"We'll dance together, someday, you and me. But first I need to ask you something."

I lean forward. "What?"

"What's baptism good for?"

I sit back on the couch, steadying my heart. This is the one thing the Voice demands of me, requires of me, but I can't seem to say yes to it. And here Emory comes, practically a pagan, asking me about it. I can never escape. "Jesus was baptized," I finally say.

"I know that. By that John guy with the funky clothes and terrible diet."

"John the Baptist."

"Yeah, him."

"But why? What does water do?"

Other than drown you? Hard to tell. "It's a ceremony Christians undertake to show they've turned from a life of sin to a life of obedience to Christ." I puppet Hap's pulpit words verbatim.

"But I don't get it. Why do you need to get wet and then come out of the water? It sounds like a dunk tank at the fair, except that God is throwing the baseball, I suppose." She shoots her legs straight out in front of her, then touches her toes. I can't remember the last time I did that.

"The water symbolizes cleansing from your old life. It means you've decided to die to that life." Hap's words again. "And coming out of the water shows that you identify with Jesus' resurrection. And that you have a new life."

She twirls her hair in her fingers, saying nothing. Then she pulls her knees to her chest and hugs herself. "That's so beautiful. I want that."

"Baptism?" Did my voice just croak that word?

"Yes. Do you think I could do it in my bathtub?"

"By yourself?"

"Sure, why not?"

"You can't baptize yourself in your bathtub."

"That water's the same water that funnels through Lake Pisgah. I don't see why that would make any difference."

"It would make a difference, believe me."

"But it's no different than those fancy tubs they use at churches, right? They're just glorified bathtubs."

I shake my head of Emory's crazy ideas. "It doesn't matter. You have to have someone baptize you. Those are the rules." I am thankful for Emory—that she wants to do such a beautiful thing.

"But who would baptize me? It can't be Hap, for any number of reasons."

"What about Big Earl?" She can do this on her own, with my support of course.

"Can you picture Big Earl dunking me in Lake Pisgah? I don't think he's up for that. Besides, call it a girl's intuition, but I think it's supposed to be someone else—like you."

"Me? You can't have a woman baptize you!" I stand and pace in front of her, stepping over her feet.

"Why not?"

"Because it's just not done. Men baptize. Preach too."

"That doesn't seem right." She sticks her right foot out. I nearly trip.

"It's right. I don't know exactly why, but it is. You have to think of another man." And as those words leave my mouth, I think of Elijah, remember him asking me to keep him secret. But inside, I've pressed down my anxiety, wondering if I'm crazy, and I've somehow made him up. If he meets Emory— "I may know someone else."

"Who?"

In this moment, I realize Elijah's been my own secret, my own imaginary friend. Only he's not imaginary, right? You've seen him. You've heard him. He's something I've cherished in a strange, delicious way. It's time to let him out, to introduce him. "This man I've met—a prophet, he calls himself. Like Hixon. His name's Elijah."

"You've met someone named Elijah?"

"He said God told him after Hixon died that he was to come to Defiance and be a prophet like him, kind of like a replacement."

She looks at me, her head cocked. "No one could replace Hixon. You know that."

"I know. He's not your typical preacher type. He's … strange."

"Sounds like it. Why haven't you told me about him before?"

I sigh. "I don't know. Just never did seem to be the right time."

"Well, I want to meet him."

I sit again on the couch. Cross my arms around myself like Emory. I look at Mama's empty chair, wishing she were here to field such strange questions and discussions. "Next time I see Elijah," I say, "I'll tell him you want to meet him. But I'm not sure he'd be interested in baptizing. He doesn't have a church. He doesn't even seem to have family. And I'm not entirely sure he's not homeless or a criminal."

I check my watch—nearly time for Hap and the kids to come revving into the driveway.

"You taking pills? You seem all twitchy and nervous."

"If Hap comes home from church and you're here—"

"Enough said." She pushes to her feet. "God, I wish Hixon were here. He would baptize me, I know. With a wide smile on his face."

I give her a hug. "He would've liked to see you get baptized," I say. "I know that would've been an answer to his prayers."

She pulls away. "The funny thing is, you're right. But I don't want to do this for him. Believe me, I've felt enough guilt about his death and how I treated him to want to follow every single thing that man said, just so he wouldn't bark his disappointment from heaven. But this baptism thing is different. I want to do this for God. Just for him." She pauses, her eyes wet. "You're going to think this sounds hokey, but I want to go under the water, and come back out to see God smile."

Her words, her simple devotion, steal my own. I wonder if I've ever said such things, or whether my life makes God smile. Hiding alcohol and sleeping away headaches would not make him smile, I don't think. Not much of anything I do would.

I walk Emory to her car. She pulls out and waves an eager hand my way. My limp-handed response cries out at me. There was a time I felt sorry for that girl, that I prayed for her soul, that I had no hope she'd ever recover from her choices. And now all I can think is this: I am jealous of such a woman. I want to make God smile too.

Later that afternoon while Sissy works on math problems and Jed plays music loud in his room, I pull out a pad of paper and a pen and write to Sheba. She has become my sounding board, and there's so much weaving through my mind that I need help to sort it out. Hopefully, she won't think me a nutcase for writing again.

Dear Sheba,

I'd like your opinion about baptism. My mother and father never stressed it, so I never "took the plunge," so to speak. And I'm sorry to say when Hap asked me whether I'd been submerged, I said a swift yes. But the truth is, I haven't been baptized. You'll think me a coward when I tell you I'm afraid of water. It's strange because I love looking at water. It calms me. And I'm one of those people who is constantly, terribly thirsty.

I put down the pen. Part of me wants to tell Sheba the famous author that it's not just water I'm thirsty for. It's liquor — in every possible form. I pick up the pen, shoving that craving way down deep, but it is with me, on the surface, taunting me to take just one sip. With nothing left stashed in the house, and no car to remedy the situation, I cannot slake that thirst. In a strange roundabout way, Hap's restrictions are freeing me from alcohol's grip. I wonder if this is what Sheba means about the benefits of submission. Hard to say.

So my question is: Should I be baptized?

I need to tell you something else. Tuesdays have turned out to be a surprising bright spot in my week. I didn't think I'd like teaching a Bible study, but now that Hap's no longer "training" me, I'm enjoying it. I love seeing the women's faces light up when they get something. You must thoroughly enjoy teaching, I imagine.

I have one last question. Do you think your husband had an exit plan? As you look back, can you figure out when he decided he would leave? And have you heard from him since we last corresponded? I ask because a friend of mine thinks I should create an exit plan for me and the kids. Just in case Hap gets violent again. But I think that might be copping out on trying to be a better wife. What do you think? Should I create an exit plan? Or is that evil?

I wish my efforts, as you've outlined in your book, consistently helped Hap to become better. Sometimes they work. Other times they're a miserable failure. (Or perhaps it's that I'm a miserable failure.) But I am trying. Really, really hard. I would like to think you'd be proud of me.

So, there's my life laid bare to you, printed as neatly as I can. It seems strange to have my words strung together like this, and it worries me to have them out there in the world in blue and white. But I trust you to keep my words to yourself. I'd imagine your publisher makes you take an oath like that, right?

Signed, Ouisie Pepper—an unbaptized,
exit-planning(?) wife who teaches a Bible study.

Forty-Eight

It isn't disobedience, I convince myself. Emory tells me she needs me to help clean up Hixon's old house. I need to be needed, except when Hap reaches a sweaty arm around me in the middle of the night and pulls me to himself, expecting me to do my wifely duty. I don't like that kind of neediness.

The day basks in warmth, thankfully, and I smell springtime. It always blesses me when God recycles the earth, rejuvenating it after a cold, dark winter. Of course I know it's colder and darker in the North, but having lived all my years in Texas, I still believe fifty degrees to be akin to frost. So seventy is heaven to me.

Emory slows when she nears her old house on Love Street. She pulls into the driveway of the once-white home.

"I can't believe the landlord painted it after all that Jed and Hixon did. It makes me feel like everything we do can be erased by some cosmic eraser."

"Tan doesn't look right on the house, does it?" I wonder why I've not noticed the change earlier.

"It looks dirty to me. I loved it pristine white, especially with it so near the rendering plant. Like a beacon on a hill, I suppose. The perfect contrast. But now it will blend right into the smell of rotting animals. Suits it, I suppose." She runs her hands along the steering wheel as if to caress it. "I wish it would've burned to the ground."

"Why?" I wonder if she means with her in it.

"So I wouldn't have the reminder of who I was."

I place my hand on hers, stopping her steering wheel rub which has now become an obsessive distraction. "Sometimes reminders are good."

Her eyes are bloodshot when she looks at me. "How can that be? You knew me then."

"And I know you now, which makes the transformation all the sweeter to me."

"But what about Daisy?"

"What about her?"

"I didn't do right by her."

I hear regret in those words, feel them inside me. They're the kind of words that blacken a person.

"I have dreams," she says.

"What kind of dreams?"

"Daisy dreams, where she comes back from heaven and tells me what I missed out on as a mama. She's not mad at me, not cross. She's matter of fact, which makes it even harder to endure."

"I'm sorry."

"So am I."

"If it's any consolation, know this: You're not alone. You share those feelings with every mama in the world, Emory. We all wake up at night worried about our past, our actions we can't take back, the words we wish we'd never said to our kids."

"It's not that, exactly" she says. "It's not that I necessarily regret what I did, although there's plenty of that to go around. I'm grieved for what I didn't do. Didn't read enough stories to Daisy. Didn't pay close attention when she skinned her knee. Didn't stoop low to her to catch a glimpse of her heart through her eyes. Didn't—" She puts her hands on her chest like she's trying to keep her heart from escaping. It doesn't, but her tears do—spilling their boundaries like Lake Pisgah after a flooding rain. "Oh God," she says over and over while tears torrent from the nooks and crannies of her grief.

I pray quietly. What else can I do? It would kill me to enter into her grief. Because I worry about this very thing. I see my children in caskets when I wake up in the middle of the night. See their hollow eyes. The stories I didn't read. The skinned knees I shrugged off. The eye contact I treated with nonchalance. These are my regrets, even though I have my children with me to remedy them.

We mothers share this grief, this worry, this grinding conscience that says we never do enough. Or that we never are enough.

She huffs in tears and air and sadness while my prayers seem to bounce off her car's roof.

"I wish I could remake the days," she says.

I want to tell her this is possible in an *It's a Wonderful Life* way. But death's grip on Daisy makes a redo impossible. She simply cannot undo what she's done. Can't love where she hasn't.

She continues her Oh Gods while I beg God to please show up in this display of grief. The Voice says, *Shoulder it.*

I try. I really try. But I have no platitudes. Just friendship. I hope that is enough.

The sun has grown taller since we've been here, taller than the pecan tree. It angles through my window, landing on Emory's burdened face. In a moment, she sniffs in her tears, blows her nose on a tissue from her purse, and folds her hands on her lap. "I know I can't go back," she says. "But I can learn. I can always learn."

"That's true."

She looks full-faced on the house where her life unraveled. "I am not who I was there. Not the same woman."

"That's right. You're not."

"Maybe me being different is my mark on this world. Maybe I'll make it up to God if I am perfect from here on out."

"That's not how grace operates," I tell her. Again, Hap's words. "You don't have to be perfect to make up for your past. No one can do that."

"Well, I aim to try."

Her voice is full of such determination that I decide to let silence be my answer. I have not grieved a child, have not lost Hixon in the same way she did. I cannot know, exactly, her grief. And, to be honest, I'm jealous of her verve. I know I've given up long ago trying to amend my life, at least from the inside. Though Hap's kept the house prohibition-safe, I still long for a touch of liquor to my lips, still think about it, pine for it. Emory makes determinations while I resign myself.

She revs the car, puts it in reverse and pulls out of her old driveway, leaving the now-tan house behind. Love Street whirs by while the opened windows glut us with springtime. Redbud trees welcome us along the road, their fiery purple blooms filtering through the air on a lazy breeze. At the stop sign, one blossom drifts into my window, landing on my lap. I hold it, turn it 360 degrees, marveling at its color, its lack of scent, its life.

"I love those trees," Emory says.

We turn on Hixon's street. It will always be his street, no matter who lives in his house after the sale. We park in front of his house, his tree, his porch. And as Emory turns off the engine, we sit, not bothering to move while the wind blows from Hixon's home through both opened windows toward Emory's old life on Love Street. The breeze seems to cleanse us both, settle us.

"Well, it's time we get to work."

She removes cleaning supplies from her trunk, then trudges them up the stairs while I haul a mop, broom, and bucket.

On the porch, I turn back to look at the street. "There will be a for sale sign in his lawn soon. How will that make you feel?"

She sets the caddy of supplies down and fiddles with some keys. "Sad. Just plain sad. You'll see. It may be a ramshackled

place, but he's in there, smelling up the place, reminding me of him."

"It's the smell, isn't it? I remember the scent of my mama's perfume so vividly that if I smell it at the grocery store, a whole flood of memories makes me tear up right then and there."

"You can smell him in this house. I have some of his shirts," she says. "That helps." She finds the key, tries it, but the lock won't budge. "That's strange."

"Maybe they've rekeyed the place."

"Maybe. There's another door out back. Let's try that."

We leave the supplies to decorate the front porch and make our way through the brambles of Hixon's yard. At the back door, she inserts the key. This time it works. "Odd," she says.

We smell it the moment we're inside. Coffee.

"What in the world?" Emory lifts Hixon's coffeepot, tethered to the outlet. "This has just been used. It's still warm." She points to a chipped coffee mug. "Someone's here,"

I scan the kitchen for other signs of intrusion, but I see nothing other than what Emory has found. And a trashcan with a bag full of trash. "Maybe we should leave."

"No!" She stomps through the living room, flings open the drapes. A sleeping bag is rolled out on the couch and the front door's deadbolt is engaged. She makes sure I see both.

"I'm calling the police."

"Just hold your horses a second." I spin around on my heels, feeling suddenly dizzy and sick. On the side table next to the couch are dozens of tiny little boxes. That's when I know exactly who's been here. "Elijah," I say.

"Elijah? How do you know?"

I point to the boxes. "He makes those. He's given me some."

She curses in that moment. "How dare he sack out in Hixon's place! What kind of man would do that?"

"A transient," I say. And that's what Elijah is. Nothing more. Nothing less. Perhaps I thought he was like Emory—that he needed me, so I needed him back. Maybe that's the story of my life, this neediness. Maybe it's time I stamp my own two feet down to the earth in declaration. And stop needing so much.

The man sat high, tracing over every line of the house. He noticed the gutters, leaves choking them. He saw the bare earth flanking the west side of the house, the nubile green stubs of something emerging from the ground—Ouisie Pepper's garden.

He climbed down the tree as quiet as a slithering snake, inched his way along the ground in case the neighbor could be watching. He crept low through the gate, past the wooden chair, the dormant picnic table, over the winter-dried lawn, until his nose and hands felt the sensation of his savior's dirt.

He brought the earth to his nose and whiffed. She touched this dirt, caressed it, sang songs over it, prayed it would give life. This was her essence, he believed. Just as God brought Adam from the dirt, then fashioned Eve from his flesh, he believed she, too, was made of man and grit and everything beautiful under the earth.

When he touched the unfurling fronds that defied infantry rows, he smiled. These soon-to-be flowers crouched like a scattered platoon—placed for the purpose of taking over this bed. He tugged at the highest sprout, uprooting it entirely. He brought the plant to the sun, let the light capture the roots still heavy with dirt. He swiftly pocketed the limp greenery.

He took the bracelet from his pocket and draped it across the stick of a rose bush, then returned the way he came, his heart toughened like leather in his chest. A noise to his right captured him—an enemy no doubt. He flattened himself on the forest floor while his heart drummed a war beat in his chest. If he stayed as still as death, the noise would walk on by. It always did.

Except that this time, it didn't.

Forty-Nine

I make dinner by rote. Butter into the pan, flour added until it becomes a paste. A cup or so of milk, a handful of cheddar. Salt and pepper. Then I strain the noodles, throwing them onto the cheesy sauce, stirring until macaroni and cheese announces itself. How many times have I created this dish?

My mind circles back to Elijah the transient. Does he have a home cooked meal? By now Emory has called the police station. And he's running somewhere new. Maybe he's camping under a tree. Hard to say.

Hap whistles his entrance, smelling like perfume again. Sissy and Jed sit at the table, but neither say a word. I spoon macaroni into bowls—no crust baked on top this time—then pull biscuits from the oven. They're the canned variety, but they'll do. I wish I had fruit to put out, but I haven't been to the store for some time. Hap never seems to be in the mood.

We bow our heads while Hap spills a rote prayer. We say Amen. Anyone looking from the outside would find us terribly mundane and pious.

"They've narrowed down the footprints," Hap says.

I give him a confused look.

"The police. Officer Spellman says they were unable to recover fingerprints on the door to the killer's lair, but they did make good casts of the shoe prints. A woman's. Size nine."

I tuck my size-nine feet under the chair. "And just how will they figure that one out?" I try to ask casually, but a quiver forms at the end my question. I pray Hap doesn't notice.

"I'm not sure."

Sissy swallows a bite. "They could do like Cinderella! And go to everyone in the town and check their shoe sizes."

Hap smiles. "That's not a half-bad idea, Sissy. Sometimes you do have some sense in you."

She looks at her bowl, sets her spoon down. She and I share a common distaste for finishing dinner, it seems.

"They're getting close, aren't they?" Jed asks.

"Seems so. I'll be glad when this whole thing is behind us and we can continue on with our lives."

Jed pushes away his food with such force that the bowl topples off the side of the table, spilling cheese all over the floor. He stands. "When will we put this behind us?" he finally says.

"Calm down, son."

I see the escalation beginning in Hap's eyes. Watch how his cheek twitches, his neck blushes.

Sissy ducks out of the room with Clementine on her heels. I hear her door shut. And lock.

"Why should I calm down? You never have to!"

Hap stands now. "How dare you talk to your father that way. I am the leader of this house, and I refuse to allow you to disrespect me."

Jed backs away.

I stand. I put a hand on Hap, hoping to settle the teakettle of anger that nearly whistles now. He pushes me away.

"Stop shoving Mama," Jed's arms are taut, his eyes full of fury.

In one smooth motion, Hap grabs Jed's right arm and twists it behind his back. He shoves Jed into the yellow wall, his cheek colliding with the plaster.

"You will respect me." His words are both command and ultimatum.

"Hap, please." My voice is small, too small to change the course of Hap's rage.

Jed spits blood between his teeth.

I try to pull Hap off my son, but he is too strong. He kicks me, sends me reeling into the spilled macaroni.

"I hate you," Jed says.

"What did you say?"

"Hate. I hate you. You can shove me, throw me, hurt me, try to kill me, but there's one thing you will never do."

He spits more blood while I try to stand on unsteady feet. "Jed, no."

"You will never make me respect you. Respect is earned, not granted. And you have done nothing to earn my respect."

In a moment, Hap lets go, moving his arms away in a strange surrender, sending Jed to the floor.

I expect Hap to kick him, to finish what he started, but he just stands there, heaving in anger. He looks at me. "I'm taking a drive." And he exits just like that, leaving behind a crumpled but triumphant Jed, macaroni-stained dishes, a cowering daughter behind a locked door, and a wife more surprised than when she found evidence of Elijah's presence at Hixon's.

Jed pulls to his feet. I offer him my hand, but he shrugs it off. "Someone's helping me find a place to stay. I'll be gone soon."

"Who?"

"It's better you not ask questions, Mama."

His words couldn't be more foolish — or painful. I try to grab him, to plead, to bring his eyes to mine, but he leaves in the same manner as Hap, only he sprints out the back door into the woods.

"You leave me be," he said to the boots near his face.

"I miss you," the familiar voice replied.

He hated to do it, but war and rumors of war demanded such tactics. He nabbed an ankle as he'd done to the sandaled girl and pulled, toppling the enemy like a felled pine. He checked eyes which rolled backward, felt the warm in and out of breath on the back of his hand. Alive. Caught foolishly off guard, yes. But alive.

He stepped over the body, then checked his flank for any observers. As usual, no one saw. Nothing out of the normal. He avoided his usual route through the woods to steer clear of the now-poisoned hideout.

Unseen again, he wandered through Defiance. If folks only knew to take account, they'd have found him and thrown him to the dogs before he spied Daisy alone in the church. But this town didn't see. Didn't care to see. Though he was as visible as the water tower at the town's west side.

He left the houses behind and hunched along ditches on the stretch of road leading away from Defiance. He felt safe from discovery in town, but not on the open road. Open places like that had proven disastrous in times past. He snuck up the incline toward the place where he choked Daisy's singing. He noted the still-open hole, where the earth yawned and took her to itself. He preferred to sprint the remainder of the way. He'd learned the importance of erratic steps, unpredictable moves. Both had concealed him this long.

Through an undetectable break in the trees, he edged through two indistinct pines, then turned abruptly right. He kept this trajectory for forty paces. The leaves crunched beneath his feet. Soon the familiar planks nailed one foot apart welcomed his feet and brought him to the sky. Perched in his tree house, he contemplated his next move.

She would be next, the woman who would free him.

Fifty

I sit at the edge of my bed, trying to wipe away restless sleep. Jed's sulking ways, his cold manner, keeps me up at night worrying. I do not want him living the transient's life at fourteen, but I can't seem to figure a way to hold him near. And every shred of my own neediness just thrusts him farther away. Will he be like a young Billy Grammer and leave Defiance for Vegas? He is fed up. Utterly fed up. I fear he's worn the mantle of protector for so many years that he's grieving a childhood lost. And no matter what I do—pray, beg, fuss, cook his favorite foods—he tastes freedom. Everything I offer is sawdust, nothing to tempt him to stay shackled to this house.

I hear Hap in the bathroom, hear the water flowing down the sink, smell his shaving cream. He slaps his face with cold water, now, so I brace myself for his entrance, his scrutiny.

"You look tired," he says.

"I'm fine."

He sits next to me. Puts a warm hand on the small of my back. He bows his head, so I do too. "Lord, wake up Ouisie so she can be the mom and wife I need her to be." He doesn't say amen. Instead he stands, a pastor smile on his face, as if to say, "There, aren't you better now?"

I tell him thanks and try to mean it.

After he leaves, I tell myself to get moving, to feed Jed and

Sissy, going through the motions of motherhood as my will breaks apart. Jed is silent—again. Sissy jabbers. Clementine follows her around the kitchen like she's queen, and Clementine is her royal cupbearer, only with a slobbery mouth. Knowing Sissy's troubles at school with teasing, I thank God for this canine friend. Toasty-O's make their way into three bowls. I place the jug of milk on the table, then pour orange juice into glasses.

Sissy makes a face. "I don't like pulp."

"I'm sorry, honey, but that's the kind we can afford."

"I hate chewing my orange juice," she whispers, but drinks it anyway, all the while keeping her grimace on straight.

Jed simply takes one teenaged gulp, then hammers down his cereal. He makes no eye contact with me, but I see a hint of sadness behind his stoic façade. Though his voice is deep now, I still hear the little boy who was always my hero, my champion, my pick-me-up. He's there, buried under anger and testosterone and a home situation I can't fix. He mutters a "Later" and heads out the kitchen to the front door. Sissy scrambles behind to catch up. Mayhem and scruffing and shuffling one minute, dead silence the next. I shiver as the door opens and closes. For the time being, I am my home's prisoner.

But it won't be long before Emory is here and I'm rescued for Bible study. Hap has somehow agreed to let her drive me to and fro, probably because he's tired of his punishment of me. Like grounding a child who's driving you crazy.

Within minutes of Jed and Sissy's slam-bang departure, I hear a car purring in the driveway—an odd thing, since Emory's an hour early. I pull back the front drapes to see Sheba stepping out of her car. She is wearing high heels, a pressed pink suit, and carrying a white purse. I am not sure what to do with such a woman, particularly today. But I open the front door anyway.

"Well, here I am!" She twirls on the porch, smiling. She reminds me of Fraulein Maria on *The Sound of Music*, how she opens her arms wide to the world. And her smile is just as wide.

"Yes, I see that."

"Well, aren't you going to invite me in? We've got just enough time to prepare."

"Prepare?"

"For your study. I've come to help you."

"All the way from Rowlett? This morning?"

"I had to wake up before the birds of course, but it was worth it seeing the pink sunrise over the horizon from my driver's side window. Pure pink on the left, dusky blue on the right, and all matters of pinkish blue in between. Stunning! And I'd have to say the sunrise actually matched my suit—a sure sign that God is in this."

She strings all these words together while she walks past me, through the door, and into the living room. She pauses briefly and says, "I like that flowery chair," referring to my mama's chair, then marches her high heeled self into my kitchen, sits down, asking for tea.

"I didn't expect you." I put the kettle on and take out my tin of tea bags. Only one left, thanks to Hap's distaste for shopping. We really need to get to the grocery store.

"I know that. God is a God of surprises. I just love following him because you just never know where in the world you'll end up. Like Defiance, Texas. No offense, but I think your mayor needs to rename the town. It's not a good name—so much like Eve's first sin that it makes me shudder inside. Why not Prudence, Texas? Or Patience, Texas?" She looks at the ceiling in rapt concentration. "No, Lord, that's not it. What is it? Yes, you're right." She looks at me. "It should be named Compliance, Texas."

While I know a watched pot never boils, I study the teakettle anyway. "My friend Emory will be by to pick me up."

"Nonsense. You call her and tell her you already have a ride, all righty?"

I dial the phone, wondering if I'm a puppet in Sheba's strange

theater, and she's pulling my strings in tangled directions. "Emory? It's Ouisie. I won't need a ride." I glance at Sheba. "No, I'm fine. I have a ride. Sheba, the author of the book we're studying is here and she'll take me. Yes, I know." The water boils, finally. I crook my neck against the receiver, then pour hot water into a clean cup, dropping in my last tea bag like an offering. "It'll be great," I tell Emory, willing myself to believe such a thing.

I hang up and hand Sheba her tea. She dunks it three times then rings it out, wrapping the teabag string around the spoon until the last bit of tea color drains from the bag. "You can reuse these, you know."

I smile. "Sure."

"Now, as far as I understand it, we're on chapter eight."

"We've actually been skipping around a bit." I sit next to her, realizing my cereal is still there—a drab bowl of Toasty-O's sans milk. I pour milk onto the cereal and force myself to eat in measured bites.

"Wouldn't you rather we pray before we partake?"

I can't answer with all the O's in my mouth.

She bows her head. "Dear Jesus, Lord of tea and cereal and Bible studies. Please show up today. Please speak through me. Touch Ouisie with your power and strength and joy. Thank you for providing this food. We serve you humbly. Amen."

"Thanks," I try to say, but my voice is liquid and my tongue is coated with cereal.

"It's not a problem. Praying is like breathing to me anyway. You'll hear me pray whenever and wherever and every cranny in between. At the grocery, folks think I'm crazy, but I'll be walking down the cleaning supply aisle and I can't help but burst out a 'Halleluiah! You made me spotless clean Jesus. Thank you for being my heavenly detergent.' Then I'll buy a bottle of Windex."

"I see." I take another bite of cereal, nearly wanting to pray, "Thank you God for Toasty O's, for giving me grain to eat, for

the way the O's float like tiny life preservers on a sea of milk."
Thinking the prayer is enough to make me smile.

"You're happier."

I look at Sheba, noticing the weariness in her eyes that contrasts strangely with her Pepto-pink suit. It's like she needs me to be happy.

"I wouldn't say that."

"But since you followed my advice about how to obey in secret, you've experienced the true joy of the Lord."

I swallow another bite, then finish Sissy's orange juice. The pulp tastes tinny, and I know little strings of orange now decorate my teeth. With Jed on my mind, Hap's tirades, the man in the woods, and Elijah's house-squatting, I can't help but spew it all. So I do. "I don't know what joy is," I tell her. "But I can tell you this. So far your method hasn't worked."

"Let me guess. It's gotten worse."

"Yeah, much worse. Hap's hurt me more, accused me more, besides the fact that he smells like someone else's perfume. My son wants to pack up and leave. I have a strange transient for a friend, and I'm worried about our safety. That doesn't seem much like God's great hand at work if you ask me."

"Oh, but it is." She rubs her hands together like she's plotting something.

"I guess I don't understand."

"The storm is always darker before it passes."

"Well, it seems my life's been one long storm. I don't know if I've seen the sun in years."

She drinks a sip of tea. "Do you have any sugar?"

I push our small cup of sugar toward her. There're only a few tablespoons left in the house. She unwraps her teabag from hugging the spoon, places it on a napkin, then shovels the remainder of my sugar into her cup. "God sweetens our lives in mysterious ways." She tips the cup toward me as if in salute, then drinks.

"Well, I've had enough of God's 'sweetness.'"

"Let me ask you this." She leans forward. I notice her perfect pink fingernails, how they match the glare of her suit and her lipstick-stained teeth. "Has God asked you to obey him in something and you have refused? Because what you're describing sounds like you're living in disobedience."

Baptism. Is she asking this because I mailed her my disobedience? I sit back. Surely he couldn't be punishing me for that, could he? Or is that how God is?

In my silence, she reaches across the table, places an icy hand over mine. The chill makes me shiver. "Honey," she says. "There's a time for everything in this world. A time for defiance and a time for compliance. Don't linger too long in the defiance or you'll risk his wrath. This is a word from God: It's time to comply, Ouisie."

My heart pounds my ribcage. I feel my pulse in my neck, throbbing all the way up to my temples. I haven't had headaches for a few weeks now, thanks to living Hap's personal prohibition. But now a headache is near. I close my eyes.

"He will press on you very hard, Ouisie, until you obey. He sent a big fish to swallow Jonah, remember? What will be your big fish? A failed marriage? Wayward kids? An adulterous heart?"

"Excuse me," I tell her. I leave Sheba to sip her tea and say her prayers to my yellow walls while I gather myself in my bedroom. The shades are mercifully drawn. I press my hands into my temples wondering how I will lead the study today, particularly with Sheba's help. I grab her book and my Bible. Without even thinking, I pray out loud. "Lord, you've gotta help me here. I can't do this without your help. And please, if this is you pestering me about baptism, would you make it clear? There are far too many voices right now, and my head's exploding just listening to them all." At my amen, I feel a tinge of peace settle into my chest, calming the thrumming. My head, though still on the edge of a full-blown headache, has tempered itself. Maybe throwing prayers into the air of my home is the way to manage after all. You learn to do all sorts of crazy things when you live my life.

I steady myself as I enter the kitchen.

Sheba stands, a pink crusader against the world, or maybe better put: *my* world. "I'm ready to take you to Bible study," she preens.

But is Bible study ready for her?

Fifty-One

Ethrea Ree sits in the circle first while Heloise, Emily, and even Flo gather like hens around newly thrown feed, squawking, pecking, fluttering around Sheba. I sit next to Ethrea, look at my watch, and hope the third of our oddball trinity arrives soon. I don't want to endure this study without Emory. The smell of coffee, the clank of mugs, and the unusual amount of banter serves as a strange backdrop to Ethrea's silence.

I bend near. "Is everything all right?"

"Delmer's getting paler and paler. Same as when his daddy passed. He won't eat, won't talk. That kid talks to squirrels and trees, but now he's mum to the world. I'm not sure what to do."

I nearly ask the question I've wanted to ask for Lord knows how long, but the gaggle of women flock around us, ruffling feathers and settling into their nests. I pat Ethrea's knee just so she knows I heard her.

With Sheba here, there are no empty chairs for Emory, so I find one more, dragging it across the floor and setting it up between me and Sheba, our apparent guest of honor. It's my little act of faith, my way of beckoning Emory here. The door opens. My heart quickens. But it's Hap who pushes through, not my friend.

Sheba stands. "This must be the Reverend Hapland Pepper," she says. "I'm thrilled to meet you. I've heard so many nice things about you!"

Nice things?

Hap crosses the room with a liquid gate I seldom see at home. He is all smiles and holiness and Christian piety. He's on his pastoral stage right now, performing perfectly. And most of his audience soaks him up. He extends his hand to the pink lady. "I don't think I've had the pleasure of meeting you."

He acts as if he doesn't know, but I've seen him examining the back of *The Godly Woman's Guide to Marriage*; he knows exactly who she is.

Sheba's face flushes. "I'm Sheba Nelson. I thought I'd pay this study a visit, let them ask me questions and all."

Hap smiles, feigns recollection. "Oh! You're the author of Ouisie's book! What a privilege it is to have you here. And what a surprise!" He sits in Emory's seat next to Sheba. "I think I'll sit in on this session, if you don't mind. It's not often a famous author comes to Defiance to grace us with her biblical wisdom. Do you mind?"

None of the ladies he can see seem to mind, except maybe Flo and Ethrea, but he doesn't nod their way.

"Great. Sheba, I'll let you proceed."

Sheba proceed? Last I checked, I was leading this study.

But Emily chimes in before I can choose my words. "Sheba, would you mind if we asked you questions instead of doing a portion of the book?"

Sheba does not mind. So they pepper her with questions, and she answers them with the ease that only comes through publication and public speaking. Every answer is articulated spot on, flawlessly argued, punctuated with a coral-lipped smile. Ethrea and I don't talk, but I consider playing tic-tac-toe with her.

As the hour winds down and I've counted every break in the wall plaster, every permanent stain on the awful linoleum-tiled floor—together a total of 89—the door flings wide. It's Emory, wild-haired. "Sorry I'm late," she says.

No one asks her what is wrong, why she looks the way she

does. So I leave my chair, and point to it. "Have a seat," I tell her. "We were just finishing up."

She flusters to the chair, opens her haggard Bible, and clears her throat. "I had a God encounter today," she says.

Flo leans forward. "What on earth does that mean?"

"Nothing, really, other than I prayed, and God answered."

"What happened?" Hap asks this question, feigns interest, it seems.

"My car broke down on the way. I barely got it off the road. Smoke poured out of the hood, and I worried the car might catch fire. So I did what I normally do. I panicked." With slender hands, she smoothes her ripped jeans. "But then I remembered Hixon, how he used to pray all the time, out loud sometimes, and I gave it a shot. I mean, what did I have to lose?"

"Other than your sanity," Emily says.

"As I was saying, I prayed. I asked God to please send some help. And wouldn't you know, but Big Earl drove by that very moment." She motions toward the other women. "For those of you who don't know me well, Big Earl's my boss at Little Myrtle's. Anyway, he opened the hood, tinkered with a few things, added fluid to my radiator, which he just happened to have in his trunk, and off I went. Isn't that amazing?"

Sheba pipes in. "That's the focus of this study, isn't it girls? That God answers our prayers—for our marriages, for our children, and even for mundane things like a car needing fixed." She stands, stoops, then shakes Emory's hand. "I'm Sheba," she says.

Emory looks at me, but I can't read her face.

"Sheba's been answering our questions," Emily says.

"Which reminds me," Sheba narrows a look my way. "I believe Ousie has a question, right? About submission?"

Hap laughs, then coughs it away.

"No," I say. "I think you've covered everything well. No need to open up a new topic."

But she doesn't seem to hear me. "Submission is God's gift a woman gives her husband."

Emily looks at Hap, then me. "I would imagine it would be easy to submit if my husband were a pastor."

"What does that have to do with anything?" Emory crosses one leg over the other, her hands on her knees, like a lady.

"Everything. It's hard if a husband isn't following God. This isn't my problem, of course, but I have friends who have this issue. Their husbands are heathens, demanding all sorts of things. But if a husband is following Jesus, leading a flock, it would be easy to submit." Emily sits back in her chair, closes her Bible as her way of saying amen.

"Husbands are a mystery. There's no telling what's really going on in their heads, let alone trying to obey their whims." Ethrea gathers up her things.

"Don't go," I say. But she's halfway across the room. She slams the door to the fellowship hall.

We sit in silence.

Emily speaks first. "It's good the Lord's weeding out the tares now."

Flo says, "I think she made a good point."

"You're weak. And gullible." Emily crosses her arms over her chest.

Hap smiles. "Let's remember to pray for Ethrea. She's obviously upset, which is why she took it out on innocent parishioners. In fact, why don't we pray now." He bows his head, settles himself. "Lord, help Ethrea to know when to speak, when to keep silent, and when to temper her words."

Is that a rebuke?

"Bless Sheba as she ministers to women around this great state. Help her to teach women submission and godly character. Walk before her. Grant her success. Amen."

Tears blur my eyes. Hap's morning prayer for me to basically behave makes me long for different prayers from his lips. Prayers like this. Prayers that show he loves me.

"Well," he says. "That about settles it, then. I best be getting to sermon preparation." He puts his hands on his knees, ready to stand.

"Wait!" Emory puts her hand in front of Hap like he's her child and she's braking too hard. "I have a question. From the Bible."

This is Hap's fodder, his expertise, so he settles back in his chair. "Of course. That's what I'm here for."

I shift uncomfortably on Ethrea's abandoned chair, wishing I could worry myself a hole in the ugly tiled floor, or that I could squeeze myself through the plaster cracks.

"Let's hear it," Hap says.

She rifles through the front of her Bible. "It's in James, but it's always hard for me to find. Here's the number. Page 1568." She turns there. "Hixon had this underlined. In the margin next to it, he wrote, 'Church should be a place where everyone's welcome. How a church greets the poorest of the poor is its definition of greatness.' Isn't that beautiful?"

Flo nods.

Emily Mohler rolls her eyes. "Just tell us the passage."

"It's James chapter two, verses one through four." She looks at me, then reads. "My brethren, have not the faith of our Lord Jesus Christ, the Lord of glory, with respect of persons. For if there come unto your assembly a man with a gold ring, in goodly apparel, and there come in also a poor man in vile raiment; And ye have respect to him that weareth the gay clothing, and say unto him, Sit thou here in a good place; and say to the poor, Stand thou there, or sit here under my footstool: Are ye not then partial in yourselves, and are become judges of evil thoughts?"

"That's simple," Hap says. "It means we're supposed to treat everyone the same and not show favorites."

As Emily and Heloise discuss the finer points of the verse while Sheba and Hap interject, I note Hap's tender prayer for Sheba, his critical prayer for Ethrea. I look at Hap's chair, how he took the place of honor next to the big-time author, how I stood to let Emory sit. It's not that I'm anyone to rally around—or pray tenderly for—but the way he treated Emory and Ethrea shouts at me. I wonder why it doesn't shout at him. He says the words, but does not obey them himself. And yet he's convinced he has.

Emory interrupts Sheba. "I'm sorry," she says. "But I guess I'm trying to say this: I want to go to the church that acts like James chapter two, like the one Hixon described in his note. My question to you all is this: Is Defiance Community Church one that welcomes folks like me?"

"Of course it is," Hap says, his smile as perfect as Emily's.

"We pride ourselves in being an open, forgiving church," Emily adds.

"So I need forgiving?" Emory stands.

"We all do," I say.

"Here's the thing I don't understand," Emily says. "Jesus died for sinners, right? For folks who do drugs and neglect their children and the like." She looks right at Emory. "But I don't really sin, so why would Jesus need to die to forgive me? I get that he died for other folks, but not really me."

Emory walks to the door, not with quickened pace, but not slowly either. She looks at Emily. "I don't understand much. Particularly not the Christian life. But all I can say in response to your words is that I thank God he's big enough to die for the likes of me. Where would I be if there were no such thing as a second chance?" She holds Hixon's old Bible to her chest, as if it's her heart. "Used to be I thought the world was one big cosmic joke, with random, horrible events flinging my way. But now more than ever, I disbelieve that notion. Why? Because I've been to the deepest, darkest, vilest pit. And God saw fit to reach

his hand down there, pull me up to flat land, and give me a place to sit and rest." She points at Emily, her eyes full of tears. "You may not think you need him. But I can't live without him."

She closes the door behind her. Amid the murmuring, I want to cheer.

Fifty-Two

I licked salty lips, looked at my seventeen-year-old feet. The Gulf of Mexico roared a welcome to David. To Mama. To me. The endless warm water terrified me, made me feel insignificant. It niggled David that I was too afraid to swim. On the shoreline, the waves circling my feet, I looked out to the great unknown. Even then I sketched darkness and endless stars and oceans deeper than buildings were tall—all in strange attempts to make sense of David's leers.

I backed away from the water, worried that if I dared go any farther, the sea's mighty tongue would lap me into its dark depths and never let me go. For fear's sake, and probably because I needed the feeling of control, I sat far away. I built a castle with a wide moat with jagged shells preventing anyone from entering my realm.

"It's time." He grabbed me from behind, wrapped strong hairy arms around my torso. "I won't have a sissy girl who can't swim. Come on."

I kicked.

I screamed.

I pled.

He pulled me toward the gulf's terrible mouth. Mama offered a faint, "Stop it, you're scaring her," barely looking up from her dime store novel. Mama had gladly surrendered her

will to this man—her terrible payment for security. She became his puppet—he the ventriloquist, she spouting his words without verve. Used to be she'd holler or cackle or cry or laugh. In the days of Daddy, Mama emoted. But under David's silent tutelage, her sentences bereft of a rise or fall of voice. When he ridiculed me in public, her "Now, David, quit kidding Ouisie," came out monotone, divorced of emotion.

Still, I called to her. "Mama!"

I thought she said, "David, knock it off," but I couldn't be sure. She did not move to save me, her fatigue trumping action. I tried to free my arms, but his hug tightened around me, nearly compressing my lungs.

"This is what my Dad did for me," he said, laughing.

The water to my chin, I pled. "I can't swim."

"That's just what I told my dad. I was only four years old, though. You're practically a woman. Don't worry. Today you'll swim. And thank me for it later."

"I won't thank you," I screamed. "I hate you! Let me go. I swear I'll hate you forever if you don't." I looked for Mama's eyes, but they're locked in a book.

"Have it your way." His arms slithered away like snakes mysteriously leaving prey. I started to call out thanks and I'm sorry I said hate, but water filled mouth. With my stepdad at six foot three and me just past five feet, I was in over my head. Water covered me. I fought with my legs. Kicked. But no air. I longed to touch the bottom somehow, to use my feet to spring to the surface, but the current pulled me deeper. Though I'd pinched my eyes shut, I opened them underwater, the salt stinging my eyes. I watched other legs kicking and wondered briefly why my kicks kept me underwater.

I only wanted air. I kicked again, this time projecting my head briefly out of the water to gulp in air. My arms flailed like a cartoon character in distress. I thrashed underwater again, kicked like I had before, and took another gulp of sunshine. On the third trip to the surface, my stepdad smiled, arms crisscrossing his chest.

The last time I plunged underwater, I knew I would die. A hurricane of white dots starred my vision. Darkness and pinpricked light swirled around my head as my lungs forced against the weight of a felled pine on it. Ocean and sky melted together. I prayed to God. Asked him if I was worthy enough to see the pearly gates.

A faint voice, the sound of a woman, sent a melody to my heart. A strong arm reached around my too-tight chest, pulling me up, up, up to the beautiful surface. I coughed, choked, sputtered. Someone pulled me toward shore. Once the sand greeted my backside, the world went black.

When I looked up, David's face scowled at me, though fear wrinkled around his eyes. "You'll learn eventually," he said. "Without the help of your mama."

"Mama?"

"She lifeguarded you. Just a few more seconds, and you would've been swimming, but she interfered. Next time, you'll learn."

The only thing I learned was this: water over my head was no place for me. Never was. Never would be.

Fifty-Three

A nd yet here I stand, shivering under a warm Defiance sky. I am not cold; I'm frightened. I'm not sure why, exactly, I decided it was time to go under the waters, awaiting resurrection. It's not like I believe Lake Pisgah's waters teem with life or magic. And, although Hap might preach otherwise, I don't feel my salvation depends on this one simple act, either. Except that on this day, in this locale, I know it would be sin for me to ignore the Lord's prodding, the persistent Voice. If you told me a year ago I'd be dipping my toes into the air-warmed waters of Lake Pisgah readying to be baptized along with Emory Chance, I would've laughed flat out, questioning your sanity.

But if you want to know the truth—and truth is not so easy for me—Emory made the argument compelling. And with Big Earl wearing a flowing white robe standing in Lake Pisgah's muddied belly, I almost can't wait to finish what was started like a seed planted in my heart years and years ago. I'm fully bloomed now—stems broken and petals falling off notwithstanding. There is no one to witness the act except God, Big Earl and each other, the perfect trio for such an event.

Emory is next to me, laughing. Big Earl tells Little Myrtle's jokes—going on about café gossip. He beckons her into the water. A rustling of underbrush tears my eyes from her. Elijah is here, looking more disheveled than ever. But he's hiding in the

283

bushes and no one sees him. He winks my way, as if telling me this is our secret. So I keep it. I wonder where he is living now, and how he's dodging the Defiance police. I look away, choosing to focus on Emory.

She wades deeper, until Big Earl's arm is around her.

Big Earl clears his throat. "We're gathered here today — "

"This ain't a wedding!" Emory laughs.

"Sorry. It seems like it though. In a way, you're marrying Jesus, the way you're identifying with his death in such a tangible way. And you'll be raised back up just like he was. Together with him." Big Earl looks at me. His kind eyes hold me there, in the moment, making Lake Pisgah the sanctuary I've always thought it should be.

No stained glass — just my stained life.

No choir — but the chirp of birds in the trees.

No Hap — just the well-rounded café owner with Jesus eyes.

No offering — except me and Emory.

No congregation — but Elijah in hiding.

Big Earl raises both hands to the blue sky. "Dear Jesus," he prays, "Help us all as we try to figure out what it means to follow in your steps. We're a ragtag bunch, but you know that. May this day mark beginnings. New life. New ways of thinking. New hope. New paths of relating with folks. Your Word says that if any lady is in Christ, she is a new creation. The old has passed away. The new has come. So this is a day of new life." He shouts amen.

"Emory Marie Chance, do you believe Jesus is the Son of God, that he died for your sins?"

"Yes sir, I do." She locks her eyes on me. They are clear eyes, not hazed over from drugs or grief. In fact, they're the clearest eyes I've ever seen — the kind you can look into and see eternity.

"And will you follow His ways the rest of your life?"

"I will try. That's all I can say." She looks at Big Earl. "Can I say something else?"

"Sure."

"A part of me is doing this for Hixon. But mostly I've come to realize, I'm doing this for Jesus, which is how it should be. I hope I don't mess all this up. I hope he doesn't regret me dipping in the water like this. I have more regrets than anyone in this town." She stops. I hear the catch in her voice. "I wasn't a good mama. I preferred the attention of men and the lure of drugs to being attentive to my Daisy. If I'd been more watchful, Daisy'd be with me here today, celebrating alongside me. But she is dead, and there's no resurrecting her now." She is crying now, but her eyes remain clear. "I have been an adulteress. I've stolen. I've used people. I pushed away the kindest man on earth. All he wanted to do was show me what Jesus was like, but I shoved him away, swore at him. I nearly spit on him. And all the time Hixon kept coming back, loving me, showing me the love of Jesus. So I do this for Hixon, but I really do it for the Jesus who gave Hixon the ability to love someone like me." She nods at Big Earl. "I'm ready."

"I baptize you in the name of the Father, the Son, and the Holy Spirit."

She crosses her arms over herself. Big Earl plunges her backward with a splash. I hold my breath while the lake makes her disappear, only breathing out when Big Earl re-emerges her to the light of day. She pushes back wet hair. The sun seems to dance upon the waters, illuminating her face. She wades through the water to me, holds both my hands, and says nothing. Her eyes say it all.

She pulls a towel around herself and sits on my Adirondack.

With every step toward Big Earl, I feel mud squish between my toes. I worry the mud will swirl into quicksand, pulling me into its depths before I can scream. I stop.

Big Earl beckons me nearer.

I am stuck near the shore.

He says, "Ouisie, it's too shallow there to properly baptize you." A smile lives in his eyes.

I force myself to take a step. Then another. The ground becomes less malleable, more firm. But as the water touches my belly button through my black shirt, I stop again. "I can't," I whisper.

"It's all right," Big Earl says. He comes to me, places a thick arm around my middle. "I'll be right here."

"Okay."

"Now I know you've been a follower of Jesus many years, so I won't pester you with questions."

For a long pause, I say nothing. Is it true? Have I followed Jesus all these years? It's hard to say. After watching Emory spill her story, I'm not sure I ever let Jesus see all the bad parts of me, certainly not in public. I've played the role so many years, I am not sure what is real anymore. A bird sings in the trees. I look from Emory to Elijah, then back to Big Earl. Maybe they are the trinity of Jesus-followers and I'm the odd girl out. Maybe I don't belong here, nearly drowning in the lake. Maybe everything means nothing and nothing means everything.

"Is there anything you'd like to say?" Big Earl nods my way, as if to say, go ahead.

"I don't know." And that's the truth right there. I really don't know.

"Would you like to be baptized?"

"Yes," I hear myself say.

"Well, then, I baptize you—"

"Wait. No. Not yet." I take my hands out of the water. I don't lift them to the sky as Big Earl did. I let them skim the surface of the water as ripples move ever outward with each swish. "I do need to say a few things."

Big Earl waits. Emory waits. Elijah waits behind the trees. I wait.

The shrubs on the periphery of the lake rustle against each other in a gentle spring breeze. The light bounces from the sky to the water back to the sky again like an offering of praise. I revel in the water's scent, remembering Elijah's stench the last

time I saw him up close. And I know that I am like that to the Almighty God—a stench. Because a lie is stench. A secret is stench. And I embody both beautifully. I steady myself, trying not to panic as the water laps my belly. Big Earl keeps his silent vigil next to me. Is he praying?

"I am no different than you, Emory," I say to her, to the trees, to Elijah, to the world, to the One who made it all. "I neglect my children. I need to drink every day. I'm unhappy in my marriage. I'm not a good wife. And I have a secret I need to tell. I can't tell it right now, but I will. Someday. I don't know if God would want a woman like me, but all I can say is I'm terribly tired. It's like I'm propping up my life with toothpicks and they keep breaking, and my only solution is to add more flimsy toothpicks."

The silence is not painful to me. I prefer it actually. My words have flittered and flown, and there is no one to rebuke them, judge them, fling them back to me in retribution. For that, I'm thankful.

Big Earl steadies me. "I baptize you in the name of the Father, the Son, and the Holy Spirit," he says. In a rush, I am under the water. I open my eyes, see the blue of the sky and the yellow of the sun just beyond me through a blurry lens. I want air, but am somehow satisfied without it. And when Big Earl pulls me back to the land of the living, I don't gulp in air like I thought I would. I simply pull in a steady stream of oxygen, thankful for life, thankful for air, thankful for truth. The world looks dewy and sweet as I drip Lake Pisgah from my arms. When I look at Emory, I see her smile. But when I pan over to Elijah, he is gone.

We leave the water together. I chew on Big Earl's words. I've seen God use Ethrea Ree. Emory too. They weren't ordinary people after all.

And Lord knows I'm different. And in the light of the sun warming wet skin, I can assure you, today I'm different. Completely so. Funny how water can do such a thing. Maybe Lake Pisgah is magic after all.

Fifty-Four

Or maybe not.

Officer Spellman's car idles as we pull into my driveway. My giddy laughter cuts short. Arms across a navy blue uniformed chest, he has a scolding look in his eyes, a tsk-tsk-tsk. I get out of the car. Emory too.

"Is there something wrong?" Emory asks.

"I need to see you down at the station, Mrs. Pepper. The Reverend said you'd be here all day." He looks me up and down. "You're wet."

"Nothing like a little spring swimming, I always say." I try to be lighthearted but my words sound muddied.

"I'll wait until you've changed." Not angry. Not impatient. Not happy, either.

Emory pulls me aside when we're in my living room. "What's that all about?"

"I don't know."

"I'm going with you."

"I don't think he'll let you."

"Well, I can pray, right? Won't that put me right alongside you?"

"I suppose."

She hugs me, then waves as she heads out the door.

In my room, I wrestle off wet clothes while my heart pounds

against my ribs. What does Officer Spellman want? Has he identified my footprint? What does he know? I pull on a pair of comfortable slacks and a light sweater the color of today's sky.

Leaving the house and locking the door, I worry I won't come back. Such foreboding I've known only in my childhood, the moment I yelled Daddy's name and he didn't answer back. It's that same dread rising up my throat.

Officer Spellman opens the car door for me, but it's the back door, not the front. From the back seat, I feel imprisoned. He does not speak as he pulls out of the driveway and heads to downtown Defiance. We pass Emory's old house on Love Street. I nod its way, hoping she'll make good on her promise to pray. He pulls into the back part of the station, opens my door, then escorts me inside.

"We'll be using the conference room," he tells another officer—one unfamiliar to me.

The man waves us on by.

My footsteps clank the flooring; Officer Spellman's do too. Ours are in opposite cadences, as if he refuses to take my pace. We sit at a small table in a fluorescent-lit room. He offers me a drink of water. Though I'm thirsty, I say no.

"You know why you're here, don't you?"

I do not meet his eyes.

"You wear the exact same size of the footprint we found."

"Lots of women have big feet in this town." I sit back, look around the room.

"Imagine how hard it would be for the Reverend to have to tell me your shoe size, to surrender your shoe to me, to know that his wife had something to do with Daisy's disappearance."

"Sounds like Cinderella to me."

Officer Spellman swears.

I say nothing. Hap gave my shoes? I think of all the times I could've exposed his sorry self to the police when his violence took over. How many wounds I endured. And here he is, giving me up. All this time I'd been protecting our marriage only to preserve him for this betrayal.

"You're quiet today. Why don't you tell me what you know about that trap door and the man who made it?"

"I am not under arrest," I say. "I want a lawyer."

"You're right. You're not under arrest yet. And if you share what you know, I'll be happy to let you get back to your family before your kids come home from school. I don't need to remind you that what you know will help put a killer behind bars."

"He's not a killer."

Officer Spellman stands. He paces the room. I feel anger emanate from him, like sweat from pores. "The evidence says otherwise, Mrs. Pepper. For crying out loud, this is your son's best friend we're talking about! Your friend Emory's only child. Some maniac choked her life from her. She's dead. Gone to heaven. Why can't you tell me what you know?"

"Have you ever read *Of Mice and Men*?" I ask.

"I'm not an idiot, Mrs. Pepper. I'm well read."

"That's not what I asked."

He throws his hands in the air. "Yes, of course I've read it. John Steinbeck. A classic."

"Well then, you'll understand what I'm about to tell you."

He waited in her closet. When she came into her bedroom, he watched her pull off her clothes, but she couldn't see him. She reached just past him, grabbing a sweater. Had her hand moved four inches left, she would've brushed his cheek. But she didn't. And when she hurried out the bedroom door and slammed the front screen door on its hinges, he crawled through the house just in time to see her ride away with the police. She would rat him out there, he knew. That meant only one thing.

Or did it?

The dreams last night came violently still. But this time, faces appeared, haunting him, shrieking his guilt. The sandaled girl who had no name. Daisy Marie Chance who choked that terrible and fascinating word, forgiveness. Sissy's lisp whispering through the night before she sought shelter in the only place he wouldn't go. All three leveraged their beauty to deepen his guilt. And its weight pushed him into the earth, past its muddy crust, to the shale beneath, deeper into the places where rock was molten and angry. He would go to hell, that he knew. The dreams proved it.

But instead of resigning himself to the place of torment, he begged forgiveness from the flames. They answered back by calling his name over and over again, as if beckoning him to be engulfed there. If they had their way, they'd burn him, consume his soul. He awoke beneath the tree house's tin roof, sweating like he did in that land so far away, with the kind of thirst gallons of water poured hungrily down his throat would never, ever quench.

He wanted relief. And he spelled it Ouisie.

But she wasn't there.

Fifty-Five

I am a wreck when the kids come home. Jed and Sissy both ask, "Are you all right?" in different intervals. I hush back that I'm fine, just feeling under the weather is all. Which is the truth, if you slice it a certain way. Hap will be home soon, expecting a meal on the table, but I cannot bring myself to make it. Instead, I walk out to the backyard under the dusking sun. I would rather spend my last hours in the garden than any other place. What kind of mama thinks that? Shouldn't I gather my children both under my wings, protecting, storytelling, loving? But my need for quiet and the smell of the earth override my guilt. And my curiosity about when the sirens will scream our way.

The next several minutes, the world is quiet except for birds. And rustling of nubile leaves through ancient trees. I make my way to the forbidden garden to see my demise—the hollyhock seeds have not merely sprouted, but have grown several inches. There will be no hiding them from Hap now. The rose bush is greening too. I see something different on the bush, but can't make it out. I come closer and then stop. My bracelet sways from a side branch like a Christmas ornament. I look to the woods and see nothing. I finger the bracelet, then place it around my wrist. It's perfectly intact. I pray through its beads, mostly for my safety, Hap's temper, and the kids. I am shaking though the

world is warm and muggy and the light is that magical time when the sun kisses the earth for a last goodnight. Do you wonder if this will be my last goodnight?

Sirens holler down the street. They come closer and closer, whirring violently until they stop in front. I run into the house, gather Jed and Sissy, and tell them to stay put. I lock the front door. But it's too late. Sissy sees the police storm Ethrea Ree's home, pounding, shoving, yelling. Barks of orders and a rush of words swirl around Ethrea's porch, then muffle from inside.

"What's happening?" Sissy asks.

"Lennie Small," I mutter.

"What?"

"I don't know. Jed, get away from the window," I shout.

"They're taking Ethrea and Delmer, Mama," he says. "Why?"

The lights flash on his face, but his expression shows fear, not wrath. "What have they done?"

"I'm guessing it's something with Daisy."

"I've got to find out." Jed runs out of the house before I can stop him. I stand with Sissy on the front porch, trying to suffocate my own wail. I'm too shaky to properly cry. Jed nears Officer Spellman who oversees the shouting. I can't make out what Jed says, but Officer Spellman points my way. Jed runs to me, then stops dead center, plants his feet. His eyes are fury now, even as strobes rhythm the back of his head. "You knew? And you didn't tell?" His eyes are Hap's now. There will be no explaining when Jed's eyes blaze this way. Jed shoves me into the clapboard.

Sissy screams. "What are you doing?"

He faces Sissy. "Mama knew it was Delmer who killed Daisy all along. And didn't tell a soul. Isn't that right, Mama?"

"I—"

"And when Sissy went missing, you knew! What kind of

mama would do such a thing?" He screams now, his voice more like a boy's than a man's.

"It's not what you think," I stammer out.

"What is it then?"

"Quit yelling at Mama!" Sissy is hysterical now, clinging to me, petting my head, shooting darts Jed's ways. If only she knew.

The roaring lights and sirens swirl around me in a maniacal dance. I look up in time to see Ethrea Ree, her arms pulled violently behind her—wrists shackled together. She looks at me with the kind of hatred Hap reserves for me. I look down. I can't. I just can't. But when they shove Delmer toward the car and he trips over his feet, I cry. Face to the dirt, he hollers.

"Squirrels? Oh squirrels? Where are you? I promised to feed you but I won't be able to a long, long time." He spies Jed. "Jed!"

Jed runs near. He looks as if he'd kick Delmer right then and there.

"Jed, you'll feed them won't you?"

"Go to hell," Jed says. He kicks dirt in Delmer's face. Officer Spellman pulls him away, but Jed throws several punches. The officer hugs him from behind, hauls him to our front steps.

"It's okay. We're taking care of it, Jed."

I look at Officer Spellman. "You promised," I tell him.

"Promises help elicit confessions," he says. He turns, leaving an angry son on my porch.

The car doors slam. I catch a glimpse of Delmer in the same back seat I rode in just hours ago. I was cool and collected then, but Delmer is neither. He blubbers, his face wet from tears I gave him. Ethrea Ree pats him, but he is not consoled. They pull away in a flurry of gravel and sirens and speed. And I'm left to pick up the pieces of my family. I glance at the bracelet, wondering what prayer is for, thinking it's more trouble than it's worth.

My foray into the depths of Lake Pisgah feels ancient now, as if it happened in another life to another woman. Another mama.

Sissy snuggles beneath me—I don't deserve such a thing. "Why did the police take them away?"

Jed slams his fist into the clapboard, but it doesn't bend beneath his rage. He pulls his hand away. Swears.

Sissy screams.

Blood dripping off his knuckles, he says, "Because they killed Daisy, Sissy. And Mama knew all along, didn't you, Mama?"

"It's not that. It's not what it seems."

"But, Jed," Sissy yells. "It's not them. It can't be. I should know."

"What can you possibly know?" Jed's voice quivers anger.

"Because I saw him, Jed. The man. And it's not Delmer. They've got the wrong man. You know Delmer wouldn't hurt a squirrel!" Her voice shrieks. She pleads with Jed with those big, big eyes. And I wonder who she saw so many months ago when she went missing.

"Sissy, you're just a little kid. How would you know anything?"

"Jed!" I say. "You will not talk to her that way."

He moves near me, Hap's fire in his eyes. "Why do you even care, Mama? You're the reason she went missing in the first place—ever think about that? And all along, you knew who took Daisy!"

I am struck dumb by his words. I hear Sissy's cries, feel her arms around my waist, but nothing of her grief registers. Only mine.

Nearer still, Jed's blood drips onto my pants. I watch it widen into larger dots with each red drop. "I'm not sticking around to find out your sorry excuse."

Sissy weeps. "Why is Jed being so mean, Mama?"

"He's angry. Don't worry. He'll be back."

But the rummaging through the house indicates differently.

He slams, throws, and hollers until he comes out onto the porch with a backpack. "I know someone who'll keep me safe. Who will take care of me."

Jed, my firstborn son, runs toward Defiance while I holler to keep him home. But he will not listen to my words. Not anymore.

Fifty-Six

It's Hap who discovers Sissy and me hunched over each other, wailing on the porch. But he doesn't console. He pulls me to my feet. Sissy screams.

"No Daddy. No." As if she's taken up the mantle Jed left behind like used clothing, Sissy flails at Hap, kicking his shins, screaming like a frightened rabbit. I pray Officer Spellman will come back to witness this—or my life will be over, I am sure.

"Let's hear your confession, Ouisie Pepper. Why don't you shout to all of Defiance what kind of monster you are." He shoves me against the house.

Sissy kicks him again. With his free hand, he wallops her across the face. She crumples to the porch, whimpering. Clementine barks from behind a closed door. I ease my hand toward the doorknob while Hap squeezes my neck. I open it. Clementine bursts through, runs right to Sissy and licks her. Sissy hugs her. Though I want to let out the proverbial sigh of relief, Hap's hand still constrains my throat.

"Why don't you tell your daughter how little regard for life you have? How you let Daisy's killer roam the woods and nab Sissy, all the while living within twenty awful feet from our house. What in the world were you thinking?"

"He's not the one," Sissy whispers. "Not the man who took me."

Hap lets go of me. He crouches. Clementine steps between him and Sissy, growling. "I don't want to hear any more excuses, any more lies to protect your mother." He raises a hand, but I grab it in mine.

"No," I say.

He turns back toward me, thank God.

"I did think it was Delmer. But I don't anymore. I don't know why Officer Spellman picked him up. I told him what I knew."

"Only after I gave him your shoes, wife." He roars his words now, so loud that Sissy's whimpers are wisps of words, so far away.

"No, it's not like that. When I thought it was Delmer, I knew it'd been an accident, was sure of it."

"You don't accidentally kill someone."

The fire in Hap's eyes must've leapt into mine because suddenly I am angry. How many times has Hap nearly killed us? I dole out my words, wondering if they'll be my last. "You're about to do that now."

His eyes ice over. He points at Sissy. "Get in the house with that stupid dog and shut the door. Your mama and I need to talk."

Sissy scurries in. My heart rate climbs. Again, there will be no one to witness this—again. No one outside my home. Not Delmer, who watched over me from smudged windows. Not Ethrea who blanketed me. Not Emory who's on the other side of town by now, driving down her country road. Not even Jed. For a brief moment, I remember Emory's boss, Big Earl. He's never been here before, but maybe he'd pay a visit. Or maybe Flo. The happenstance of that is smaller than my chances of overpowering my cold-eyed husband.

He sits on the porch swing and motions for me to take a seat. For a brief moment I think I see worry in his expression, not wrath. Perhaps he's counted to ten. Or one hundred. Maybe he will relent. So I ease myself in beside him.

"Tell me about your garden," he says. I hear nothing in his voice, see nothing in his face since we both look forward to the front yard while spring teases me with a sweet breeze.

"Hollyhocks," I choke out. "The ones Jed gave me for Christmas. I planted the seeds is all." It feels good to say it, like I'm washing my soul with soap when I let out the secret. "And there's a rosebush too—I rooted it from one of Ethrea Ree's."

"I see. Care to tell me what other secrets you're keeping from me?"

"I don't understand."

"How about your fake baptism today? For crying out loud, how big do you think Defiance is, Ouisie? Word gets out! You being baptized by that fat old man? You've already been baptized. What kind of deception is this?"

More soap. "This was my first time." Suddenly I see the picture I want to paint—how the light plays on the water and my face, where the sun is in the sky, how the horizon is bluer toward land and periwinkle near the clouds. Like the skilled Old Testament people who God gifted to build the tabernacle, I am imbued with his artistic knowledge. I know the colors to use, which to avoid. I know what kind of strokes will create my hair, which will pearl the sky. And I know that pointillism will dance wonders on the surface of the resurrecting water. My hand twitches its urge to paint. But I watch Hap's face, wondering how he's taking all my words—my confessional time, with Hap as my angry priest.

"Any more secrets? What about your relationship with David?"

"You know he's in a wheelchair in Burl. I've never visited him," I say. "We broke up long before I met and married you. How many times do I have to say it? I've never been remotely near him since. That's the truth."

"That's hard to believe."

"I'm sorry. But it's the truth."

"You paint."

"Yes, I paint."

"You hide that from me."

"Because you don't approve. You seem to want me to only be your cook, the maid, our children's mother, a Bible study leader. Nothing more."

"There's something more."

"What?"

"You drink."

This is not news to him. But it's nice to let everything out. "You're right. I do. But I haven't had a drink in many days. And I'm okay."

"A few days is nothing. You can't be trusted on your own. You know what they say about the weaker sex."

"No, what is it that *they* say?"

He looks at me, warm tears in cold eyes. "Women need protecting. They need strong men."

"Unlike your father." I wonder if I should've let those words free. I study his face, the way the lines around his eyes tell me stories of rage or fear or indifference. Right now? I can't really tell.

"Yes," he whispers. "Unlike him. Haven't I been strong enough?"

I let his words hang in the now-gentle breeze. I've been his grand experiment, his atonement for his father's suicidal life. In rebelling against his father, he's swung to the other extreme. Not neglectful, but mean and intrusive. The swing stops—my cue to speak. "You've been far too strong."

"I love her."

What?

He stands, puts his hands in his pockets, and swivels to face me. He seems taller, like a hundred-year-old pecan tree rooted to the earth. I feel my pulse throbbing my head. My thirst—the thirst I hoped would die with baptism—returns. I wonder if I

can drink perfume. "It's Emily, isn't it? I've smelled her perfume on you."

"No. Emily's going through a crisis. I've simply been her confidant."

I wonder how many times I've longed for Hap to hear about my day, to erase my worries. Instead, he runs around town being Mr. Counselor to other women. Their blessed pastoral hero. I'm left with his angry leftovers. "Well, then, care to let me in on the secret? Who is the lucky girl this time? I mean you've already had your way with Emory. Who else? Ethrea Ree?"

"Don't be ridiculous. It's Sheba. She understands me. She needs me."

Sheba the Bible scholar? "Last I checked she was another man's wife." I stand, shove my finger into his muscular chest. "Last I checked the Bible says it's wrong to lust for someone like that. I believe it's called adultery."

"He left her. You know that."

"So then it's okay for *you* to leave your wife to comfort poor Sheba whose rat of a husband left her without so much as a note? Well, at least you have the decency to let me know your course of action. Can't you see the irony there?"

"I didn't say I was leaving. You did."

"Oh, great. Make me the bad guy." I remember my letters to her, my private thoughts, and nearly vomit. Has she disclosed them all? He didn't know about my lack of baptism, so perhaps she hasn't. A regular confidant—a Dear Abby bent on stealing my husband.

Hap paces. "You know what? I don't care what anyone thinks. This town, my church—they're like straightjackets."

Really? "I thought you liked that. Thought you loved the spotlight, the renown of being the Reverend."

"You don't really know me, Ouisie."

"I know enough to be afraid of you."

"Sheba's not afraid. She's written me letters, dozens of them, all full of Scripture and encouraging words. When was the last time you sought to encourage me that way?"

"I get the mail every day and I didn't see any letters. How did she send you them?"

"To the church."

How interesting. I worried so much that Hap would read her letters to me that I had them sent to Emory. "Perfect. Right behind my back, and all couched in flowery religious terms, no doubt."

Hap covers his mouth with his hand for a moment, then places it back on the porch ledge. "She understands my heart. My hurt too."

"How poetic."

"You don't know what it's like for someone like me — the pressure of trying to fill everyone's needs."

"I do that every day of my life. Believe me, I understand."

"I'm tired."

"I can see why. It must be exhausting for you to be so good in public, covering up for what happens in this house." I feel my own anger rousing again. Soon I'll be Hap, though I don't have the strength to fist him until he doubles over.

"You want to know the truth?"

"Yes."

"If I had a preacher's collar on today, I'd rip it off."

"I'd do it for you."

Hap swears a blue streak. Then he pins me with his blue-eyed gaze. "I don't love you. I can't even remember the last time I liked you."

All that energy wasted. All those promises Sheba made about my toil and my marriage while she spent her ink "encouraging" my husband. I am bare-naked of secrets and it means nothing to this man. Hasn't for a long time. I sink back into the swing, wondering if tears will come. But they don't. "So you love Sheba the writer."

"It's not what you think."

"How do you know what I think? When was the last time you ever asked me what I felt, how I was, what I wanted out of life? When was the last time you took a moment to explore my heart? And now you're off exploring someone else's." Should I say what I want to say? Do I risk it? Might as well. "You're a hypocrite."

He is deadpanned. Not a twitch of anger. And yet, he doesn't smile either. "At least I'm happy."

"Oh really. Happy. How convenient. Is Sheba happy? How about her husband? Would he be happy if he knew?"

"Nothing's happened, Ouisie."

"Except that you fell in love with someone other than your wife. Nothing's happened except that." Mine is the raised voice now. He is all calmness and peace.

He settles against the porch railing. "I didn't plan any of this to happen."

"Oh really."

"She understands me."

"Does she understand your temper? Does she bear the battle wounds?"

"I couldn't raise a hand to her."

"How kind," I spit.

He says nothing, fidgets with his ring. Around and around he twirls it, finally taking it off and placing it on the porch railing. "I have a feeling you won't grieve this loss. You'll be rid of me."

Tears come now, though I don't want them to. "You can't leave," I say.

"I'll go back to carpentering, find a place to stay in another town."

"Would the town be Rowlett?"

"Stop it."

"So you're leaving like your father did. Just up and abandoning your family." Fear trembles my words, fear so present I can taste it on my tongue.

He narrows his eyes, the fight returning. He walks to his car, opens the door, sits behind the wheel. I can't help but remember him the first time I saw him, offering to fix my car, my heart, my imprisoned life. Only to woo me to himself to destroy me. Take the gas from my car. Beat the life out of me. Rip out my heart.

I cry now, letting every sob, every worry, every regret fuel a torrent of woe and darkness. Hap just sits on the Chevy's pristine seat while I try to figure out what life will be like, just me and Sissy, Jed away somewhere, Hap living across the state. I think of Delmer, bewildered in jail, Ethrea Ree nursing a grudge, and Emory and me commiserating about our husband-less lives. This will be my life. I'll be free, but shackled to so much grief I'll never smile again.

Sissy runs out. The screen door slams on itself as she runs toward Hap who holds the steering wheel. "Don't leave us, Daddy," she cries. He pulls her to himself, pets her hair. I cross the yard to him, hoping maybe this is the breakthrough the enigmatic Sheba hinted at. Maybe a man has to get to the end of himself, to see his losses in plain day to realize his life's worth resurrecting. Maybe he's tired of being so mean.

His grip seems to tighten on her. "I won't leave you behind." He enunciates the words into Sissy's ear, but he looks at me.

"No!" I lunge toward the Chevy's open mouth. I grab Sissy at the waist and pull. She screams. Hap's grip is too tight, too firm. But I cannot lose Sissy. I persist. But she is the rope in a hellish tug-of-war, her screams echoing in my head.

"You can't expect me to entrust her to you," Hap says. "You can't even take care of yourself."

"She needs her mother." I tug.

"Please, Mama. You're hurting me."

I let go.

Hap does too.

Sissy runs into the house. I look up, and Emory's car stops

on the street with a screech. I am panting. Hap, too. He looks at me. "Happy now? You scared our daughter to death. I'm going." He slams the door, turns on the engine. Emory gets out of her car, heads my way. Hap yanks the car in reverse. I say, "No," but the engine kills my voice. He is at the end of the driveway in his perfect car, heading off to his perfect woman. In a snap of a moment, I run toward him. He stops. I hear Emory shouting something, but I can't make out her words. I raise both fists, then bring them down on the hood. Hap jumps out of the car. He grabs me. "Don't touch my car," he hisses. He shoves me to the ground. My head hits something—a rock? In a hair of a second, the world spins, then darkens. I hear the revving of his car, and pray for the light. I am underwater, looking skyward, when strength rushes me to the air, the sweet, sweet air of life. I drink oxygen hungrily, joyfully, tasting the beauty of life in that halcyon moment. The picture of water and air is God's second wind to me—his willing me to fight for this life. I remember the bracelet, the Jed and Sissy charms, and decide life's more than simply fighting for yourself, it's sacrificing for those you love. Jed needs me here, to explain things. Sissy needs my attention, my protection. The revving will be the death of those plans—the end of my own strange resurrection. But I cannot move. I will the revving to back away, but I know that won't be Hap's plan.

Hands grab me. The engine roars. I am being pulled through gravel, then let go. I smell the spinning of tires. Hear a scream—is it mine? Then, sleep.

Fifty-Seven

I stroke Emory's head. She is all tubes and monitors and beeps. Sissy slumps in a chair next to me, her face angelic. Sissy and I rode behind the ambulance, me with a bandage across my head and a roaring migraine and a chastisement from the EMTs for driving Emory's car in my state. The scream of the siren still wails in my head. And though the doctor wants me to stay in my own bed for observation, I can't tear myself away from Emory.

Hap's Chevy growled over her after she pulled me free, at least that's what Sissy said. Emory survived, but her spleen did not. Her hair is corn silk splayed on the pillow.

Sissy rouses. She watched the whole thing, she told me, from the front picture window. I can't imagine the haunting this will do.

"Ith the going to be all right?" Sissy's lisp, nearly confined to an afterthought in the past month now colors her words. I don't wipe my own tears. This is grief. All of it.

"I don't know, baby. The doctor says she's strong. We can pray that's true."

"If the dieth, the'll be with Hixthon."

"Yes, baby. That's true. But I'm not ready for her to meet Hixon. Not yet. She's my dearest friend."

"I know." Sissy places her hand in mine, squeezes, then lets go.

I pull her onto my lap, wrap my arms around her. If I hug her forever, will I push out all the pain that's invaded her life?

Will I atone for pulling her near apart from Hap's vice grip? Is such a thing even possible? Can a mama's love protect a child from hell-bent evil? I wonder if my love is enough. God, I hope so. I do.

A nurse comes in, fiddles with some tubes. "Are you next of kin?"

"Yes," I say. "I'm her sister."

"Good, because we only allow next of kin in the rooms."

"What do you think? Will she—"

"I'm not a doctor, ma'am. I've seen worse pull through. But then again, I've seen easier cases die. Let's hope for the best."

"The best," I say as she leaves the room. I'm not sure I know how to hope for the best.

He watched the men in black haul them away, those two. All was fair in love and war—poet's words, not the police's. In this Defiance war, the innocents faced incarceration while the perpetrator perched nearby, freer than a jaybird. Delmer, he worried about squirrels, and Ethrea, well, she was her hard, bitter self, as usual. He should've felt a certain relief in their capture knowing the police were squirreling up the wrong tree, knowing his own tree full of shoes and tokens was safe as safe could be. But he only felt the fury of his heart against his chest.

He watched it all, but did not rescue. Saw the sticks and stones and names that hurt. Watched the Reverend Hap Pepper get in his car.

He should've blown his cover beneath the underbrush to intercede. And he planned to do so until Daisy Marie Chance's mama came to the rescue, halting his efforts.

Fifty-Eight

When Mama got sick, I really did figure cancer. She'd worked herself to exhaustion, and everyone knows a tired body welcomes sickness. And cancer being the scariest of the diseases, and me being pessimistic in nature, I deduced it. What I didn't deduce was the sly way David never managed to eat while Mama ate dinner. I'd taken to eating less and less, but he stopped altogether, preferring to cook her meals, plate them, and bring them right to her like he was a waiter in a fancy restaurant.

"It tastes funny," she'd say.

Which would launch him into a diatribe about her ungratefulness, how she judged him because of her own superior culinary skills. She always backed down, always swallowed every last poisoned bite.

David skipped town while Mama sucked life in little sips on her deathbed, the poison far too integrated into her system to be detoxified. The doctor told me plain out it was poison, that he'd seen a case like this once in his residency. He said he filed charges then and he was obligated, thanks to his Hippocratic oath, to report this. Of course David had probably ventured to some other small town to prey on another gullible widow by then. He's never been found.

I had my first black eye the day Mama died. She saw it too.

She pointed to it with a sadness in her own eyes that made me want to hide under her adjustable bed. "Eye," she said. She pulled in another rasp. "Hap."

"I fell is all," I told her. "You know how clumsy I am, Mama. You remember how I used to be when I first sprouted hips? How I used to ram my pelvis into doorjambs because I wasn't used to being that wide? I guess I haven't adjusted still. I'm a klutz." I filled the room with an onslaught of words, hoping she wouldn't say another agonizing one. The last thing she needed was to have a daughter who walked in her exact shoes. The last thing she needed was more worry. I sheltered her from the sad truth that the house was in David's name, that he had sold it out from underneath her the moment the hospital admitted her.

"David?" Another ragged word.

"He's not here, Mama. I told you that. He's away — on business."

"Hand." She lifted her hand, a whisper, barely detected.

I held it, felt her papery skin, watched her veins bulge, wondered how long it would be before her arteries would circulate the poison until she died.

"Thirst."

I lifted a cup to her mouth, tilting it the slightest incline, but the water meant to slake her thirst poured down her face in rivulets. I captured the water in a clean cloth and tried again, but no matter how much I tried to gentle its descent, the water dribbled.

"Thirst!" she said.

I tried a third time, but it was useless. I could no more quench Mama's thirst than she could save me from Hap's fist. I stroked her head, tears weeping from my eyes. "I love you, Mama. You deserved much, much better." I nearly added, "than him," but I kept the secret alive for the sake of an anguish-less death.

"Eye," she said again.

I took her hand, my tears warming the dry skin. "It's okay,"

I told her. "Daddy's waiting for you. Give him a big hug for me, you hear me?"

"Love," she said. And nothing more.

Black-eyed like a pea and grief-pocked, I didn't drive home after I signed papers and released Mama to the funeral home. I only knew I was thirsty and I needed a drink.

Fifty-Nine

Who will I send to look for Jed? Hap is nowhere to be found. Sissy is a tangle of hair and tears on my lap as I sit next to pale Emory. What about church folks? By now word would've ignited like a well-placed spark, folks cackling and wagging their heads, fueling the gossip into a firestorm. I doubt they'd have energy left over to look after my concerns. And Ethrea and Delmer sit in a stale holding facility, answering questions that lead to no one and nowhere.

I marvel at the crucible of life while Emory clings to it in threadbare breaths. I breathe along with her, willing my strength into her lungs, but she seems far too frail to take in my life. Emory who worked Muriel's run-down farm and made it her own. Emory who stood up to Hap when no one else would. Emory who wrote a note to Jed, forgiving him for leaving Daisy. Emory who took the baptism plunge before me, almost daring me to follow. *That* Emory warbles in oxygen. *That* Emory looks like death. You can see a thing like that, but pray it isn't so.

There is a phone in the room. I call the hospital operator, tell her I need to phone the Defiance police station. She connects me.

Officer Spellman picks up. His voice is beyond edged, hinting at deep disappointment.

"It's Ouisie Pepper," I tell him.

"I'm busy, as you can imagine. Sending patrols out after Mr. Pepper, questioning the Ree's."

"It's not Delmer you're looking for."

"Do you fancy me an idiot, Mrs. Pepper? Of course I know that. Did it occur to you that I brought them in for their own protection?"

"No, it didn't." I swallow.

"I need to go."

"No. Wait."

"What."

"Sissy says that the man she saw when she was taken from Hap's car wasn't Delmer."

"Hap said she wouldn't talk about that night—that she was traumatized."

"When you took Delmer and Ethrea in, she remembered."

"Does she know the identity of Daisy's killer?"

"Not by name, but by sight."

"When can I question her?"

I look at Sissy, exhausted and lifeless, her breathing steady. "I don't know," I say.

"How about if I come there. I'll be delicate, I promise."

"Only if I'm allowed to be with her."

"All right."

I let out a long sigh, my head still throbbing. "Officer Spellman?"

"Yes, ma'am."

"There's something else."

"What?"

"Jed. He left when he saw Delmer and Ethrea leave. He thought I knew—"

"Left?"

"I know you're overwhelmed. But you have to look for Jed. I can't leave Sissy or Emory right now. Promise me you'll find him."

A long pause crackled between us. "I'll call in extra help—the sheriff, the rangers."

I tell him thanks as I hang up.

Lord, I can't lose Jed like I'm losing Emory. You have to help me find him. Please. Please.

I nearly say the last Please out loud when the door opens and in steps Big Earl, the answer to my pleas. His shoes are scuffed brown leather with mismatching laces, and he's still wearing his grease-and-ketchup-stained apron.

"There she is." He sits opposite me. "I can't—" He puts his face in square, strong hands and lets out a sob, rousing Sissy.

"What ith it, Mama?"

"It's Big Earl come to see Emory."

"Oh." She looks at the crying man, then shimmies off my lap. She soft-shuffles around the bed and puts her hand on his. She says nothing, just holds his hand while he cries. Eventually, he looks up, sees her, then startles. "I'm sorry to carry on. It's just that, she's my—"

"Friend," Sissy finishes for him.

"Yes. A very special friend."

Sissy returns to my side. I pull her back onto my lap. Her legs dangle from me like I'm a dock and she's about to take a dip. She slides off again and heads to the long gray heater, preferring to perch there.

"What are they saying?" Big Earl blows his nose in a hankie.

"They don't know. Could go either way."

He bows his head and prays out loud. I quickly bow my head.

"Lord, you hold life and death in your hand. You are the God of the living. This morning you brought beautiful new life to Emory as she came out of the water, resurrecting her from death. Her life wasn't pleasing to you for many, many years, but it is now. Please don't take her. Please give us the gift of enjoying her many more years. Touch her. Bring her from the grave. Please, Lord."

So Big Earl says please too.

"Thanks," I say. "Do you mind if I ask you a favor? Feel free to say no."

He takes Emory's hand, pets it. "Anything."

"When you leave, could you look for Jed?"

"Is he at home?" He holds my eyes in the moment, Emory alive between us.

"No. He took off before the shooting. He thought I knew about Daisy's killer and didn't tell."

"Did you?"

I look at my hands, then at Sissy. "Sissy, can you run to the cafeteria and get me a cup of tea? It's just down the hallway to your left." I hand her a dollar. She nods, then leaves.

I turn to Big Earl. "To answer your question will make me sound like a horrible, terrible person."

"Tell me." He continues petting Emory's hand.

"I ran into Delmer Ree soon after Daisy went missing. He was acting strange, talking strange—almost cryptic. He gave me something—the eyelet ring from Daisy's shoe. I have it here." I expose my bracelet and point to the eyelet.

"You think he killed Daisy?"

"I did at the time, and thought so for most of the past few months, but then someone grabbed me in the woods, scared me. And my theory about who did it collapsed."

"Who grabbed you?"

"I don't know, but it couldn't have been Delmer."

"But even when you did think it was him, you didn't tell anyone."

I look at my wrists, hands and fingers, noting how old they look. Decades older than Emory's young skin. "No. I felt like it was my job to protect him. I assumed if he had taken her, then killed her, it was some sort of mistake that wouldn't happen again." As I say the words out loud, I realize how ridiculous they sound. Why didn't I just tell Officer Spellman my worries?

"I agree it would be hard to believe Delmer could do such a thing, but you really should've shared your concerns—and the evidence."

I wonder if Emory is hearing all this, wonder what she thinks of me if she does. I look at Big Earl. "Guilty," I say.

"I'm not trying to condemn you, I just want to understand what you're trying to say. You felt Delmer made a mistake and you were protecting him."

"Yes."

"And you were questioned by the police, right?"

"Yes, today just after the baptism."

"But they didn't arrest you for obstructing justice? For keeping this to yourself?"

"No."

"They took in Delmer and Ethrea right before Jed left, is that right?"

All these questions burn inside me. I am with Officer Spellman again, only his uniform has turned from navy with a badge to stained apron with kind eyes. "Yes," I finally say.

"It couldn't have been Delmer. You have to know that. But did you consider it might've been Ethrea?"

"Not for a moment. Emory said it was a man chasing after her, and he had a tattoo."

"Tattoos can be manufactured."

I shake my head.

"Maybe your tip off about Delmer brought in the real perpetrator. Have you thought about that?"

"No."

"Listen." Big Earl let go of Emory's hand. "I don't know what the reality of the situation is, and I'm not here to judge you, just to clarify things. If they haven't taken you in, it's likely you didn't obstruct at all. Think of it like bread crumbs on a trail. You simply pointed out some; that's all."

"Bread crumbs on a trail," I say. "A bit too late, I'm afraid. Now the birds have eaten them up."

"And Jed's missing too?"

"Yes, he took his backpack. Said he knew someone to help him."

Big Earl shakes his head. "Who?"

"I don't know."

"Don't you worry. I'll find your son. Might be camping out in the woods."

At the word *woods*, I retrace my interactions with Elijah, wondering if he created the lair, if he grabbed me from behind, if he's been watching me from the woods, if he has a tattoo. "Oh dear God," I say. "You have to find Jed. Please."

Big Earl stands.

Sissy comes in the room, walking very carefully. Hot steam warms her face. She presents the tea to me.

"Here you go, Mama. There'th change, too."

"Keep it," I say.

"I best be going. Don't worry. I'll find Jed."

"Mama, where ith Jed?"

Not wanting to worry her, I say, "He took a walk and Big Earl's going to find him."

Big Earl ruffles Sissy's hair. He bends on his haunches, nearly toppling over. He steadies himself by holding Sissy's shoulders. "You and your mama are here. And your daddy's not at home, so Jed needs to know where he's going to sleep tonight. I've got to find him so he knows to come to my house. Understand?"

"My protector," she says.

"Jed's your protector?"

She nods. "And Mama'th. That'th why daddy tried to run over Mama and then Emory becauth Jed wathn't there to protect. You need to find him."

Big Earl struggles to his feet. He puts his arm around Sissy. "I will find him." He takes my hand, squeezes it. "Don't worry."

But worry is all I know how to do. That, and blaming myself for trusting a man who fancied himself a prophet.

Sixty

I can't see Hap, but I feel his hands around my neck, startling me awake. I try to flail under his grip, but my arms are as limp as Emory's. He says nothing while I beg silently for oxygen. I am drowning without water. Drowning in the hospital's sterile air.

Only prayer makes it through my head—my new way of thinking since the baptism. God, if you're there, unstrangle me!

In a moment, hands release, and I choke in air. Blessed, blessed air.

I turn in my chair. I see no one, only Sissy curled up on top of the heater covered in a hospital blanket and Emory plugged into machines. The room is silent but for the whirr of medical science. It must've been a dream, I tell myself. A nightmare.

I stand in the gray-green light of the room trying to uncrook my neck from sleeping in a Nagahide chair that doesn't recline. I place my hand on Emory's head. She feels neither cold nor warm. But as I release my touch, her eyes flicker. "Emory?"

They flicker again, eyelashes knit shut, then open to show the most beautiful eyes a friend could have. She is awake. She struggles against her tubes. I holler for the nurses.

A new nurse comes in. "What do we have here?"

"Her eyes," I say, pointing.

"Looks like someone's woken up." The nurse puts a hand on Emory's arm. "Don't thrash about, okay? These tubes are in you

318

for good reason, and you'll make my job easier if you stay put."
She turns to me. "Let me get the doctor."

In the interim between meeting nurse, then doctor, I take this
moment to thank God out loud for sparing Emory. You may
find it irrational to foster such strange hope. After all, flickering
eyes and struggles against tubes don't mean she'll recover, but
deep down, I feel she will. It's not the kind of knowing I had
about Delmer, which, in retrospect was based more on intuition
than God's guidance. This is a God-knowing. A reassurance
from the Voice. I hold Emory's hand, warming her with my
warmth. She squeezes back. And when she does, she presses
more tears from me.

Sixty-One

In the aftermath of Emory's eyes, I dare to hope about Jed's whereabouts. Sissy does too. But a phone call breaks my hopes like glass shattered underfoot.

"We haven't found him, though the county dog unit tracked him into the woods near where Daisy—"

"Don't say it," I tell Officer Spellman.

"I don't need to remind you of the gravity of the situation."

"No, you don't."

"But wherever he went, he spent the night out there."

"Oh God."

"We haven't found Mr. Pepper, either."

I marvel at how quickly the Officer changes Reverend to Mister. "You might try Rowlett," I tell him.

"Why there?"

"There's a woman there, Sheba Nelson, whom he has an attachment to." I am thankful Sissy is out of the room for the moment.

"An attachment," he says. "Why didn't you tell us this yesterday?"

I could think up excuses, but instead I say, "I really don't know."

"Okay, I'll keep you posted on Jed and Mr. Pepper's whereabouts."

"I really don't care about Hap's whereabouts."

"You should care, because from what I'm gathering, he could be dangerous."

I sigh, letting out my frustration before I speak. "He's been dangerous a good long time. I can handle his kind of danger."

"Like Emory Chance did?"

I look at her, sleeping there, and remember all she told me about having an escape plan. "Just find Jed," I tell Officer Spellman.

We spend the morning with Emory while she fights doctors and spits out food. At least her feistiness has returned. But through it all, I am torn between searching for Jed and attending to the friend my husband nearly killed. I shoot silent prayers heavenward for Jed. After all, God knows where he is, and he can find him. But by the day's middle, I am ready to leave Emory.

"I need to go," I tell her.

She shakes her head no. Tears spill out of her eyes. I wipe them with tissues next to her bed. "Jed's missing. Do you understand me?"

She nods, but more tears leak.

"I'm sorry," I tell her.

Sissy pats her hand from the other side of the bed.

She doesn't speak, but her eyes seem to understand. I hate to leave her, but I must find Jed before night descends again on Defiance. The thought of him out there by himself—or with someone else—suffocates me.

I rise. I place my hand on Emory's head, which is blessedly free of fever. "I'll be back as soon as I can," I tell her. When Sissy opens the door, Big Earl is there.

"The nurse said she's awake." He smiles, but I see more in his eyes that I can't read.

"She opened her eyes and squeezed my hand. She cries, too."

He comes to her bedside, and takes her hand. "An answer to prayer, thank God."

I hate to barge in on his joy at hoping for Emory, but my worry for Jed has grown bigger than a wild hog come autumn. "Any news of Jed?"

He keeps his head down, watching Emory's hand as if it would offer up an answer in the silence. "No ma'am. Afraid not."

"Mama, where ith he?" Sissy tucks herself under my free arm, secure in my embrace. "And where ith Daddy?"

"Daddy drove somewhere," I say. "I don't know where Jed is just yet. But Big Earl is helping us find him."

"You have to find him," she tells Big Earl.

"I am doing my best, little lady. Once I leave here again, I'll be driving the streets of Defiance, hollering out his name."

"Could you stay with Emory until she falls asleep? I need to go to Defiance to look for Jed myself. I can't live with myself if I don't. He's my son. You understand, don't you?"

"Of course. But be careful. What about Sissy?"

I hadn't thought of what to do with her. "I'll figure something out," I say. My words don't sound convincing.

The dream was a nightmare. He, blackfaced, crawled along the underbelly of Vietnam, clutched at an ankle, shoed in an overlarge sandal. When he looked into the muggy sky, he didn't see her face, the girl's. He saw his own. Something inside him recoiled, turned back, and bit him, the poison of his own venom slipping through his veins. It's what murder did to a man, made him elusive from his own self, divorced from empathy forever. Murder was why he couldn't live his story in the present, in the great "I am." It's why he felt compulsion to tell it backwards like he could observe himself in the "he was." If he could detach like that, perhaps he could prevent himself from severing his soul completely.

Only it didn't work, this living in the past. This referring to himself as he back there. All this came to him in the dream like a flash of white after a buddy's foot tripped a body-dismembering mine. None of that—not the mines, the raids, the fire blowing hot from the sky, not the pot, not the death of friend upon friend—none of it registered in the moment. It couldn't. He became a "he was," a walking zombie of war, a zombie in the landscape of dreams.

He begged for release, hoped he could change, but he stayed pinned to the jungle earth, grasping his own ankle in his own hand, staring at his own anguished face.

"Release me," he told himself.

He couldn't release his grip. "I'm sorry."

"You have to. It's time. You've killed long enough. You're not in 'Nam anymore. You're in Texas, for crying out loud. Jungles are gone. Vietcong, too. There is no enemy." The face above him, the face he saw reflected in Lake Pisgah from time to time, said, "It's time you came home."

"I can't."

"You will. And she will help you."

The night terror shifted. He was no longer holding his own ankle, but hers—the little Vietnamese girl. She couldn't speak, *really, though she pushed out a gurgled please his way to make him stop. But he didn't stop. He pinned her to the earth, swearing every American curse word he could muster, the sound of helicopter blades thrumming behind him. She was the enemy, this girl who barely spoke, who somehow learned enough English to say please. He couldn't abide her one word, the way it gained strength on dirtied lips, how her hair slicked sweat in the effort.*

"Please, please, please."

He placed his strong hands around her frail neck. Just a baby bird without its mama who wouldn't survive anyway, he told himself.

"Please, please, please."

He squeezed the please right out of her.

Eyes, once alive with light and a fierce will to exist, now stared blank back at him. He watched his arms fly from her, watched as if he were God looking down on a pitiful creation. He saw himself pull an alcoholic breath into awaiting lungs. He watched the lungs rise and fall, but never take root. He watched himself push on the girl's small ribcage, but her heart never jumpstarted.

He stayed above himself like that, suspended like a medevac, the blades whirring, twirling, slicing hot air. He wanted out of the dream, out of 'Nam. Out of the place where he was forced by an unseen hand to stare down upon the mouth he silenced, the eyes he shuttered, the nose that couldn't smell the stench of rotting flesh, the ears that couldn't hear her own screams, the feet he unshod. In that hovering, he heard the words, "I am sorry" release from clenched teeth.

Sixty-Two

I am a beggar come suppertime, imposing on the first house I
see as I drive into town. It's Heloise's—the cat woman who
saw the evidence of Hap's rage not too long ago. Her lights are
on. From the car I can see her and Harold around the dinner
table. "Sissy, it will be fine. Mrs. Dickson will take care of you."

"But I barely know her." Her voice is quiet, tense, shaky.

"I'm sorry honey. I know that. But I have to find Jed. You
understand that, don't you?"

"Why ithn't Daddy looking for him?"

"I don't know." Which is the truth.

"I'm thcared."

"I know, baby. I'm scared too. Please just trust me on this.
Mrs. Dickson is a good Christian lady. Her husband helped
Daddy at church. And she's got cats—maybe even kittens!"

She nods, which makes me feel even more pathetic, but each
moment we delay is another moment I'm not hollering Jed's
name.

I take Sissy by the hand. We mount the stairs. I ring the
doorbell.

Heloise greets me at the door, her face flushed. "Ouisie. I've
heard the news."

"I don't have much time to explain, other than to say I need
a favor."

"Of course. Anything."

"Can you watch Sissy for a spell? I've got to go find Jed. He's been missing since yesterday."

"I know. We've been searching too. Do you want Harold to go with you? It's getting dark."

"No, I'll be fine. I've got Emory's car for protection."

Heloise crouches down to Sissy's height. "We're sitting down to dinner right now. You like fried chicken?"

Sissy nods.

"Don't worry. We'll take care of her."

"I appreciate it."

Before she closes the door, she whispers, "Just remember, God doesn't put us through more than we can bear."

The same words she tells me after Hap nearly strangled me to death. Ironic. I nod, then run down the porch stairs. Once I pull away from her curb, I am lost in more pressing thoughts. Where do I look for Jed? Where would he go? While the car idles, I know. Daisy. The burnt ruins of the church. The mural he helped paint in his grief. Her last resting place. And as I turn to head toward the church, I remember poor Clementine. I make a 360 in the middle of the road and head toward home, my heart pounding in my chest to the rhythm of find Jed, find Jed, find Jed.

From the driveway, no lights illuminate a family around a dinner table. Only the sound of desperate barking breaks the dead silence. I let Emory's car idle while I run to the door and unlock it. Clementine nearly knocks me over, wagging her tail. I smell excrement from the living room, which I know pains the dog who hates to disappoint us. After licking me, she runs to the yard to relieve herself.

I run by the stench into Jed's room, hoping to find something—anything. I rummage through every drawer but find nothing. When I open a shoebox in his closet, I weep. It's full of dried flower petals, remnants of the mom I was long ago—each

shriveled petal once full of messages to Jed. He saved them. A boy like that must still love his mama. "Oh Jed," I say to the petals. "Come back to me. I'm so sorry." But the house's walls absorb my words.

Outside again, I open the car door for Clementine. She enters the backseat only to jump the console to sit next to me.

I look beyond Clementine and see Ethrea's rose bush—the one I rooted and planted. And in that moment, I remember Heloise's words about God not putting us through more than we can bear. I wonder, though. Maybe God puts us through hell so we'll long for heaven. Maybe all this pain points somewhere— to my own frailty in facing it, to my own need for help, for my longing for a world where everything's made right, where hidden blows become public knowledge.

Mama said, "Hard times are God's gift to us, to keep us hoping in him alone." And she said those words before she journeyed down the road toward her death. She had hope.

Hard times indeed. I certainly can't hope in me.

Not in Daddy.

Not in Mama.

Not in my stepdad David, heavens no.

Not in Hap—which, you know, goes without saying.

Not in Sissy.

Not in Emory.

Not in Big Earl or Ethrea Ree.

Not Hixon or Muriel.

Not in Elijah.

And, sadly, not in Jed.

Clementine, though, tries to prove her worth by licking me and looking at me with I-will-be-there-for-you eyes. "Not even you, Clementine. It's just me and Jesus. But you can come along."

Now in the car, I look toward Ethrea's living room window, as dark as mine has been. She is not home. I wonder what she thinks of me. I tell God I'm sorry again for my betrayal, that I can't even hope for reconciliation. I've learned friends come from God in the most surprising, perplexing packages—Ethrea Ree notwithstanding. I shudder to think of my life today had I not opened the brief yet brilliant gift of Ethrea Ree.

With Clementine as co-pilot, I drive past Emory's old house on Love Street, park at its dead end, and venture through the woods until I hit the clearing where Crooked Creek Church once stood.

The air still reeks of smoke—as if it gathered all the fire to itself and hoarded it just to spew it my way when I come upon it—to prove its own penchant for treachery. Parts of the building still stand, but most remains piled in an ashen heap. As the sun burdens the horizon, and the orange-honey glow of the trees belie the tragedy before me, I call out Jed's name. Over and over and over I holler until my voice grates my throat. I walk around the ruins, reliving all the tragedy marked by this one church. Daisy's disappearance, then death. Jed's overwhelming guilt over the tragedy. Emory's near-suicide. Hixon's heroics rewarded by death. Jed's heroics rewarded by life—at least until yesterday. I hope and pray he still lives.

But as I circle the ruins one last time I wonder what kind of sadness comes from Defiance Community Church, a church unburned, where the Reverend Hap Pepper presides like a king over his kingdom. Countless bruises and injuries came my way. Jed's and Sissy's way too. Not to mention how folks must've felt when the façade of peaceful Reverend Pepper was violently ripped away in his hit-and-run of Emory. Would the bricks, the entryway Hap so painstakingly made Greek, the floors, the windows still stand? Or would they burn to the ground as Crooked Creek did? Would the people suffer the kind of bruises I have? Or would they find another pastor and move on as if nothing happened? Walking toward the woods, I pray that somehow, someway, folks would be changed through it all—for the better. An impossible prayer, but one I mutter with every step.

In the woods again I feel fear, taste it. I am near the lair I found. I cut to the left, dodging underbrush. Clementine whines at my heels. She senses it too. Shadows of trees fade into the gray night like giant pillars supporting the sky as a roof. When I come upon the gaping hole surrounded by yellow police tape, I startle when an impossibly cold breeze sends shivers through me, rattling the tape like flags. Clementine barks. "Jed, come out," I yell.

But nothing comes out of the hole in the earth. Not Jed. Not noise. Not anything. "Clementine," I say. "I'm afraid we need to go down the steps."

Clementine whines again as I walk downward into the forest's mouth. Each footstep she is next to me, her warm fur brushing my leg. I descend until I am surrounded by dirt and darkness. "Jed? You in here?"

Nothing. I feel along the walls, touching, hoping, wondering, worrying. I get on my hands and knees, level with Clementine. She growls. I feel my heartbeat in my throat. I touch the ground, hoping it will speak to me, show me something. But all I get is dirt under my nails.

I leave the lair, blinking at the dim that feigns daylight. Clementine and I hurry back to the car. We both run like crazy, some unknown evil in pursuit. I tear away from the dead-end street, turn a hard right, and park facing the long cement mural that leads to the rendering plant. Clementine whimpers as if she knows how near she is to animal doom. Her head rests on my lap.

I scan the mural that Jed, Muriel, and Hixon painted. Sissy told me she helped once, but the fact that Sissy didn't paint the whole thing presses in on me. Was the mural a prediction of doom? Muriel first, then Hixon. Would Jed be its third dead artist? I holler his name, but the mural echoes it right back at me. I'm yelling at myself and Clementine. And not one soul echoes back. I almost turn to leave, when a picture catches me. It's Jed,

Hixon, and Muriel walking toward a horizon line along a narrow path. Though rudimentary, the painting is full of light and life—the kind I've longed to paint. I hope someday when the pieces of my life fall where they may, I'll be able to have Muriel's vision to paint with light. Perhaps the baptism will be that painting. But as I think of hitting the water, then emerging into life—trying to captivate the spray of water with paint seems impossible again. The whole image is vibrant life, but first it must endure the darkest death. Oh God, why can't I have life without the death? Clementine looks at me, whimpers again. I look at the painting once more, then pray Jed is not holding Hixon and Muriel's hands in the afterlife.

I leave the mural behind, the scent of rendered animals chasing after us. Clementine cocks her golden head out the window. As if she needs extra air in her lungs, she gulps in the evening.

I park in the ditch next to the place where they found Daisy. I kill the engine, pat Clementine, then open the door. I'm struck by silence. No cars. No birds. No trees bending in a breeze. "Come on, girl," I tell Clementine. She follows.

The sun is officially setting now, sunk below the trees. Its departure tints the sky a brilliant magenta, orange, and dusky purple. I watch it and wonder why it is that I love sunsets more than sunrises. You'd think all of us here on earth would relish the rise of the sun, the way it chases away the night, replacing it with pastel light. But there's brilliance in the sun's setting—something about the contrast of the creeping night against the last hurrah that makes it more beautiful to me. In that moment, nearing Daisy's last known place, I understand why this is so. I want the latter part of my life to be as beautiful as this sunset, the darkened parts making the colors even more stunning. It's an impossible prayer in light of everything that's been taken from me. But it's my prayer nonetheless.

I stand above the second hole—the gouge in the earth where a strangled Daisy once rested. I call out Jed's name. I search the dirt and brambles, hoping for a clue—something to connect me to my son, perhaps a Hansel and Gretel trail of crumbs. But there is nothing.

I venture further away from the car toward the dark woods. With each step closer, Clementine's growls grow louder.

Come closer. Come closer. I am here. In the great Right Now.

I see her there, the sunset warming her face. Ouisie will understand. Will know what it's like to feel regret like I do. Hers is a sin of omission, mine of commission, but sin nonetheless. She will listen to my words, will hear my confessions. I need her to.

I slip noiselessly down the tree, one foot per nailed rung, and wait for her to come to me. Her trajectory is homing in; I see that.

So I wait.

Sixty-Three

The woods darken the dusk further. I stop, compose myself. I holler Jed's name, venturing further and further into the forest. A noise to my left like the rushing of a river stops me. Then a voice.

"Hello, Ouisie."

I spin, trying to locate the giver of the voice while Clementine circles me, her head low to the ground, a growl through her teeth. I see no one. A hand touches my back. I turn.

I've seen this man before, but cannot place his face. He doesn't move, doesn't motion for me to follow him. He simply stands in the dark, then pulls out a flashlight. He clicks it on, shining it from his chest to his face, ghosting him.

I should be scared. I should run. Maybe Hap's cleaned me clear out of all my fears, or maybe I've exhausted them in running from him. I stand in the dark, Clementine close to me, my heart pounding a normal rhythm. "You killed Daisy," I say.

He unclicks the flashlight. "I need redemption."

Simple words said in the night. He wants redemption. Don't we all? "That's not for me to decide," I say.

"Let me tell you my story."

Something in me knows I shouldn't stay and listen to how this so-familiar man strangled life from Emory's daughter. But I don't move away. I don't move toward him, either. "Who are you?"

He clicks the flashlight on again, this time illuminating a pathway out of the woods toward the field. "Let's walk."

Clementine is my Siamese twin, pressing up against me, a barrier between me and this man. In the clearing, I see his arm fully snaked. "I need to go."

He grabs my arm, pressing strong fingers into my flesh. "No. Not yet."

"Please," I say.

"Don't say that word."

"I'll scream." I hear my voice quiver, confirming the fear that has been strangely elusive in the woods.

"No one will hear you." He pulls me toward Daisy's hole.

I feign resistance—at least he's bringing me closer to Emory's car.

He shoves me to the earth. A rock bites into me. I put my hands in the air. "Listen, folks know where I am. They'll come looking for me." Clementine growls, adding her own period to my desperate sentence.

"Just listen."

I nod, noticing how muscles flesh out the snake, even on this man's forearms, how strong he is in the dusking light. I try to locate his face from picture albums in my head, flipping, flipping, only to suck in a frightened gasp when I finally locate his face in his son's.

"I'm good at my job. Papa says I'm a good chopper."

Ethrea's whispered, "He has a hard time with Slim being gone."

I watched as Delmer ambled to their ancient piano, strewn with framed photographs, some dusty and upright, others prostrate. He lifted one—a man in a uniform. "My papa." He pointed a thick finger in his papa's belly. "He killed people over there."

"Delmer," I say out loud. "He's your son. But Ethrea Ree said—"

"Never you mind what that woman said." He spits at the ground. "Do I look dead to you?"

No, I want to say. You look hauntingly alive. Especially as night falls, and Sissy waits for me. And Jed faces another night alone in Defiance—or has this man taken Jed's life? I try to stand, but his snake arm shoves me back. This time I lose my balance and tumble into Daisy's hole. Clementine barks.

"Make your dog stop or I'll wring its neck."

I try to soothe Clementine. She sits with me in the hole, her body a barrier between me and Slim Ree, back from the dead.

He paces in front of me while I shoot prayers to the darkening sky.

"I didn't die. I came home. But Ethrea, she didn't want me back. Said I was too crazy. Too angry. She didn't understand what it's like to fight in a jungle war, didn't know what I had to do over there. If she would've given me more time, just a little more time, she would've seen that I would be okay eventually."

"You're not okay eventually."

He curses. Keeps his pacing. "That's because she killed me off. Like an author would a petulant character. One day she said to me, 'Slim, you've died a heroic death in Vietnam. I'm buying a headstone, grieving your loss, and moving on. Delmer's afraid of you. I'm afraid of you. So it's best you go.'" He says the words with Ethrea's voice, a near exact imitation.

I don't say anything. Instead I finger the bracelet Slim must've slipped back onto the rose bush. I touch each bead, praying for Emory, for Elijah, Jed and Sissy.

"I see you got your bracelet."

"Yes." The car is not far. But how will I get there?

"So she killed me off, told me to leave her. Which I was glad to do. Only Delmer didn't take too well to me leaving."

"He took your picture ... "

He doesn't pay mind to my words. "They secretly moved to Defiance. And I was left to eke out a life. Eventually I found them here, built a little house in the trees, roamed around, stole for food, watched Delmer when I could. Then the little girl in the sandals cried in my dreams, came back to life, though I couldn't see her face."

He is darker now that the sun has slept. His words, darker too. I inch my way backwards, trying to move undetected.

"I didn't mean for the second girl to happen. She forced it, really. I heard singing. A wedding song of some sort, coming from that old church. I stepped inside, startled Daisy, and, well—"

"You killed her." Another inch.

"Not right away."

"I am friends with her mother. I am a mama to Daisy's best friend. Don't try to sound as if you're a saint in this. Not right away? What kind of man would—"

"A war-torn man. A damaged one."

His duo of adjectives belie the sinister way he paces. Am I supposed to feel sorry for him? I'd just as soon feel sorry for poor Hap who blamed his father's death for his rage. Poor, poor Slim. Another inch.

"I see you lack sympathy." He paces more.

Clementine growls again. I pat her head, hoping to shush her. "Killing is evil. It's wrong. And it's vile."

"You're supposed to understand!" His voice shrills the night. "My redemption!"

Now my heart beats faster.

He lunges at me, grabs my blouse in his right hand and lifts me to my feet. Clementine bites him. He lets go, recoils, then kicks the dog swift in the belly. She yelps away. I beg her to return, calling, "Clementine, Clementine." But her name flies away with her, gone and lost forever.

I try to run to the car, praying my legs are stronger than Slim's, but he catches me as I crest the hill. I kick his shin, then try to trip him, which works, because he tumbles down the steep

incline toward the car, pulling me with him. We are near the road, thank God. And near the car.

He pulls me into the ditch near the passenger side. Here, we are hidden from traffic—something I'm sure he knows. He straddles me, then places both hands around my neck. I grab his arms, scratching, clawing, drawing blood from the snake. I feel it wet my fingertips. Still, he keeps his hands over my neck, not squeezing.

"You understand. You know what it's like to live with someone who hates you."

"That didn't make me kill children."

His hands tighten. I drink in air, but it's not easy. I tell myself not to panic, but I feel my body tremble beneath his hands.

"I saw her face."

"What?"

"Her brown, pleading face. She had Delmer's eyes."

I struggle for air, digging my fingernails into Slim's flesh.

"Please," I say.

He shakes his head. In the shaking, he shifts from remorse to rage—so unlike Hap who never camped in the remorse. In the faded light, I see Slim's hyena eyes. He screams into the night, a gut-curdling wail that wakes a crow that now caws his response over and over and over. I coddle hope—perhaps someone will hear Slim or the strange cawing. I wriggle beneath his weight, but cannot get free. His grip tightens, starving my lungs.

The colors. The beautiful colors I'll never be able to paint. They're dancing before me now, animated by voices and instruments and halleluiahs. I shut my eyes, resigning to the irony. I survived Hap, though Emory nearly didn't. But I cannot survive a dead man.

Beyond the singing and the colors I see water, flowing, showering, flooding. My thirst, I can feel it on my dry tongue. Oh God, how I need that water. His Voice, as fluid as the waters showering the beauty, tells me the water is living. "It's for those who live forever."

"Please, give me a drink. Just one sip."

He calls my name, over and over, but does not bring me a cup of water from the gushing to slake me.

The colors fade to black and white.

Sixty-Four

Slim is no longer on top of me, no longer choking me. I cough. Then open my eyes.

"Are you okay, Mama?"

Jed.

"Oh dear God." I grab at him, pulling at him, wanting to make sure he's really him. He secures my hand and lifts me to my feet.

I cling to him, my arms around him like a fortress. "You're alive," I say. "Thank God. Thank God." I sob against him. Smell him. Muss his hair.

"It's okay, Mama."

"Where's Slim?" I dart my eyes, squinting in the night, but can't find him.

"In the back of Emory's car," Jed says.

I look. Slim reclines like a dead man along the back seat. "You did that?"

"No, Mama." Jed turns his head. I follow. Above us, nearly concealed by a tree above the ravine is Elijah, hands in pockets. He cocks his head, says nothing.

"You know Elijah?" So I'm not crazy?

"Yeah, he's that Santa we saw, remember? We've met just once before, out in the woods, but I knew where to find him. I told you someone would take care of me." Jed's voice is not defiant, not emotional, just plain old matter of fact, as if he'd been spending the night at a friend's.

"You had me worried sick." I say this to Jed, but my eyes are on Elijah.

Elijah pulls something out of his pocket. He scuffs down the hill and stands before me, still silent. He hands something to me. It's hard to make out in the darkness, but I feel its boxiness. "Another box?"

He nods.

"He's on a talking fast," Jed says.

"How convenient. Especially when a mama is worried sick about her son's whereabouts." I throw the box at my feet, smash it underneath.

Elijah shakes his head.

"What'd you go and do that for? He's the one who knew to come here. He's the one who pulled Slim off you, then knocked him out. He's the one who knew, Mama."

I look at Elijah, say thanks, but I leave the smashed box where it is. "We need to go to the police." I touch Jed's arm.

He jerks it away. "Just stop it, will you? I'm not a kid anymore."

"You're my son. You'll always be."

"I'm a man."

"A man who runs out on his family? That sounds like your father, like what he did last night."

"I heard what Hap did."

"You did? Then why didn't you come back?"

"I did, but the house was empty. I had no key. It's not like Elijah kidnapped me. He understood. He encouraged me to come back. But when I couldn't get in the house, and he advised me against breaking a window, we spent the night outside. It was fine, Mama."

"Emory's really bad," I tell him.

He says nothing back, just looks at the car. Slim stirs in the back seat—our cue to leave—and in a hurry.

I turn to see if mute Elijah will drive us, but he is gone.

I bend to the ground, picked up the smashed box, then get in the car.

Sixty-Five

Screams of "forgive me, forgive me, forgive me" rattle the police station thanks to thin walls and Slim's large voice. When Ethrea Ree enters the station, I am sitting next to Jed who's taken Elijah's silence oath and Sissy who clings to me like static in winter. I stroke her hair, noticing wiry gray strands. I say a prayer for this girl who's endured so much. I rise to meet Ethrea, but wonder if I'm in for another walloping.

She faces me. For a long moment, she says nothing while Slim's pleas for forgiveness go unanswered. Then she reaches a hand my way, pulling me into an awkward embrace. "I couldn't tell anyone," she said.

"I understand." Oh how I understand. So many secrets I've kept. Secrets that had held Jed captive enough to make him want to flee. Secrets that lisped Sissy's mouth, grayed her like an old woman. Secrets that nearly destroyed me. I pull away from Ethrea. "How is Delmer?"

"Confused."

Jed rises. "Please tell him I'm sorry I hollered at him." He extends his hand Ethrea's way.

She takes his hand, holds it, then lets it go. "I'll do that."

Sixty-Six

The sound of metal clacking against metal brings the visit back to reality. Texas state prisons are not for the faint of heart—especially those locking up violent offenders for life. But this is a visit I must make alongside her. And she is the one I'm going for after all, though my own task blurs my mind. Emory fiddles with her hands, twitching nervously as we enter the small room where the booths are. We sit in two plastic chairs, framed by a metal cubicle and one solitary phone.

"I can't do this," Emory says. But I assure her she can. She's traded her frail faith for something more tangible than the bracelet that still hangs from my wrist, although I've replaced the ratty string with a silver chain. I put my arm around her.

A door opens on the other side of our barricade. A corrections officer pushes Slim Ree toward us, his hands shackled together, his feet shod in black prison-issue shoes. He's lost weight, his snake tattoo shrunken, more wormlike. I feel Emory tense beside me.

Slim picks up the phone.

"Would you rather I stay or go?" I ask.

"Stay," she answers. She picks up the phone.

Slim's exact words don't make their way to me. Only Emory hears them through the receiver, but I see a more contrite man than the man who turned on me, choked me. Still, seeing him makes me shiver.

Emory looks at me. "He wants to talk to you."

"I have nothing to say." Which is the truth. "You say your piece. Just give the word and I'll walk away."

"No, stay."

She swallows, then looks at Slim. "You killed the best part of me," Emory says.

A long pause. Slim says nothing, just puts his face in his hands. When he lifts his head again, his eyes are piggish, his face a torrent of emotion. He looks to me, a begging look, but I feign interest in my fingernails. He needs to hear Emory, not examine my face.

"Only monsters kill young girls, Slim Ree. Only monsters scare a town out if its wits, stealing shoes, choking—" She melts into tears.

He covers his face in wrinkling hands. Seeing him like that, I can't help but think through all the times I wanted Hap to be dead, how I pictured myself standing before his coffin without tears. So much premeditation lived in my head, I wonder if I shouldn't be in Slim's place. Thank God I didn't kill Hap. Thank God. Though the wanting was there.

Emory steadies herself. I feel her relax under my arm. "Slim, you killed that little girl in Vietnam. I read it in the paper after the trial."

He does not look up.

"She was addled, I hear. Like your Delmer. And you took her life, kept her shoes. What kind of madman—"

He removes his hands, stares crystal blue eyes her way, then looks at his hands as if he blamed them for doing such a thing.

"Look at me," she says.

He obeys.

"You killed my daughter. My Daisy."

He doesn't utter a word into the phone, but he holds her eyes.

"And Hixon, in a way." Her voice quavers now, but she inhales her tears while she touches her ring.

Slim clears his throat in a consumptive cough. His body doubles on itself. The plain-faced guard pulls him back upright. He holds up five fingers. Five minutes for Emory to begin to make some peace. Not nearly enough time for such a task.

"I'll get right to it, then." Her voice is tiny, frail. "When I look at the mountain that God's forgiven me, it stands taller than the pine trees, the courthouse, the sky. I've done one million things I regret and those regrets heap up and up the more I rethink them. If I can accept God's pardon for sins so great, who am I to withhold such a grace from you?"

Slim shakes his head, as if Emory's words are poison. I wonder if Ethrea Ree has said such words to him, if Delmer's talked squirrels with him or weightier matters during their visits. I wonder if Slim wishes the Vietnamese girl's mother were here, giving full vent to her grief. Would all of it kill this snake-tattooed man? Would he welcome a death like that? Death from grief? Regret?

Emory puts her hands on the table, examines her palms. "I shudder to think of what I've done with these hands." She looks at Slim. "But I worry even more what my heart would look like if I kept nursing my desire to see you pay. I've spent too many years in my own prison, Slim Ree. You'll be spending the rest of your days in one, that's for sure. But I don't take kindly to prisons."

The guard holds up two fingers.

"I'll be done with it then. Slim Ree—"

He looks at the Formica.

"Knowing my Daisy, I'm guessing she forgave you. That's just how she was. Lord knows how many times she extended her kindness my way when I didn't deserve any of it, or even ask for it. And Hixon—I sliced through that man's heart only to have him forgive me. They've given me a gift, and now, for my sake and yours, I'm extending that gift to you." She steadies herself, "I forgive you."

Slim doubles again on himself, this time from weeping. The guard pulls him to his feet and shoves him toward the metal door. Slim looks back, his hands still shackled, a thank you forms from a mouth we cannot hear.

But I can hear Emory's weeping. I'm sure Defiance can too.

Sixty-Seven

Emory understands my need to be alone with him. She waits in the stark room while I anticipate the metal door's opening. Like Slim, Hap is shoved through the doorway, his hands in shackles, feet in the same black prison boots. Mama did always say you could tell a man by the shoes he wore, and now her words finally ring true.

Hap sits. I can't meet his eyes, preferring to stare at the bracelets of his imprisonment. Eventually, I look at him. His hair is not preacher-slick. But his eyes have the same fight.

We pick up the phones.

"Who bought the car?" he asks.

"Does it matter?" I say.

He stands. The guard pushes him back down.

"That car was mine."

"Not according to the state. It became mine, so I sold it."

He slams his fist onto the counter, jangling both wrists.

"The house closes this week."

"You sold that too?"

I nod.

"We'll be living with Emory until I can figure out what to do to make a living. Then, who knows?"

"How is she?"

"She's recovering. You ought to thank your lucky stars she didn't die."

He makes no response.

I twist my wedding ring around and around, hoping that in the twisting the perfect words will form in my mind. They don't. I do not have Emory's heart, but I pray for it, hope for it in that moment.

"If you hadn't made me so angry, I — "

"Shut up, Hap Pepper." My voice surprises me. I'm not loud, not angry, just resigned and firm.

He reels back. "You should respect your husband," he says.

"We're divorced, Hap. By the way, how is Sheba doing?"

He shakes his head. "You changed the subject."

"I can do that, particularly from where I sit. Besides, that's where the police found you, right? With her? Doing Lord knows what."

"She respects me." He hisses these words.

I hear the tension in his voice, but I am blessedly safe from his fists.

He tries to settle himself. "That's what I can say about Bathsheba. She loves me. Understands. Because her husband left her high and dry, alone, and found himself another family. He was an adulterer, Ouisie. And he divorced her. Did you know that?"

"Of course. You forget about Defiance's love of gossip. I'm sorry for her."

"Ouisie," he says. "Don't you believe in grace? In second chances?"

"I have to. And, oddly, I believe that because of Bathsheba's words in her book. She wrote about that, you know — in the final chapter. About marriages being an example of God's grace, his mysterious way of showing the world his church."

"Not our marriage," he says.

"No, not ours. I'm still doing my best to bring those grace words into my heart, without hearing your voice in my head or being tainted by the way Bathsheba colors them."

"She's a wise woman."

I shake my head. Want to spit. But I tell myself to finish this conversation, painting it with as much grace as I can muster. "You yourself were right about something—I do have a problem with drinking. I have neglected the kids in the midst of it. And I could sit here and point my righteous finger at your sorry face and blame you for it all. Lord knows I have plenty of evidence. But I'm not going to. It would take far too much energy—energy I need to go forward, to move on with my life."

"That's easy for you to say. You're not locked up."

"Yours is a prison of law, of justice. Mine is a prison of choosing, if I don't say what I came to say."

He stares at me.

I twist off the now-token ring, place it on the counter. Its circularity, how it never ends, never begins, stuns me in the moment. I remember the words I sputtered to Hap so many years ago. Rich and poor. Sickness and health. I meant every word. But I didn't know the man I married would Dr. Jekyll me, would shift ever so slightly each year until his opinions ruled my soul. I lost all my opinions under the tyranny of his voice, his fist. The kids too. The fact that he's divorced me from prison so he and Bathsheba can pursue their strange dreams makes the circularity of the ring even more mocking. "You go ahead and marry her, then. Be that example of grace."

He says nothing. I know my time is nearing an end, thanks to the guard pointing to the plain clock behind him.

"I'm moving on." I touch the ring, then recoil from it. "Without you."

I see a hint of regret in his eyes for a flash of a moment. An ache from deep inside purrs, then roars inside me. This is the end of my life. Of the man I spent years trying to appease, to make love me. All for our painted story to end on an over-painted black canvas. It's up to me to sign my name to the Jasper Johns imitation, to hang it on a museum wall and walk away.

"I am trying to forgive you, Hapland James Pepper," I say.

And in the saying, I realize signing my name to the black canvas is not enough, so I say my words again, this time with fervor. "I choose to forgive you!"

He looks at me, his eyes noting my voice, I'm sure. "You always were an emotional wreck."

I say nothing. The eyes I used to get lost in, seeing the sky of Defiance alive there, are now prison gray. He shakes his head as if he needs to scold me—for old time's sake. "What's there to forgive?"

I will not let him end it all with that question floating in prison space, will not let him sign his own name to our painting. "You," I say. I let go of the receiver, turn away. I don't watch him leave the tiny room, though I hear the sound of his boots on the floor and the clank of the heavy door shutting. I don't retrieve the ring. I walk on unsteady feet toward a different future. And though I want more than anything to take a deep, long drink, by God's strength, I'll settle for water.

Sixty-Eight

We are barefoot for our makeshift Bible study. I feel the soft now-green grass tickle my toes as I shift my weight. The light of midmorning isn't exactly perfect, but I'm thankful for it nonetheless. The picture in my mind is lit correctly, the sun angling at dusk bringing a hint of sunset to the canvas. I lift a paintbrush to the image, then pull it back. It's perfect. Not perfect in a Renoir way, but perfect for me.

The sun ignites the image, glinting golden and silver on the surface of the broken open lake. I am emerging from the lake, violating its peace. I am blurred, multi-hued, vibrant, full of life. Big Earl, his arm around my waist, wears a laughing smile. Others from the shore stand as witnesses. They throw rose petals my way, littering the lake with scent and beauty. I can almost hear the painting laugh. Almost.

"Breathtaking," Emory says. "I think you should sell it, make a living by painting."

"That I may do," I tell her. "Make a living, that is. But this one's not for sale."

Emory motions for Ethrea Ree to come near. She's been sitting in the Adirondack watching Lake Pisgah ripple under the sky. She's been quiet, like a ghost between Emory and me these past few weeks.

She nods when she sees it. "Your baptism?"

She speaks.

"Yes. I was terrified," I tell her.

"But you're not anymore, are you?" Ethrea smiles. "Because you're free."

"Free," I say. And it's true. Not merely free from Hap's wrath, but free from all the angry voices he inflamed in my head. Free to hear the Voice who whispers grace over me like the first rosebud of spring. Free to be the mother I long to be. Free to live. Free to turn my back on alcohol, though thinking about it plagues me still.

Ethrea looks at the lake sparkling on the canvas, then to the real lake. She sits on the grass at my feet, then opens her worn Bible that bears Slim's name. "Psalm 63:1," she reads. "O God, thou art my God; early will I seek thee: my soul thirsteth for thee, my flesh longeth for thee in a dry and thirsty land, where no water is."

Emory sits next to her cross-legged.

I do too. I let the verse soak into me. I've been so thirsty, and the land of my life's been so dry. This is how it goes for the three of us in our Bible study under the sky. A verse shared, mutual silence, God thick in our midst.

"My mama used to say something," Ethrea says. " 'When it comes to God,' she said. 'We draw from a well we didn't dig.' Her words figured into my thinking when I was a child, always remembering that God supplied me his living water. But after Slim returned from the war, I forgot all that. I dug my own wells, coming up dry every time. Came to the point where I believed my life's ambition was to simply struggle well, thirsty all the way."

She says more words today than she has the past several weeks together. I let the silence between her sentences grow, comfortable in them like wearing gardening clothes. But she says nothing more as the sun dapples the lake.

I notice our bare feet, how they all take different shape under

a peek-a-boo sun. How, we, barefooted, all mourn men. And though it took me some time to tell you, and my intuition was wrong, you probably figured out Slim before I did. Slim, whose painful fetish with children's shoes was merely a trifle to the places his own feet took him. Hap who trampled through my life, not bothering to look behind to see the aftermath—even now. And Hixon whose feet probably resembled Jesus'—a man who walked the streets of Defiance as a good man, a forgiving man. Emory's grief must be larger, I think.

Emory stands. She looks at my painting. She reaches to me and lifts me up. Ethrea follows. "I have one question," she asks.

"What?"

"Those people. Who are they?" She points to the figures at the painting's lower left corner, those who throw rose petals.

"Jed, Sissy, you." I point to the three of them.

"But the others?"

I point to the next three people. "Muriel, Hixon, and Elijah."

"Do you think he's dead, Elijah?"

"No," I say, "but I'm not sure what to think. Jed says he kept him safe overnight, took care of him, fed him even. Said Elijah knew exactly where to go to save me from Slim. Told him God revealed my location."

"Have you seen him since?" Emory puts her hands on her hips, then slips them into her back pockets.

"No. Not since he knocked out Slim. Jed hasn't heard from him or seen him either. He just vanished." I half expect Elijah to start laughing from the bushes, but the shrubbery is silent. The now-silver bracelet he gave me hangs from my wrist. It reminds me to pray, to believe, to remember. His last box to me, the one I flattened under my shoe is resurrected there—reboxed and silver leafed, thanks to a jeweler in Tyler. The other box, with God's love tucked inside, is gilded gold. The chicken bone, too.

I leave Ethrea and Emory, just a few paces. The water beckons me, slips its warmth around my ankles, my calves, my knees. I'd keep going, but Emory interrupts my journey.

"Who is that on the right of the painting all alone?"

I turn to see.

Emory nods toward the last image, taller than the rest, bare-footed, submerged to his ankles like I am right now.

I say nothing. She doesn't prod. Ethrea either.

Because we all know who he is.

Acknowledgments

Patrick, thanks for being Hap's antithesis. You are everything he is not. Your patience, kindness, hope, forgiveness, sweetness, and encouragement bless me and make me want to be a better woman. Sophie, thank you for moving from girlhood to womanhood with such grace it makes me cry. You're beautiful. Aidan and Julia, I'm so glad you're beginning to devour books—perhaps one of mine will be your next. Thanks for cheerleading me through this sometimes-painful, sometimes-exhilarating journey called writing.

Leslie Wilson and D'Ann Mateer, I stand on your shoulders as a novelist because of your dedication and keen editorial eyes. You've propped me up, pushed me to grow, and rejoiced when I rejoiced—the measure of true friendship.

Andy Meisenheimer, I'm a better storyteller and self-editor because of your intelligent critique. Who knows, maybe someday I'll plot my next novel.

Beth Jusino, you're sassy, fun, smart, and cool. I'm thankful we sojourned together.

Esther Fedorkevich, what can I say? Your belief in me blesses me.

Karwyn Bursma, I love that you love these books. And that they've changed you.

Thank you, prayer team, who prayed me through: Ashley

and George Weis, Kevin and Renee Bailey, Carla Smith, Caroline Coleman, Cheramy Mayfield, Colleen Eslinger, Jeanne Damoff, D'Ann Mateer, Darren and Holly Sapp, Dena Dyer, Dr. Dorian Coover-Cox, Elaine Sims, Erin Teske, Ginger and JR Vassar, Helen Graves, John Davis, Katy Gedney, Denise Willhite, Jim and Darci Rubart, Anita Curtis, Diane Klapper, Cyndi Kraweitz, Lesley Hamilton, Leslie Wilson, Lilli Brenchley, Paul Napari, Holly Schmidt, Jan Winebrenner, Jen Powell, Kathy ONeall, Katy Raymond, Liz Wolf, Marcia Robbins, Marcus Goodyear, Marilyn Neel, Marion-Grace Bower, Mary Vestal, MaryBeth Whalen, Michael and Renee Mills, Pam LeTourneau, Pamela Dowd, Phyllis Yount, Don Pape, Paula Moldenhauer, Rae McIlrath, Rebekah Jowers, Becky Ochs, Sandi Glahn, Sarah Walker, Shawna Bryant, Sue Harrell, Stacey Tomisser, Susan Meissner, Tiffany Demien, Tim Riter, Tina Howard, TJ Wilson, Tracy Walker, Twilla Fontenot and Heidi VanDyken. I pray many in difficult homes and lives will be touched by this book precisely because of your prayers. May the healing begin.

Jesus, thanks for bearing defiance on the cross. We're all the better for it.

Daisy Chain
A Novel

Mary E. DeMuth

The abrupt disappearance of young Daisy Chance from a small Texas town in 1973 spins three lives out of control — Jed, whose guilt over not protecting his friend Daisy strangles him; Emory Chance, who blames her own choices for her daughter's demise; and Ouisie Pepper, who is plagued by headaches while pierced by the shattered pieces of a family in crisis.

In this first book in the Defiance, Texas Trilogy, fourteen-year-old Jed Pepper has a sickening secret: He's convinced it's his fault his best friend Daisy went missing. Jed's pain sends him on a quest for answers to mysteries woven through the fabric of his own life and the lives of the families of Defiance, Texas. When he finally confronts the terrible truths he's been denying all his life, Jed must choose between rebellion and love, anger and freedom.

Daisy Chain is an achingly beautiful southern coming-of-age story crafted by a bright new literary talent. It offers a haunting yet hopeful backdrop for human depravity and beauty, for terrible secrets and God's surprising redemption.

Available in stores and online!

A Slow Burn
A Novel

Mary E. DeMuth

"Beautifully and sensitively written, her characters realistic and well-developed. Mary DeMuth has a true gift for showing how God's light can penetrate even the darkest of situations."

– Chuck Colson

She touched Daisy's shoulder. So cold. So hard. So unlike Daisy.

Yet so much like herself it made Emory shudder.

Burying her grief, Emory Chance is determined to find her daughter Daisy's murderer — a man she saw in a flicker of a vision. But when the investigation hits every dead end, her despair escalates. As questions surrounding Daisy's death continue to mount, Emory's safety is shattered by the pursuit of a stranger, and she can't shake the sickening fear that her own choices contributed to Daisy's disappearance. Will she ever experience the peace her heart longs for?

The second book in the Defiance, Texas Trilogy, this suspenseful novel is about courageous love, the burden of regret, and bonds that never break. It is about the beauty and the pain of telling the truth. Most of all, it is about the power of forgiveness and what remains when shame no longer holds us captive.

Available in stores and online!

Share Your Thoughts

With the Author: Your comments will be forwarded to the author when you send them to *zauthor@zondervan.com*.

With Zondervan: Submit your review of this book by writing to *zreview@zondervan.com*.

Free Online Resources at
www.zondervan.com

Zondervan AuthorTracker: Be notified whenever your favorite authors publish new books, go on tour, or post an update about what's happening in their lives at www.zondervan.com/authortracker.

Daily Bible Verses and Devotions: Enrich your life with daily Bible verses or devotions that help you start every morning focused on God. Visit www.zondervan.com/newsletters.

Free Email Publications: Sign up for newsletters on Christian living, academic resources, church ministry, fiction, children's resources, and more. Visit www.zondervan.com/newsletters.

Zondervan Bible Search: Find and compare Bible passages in a variety of translations at www.zondervanbiblesearch.com.

Other Benefits: Register yourself to receive online benefits like coupons and special offers, or to participate in research.

ZONDERVAN.com/
AUTHORTRACKER
follow your favorite authors